No Demons But Us

Sister Seekers Book 1

BY
A.S. Etaski

Published by Corpus Nexus Press
ISBN: 978-1-949552-01-0

etaski.com
etaski.com/sister-seekers
miurag.etaski.com
www.patreon.com/etaski
www.goodreads.com/etaski
www.bookbub.com/authors/a-s-etaski
www.facebook.com/asetaski
mastodon.online/@etaski

Cover Design by Eris Adderly
Book layout by DocKangey

Dedicated to my husband and companion, who did not know on our wedding day he had married one of his favorite authors.

Dedicated to every fan who wanted more, and to my patrons who have directly supported this new world.

CHAPTER 1

I can speak.

I trembled, hidden in a small, dark pocket of the stables, as a nameless, hard sickness broke at last and seeped out of me. I felt my throat loosen as the curse unraveled; tears leaked from my eyes. I opened my mouth with full intent to accuse her. Nausea did not rise in my stomach. No headache threatened to split my head apart.

I could tell someone.

"Your own doing," I whispered to no one. "You deserved to die."

The body lay in the barn next to the stables, but I hadn't lingered there after it remained unmoving long enough. I pictured it now in that awkward sprawl at the foot of the ladder, the neck in an unnatural twist. The chest would never swell with breath. I would never hear her voice next to my ear, would never feel her hot breath on my skin. I would never taste her again.

Half my life ago, I'd been forcibly silenced. Now, I could speak of it if I wished. I could accuse her.

But she's dead now. The First Daughter is dead.

Speaking wasn't the wisest thing to do. Not yet.

Someone would find her body soon, and I wanted to live past the next wake cycle.

I wanted to live far beyond the next *century* without her if I could.

"SIRANA. WHERE IS SHE?"

My other sister blocked my way. Kaltra Thalluenduv, the Second Daughter of our House, stood with me in the hall leading from the kitchen to the space for lower guests. This wasn't unusual; I often tested my sisters' desires to locate me, creeping around the places we Nobles weren't supposed to dirty ourselves. I glared up at Kaltra in silence, also nothing unusual.

"Where is Jilrina?" she asked again.

"Haven't seen her," I said, attempting to slip by her.

My sister wasn't quick, and I knew I could slip loose if she grabbed me. My eye level was at her shoulder, however, and she weighed more. She used her larger size to pin me against the wall in the tight hallway. The halls of our own quarters would have been too wide for her to achieve that.

"Get off me!" I shouted.

My protest was louder than it had ever been. If this surprised her, she didn't show it. I wagered she didn't understand the significance.

"Is she out back?" Kaltra asked.

"I don't know!"

I struck her thigh with my fist, expecting the retaliatory slap to my sensitive, pointed ear. Kaltra always hit hard, and my head thumped against the wall this time. I groaned, and I sank down to the floor as if suddenly giving up fighting. I tried crawling past her. She blocked me with her legs.

"Get up! You're going to help me find her. It's time for more practice."

"Fuck Braqth's Tits I will!" I snarled, and her eyes widened in horror. "How dare you?"

Kaltra looked around us as if the Spider Queen Herself would be there, ready to judge my blasphemous mouth and doom us both to the Pit. I scoffed, straightened up, and took a step back. Subtle footfalls and shifting shadows behind us meant several servants were aware of the conflict and making certain to stay out of it. I could turn around and run toward them, but I already knew how petulant my older sister could be if a poor, fool servant wasn't fast enough to get out of my way. It had never helped me in the end.

"Speak the prayer, Sirana," Kaltra said. "Show humility."

Defiant, I pursed my lips. For courage in the face of her fury, I called back my loathing of Jilrina and the sweet memory of our eldest sister's body in the barn, of the life-heat fading from my Dark Sight.

My calm returned, and I reigned back on my protests and held my ground. This had never changed anything before, but now there wasn't a would-be-Priestess, sitting with legs spread, in front of whom Kaltra could force me to kneel.

The outcome now was anybody's guess.

"SHE DID IT!" KALTRA SCREECHED. "SIRANA PUSHED HER!"

"I did not push her!" I barked back. I shook with rage and fear the same as she, but for different reasons. "We found her like that! You could see as I did that she fell!"

"Lying slit! You found her before I found you, I know it! You treacherous, traitor cu — !"

"Kaltra," our Mother commanded. "Hold your tongue."

"Why?" the Second Daughter flung at the Matron. "You know the truth, Mother. Sirana has always threatened at Jilrina's back! She's a proven Sister Killer! I hope the Red Sisters flay the skin from her entire body for what she's done!"

"*Enough.*"

Matron Thalluen held us both in her office. The door was locked, and a Ward set against the sound carrying into the hall, even though by now the entire plantation knew what had happened.

I was glad that Kaltra had spoiled so much of the barn when we found Jilrina. I relished how she had landed on her knees and shook our sister's unresponsive corpse, calling her name, before pulling the body up into a wailing embrace. It had taken the Head of the Guard and several Guardsvrin to pull Kaltra away at our Mother's command, to keep some semblance of order until Matron Thalluen could decide what to do.

Within a mark of the candle, Mother had sent a magic missive to the Palace.

I hadn't expected her to invite anyone from off the plantation for at least a cycle or two. Barely two candle marks had passed since Kaltra found Jilrina's body, and it scared me now how swift was the Sisterhood's response. First, to hear they were coming, and then to watch them arrive from out of the darkness of the Great Cavern, their red uniforms the first thing I could make out as they approached the lights of our manor.

Now I worried that I underestimated how much anyone besides Kaltra might care about Jilrina's death. Even Mother had been at serious odds with her own First Daughter since my earliest memories.

She deserved to die. Don't panic, or it will show as a confession.

The Guardsvrin of House Thalluen had been confined to the barracks, the servants to their quarters, and our Matron was tasked to keep her two surviving Daughters "secure" and within her sight. Matron Thalluen herself had been commanded to give all search and study over to the Red Sisters.

That my Matron bowed so readily, agreeing to be ignorant of anything the Sisterhood may be doing on her plantation, only reinforced my miscalculation of their power. There had always been the reputation, the gossip and stories meant to scare the young and gullible into fearing shadows. Until now, nothing had happened on this plantation to warrant their direct attention, and I had never set foot outside of our borders.

While Kaltra yelled at me, my Mother and I waited for the Red Sisters to finish in the barn and come to us. They did after only another mark, and then Kaltra and I were separated from our Mother. Each of us was taken to our own bedroom while the Matron Thalluen remained in her office.

I wondered whether all three of us would step out again. I wondered; if one or more of us did not, who would it be? If any female family was taken yet I survived, what would I feel then? I could not decide while I stood in familiar surroundings with a wholly unfamiliar type of female in the room with me.

"Hmph," she grunted, probably as a laugh, as she looked over my room and gestured for me to sit down.

I obeyed, and I dared not let my thoughts stray from the Red Sister's stance, from every motion or expression she made as she casually handled my belongings. I didn't know her skills or her magic — be it mage-born or magical tools in her possession — so it was best to keep my mind on the present.

This Red Sister was a warrior, visibly powerful in form and reflex. She wore a leather uniform, protective, flexible, quiet, and flattering her shape. Her hair was cut short enough to hide any hint of white beneath a slim, open-face helm fitted just for her. A fine quality cloak with a hood hung from her shoulders, and her boots reached just above her knees; not a buckle glinted in the light to warn others of her movement. Her gloves hid the dark skin of her hands but not the apparent strength and competence I could read in them.

The entirety of her uniform and cloak was dyed the color of fresh blood. This color could not be used by any Noble House in the Deepearth City of Sivaraus. Only the Red Sisters of our Queen could wear it. By design and reputation, it terrified citizens at the slightest glimpse in real light yet appeared black as the rest of the shadows whenever fire or magic glow went out.

Even our Elven ability to see in the dark, it was said, would fail to detect the elite enforcer's outline or the heat of her body. For now, a smokeless candle burned on my dresser — the only light source in the room, also counting the time — making it impossible to ignore the red filling up space which led to the exit. I couldn't test the rumor of lightless invisibility, but I also hoped the opportunity might pass me by.

"You don't care what I touch," the Red Sister murmured, lifting a hairbrush from my vanity which I thought was too heavy for its ornament. Then she exchanged it for a hand mirror I barely used.

Glancing at me, she saw me shrug. I jumped when she slammed the hand mirror against the edge of the dresser, the candle jostling and dancing, threatening to topple over and plunge the room into darkness.

The light held, barely, and I watched as expensive glass tinkled down over the chair and onto the throw rug beneath, glittering as the candle remained upright. She turned to face me, unmoving, with the broken mirror in her firm grip.

The Davrin Elves all possessed keen hearing. If this Red Sister couldn't detect my heartbeat before, I was confident she did now as it throbbed in my own ears. She lifted her chin and inhaled the air; whether that was only for show or whether she really could detect a change in my scent, she at least wanted me to see her do it.

"Nervous, not angry," she noted, walking toward me. "But not pissing your gown."

Her assessment was accurate enough. I could oblige her my fast heartbeat and the grey-knuckled grip on my seat, but I had firm control of my bladder. I hoped it was enough to satisfy as she stepped up to me and leaned down to meet my eyes. Belatedly I realized she hadn't asked me to look her in the eye.

Fuck. Well, now you're there, Sirana, don't look away.

The Red Sister smirked as she studied me. I expected her to slap or hit me; it was what Jilrina would have done to feel more powerful. This older female didn't. Instead, another deep murmur eased its way out from her mouth.

"Blue Eyes doesn't care about her mirror, hm?"

It had been a while since anyone had commented on that. My eye color had become ordinary on the plantation, and I didn't need a mirror to continually remind me when Jilrina had so often. I'd almost forgotten there was a whole city out there which hadn't seen my eyes yet, and I didn't know how many other Davrin might have been born with a similar color.

By contrast, the Red Sister's eyes were a natural color: a bright, coppery red, almost like magma without the glow, or maybe flakes of rust ground into powder.

"No, Red Sister, I don't care," I said. "Break any piece you want."

She chuckled in a way that slid down my spine like a slime. "Careful what you suggest, little Noble. You're almost the right age."

I smelled the threat then, a musk coming from her, and I swallowed. I knew she could do as she liked to entertain herself or torment me, and I couldn't stop her. The helplessness which gripped me was familiar, but I knew I could face it.

If this Red Sister's tastes were like Jilrina's, then I wouldn't be surprised by anything she demanded. The Red Sister would leave House Thalluen at some point, unlike the First Daughter before her death. I'd either be alive when the Sister departed, or I wouldn't be. But she *would* leave.

This is a separate test from Jilrina.

I trembled despite myself as the enforcer stared at me unblinking. After some very long moments, she straightened up and stepped away.

We returned to waiting — that's what we were doing, I realized — and the uniformed female looked through my room, in all corners and drawers and cubbies. I let her do it. She seemed to be gauging my every breath, but there was no possession here in which I placed value over my own self. She touched everything but me, so why should I care about anything else? These were things I used, nothing more, and they all belonged to my Mother, anyway.

I thought I heard Kaltra cry out at one point, and I straightened up, straining my ears to hear more. After that first noise, there was nothing. Silence returned but for the shift of my body in my chair and the careful placement of red boots upon the floor and its rugs. The smokeless candle burned down another two marks, and I was getting stiff, hungry, and thirsty. I neither voiced nor motioned anything about it.

There was a knock at the door, and I was almost relieved at the sign of change. The red warrior let her superior inside the room with us, providing a ritualized gesture of welcome and respect after the door was secured behind her. The gesture seemed genuine, as far as I could tell; habitual, but not reluctant or ironic.

"Sirana Thalluensareci," the leader said, announcing me before herself. She wasn't looking at me yet; she adjusted her gloves as if she had recently put them on.

"Yes, Red Sister," I said obediently.

"I am an Elder, Third Daughter. You will address me as such."

"Yes, Elder Sister."

This one wore a uniform slightly different than the warrior but, from a distance, I wouldn't have known she was the leader. Up close, I could say it had seen less activity, was less worn in places, and something about the cut of the body harness accentuated her breasts, lifted them up instead of flattened them down, without exposing any skin.

Up close and standing beside the warrior, I could also guess she must be a mage, notably when she lifted the thin helm from her head. I saw how much thicker her hair was, bound up off her elegant neck but kept long. I didn't doubt she could use the dagger and sword at her waist; her body looked toned and powerful inside that red uniform, but her hands somehow suggested familiarity with the grace of magic more than it did fists and hand-to-hand combat.

A fundamental rule of the Queen's City was that the powerful mageborns gained more status than the best of fighters, as long as they were female. I wasn't sure what happened to those mages born male, but that wasn't important now.

The Elder Red Sister approached me as the warrior had, although staring down at me without leaning over. Again, I met a Red Sister's eyes — a much darker crimson than the light copper of the warrior — and I wasn't punished for it.

Immediately.

The sorceress tilted her head this way and that as she stepped around my chair. Her eyes seemed to scan the air touching my body, my gown, and my hair rather than my physical form. After completing a circle, the Elder stood in front of me once again and reached out with her gloved hand to wrap it around my throat.

My pulse beat like the wings of a panicking moth trying to escape a spider's web; somehow, I hadn't expected a direct touch without so much as a question asked. My throat closed as it had whenever I had wanted to speak out against Jilrina, and it hurt. I worried that the compulsion had returned, there was no stomachache or headache or bright lights before my eyes.

"Residual effects," the Elder commented. "A recent dispelling. What spell, Sirana? And who lifted it?"

I quivered like a tiny burrower beneath a hunter's paw. I'd already looked down voluntarily. This wasn't an interrogation I might have imagined in the lengthy time I'd waited in my chair. She never asked me what I thought happened to Jilrina, where I was when she died, who was my witness, and so on. The Elder asked directly about a magical compulsion being gone; one that my own Matron hadn't known about.

Yet this sorceress could see its recent passing. It was a spell that gave me undeniable motive to murder a First Daughter, and the incentive to assassinate a family member.

A Sister Killer, as Kaltra claimed.

I didn't kill her. I didn't push her.

"S-Silence compulsion," I whispered. "No one lifted it, Elder. The Silencer died in the barn."

The warrior snorted softly, standing as a bodyguard to her Elder though I was no threat.

"How long since the compulsion was placed?" the Elder Sister asked, her gaze too intense to meet again. She could feel my every twitch and tremor running up her arm as she held me by the throat, yet she allowed me to breathe. She wanted an answer.

"T-Thirty five turns," I murmured.

The warrior grunted, speaking to her Elder. "This cait can't be more than, what, seventy-five?"

"Seventy-nine," the sorceress answered. "She was still a child when the spell was set."

Unlike the broken mirror, the Elder Sister caring enough to know my age down to the exact turn now brought on the urge to piss. I squeezed my thighs together and stared at her red forearm, swallowing against her palm again.

"What did First Daughter Jilrina Compel to Silence?" When I didn't respond quickly, she commanded, "Speak, Sirana. Now."

I gritted my teeth; after a moment my jaw hurt. "The fact that she likes the taste of a child in her bed. A child, and her younger sister."

Even the residual pain faded now, and I felt so light-headed I almost passed out.

I said it. Braqth tied in Her Web, I said it!

CHAPTER 2

THE FEW TIMES WE GLIMPSED EACH OTHER OVER THE NEXT HALF-SPAN, KALTRA wouldn't look me in the eyes. For a full four cycles, whenever we saw each other in the hall or were required to share a room, she looked anywhere else but at me.

The infrequency wasn't unusual. We had barely seen each other without Jilrina between us anyway. Not even mealtime had put us in proximity, as meals were often delivered to an office, to one's quarters, to the garden, or wherever. The few times we had guests of some status were the only times we sat together as a Noble family in the dining hall.

The consistency of her avoidance, however, was notable.

And enjoyable.

I didn't know exactly what happened between the Second Daughter and the Red Sisters during her interrogation, but I had been released back to my Matron unmolested but for that throat-grab. This, I had no doubt, was in large part due to my own effort, cooperation, and relative honesty.

The Elder had determined, without physical torture but with a magical will, that I was telling her the truth: I hadn't pushed Jilrina to her death. The sorceress had also pulled just enough of the lurid story of my oldest sister's designs on me to understand why I wasn't upset with the First Daughter's demise.

The Elder had brought me out of my chair after speaking my decades-old secret and made me stand. She inspected my body with magic, lightly touching me with her gloved hands now and then. I couldn't say what she searched for; I knew she was doing something, seeing things I couldn't. I felt something tickle or flutter along the edges of my ears or at the back of my teeth, heard her murmur unknown words, watched her hands move with precision.

I had started to sweat, wondering if her casting on me was permanent unto death, as the Compulsion potion had been. Instead, the Elder Red Sister had finished, studied me some while longer in silence, and then she and her warrior escorted me back to Matron Thalluen without another word of my fate.

Mother had been standing in her office, as poised and quiet as when I'd been taken away, bowing gracefully to the Elder. She watched me sit on a chair with her usual impassive expression and those familiar, scarlet eyes which always cloaked her real thoughts. My Mother waited and said nothing.

"Consider yourselves under House arrest until we finish our investigation," the Elder had told the Matron. "I see no reason to take any of the Noble family away, but leave the grounds before I return, and that one will be hunted and taken, unlikely returned. No matter who it is."

My Mother nodded, kept her chin high. "What of our business with others, Elder Sister? My liaisons and Guardsvrin must leave House Thalluen to complete our trades."

"They are to remain here for three cycles, under the same consequence if they leave. After that time, they may conduct regular business on your behalf, no one else's. The Noble family will remain here until I return, however long that may be. I trust you can work with this, Matron?"

"Yes, Elder."

As if she has a choice, I thought.

This also wasn't much of a restriction. I had never left the grounds around House Thalluen; Mother, Jilrina, and Kaltra had on occasion gone to the city or another plantation for political purposes, but I could count those times on one hand in my short life.

As a middle-status House, we were withdrawn from most of society, spending our cycles, our spans, and our quad-spans here doing the same thing through the turns to produce the various mushrooms, fiberstalk, and animals which helped feed all Sivaraus. We worked seeming to hope we'd avoid being noticed by stronger, more militant Houses who might want to claim what we have by force.

We stayed here, taunting and trapping and feeding on each other like too many spiders sharing a single web.

At least there was one less female spider in the web now.

The Elder Red Sister had left with all but one of her Sisters, taking Jilrina's body plus whatever else of ours they wanted to claim.

One Red Sister remained behind to enforce the edict. She wore the same uniform, cloak, and helm, but it wasn't the same warrior who had handled every item in my room. We didn't know this Red Sister's name, either, but she had asked — insisted — to dine with us in our great hall while she was here. Of course, we obliged her.

Over the first span of the Sister's residence, I watched her leering at Kaltra across the table and recognized her flustered response, the familiar shame. That was when I thought I might enjoy having a Red Sister as a guest for a while. Anyone would have told me I was insane for thinking that, but at least this even had put a prideful Second Daughter in her place.

"Don't you look at me like you won anything yet, little slit," Kaltra muttered to me after one such dinner when we both left in the direction of our quarters. "They'll come back and condemn you for what you've done, and with your disrespectful mouth, I have no doubt they must have punished you as well while they held you in your room so long."

"As well?" I repeated slyly, narrowing my eyes in triumph. "Mm, no, I don't think they did. What did the one dining with us do to you? Make you breathe through your mouth with your face in her cleft?"

My bigger bully of a sister shoved me against the wall hard enough that it hurt my shoulder. She said nothing else and stomped off. I sneered at her back.

You deserve that Red Sister's attention, you dullard, whatever she's doing to entertain herself. I'm just glad it's not me for once.

The Elder Sorceress took her time returning to House Thalluen. She finally did nearly eight spans later, and I wagered it had been a long sixty-four cycles for my dullard sister to become familiar with entertaining another superior besides Jilrina. I stayed out of their way and worked the plantation more than I ever had before.

Now back in my Matron's office, we listened intently as the Elder deemed the First Daughter's death officially an accident. Our Matron accepted the ruling with grace and requested no further resources; she seemed satisfied that no one else would be taken from her House. Yet even as Kaltra was now the Heir, this covetous status seemed to pass right by her as her first response was denial.

"No!" Kaltra pointed at me, trembling. "Please, Elder, you must know! Sirana did it!"

"Shut that hole before I fill it again, sweetmeat," growled the Red Sister who had been with us this entire time.

That was the end of that argument, at least until the Red Sisters left our lands. I wished my Mother could shut Kaltra up that readily, but I would hear growling accusation over and over again for nearly five turns until I was eighty-four. Be it alone, in front of servants, in front of Mother, Kaltra just would not let it go.

You are such an idiot. Focused on the wrong source of power, tripping over our dead sister's corpse when you are supposed to take her place. You can't represent us. You aren't worthy to be Thalluendara.

My instincts told me I had only to wait. I had waited for thirty-five turns for Jilrina to die, to be free of her. I could wait a little longer for the unbalanced Second to make a similar mistake, then I could prove myself. Mother may have ignored me, ignored what was happening between her Daughters right beneath her nose for decades, but she wouldn't be able to continue ignoring me when I was the only Daughter left to inherit our House.

I would prove myself better and smarter than all the females with whom I was forced to live. I would make something of myself beyond the "slutty sacrifice" Jilrina had always told me I was.

I'll prove it.

"WHAT?!" I CRIED, TREMBLING WITH RAGE AS I HEARD MY MATRON'S DECISION. "You jest! Kaltra tried to kill me! She was so sloppy anyone can see it!"

"Tried and failed, Third Daughter," my Mother said, staring at me alone in her office.

"You agree, yet you won't call the Red Sisters? They won't need nearly the two quad-spans they took last time! It'll be done in a cycle!"

My Mother shook her head. "It is not required to involve the Red Sisters if the assassination fails. It falls to the Matron of the House to manage her own living offspring."

"She'll try again!" I barked. "You know she will! And if she does, I'll defend myself again no matter what the outcome!"

The Matron nodded in agreement. "I believe you. That is why I am sending you to the Palace Court, Sirana. You will be my representative there while I train Kaltra to focus on our holdings. It will be better without you here to distract her."

I felt something like a fist slam me in the gut. I stared in disbelief. "You're … sending me away? And keeping her?" I couldn't stop shaking. "As if I am sabotaging her lessons?"

"You are," she said plainly. "You provoke her with intent. You wanted her to attempt murder."

"If you see it that way, then you know I'm smarter!" I shouted. "I've learned twice as much as her about managing the plantation since Jilrina died, and I'm half her age! Dare try to tell me I'm not the better choice for Heir if you must send one of us away!"

My Matron's icy, formal mask remained in place as she lightly touched the tips of her fingers to her desk, which she kept between us. I'd never forgotten the next words she spoke.

"Kaltra is still fertile," my Mother said. "She can bear children. Elder D'Shea told me, five turns ago, that you cannot. You are scarred on the inside. I cannot name a barren Daughter as my Heir, Sirana. I regret it, but it is the way it is. You will go to Court, and you need not be near Kaltra ever again if you do not wish it."

THE COACH WHICH HAULED ME OFF THE PLANTATION OF MY BIRTH WAS DAMAGED on the inside by the time it stopped in front of the tallest structure I had known could exist in the Great Cavern. The driver had been ignoring the noise, and she would guide the less-than-perfect property back to return to my Mother.

Damaged inside, like me. She can deal with the coach the same way she dealt with me, I don't give Braqth two fucks!

I dared not show how angry I remained as I met the liaison who would take me where I was supposed to be tucked away out of my Matron's sight and forgotten. At least if I needed to cover up fury and resentment, the two were too loud for me to worry about covering up fear, also. That would work in my favor.

"Thalluensareci," was my first and only greeting from the older male.

I nodded confirmation, stared directly at him as he kept his eyes down from mine; he seemed aware of my foul mood all the same. He was my height but easily a century or two older; typical for the smaller Davrin males. His uncovered, white hair was cut straight across at jaw length; his skin was dark and clean, and he wore some powder that kept it dry and smelling sweet. I couldn't tell the exact shade of his eyes in the streetlights but saw a red that was common enough. He seemed competent and respectful for a Doorsvrin.

For appearances, I was surrounded by several trunks set to be carried away by Palace servants. They were all locked by a magical inset that required a specific word to release — a reasonable deterrent for non-mages — but I bore in mind not to take their security for granted. Something unpleasant might jump out at me during the very first cycle or span I was here. Nothing in them was important to me, though I was told I would need the variety of clothes.

There were sources of light which illuminated the dressed pathways and streets around me, even if the lanterns didn't reach very far up the curvaceous, looming architectures of the Palace and the Sanctuary constructed right next to it. What struck me more than any sight, however, were the smells.

The scents were dense and foreign to me. I quickly caught strong fragrances clinging to gowns and robes as any Palace resident walked by. There was a hint of a water-and-web garden somewhere nearby, and for me to smell it from here, I knew it must be much larger than the one we had at home. Clusters of nervous bodies and animals living too close together, and a whiff of the garbage in the city streets, which were only a brief jog on the other side of the Palace Wall.

All this scent and visual movement around me, and I realized I was unsettled. This space didn't seem as loud as it should be. I heard the low drone of murmurs and the shuffling and clacking of work beasts being moved and work being done, but there was no shouting, no raised voices. They were all hushed, stepping light and often silent. Given how much yelling had been going on at my House lately, with far fewer females, this seemed unnatural.

"Allow me to guide you to the quarters set for your House, Thalluensareci," the liaison said when I just stood there watching as the coach pulled away.

"Go ahead," I said with impatience. I had my own bag of things I didn't want servants touching over my shoulder; I jerked away in warning when the Doorsvrin silently offered to take it, and his hand dropped again to his side.

A lot of eyes watched me as I entered, most of them common-blood servants but a few slaves of the short races: a well-groomed ketro-slave holding a bucket for some reason and several low pytes polishing the floor clean of dusty footprints. I kept my chin up and never looked down — one of the few bits of advice I let my Matron know I had heard her — and walked deeper into the Palace of the Valsharess.

I was led through wide, opulent hallways made of dark grey stone shaped by magic, yet it was hardly as dark and drab as it looked from the outside. Carved into the stone walls were symbols of spiders, webs, and Abyssal eyes in many places. At least some of them were functional, I wagered.

Those walls not etched with decorative inlays of gold, silver, or another shiny metal were covered with some of the most detailed and finely crafted tapestries I could have imagined, suggesting events and places I had heard about from my tutors. The floor was polished in such a way as to allow candlelight to reflect, seeming to double the number of torches down any hallway I passed.

The Doorsvrin guided me up both straight and curving stairways fixed with plush, woven carpet which absorbed all sound. I paid attention so as perhaps to be able to find my way back to the front door, if need be, although I was starting to get confused already which direction that was. The servants who had taken my trunks weren't coming to my "quarters" through the same route I walked. I'd have heard them ahead of me, or at least seen more than the few little sniffs I got from the other Nobles whose conversation I disturbed by walking by.

Most female Noble Davrin glanced at me then ignored my passing, and if the males watched me any longer than a glance, they were subtle about it. I clenched my jaw and kept it level with the floor, still angry and hiding it.

"These are the same quarters your Matron used when she was last here, Third Daughter," my guide volunteered as he demonstrated how to disengage the Ward without breaking it.

"Oh, are they?" I said, uncaring.

"They are sometimes let out to other Houses as we cannot afford to have space unused for half-centuries and more, but we are usually able to accommodate the established Houses in intimate spaces for each Worship Ball at least. These should already be clean and ready for you."

The Doorsvrin then turned the handle to open the door, entering first and gesturing for me to wait in the frame while he performed a brief sweep to make sure the place was empty. It took him some time — I counted twelve doors being opened and left open.

When he returned, he smiled in satisfaction and bowed his head to me, indicating without speaking further that my trunks were already here. He was preparing to leave.

What do I do now? I wanted to ask but bit the inside of my cheek rather than show a servant such drifting uncertainty.

"Very well," I said coldly. "You are dismissed."

He left me, and I stood alone staring at my trunks in a hollow, quiet, series of rooms intended to contain a visiting Matron and all her children, sisters and brothers together. There would be a lot more noise in any of these suites during the preparation and the seasons of a Worship Ball. Right now, placed neatly where I had been sent, I was the only Noble from House Thalluen in residence at the Palace. By the Abyss, I was the only Davrin from House Thalluen of any kind.

Mother had offered a tender, a tutor, a maid, anything. I had refused and come here alone. Just a worthless Daughter with whom my Matron didn't know what to do, thanks to my oldest sister's fanatical delusion and twisted tastes.

I cannot name a barren Daughter as my heir, Sirana. I regret it, but that is the way it is.

She regretted it?

She could have *stopped* it whole turns of the core ago!

If I could have spoken. If she had noticed.

I got to work unpacking my trunks with my own hands, distracting myself by inspecting every piece I lifted, searching for anything that didn't belong. My throat hurt, but for a different reason than forced silence. I kept blinking away any blur to my sight, listening to the silence around me, breathing deeply of this new place that was to be my exile while Kaltra struggled to learn how to keep our heritage.

She will fail. And I'll have to watch it fall. What a waste.

I breathed deep and kept working, unconvinced that I had the privacy I craved to weep my frustration. It felt like someone was watching, and here at the Valsharess's Palace, someone probably always would be.

I BEGAN MY STAY AT COURT CAUTIOUS AND QUIET. WITH NO ENTOURAGE, NO announcement, no allies, and no enemies, I had a chance to observe the new rules here and learn my way around the Palace before anyone said or did anything beyond commenting on my blue eyes — always assuming the light was good enough for them to see the actual color.

"Consort's lineage somewhere," I overheard someone say. She was talking about me but not to me, and she let me hear her, I was certain. "One of the fashion statements."

"Indeed? Who is she?"

"I'm not sure. She is very young to be here without an elder female escort, though, isn't she?"

"A little young. Not *too* young."

I left before they could call me over and ask whose Daughter I was. *Consort's lineage, huh?*

Not as far as I knew, and my stomach roiled at the thought. Jilrina and Kaltra were both Consort-sired; they made certain I understood. Our Mother had been dubiously Blessed by a Grandson of Braqth during two Worship Balls. She hadn't claimed a third Consort to conceive me; some young pole at House Bovritz had conducted that trade.

The Matron of the Eleventh House was one of our occasional visitors when she deemed Thalluen, of the less-populated Twelfth House, was worthy of her time or the time of one of her many family members. The Davrin who had sired me was one of her cousins, I thought, though I couldn't even remember what the record had said was his name.

How often had my two sisters described to me *their* sires? Perfect skin, dark as shadow with flowing hair stark white at both top and bottom. Beautiful, exotic, talented in bed. Bred and trained by the Priestesses to please any female. Each had been kept at the manor for only a few short turns while our Matron entertained herself with him, many decades before I was born.

Mother would never own a Consort permanently; all belonged to the Priestesses and the Valsharess, as the highest studs a Noble could claim.

He would always return to the Sanctuary for the next Worship Ball, then he would be given to another Noble who had done enough favors for the right slits in high places.

Unless my sisters had taken after Mother in ways I could not see, I thought the choice of sires was to blame. The first Consort to visit our home must have thought so highly of himself that he could not couple without a mirror in one hand. The second Consort must have been so dumb as to run face-first into things in the dark, and he only found Mother's breeding hole with his prick by accident.

It was only a matter of time before someone here recognized Matron Thalluen in my face. Of her three Daughters, I was the one who looked most like her upon seeing past the odd blue color. Yet my eyes alone seemed to provide me that real distraction, a level of camouflage with no family standing by my side.

That weird anonymity would only last so long, I knew.

Still, I avoided spats and petty squabbles for the first twelve spans — a full quarter of a turn, which I thought was impressive. To be not worth anybody's time yet still be able to watch their eyes and hands, the tilts of the heads at formal meals, in the gardens, the halls, and the bathing rooms? Beneath the actors' notices, I started to feel safer, more confident. Bolder ... and curious.

I began to meet the eyes of more young, male Nobles. I would catch a drifting gaze, one bored or embarrassed by a public display, and I would hold his eyes for a few moments and share some unspoken, snide comment about our so-called "betters." As long as the politicking females weren't hurling toward a known crime or physical conflict with the bua in the middle, he and I could snicker oh-so-subtle behind their backs from the fringe.

More of these Sons smiled when they saw me enter a room, yet they didn't stumble forward to gain my attention and pull the judging glare of their chaperone. I would prowl behind a few proven able to control himself and do it slowly — usually at a dinner party or in the web gardens — letting him lead the chase no one could see, and the secret game seemed to delight more than one of them.

I was delighted myself, especially when one wiggled his backside suggestively for me, or another adjusted his robe just so, allowing me to see a glimpse of the turgid outline of his staff. The game offered a far better buzz than the wine at dinner, and alone in my too-large quarters, I kept dreaming about what I would do with one of these Noble buas when I finally caught him.

Then one eve, the drink at dinner proved far stronger than the high of my personal game, and many Davrin returned to their rooms early or would be found dozing openly in unsecured places. There would be many and varied accusations awaiting the Court upon sobering up. I had managed to stop before I got halfway through my first glass, and I still felt the dulling of all my senses. I didn't like it one bit.

In no shape to play the floor now. Return to my rooms. Get safe.

Yet on my way back, I found one of the young, Noble Sons for whom I'd prowled before. He was alone, unprotected, and passed out beneath a tapestry of our Valsharess facing off with some giant, black snake of the Deepearth. I crouched and shook his shoulder, sluggishly trying to think of his name.

"Micraen," I mumbled.

My head pounded and swirled a moment, and I stopped shaking him, resting my face in one hand, breathing deep. *I think someone tampered with the whole cask at this dinner. Who was it? The Priestesses? The Red Sisters? The First House? Bah.*

I tried again. "Micraen, wake up."

The most I got out of him was a groan. The sound was unfamiliar because it was unguarded; I was a little surprised how my heart sped up, a rush of heat passing through my body. I leaned closer, shook him again, and he made that noise again. Annoyed. Confused. Harmless. I could smell his scent, too; the natural one rising from his chest, not the fragrance he wore just behind his ear. It made my mouth water. I'd never been this close to any of the buas with whom I'd been sharing smiles and jests these many spans.

"Micraen." Another shake.

No response now, not even a grunt.

Well, I could leave him here for his chaperone to find him — she should be looking for him this very moment if she were to do her job — or I could watch over him myself. A few moments' worth of thought, where I imagined leaving him and waking later after an eve's Reverie, only to hear some drunken group of caits had gotten hold of him and violated him while he was unconscious. I didn't like it.

Fucking slits would do it, too. My room it is.

Part of me was surprised no one stopped me, or that a servant didn't report seeing me. It had taken some work, but once I had the young Noble flung over one shoulder, I was stumbling alone toward a quieter side of the Palace. Everyone must have been feeling like dung heaps to ignore this, not just me.

I forgot about that curious thing as soon as I released the Ward and lurched into my own chambers, shouldering the door closed again to reset the Ward with a swipe of my hand. I had so many rooms to choose from, sometimes I rotated between them just to change my routine. I didn't consciously decide this time; I made my way to the nearest one with a bed, which also happened to be the smallest.

Fully clothed and my head swimming, I dumped Micraen onto the well-padded mattress and followed right behind him, shoving the warm body almost against the wall to make room for me.

My head touched down; I closed my eyes and slipped away.

WAKING UP IN BED NEXT TO ANOTHER DAVRIN HAD ALWAYS BEEN HARROWING for me. It almost always meant I was naked, sore, and suffering aftereffects of whatever "ritual tonic" Jilrina had given me. From what I'd seen and heard so far at Court, I wasn't alone in this desire to wake up alone. Perhaps waking from Reverie in twos and threes on a regular basis was done among the fighters and the servants who had no status to lose or assassination to fear, but the Nobles at Court avoided falling asleep together mainly for those same reasons.

When I opened my eyes in the pitch black, I saw a body so close I couldn't help but recognize it. Micraen was already awake and staring at me, lying on his side. I sensed the heat of his skin immediately, smelled both him and the rumpled clothing he'd worn to dinner. I read confusion and wariness in him, even as I saw him mostly as an Elvish shape without color.

I bolted upright, identified the room as mine, saw I was still dressed and covered down to my formal slippers. I could breathe. Then I noted sandals on his feet, tiny beads, and decorations tied around attractive ankles. I shook my head, trying to clear it.

"What the fuck?" I said.

"What I was going to say," the bua murmured ruefully. "And, where am I?"

"Thalluen quarters," I grumbled, rubbing my face and the grit from my eyes.

"I see. How did I get here?"

I tried to remember. I shrugged and said, "I don't know. Either you walked here, or I carried you. I doubt you carried me."

He swallowed subtly. "Do you know what mark of the cycle it is?"

I exhaled. The room was dark without candles, smokeless or otherwise. It was barely prepared as a living space because I hadn't used this one much. I didn't keep a timepiece in here.

"Nope," I said, fumbling in a side drawer to light one of those candles so I could begin keeping time at some point. I waited for him to spring up and straighten his clothing in vain, to explain that he needed to rush to find his chaperone or his governess, his sister or cousin. I waited for him to say he needed to leave my rooms.

He didn't. Micraen just looked at me like he expected something.

I narrowed my eyes suspiciously. "Aren't you going to be punished?"

"Probably," he agreed.

I watched him shift on my bed as if he was comfortable yet intended to relax further; he tugged up his shirt to show me his taut belly and sickle-shaped navel. Resting his head on one arm and turned so that he was in a suggestive pose, the cup of his crotch hanging heavy. He drew in a breath through his nose and watched me hopefully with wide, pretty eyes.

I huffed a laugh even as my eyes trailed with appreciation over his form in full color. I twisted a handful of my dinner gown in one hand, wiping the sudden sweat off my palm, but then made myself stop.

"You're offering," I checked.

"I'm here," he replied. "You finally caught me, even if I can't remember how."

He was hard, too. He wanted it.

Sitting there, I felt like the rat hunter that had stalked and toyed with its prey for far too long. Now I had it under my paw, the rat had gone still and wasn't trying to get away, and I didn't know what to do next.

"You've been fucked before," I guessed. "This isn't your first."

Micraen was coy and shifted sensually, now pushing down the fine fabric covering one hip. I could see not only more smooth, dark skin but also the contrasting white fur crowning his cock, as well as the base of it. Clearly ready to ride.

Teasing slut.

I shivered involuntarily, and my dark nipples stood up through my pale dress. It had sunk in. The bua was here in my bed, and I had decided.

I was about to lay the first male of my life!

Let's aim not to let him guess that.

We stripped down and slipped under the covers, and I dove right onto him, wanting to explore all of him with more than just my hands. Goddess, but I did enjoy using my lips and tongue; his skin tasted good! So good, in so many different ways. Every place was new to me, and I loved that he didn't smell female at all, didn't taste or sound like one. I loved the way his phallus fit in my mouth, how I could suck to make him shudder. I enjoyed listening to his whispered submission to me. He didn't once try to climb on top of me.

"Please take me," Micraen said, eager and willing by the time I finally got to my knees and straddled him. "Oh, yes. Sirana."

He was good at making sexy, encouraging faces. Pretty masks, practiced for the female's pleasure and ego, of course.

Oh well. Give me that bua-pole.

I was a little too quick and eager myself. My impatience got the better of me as I found myself moist but not as slick as I could get just dreaming about buas. Either my nerves or the drink last night — or both — made me a little dry despite the foreplay. I got the head in but really should have given myself more time to work us both, or just give up and use some spit.

I did neither; I took him most of the way in on the first lunge down, and the searing fire that scalded the entrance of my sex shocked me. I sucked in a breath and emitted what sounded like a roar to my ears; my body clamped down on his, and my torso fell forward into his arms as I bit the pillow, willing the pain to pass.

"A-Are you well?" Micraen asked, sounding afraid. "Mistress?"

Mistress. The first he'd called me that since we woke up. Now I *knew* he was scared, believing I was about to get violent.

Meanwhile, my needy, fresh-speared slit burned, throbbing a little around the stiff rod I'd jammed into it.

Stupid, stupid …

I hadn't put anything in there since Jilrina had nearly killed me on her homemade altar a decade ago. *So glad she's fucking dead. I hope Braqth ties her up in her metal web for playing a fake Priestess.*

Sweat dotting my forehead, I lifted my head from the pillow and tasted Micraen's skin again with my lips, trying to calm myself. I explored his throat and shoulders and collarbone. His tense muscles relaxed a little, my sex seemed to loosen its death grip on him; we made eye contact. He stroked my thighs and, trembling, I nodded, tentatively rocking on him. There seemed more wetness to spread along his length, which had gone slightly soft.

Finally, I nodded again. "I'm well. Whew."

"Y-You've never — ?" he began.

My face flushed. "It's not my first time, alright? I know what I'm doing. Just wasn't wet enough."

Micraen exhaled and accepted without question. He looked down to admire my breasts, touching them, stroking one hand along my flank and over my hip to really reach and squeeze one buttock. I felt him regain what rigidity he'd lost in his fright, and he even thrust his hips up, moving with me as I sorted out my rhythm.

I managed to fuck him properly, working out something familiar in theory but not in practice, using an orifice that I both loathed for it costing me my inheritance and still wanted to reclaim for myself.

If I didn't, the first century at the Palace would feel even longer than it was shaping up to be.

"Mmm, yes, Sirana, like that," he whispered, caressing my thighs as I pushed myself up again to regain leverage.

I went faster on him. I listened to the smacking and slapping of my flesh on his; I squeezed his pole tight with my muscles as I got wetter, as the burning eased, but the soreness remained.

Braqth's Tits. This feels alright but … strange.

A small, childish part of me suggested that now I'd tried it, it was kind of disappointing, and I didn't know what anyone saw in lodging blunt, unwieldy, uncomfortable things up inside like this. Tongues and fingers had more fine control.

You sound like Jilrina.

I growled. If I stopped riding my first cock now and ended on a note of disgust, the cunt's memory would win. I wouldn't let her. I wouldn't give up. I kept going.

I hadn't figured out how to climax before I was out of time. The candle told me I risked someone knocking on the door searching for their missing Noble Son, and simultaneously the same, slutty Davrin in my bed was now to the point that he might choke if I didn't let him—

"G-Goddess, please, Sirana!" he wailed.

"Do it!" I commanded. My palms planted on his shoulders to hold him down as I sped up. "Let it loose! Now!"

His naked body was anything but passive beneath me then. I watched his face as he pitched himself over the proverbial cliff. I felt him writhe, and his cock twitched and pulsed deep inside, seeding my sex for the first time. I listened to those genuinely uncontrolled noises through gritted teeth, and I stared at him wide-eyed, my fingers gripping him, my mouth gaping. I may not have climaxed myself, but …

Wow. That was a very close second.

His member softened, and I lifted my soggy sex off him, landed beside him with my crotch buzzing. He had sweated enough as to smell delicious, and I gathered him closer while the bua caught his breath. I meant to rub that scent all over my chest where I could enjoy it after he left. He nuzzled my tits with his face, and I chuckled, touching his back and soft hair while he fell into a light doze.

He was so pretty when he relaxed.

I knew it now. There were qualities in bua I sought to enjoy, despite my never having the chance to explore it until now. I'd always known it.

I'm not like my sister. I'm not like either of them.

I could peak taking a bua this way; I had only to practice. Tracking and catching these eager members on which to practice would be my new task. Tittering with the children behind older female backs was a youth's game. Now I was ready to play the bigger one.

When I returned Micraen to his female guardians in House Kelnic suites, I realized I had "jumped up" a few levels in stud quality. The less important Daughters of the Ninth House were themselves still bleary from last eve. Since the Matron and First Daughter weren't present but far away on their own plantation, I enjoyed the bluster and predictable chiding, which failed to hide their personal embarrassment at the blatant filching of a Son from their nest beneath their own noses.

"You should thank me," I told them after they had run out of hot air, patting Micraen's bottom while he stood demurely. "The Red Sisters might have gotten to him instead."

It was a cheap shot to make them pause and give me an out, and I would learn to do better in time. I would finally be noticed and would make the necessary allies alongside the inevitable enemies.

That first early cycle, however, in the hushed, whispering Court of the Valsharess, I remembered laughing out loud before I left.

The new sound of my own delight echoed back at me.

Chapter 3

Spectacle was a regular part of our sustenance at Court.

Within another decade, I would approach that important marker of having survived my first century among the Davrin Elves of the Deep. Over the next five turns, I recognized familiar, mortal wounds in pride, and I observed the arrogance of simultaneously testing and knowing one's place, of playing for better rewards or besting another. I saw, somehow, this often led to inertia after the flavor of victory wore off.

Life at Court was very much as it had been with Jilrina and Kaltra always on my tail. On occasion, Mother did something that made them shrink back and rethink their fantasies of outright killing her or me. But not often enough, in my opinion.

Without an army at one's back — the reason the members of the House Barracks were banned from Court — there were only the periodic, successful poisonings or "accidents" which changed the status quo. Even when those happened, it did not mean that either the killer or the real hand behind the assassination received precisely what she wanted. There were always females tumbling and stumbling in the wake of the death of another, whether one could argue they should have seen it coming or not.

The Nobles together at Court, all from different Houses, were like home but with far more variables. This was why the Davrin at the Court needed the Valsharess, the Red Sisters, and Braqth's Priestesses. This was why we needed the glimpses of royal purple robes and blood-red uniforms. We required reminders of structure, of order and consequence. Otherwise, the escalation of petty hubris never paused.

This was why I focused my energies on male conquests and bedroom antics for my first turns at Court. I could learn to plot and move at my own pace; I could enjoy myself and never worry about stuffing my gut with an unwanted child. And, perhaps most importantly, no one died. Rarely was anyone even injured.

I built my own reputation, such as it was, as a "safe" cait who didn't lose her temper, who didn't invite other females to humiliate a bua, who didn't tend to brag to others about the details. I kept my mouth shut, most of my bragging held within the smirk on my lips.

From this, I enjoyed popularity among the bored and curious sons wanting sensual indulgence with only mild social consequences for them or me. As a solitary, middle House representative with small actions and plots that mattered not at all in the long run, they soon learned I was there to play.

None of the Top Five Houses got near me, male or not, and the rest sniffed and sputtered a bit as I slipped away with their Sons, but again, my relative discretion saw few elder females seeking more than a snide, public comment or an attempt to slip a purge potion into my dinner as her revenge. I could handle that.

I always made sure these buas were sensually rewarded for their efforts, giving me a sign of their interest. I learned so much of the male form, of their physical limits and mental boundaries. Once naked, they were endlessly fascinating to manipulate.

I was not the only Noble female playing this way, yet this game did not see all that many children conceived and born as far as I could tell. Transactions and alliances of this nature were short-term goals, diversion, and excitement, and any disappointment when conception did not happen was brief and transient.

I barely understood how fertility changed in buas and caits anyway, and I had none of my own to consider. For all I followed, it required a fertility potion to plan for it; otherwise, it seemed to happen at random. This was fine with me. I knew if it worked every time a cock seeded a slit, if many pregnancies occurred all at once, it would throw things out of balance down here. We needed a lot of slaves and Houses working to feed those in the Great Cavern as it was.

This game of mine was pure entertainment, a type of theater that appealed to Davrin nature, and a chance to pretend to be somewhere else for a while. Some of us wanted to be because every cycle indeed was the same, broken only when we received another reminder from the Valsharess that She still held absolute power over us all.

In addition to the numerous chances to seize and ride cock, I witnessed many more formal tortures, executions, and rituals than I ever had at House Thalluen. Not only me and the rest of the Court but many times, much of the common bloods of Sivaraus bore witness as well.

These events all had the intended effect: my fears and emotions were in a whorl at the grating sounds, at the scent and sight of blood, and the shock of such creative or magically inflicted agony. I was afraid, but hiding it from everyone else, and I was fervently glad it wasn't me on the platform or the altar.

Once was more than enough. Let it never be so again.

By my fifth anniversary residing at Court, I had built a stable of Noble sons I could tick off as knowing the shape of their cock and not once had I returned to see Mother or Kaltra. I had expected to continue in this vein when, upon waking one cycle, I was "selected" to participate in one of the few Priestess rituals that required a fair number of Nobles to complete.

"Take this with you to the eve meal," a messenger cait from the Sanctuary said at my suite doors, delivering a small, blushing vial sealed with wax and imprinted with Braqth's Spider symbol. "Do not drink it until after you've eaten."

Uh-oh.

I knew better than to display any reaction but that of thrilled elation, despite the shadow of wariness in my heart after I closed the door.

"Fortunate Pole-Clutcher," remarked Baedit Lospursareci later on, at the formal dining before the ritual. She had noticed the sealed vial near my plate. "Most of us need to be here a decade or more before we were noticed for such honor."

She was an older female, a Third Daughter like me but quite a few steps higher in the Seventh House, yet our similar title was enough justification to be seated next to me if she wished. Baedit was one of those Nobles not at all pleased I had lured her nephew into my arms in the web garden just a few cycles ago, and I knew to be wary of her smirk.

She said, "I dare say you've been honing your skills for this moment since you arrived, Envi's Daughter."

"Rohenvi's Daughter," I corrected, holding my chin up at the name, if only for pride's sake.

"Oh, I am aware, little Thalluensareci." Baedit chuckled, sipping delicately at a taste-tested glass which had not left her hand all eve. "I remember Rohenvi when she was here parading around for her own studs. She avoided nursing her haughty mouth on slippery netherlips, too, and from what I heard, she was only interested in the swords going in one particular sheath. She must have been rather modest teaching you the way of things."

I gave her a wordless look, and she snickered.

"From the way you go at things, I'd say she sent you here to catch as quickly as possible, even from a male at random, and give her a grandchild. Maybe more than one?"

All my effort went into the restraint of grinding my teeth; if I didn't, she would hear it.

The Noble shrugged, sipped from her glass again. "But I understand the Twelfth House needs more children to survive, else I shouldn't be surprised if it is simply absorbed into another within the next hundred turns. The First Daughter, strangely, seemed neither tempted nor was required to perform her primary duty before she died, and I haven't heard any happy news in the new Heir. The only female bearing any Nobles at all for the last three centuries is the Matron herself, isn't it so? One Daughter a century? No Sons? Rather stagnant for a middle House."

Not the first time I'd endured such talk — threats and insults disguised as curiosities — but this was one of the most precise collections of needles to be jabbed in a tiny area, one after another. Baedit must have been collecting comparison details between my Mother and me almost since I got here.

I had never offered even a hint of my barrenness, however, and I knew my Mother hadn't shared that detail with any contact upon sending me here. The Red Sisters knew of my condition, though they weren't known for spreading gossip but instead collecting it into a bottomless, black cave, where it never came out except with a poison dart attached.

"You haven't taken your tonic yet," the elder nudged me. "Be certain to quaff it before they come to collect you for the ceremony. Even the novice Priestesses will be able to tell who hasn't drunk their 'aid' for the ritual, and they never treat gently those who delay them."

Controlling my expression lest someone connected to the Priesthood see it, I glanced at the vial sealed with wax. I thought again of Jilrina's plays at being a Priestess, of her scouring unreliable sources for details of what went on inside the Sanctuary. I thought of all the potions she must have purchased to force down my throat on her little altar at the back of our estate. Most of them seemed to have no real effect beyond sedating me, sometimes leaving a headache or nausea afterward.

Sitting at Court decades later, an ugly, cold fear spread over my stomach as I admitted to myself that I didn't want to break that seal and drink whatever was in that vial.

This one is real.

My mind raced through possible means of evasion, of bowing out of the ceremony and still be blameless. Maybe I could manage food poisoning in a quarter mark.

The tall, main doors opened, and everyone dining now stood at the first flash of elegant, purple robes and novice gowns in black and white. A shudder of terror gripped me which Baedit noted with a raised brow, and I cursed myself lividly in my own head.

They'll see! Do it! Don't think!

I reached for the vial, broke the seal, lifted it to my lips. A thick syrup touched my tongue just as I realized that everyone else who had been chosen got up but needed assistance to walk; most were guided toward the Priestesses by someone from their own House. A luxury I didn't have.

Fuck.

I swallowed, nearly gagged at the bitter-sweetness, and scooted back my chair to slip by my dinner companions of the eve. I approached the Priestess novices and curtsied in my pale green, spider-silk gown beside another female Noble showing more drunkenness and attempting to do the same.

The apprentice frowned at my relative sobriety, whispering something under her breath to scrutinize me and I waited, offering another curtsy as I hadn't the fucking clue what to do next.

"Good," the novice Priestess said, nodding in satisfaction even as I expected her soon to report to a superior how I'd delayed quaffing the vial until the last possible moment.

A good fourth of the dining hall had been gathered up, and we were now escorted out. Equal numbers female and male, all Davrin, of course, and each of us under two centuries old. The Priestesses had chosen only those with less experience and more youth.

I couldn't help wrinkling one nostril in bleary, private comment as my stomach rebelled at this apparent requirement. Perhaps Jilrina had heard about it and sought to mimic it as well, except she had chosen much younger than anyone here. This may be the most for which I could be grateful this eve: no children were collected to bear witness, not as there often were at executions.

This was the first time I would pass outside the Palace and its grounds since I'd arrived, although we as a group never went outside the massive structure. The Palace was connected to the Sanctuary by open public doors and hallways, and probably many private ways unseen.

Even the public doors were well-guarded. Any time prior, when I'd crossed in front of them on my way somewhere else, I'd never done more than quickly appraise the value of the gold webbing and amethyst spiders which decorated the entrance to the Sanctuary.

When our dinner group arrived at the entrance, those extravagant, giant doors were already open. A Red Sister stood on each side, standing tall and intimidating even without clear weapons in their gloved hands. Their hard, unreadable eyes were on us as we were shuffled through the archway into a long, void-black hallway, clustered together. I could barely sort out my quickened heartbeat from those others around me.

Someone slipped a hand into mine, either seeking mutual protection or merely preventing me from falling over as the Priestess' potion spread through me, twisting my vision and lightening my head. I looked over before I could decide whether to pull my hand away.

Micraen.

I left my hand resting in his.

We were herded into a large altar room lit by standing, iron lanterns drawing a rectangle of light along the stone walls. The Priestesses-in-training moved through various clusters, flashes of black and white pushing a few staggering, young Nobles into different groups.

"No sisters with her brothers!" one of the novices shouted. "No brothers with brothers! Sisters and cousins may remain together."

Without needing such shoves, I noticed that Micraen wasn't the only bua I'd once bedded sidling up to me now. I recognized Yeri, Tohni, and Reaf along with Micraen, as individual conquests from four separate Houses. Fuzzily I detected a pattern; each of them was the only bua from his House here this eve. He had, at best, a sister here. No cousins, apparently; too old to be selected, perhaps.

Above our heads, the ceiling was bedecked with purple and gold banners, and the walls were clothed in rich, colorful tapestries meant to convey Braqth in Her Aspect of the Queen of Intrigue and Sensation. It was my first solid hint why we were here. I swallowed in relief that I wasn't in a room with the Aspect of Endless Descent or that of Battle Madness and Blood Drinking.

We were all ordered to kneel; she who spoke must be the elder Priestess, I guessed by the dress and appearance. I stood up on my knees, weaving to remain upright while some sat down on their haunches with legs folded beneath. My vision wasn't clear, and some of the words the Priestesses spoke next seemed muddled; I vaguely worried I'd miss some vital instruction that would ruin the ritual, yet any fear at the thought was muted and numb. I felt in full the effects of the vial by now; I was warm, floating, and open to whatever would happen.

As chanting-turned-singing began to rise from the front platform, three hands touched my backside through my dress while we listened. I glanced to one side, nearly fell over, and the Noble Sons surrounding me caught my fall, one caressing my breast while he had the chance.

We seemed to be floating. The buas' hands were almost reverent, even being too bold and familiar. My heart pounded, and I didn't tell them to stop. I glanced around and saw their erections in top shape, be it through trousers, robe, or sarong. Licking my lips, I smoothed my hand over my crotch; my breath hitching at the sensitivity. Watching me, they began rubbing themselves through their clothes, too.

Goddess, yes …

The Priestesses' voices became a drone, the air seemed hot, and my little group was not the only one daring to relieve boredom in evident and flirtatious lust. Most seemed to be pairing up, with the female the clear dominant. A couple collected in threes — two caits roughly and greedily sharing a bua — and some of the pairs and small clusters were entirely female, struggling for control even before their clothes were off.

I saw no twos or threes which were all male; every Noble Son was attached to at least one Noble Daughter, not of his House, and she often held his cock by the figurative leash.

My group was unusual. Four Sons serving one Noble Daughter. Eight dark hands touching me. Over my buttocks. Between my legs through the gown. Now tugging at the threads and laces, exposing my breasts and my shoulders. One dove in to suckle a turgid, purple nipple.

Oh, Goddess!

"Braqth'ne Kash'et!" cried the elder Priestess, lifting a scepter high in the air from atop her platform.

With the writhing lake of bodies spread out upon the floor, I could barely see what was happening upon the Altar. I also ceased to care when Micraen and the others eagerly stripped me nude and, in the struggle to get free of the confining dress, I fell forward onto my palms, barely remaining on my knees. My legs still parted, I flinched when the pads of fingers glided over my netherlips, testing my receptivity. I needn't worry about a repeat of my first time with Micraen; I was dripping, my fluid oozing with abundance.

"F-fuck me," I growled, quivering in that undignified position. I didn't want to move; I only wanted to feel—

One of them plunged his cock into my sex, and I sucked in a breath and wailed in relief. The other three pinched my nipples and caressed my belly and flanks while the first stroked and serviced me like a well-trained stud. I climaxed swiftly; I should have been surprised about that but was drowning in the gasps and cries surrounding me while the Priestesses whipped the Nobles into a drunken orgy.

The quality of the light seemed to change, from crisp, silvery blue from the lanterns on the side walls to a warm red glow from the direction of the high platform. I couldn't lift my head to make out the reason for the odd light as the first bua to mount me now pulled out, having spilled inside me at some point during my own gripping peak. I waited for the next in line to seek his relief and help me come again.

I yelped to feel something *entirely* different and intensely sensitive. Looking over one shoulder to blink, I was shocked to see the next male — Reaf of House Bovritz — with his face buried between my buttocks. There was that startling, wet swipe again.

He … he's licking my netherhole!

In all my conquests, this was the first time I was bent over exposing my slit and bud at the same time, and I'd never asked for a service such as this! My mouth hung open as the knowledgeable tip of his tongue stroked and teased the tight pucker open, making it flutter around his probing tongue, out of my control. Somehow my drenched folds swelled even more as my breeding hole ached for another rut.

H-He knew how to do this, and he didn't ask before? Oh! Fuck, yes!

Reaf stopped slurping my ass and had finally mounted me properly, taking my cunt despite my inability to articulate that command. I grunted and blubbered something like approval as his hips slapped my haunches, my eyes rolling up. Goddess, I was wet! Too wet. He might have to go for quite some time to reach his summit.

The third bua couldn't wait. He slithered on his back underneath me, slipping his lovely feet in between my parted knees and encouraged me to resettle my hands just to the outsides of his shoulders. I chuckled as my tits jiggled above his face with Reaf's thrusts; I looked down at this new one with his sweet face and wide, eager eyes.

Tohni, I recalled though failed to think of the House. Instead, the next thought was, *He likes kissing.*

I settled down on my elbows, pressing my tits to him while keeping my hips in the air for Reaf. I pressed my lips to Tohni's mouth, and he kissed me back; I felt his shaking arms go around me as he hummed. I didn't think Reaf had climaxed yet, but he pulled out and, solely by pressing down on my butt, encouraged me to sit and take Tohni's cock next. Eagerly, I did so, and my new bua groaned and humped upward as Reaf guided him inside.

Three in my snatch without even wiping down. A personal best!

Almost immediately, I would perform another.

Reaf didn't move out of the way but instead climbed over me, gripping my shoulder and wedging the head of his unsated pole between my ass cheeks. Without pause, he pushed on the bud he had teased so delightfully before.

"W-What — *Oh!!*"

My netherhole held little resistance to any pressure, despite it knowing only a tentative finger or two until then. Wet from Reaf's saliva and now meeting his blunt spear coated thick with my own lubricant, the virginal hole splayed open for him in obscene submission. Such a stretch seized my mind! I hardly felt a twinge of pain, and no burning as I would have if I had been sober and not surrounded by chants and grunts of other Nobles receiving the same.

I cried out loudly as Reaf penetrated his full length, my voice lost among many others and held still while both pricks were squeezed together, tight inside my body. I was suspended within the sensations of our Goddess, held tight in the grip of ritual magic. I didn't fight or protest straddling one bua from above with another on top of me, his cock deep in my ass.

"Sirana!" Reaf gasped, drawing halfway out and pushing back in all the way to his white fur. "Yes, oh my Goddess, *yes!*"

"Yes!" I echoed, shaking at the unfamiliar invasion, yet still, I relaxed back against him and wanted more.

"Yes! More, Children of Braqth!" the Priestess commanded, her rich voice filling the chamber above us. "Each climax, every one of your screams gets us closer! Deny Our Mistress of the Web no part of your body which She demands! Submit to us! Spread your young legs wide, Nobles! Service them, young Sons, until they can take no more!"

Tohni and Reaf fucked both my orifices with such enthusiasm, pinning me between them and moving together such that I couldn't catch my breath. My mouth was open, drooling when I was caught up in an unexpected rise, groaning through a second, shuddering orgasm.

When a hard, smooth phallus slipped between my lips and settled on my tongue, I sucked him readily, delighted and proud to be pleasuring so many at once! Reaf slammed in a few more thrusts and grunted, going still so that I could feel the pulse and throb of his member inside my initiated netherhole; he had left his offering behind at last.

At this point, the male inside my mouth took my once-styled, well-braided hair in his fist and thrust harder past my lips as Tohni hurried to finish inside my swollen cunt. Held in place and waiting for those two anticipated moments, I didn't know who parted my cheeks and pierced my netherhole again. I cried out, heard Tohni do the same as he seeded me at last, and looked up to see my fourth, Yeri, ready to paint my tongue with his cream. He quickly followed Tohni, and my slit clutched one while I swallowed and slurped the other.

"Wraph't'ren Galla!" shrieked the Priestess, and something like torn cloth sounded through the very air itself.

I was dripping male seed when Micraen — the one now inside my loosened back hole — pulled my hips up off a momentarily-spent Tohni. I settled on all fours again with my head lolling, a hum of the Priestess's power rushing through me as I trembled, caught helpless in ecstasy. My first conquest of the Ninth House reamed my netherhole for the second time, intending to finish there, and I wanted him to.

And I wanted another after him. Whoever was ready!

I neither could move nor wished to, as Micraen slipped his member back out, as mixed fluids dripped down my thighs.

Yes ... yes ...

A scream.

One of pain.

With effort, I lifted my head, tried three times to focus my eyes to see that far; meanwhile, a faceless male got behind me and squished his rod inside my soaking slit.

Oh, Goddess. Ugh. Th-there is a creature in the chamber. In here, with us.

Not a Davrin. Huge. Wings like a bat. Spikes on his elbows — *Four of them?* — and hooked spurs on his knees; more sharp edges jutting from his shoulders. A mane of long, russet red hair flowing down his spine. No tail. No clothes.

He rutted a Priestess on Braqth's Altar, his hips thrusting between her spread legs. His wrists were chained down to the stone through the spellcraft of one Priestess. Another Priestess maintained the magical muzzle keeping his bestial mouth shut and his jaw up as if it was tethered to the ceiling. He couldn't rip her flesh.

Or, not more than he was doing.

Spikes on his cock ... blood on her thighs.

She endured it bravely.

I shuddered, felt someone withdraw from my cunt as semen splattered the stone beneath me. A blessedly normal Davrin cock pressed into my yielding netherhole, filling me up as yet another bua kneeled in front of me, blocking the view of the altar. Closing my eyes, I lowered my willing mouth onto his erection, tasting a previous mix of female fluids on his prick.

I might have come again, once or twice more while my holes felt more pleasure than I could ever have imagined. I knew Tohni rolled me to feast with his lips on my mouth regardless of semen still dripping from my own, while Yeri lifted my legs and mounted with me while I was on my back. Beyond this, I could barely focus.

At some point, there was an explosion; not of fire or destruction, but of raw power, of controlled magic. I heard and felt the roaring completion of a spiritual ritual I would later learn defied mundane forms of conception. It created something exceptional within the Valsharess's control.

Long before then, I regained consciousness along with the other young Nobles on the floor of the Altar room. All of us. Naked. Sticky. Sore. Looking furtively at one another, wondering, *Had I really … ? Did she, did he — ?*

"Return to your families and your quarters, Nobles!" a Priestess commanded. "Stand up! The novices and the Sisters will guide you back to your rooms. Do not take time to dress; let your elders be reminded when they were once in your place!"

Return to your families …

My four conquests did so, meekly joining their sisters and leaving me standing alone. My elbows and knees were scraped, my muscles tired and my neck stiff as I got up. For the moment, my nipples were somewhere between tingling and numb, and I couldn't tell how many poles had served me in such quick succession. All three holes felt sated, pleasantly warm.

It wouldn't last once the contents of that vial wore off.

Surrounded by blood-red leather and white-black spider silk, and once again herded like livestock, we clutched our clothing to us, many of us wearing only our slippers as we made our way through chilly hallways back to our respective parts of the Palace.

Some of the group whimpered; others sighed and took pride in the apparent success of our participation, what it might mean for their status. Some of them would speak of what just happened while some would spurn the opportunity. I stayed silent because there would be no one waiting at my quarters — be it to mock me or help me into a bathtub; no one to choose whether to let me sleep this off.

I broke off from the herd as soon as I could, evading a few older females who tried to get my attention and hurrying down a familiar hallway. My head pounded as I prayed I wouldn't collapse before I got into some warm, clean water. There were so many scents on me I couldn't enjoy one in particular, and I needed something to soothe my inspection of sensitive, tender flesh.

I reached my quarters, fumbling with the Ward before I got the door open and took a step inside.

I heard, "Hold the door, Blue Eyes."

I didn't know the other Noble's voice, and I didn't care. I nearly stepped inside, ready to close the door in her face.

Or do I? Should I?

I hesitated, glanced to my right.

It wasn't another Noble.

One of the Red Sisters strolled her way toward me, apparently relieved of her duty in escorting the mass of us back. I froze in terror, holding the door by happenstance instead of cooperation. The fighter female took my naked shoulder and pushed me inside my own suites, closing the door behind us as I gripped my ruined evening gown to my front, already shaking.

In the state I was in, my mind was not remotely prepared to deal with a Red Sister. We were alone. No one even to see what became of me.

I'm going to die.

The Red Sister left me to quake as she swept my suites for me, checking every empty bedroom and living space before showing herself again. She then lit a few candles around the sitting room, her rust-red gaze returning to me.

"Ah, good, you didn't move."

She smiled as she removed her cloak, gloves, and helm. Hearing her speak again and given a chance to see her face again, I realized I *had* known her voice outside in the hall. She was the Red Sister who had guarded me in my room back home five turns ago, the one who had broken my mirror while waiting for her Elder to interrogate me.

Maybe they found something they'd been keeping in reserve in judging my supposed guilt? Perhaps they were just picking an unexpected time that I should be taken away and locked up? Would my Matron be informed, or would she even know what happened to me? Would she react with more than a mildly regretful sigh, as she had hearing Jilrina had met her death by accident?

Or maybe now I'm the "right" age for this Red Sister when I'd only been "almost" then.

It wasn't unheard of that Red Sisters would occasionally harass a Noble who needed to be reminded of her place. I'd heard whispers. Maybe I'd drawn that attention. Maybe I would learn what Kaltra already knew. I swallowed.

She approached to take my bare, upper arm in a firm grasp, dragging me with her to the bathing room. Setting her cloak, gloves, and helm on a counter, she placed the stretch-funnel attached to my rune-marked cistern into the empty tub and opened the valve. As clear water spilled in and began climbing up the smooth sides, the Red Sister turned around and kept herself between me and the water basin.

"Have fun, Blue Eyes?" she asked, arms crossed as her eyes raked over me. Her poise was intimidating; I got the impression a single punch from her would knock me out.

"S-Surprise, but lav'sh, Red Sisster," I slurred.

I wanted to slap my own face. What kind of answer was that? I couldn't think!

As the tub continued to fill, she chuckled and motioned for me to drop the stained dinner gown; slowly, I obeyed, letting it crumple to the floor. I stood nude with hot and protesting joints, wearing only my eve's slippers on my feet. I was filthy, covered in sweat, spit, and the semen of no less than four males. Maybe more.

"Show me your netherhole," she said, casually and without preamble.

I resigned myself to let the funnel drain the entire ration of heated water from my cistern into the tub. The servants only refilled the water by bucket every three cycles, and it took time for the magical runes to warm it up to a pleasant temperature.

You're stalling, Sirana.

I turned around, my knees growing weak, and bent over.

Or rather, I tried to bend over. My head revolted, I lost my balance, and soon I was splayed on the floor. Within a moment I felt the tap of the Red Sister's boot.

"Come on," she said. "Show me."

I couldn't stand to try again with my head toward the floor, so I opted for elbows and knees again, whimpering slightly at the renewed rawness. Her boot tapped the inside of my knees, wordlessly instructing me to spread them wider, and I did. She pushed her palm down on the small of my back, and I took the cue to roll my hips up to present myself in a way I had only just now learned to do for Micraen and the others in mutual service to Braqth.

"Good cait," she murmured, touching my buttocks and gently parting them with a thumb, studying my holes while I couldn't even imagine how they might look right now. "Ohhh, little Noble. Unless you've got a potion hidden away somewhere, you're going to waddle when you walk the next cycle or two."

Her eyes lingered to drink their fill of my soiled and swollen flesh, and her bare hand squeezed my rump, yet she did not try to jam her own fingers inside either orifice as I expected her to. I was silently grateful; I could feel exactly what she meant about waddling.

"Into the tub," she ordered.

"Y-yes, Red Sister," I mumbled.

I found myself unable to securely attain my feet, so instead crawled to the edge and pulled myself up. Eventually, with sloshing and some water on the floor, I managed to shed my slippers and get into the tub. I groaned in bliss as the heat seeped in.

"Don't fall asleep," she said.

I snapped my eyes open, my heart pounding as I realized I could easily drown because I could in no way expect her to save me if it suited her otherwise. So I forced myself to use soap and cloth to scrub the ritual's stains from my skin. While I worked on this, the Red Sister smirked, watching me like I was a fly caught in Braqth's web and dancing to provide much amusement.

"Was that your first time?" she asked.

"H-huh?" I bit my lip at the half-witted response, but fortunately for me, she overlooked it in favor of an answer.

"Taking three at once," she clarified.

Shivering in the warm tub, wincing as I shifted on my sore backside, I nodded. "Y-yes, Red Sister. My first."

"What about having your shit chute ridden like a collared male at an execution party?"

My face flushed and my scrubbing faltered. I hadn't heard a description that crass since I'd been near my Matron's fighters at our Barracks, even though Mother didn't tend to have "execution parties" like that.

"Also my first, Sister," I answered, not arguing with the degrading likeness. It wasn't as if I'd been in any shape to pick which Nobles mounted me that way, and I still remembered the way I'd cooperated and moaned for more.

Because of whatever was in that vial.

The Red Sister chuckled, her eyes trailing over me in obvious appreciation of my used, naked body. My gut rebelled against whatever she imagined, yet my head knew I was trapped into whatever she wanted until she decided to leave. To my intense aggravation, I felt my eyes ache as if they might tear up.

No! Fucking deal with it, don't dare weep like a weak, little child. I can take it, I've done it before.

I washed my hair, got my body clean, answered her other questions about my part in the ritual. I asked no questions of my own even though plenty ricocheted through the stubborn bits of my mind. The water raced toward tepid and about when my toes might have been wrinkling, the Red Sister stood up and held a dry towel out for me. Her hungry eyes never left my body as I stood up, set the tub to drain, and accepted the plush cloth to dry myself. She offered a second one for my long hair. I doubted she ever needed two; her hair was far too short.

"Where do you lie down?" she asked as she escorted me out into the narrow hall.

I shrugged, nauseated but resigned. "Wherever, Red Sister. Pick one."

She looked up and down the near-empty quarters, still amused, and pushed me toward a middle-sized bedroom two doors farther back. I cursed myself for not even resisting her for two instants, for swallowing all my defiance as if Jilrina was still alive.

I was a pathetic Davrin in front of stronger females. No wonder the Court sneered at me for only being able to handle buas.

She's a Red Sister. What good has it ever done anyone to defy a Red Sister?

One of the last torture-executions I saw had been conducted by them. I nearly heaved just thinking about it now.

I exchanged a Reverie-gown for my damp towels — at least to give me some brief moment of protection, and she didn't stop me — and readily climbed onto the clean bed, above the covers. I kneeled, waiting for her to tell me what she wanted first.

The short-haired warrior sat down on the edge of the bed, her legs splayed comfortably, boots flat on the rug. Her scent of skin and leathers was musky and suggestive that she spent more time outside of fancy shelters than I ever had. She hadn't shown me one spell or tool or weapon, yet I sensed the power and confidence such that I knew there were times when she didn't need them.

She must be four times my age. And she's still alive. How long has she been wearing that uniform?

After a few moments sitting there in silence, I realized I envied her.

Nobles fear her. Even Matrons. She goes into whatever room she wants and doesn't have to threaten. She sees things, hidden things. She can fight, can defend herself; she isn't humiliated no matter who she fucks. Meanwhile, I'll sit here like a dumb beast distracting myself with young poles until the Priestesses need to herd us from our holding tank again.

Five turns at Court, and I already hated my life as much as I had back home.

"You started combat training at House Thalluen. Why did you stop?"

She had spoken out of thin air, yet her words clubbed me over the head. I swallowed another stupid reflex and answered her.

"Jilrina made me stop," I said.

"She's dead."

That reasoning had been swept aside like cobwebs.

"I w-was trying to learn how to run a House as an Heir," I explained.

"You're barren."

I shivered, the statement spearing me down to my core. My throat flexed painfully. My next excuse would have been related to how no fighter groups except the Red Sisters and the Palace Guard was allowed at Court, but I already knew the Valsharess still saw some Nobles taught how to use a sword or dagger at least, one-on-one, upon the request of their Matron.

"I don't know," I said.

Finally, the Red Sister nodded. Although she took that, the answer felt unacceptable.

"Send a letter to your Matron," she said.

As soon as she saw the stubborn expression flitting unwisely across my face, she barked a loud laugh at the ceiling. I jumped and shrunk back at the sound, but she reached out and took my arm, yanking me onto the bed and pressing me down with her body. I screamed once — I couldn't help myself — but silenced myself as I found her mouth on mine, her tongue forced between my lips. She kissed me, sucked on my sore lips harshly, a firm hand palming my right breast through the thin sleep gown to pinch my nipple. Though it grew hard under her fingers, I discovered it still tender.

I squeaked in protest, which amused her as she hummed against me. *So be it. Don't fight. Don't offer a reason to kill me if she wasn't sent to.*

The Red Sister finished claiming her kiss from me and lifted herself off, next slapping my cheek open-handed. Its strength was somewhere between an insulting tap and a bone-cracking backhand. I stared up at her, unblinking, frozen, and unable to move.

"Rest well, Blue Eyes," she said, grinning as her eyes trailed over me one more time. "Dream of me instead of those lucky fucks who broke in that tight ass for you."

The Red Sister stood up, collected her helm, gloves, and cloak, and left the Thalluen quarters of the Palace, snuffing the candles she'd lit on arriving. Stunned several long moments, waiting in the dark and fearful of her to return, I crawled beneath the blankets when she never reappeared.

My throbbing head was so confused. I felt fortunate to be given the reprieve, and yet I felt condemned to bear the specific attention of a Red

Sister who looked at me like a tasty morsel.
Probably the intended effect.

CHAPTER 4

THE RED SISTER'S LAUGH RETURNED TO ME MOST AS I WAITED IN VAIN FOR HER to arrive at my quarters again. That braying, uninhibited bellow such as I'd never heard from the often-solemn, stone-faced enforcers of any ilk inside the Palace or Sanctuary. I recalled the way her eyes twinkled in candlelight when she smiled at me as if there was something in me to want. Or admire.

When had I ever heard or seen that before? Not at the quiet, sullen plantation of my birth. If someone laughed like that — a servant or a soldier — they didn't do it where their Nobles could hear them. At Court?

Hah. All the laughter here has a double edge to it. To cover fear, to carry insult or anger. To wear a mask.

The first turn since that orgy ritual wore on past its first quarter and then its second, and I remained unmolested by leather-clad females in my empty quarters. I was alone unless I invited my own male companionship. I dared to wonder if that Red Sister hadn't been showing me a mask. Was that how she was? Did Red Sisters, in their power, have that luxury to strut about however they pleased, to laugh when and how they liked?

Why not? How can any of us manipulate it for our own ends, if there is no shame to exploit? I snorted to imagine a Noble attempt some judgment or insult for it. *No judging.*

That was the other thing. I'd just been used by multiple buas — Noble Sons who now avoided me for fear of what I might do in retaliation. I hadn't gone looking for them yet, and I hadn't even decided what I would do if I caught one of the four again. There would also be others whose names and faces I didn't know, yet he might remember knowing my holes well, and it could be his secret pleasure to enjoy that memory without consequence.

It wasn't unheard of for a Noble female to "submit" herself to receive that much service at once, but she "directed from the center," as the saying went. Anyone watching that orgy — and I was sure the Red Sister had been, and she had focused on me — would know I hadn't been in control of them.

They used me under the influence of Priestess magic. Afterward the Red Sister ... looked at me as though standing so filthy and defiled made me desirable to her.

Desirable. Not contemptible. *Weird.*

Her first question after I'd shown her my swollen and sticky nethers stuck in my head. *"Was that your first time, taking three at once?"* Why would *she ask me that?*

A first time implied a second — a time where some skill could be honed. It suggested she wanted to see me do it again and be proud of it. I wasn't sure that I could. Wouldn't I just be like a meek male then, getting on my knees waiting to be done to, not taking what I wanted?

Maybe she's only aroused by females who act like males.

There weren't that many of those types of females at Court — or anywhere, as far as I knew. Given how such Nobles were treated by everyone — mocked, disrespected, making even the males bold around her — I didn't want to become one of them.

The Red Sister had left my quarters with a clear directive, however: write a letter to my Matron asking for formal martial training at Court. I did not ignore that suggestion, and doing it even made me feel less like the kind of female who would crawl in front of a male and ask to be used and humiliated.

Jilrina is dead. I am not an Heir. Nothing holds me back from taking up a sword and training to fight. I was desperate to learn when she was alive.

Although the males at Court and their female relatives had distracted me for my first five turns in taking all of my focus, I knew I could do better for myself. I *would* do better.

My Matron responded quickly to my letter, and I had what I needed to request a formal apprenticeship from among the Palace Guard. The approval, I was told, ultimately came from the Valsharess but I never saw Her in the process. I also doubted the Queen looked that carefully at every Noble application.

At first, I spoke only with bored, older administrators sitting behind large desks with quill in hand, wearing the blue and purple uniforms of their station. In almost three spans, before the full quad-span had passed, I started novice training with some other Noble Daughters.

The Guards who could genuinely teach us something wore blue, purple, and a stripe of orange. Most tutored in the way of enjoying the opportunity to floor a Noble now and then, just short of the humiliation which would invite vindictive responses from a House. They always pulled their hardest strikes, though sometimes, with me, I wished they wouldn't.

Once my first half-turn of training was complete, I had moved beyond the group lessons to regular one-on-one with three different veteran Guards. I managed a better balance between the sex, the intrigue, and sparring, and I gained in the martial skill I'd always wanted. My confidence rose with it; so did my laughter, which sometimes filled and bounced off the high walls of the practice chambers.

"Braying Uroan," Wixara of the Sixth House said once at dinner, though I'd never seen her in a match, only as a pillow-sitting spectator.

"So knock my wind out," I challenged with nonchalance, "if you can."

She tried to make me regret saying that. I almost did a few times.

This ill-considered taunt began another source of welcome entertainment to pass the time at Court. I received challenges on behalf of lazy Nobles like Wixara, fulfilled not by them but by relatives and servants who could display their skill. I got the wind kicked out of me more than once by fighter females, and the observing Noble would smirk and snicker, rewarding her chosen champion in various ways.

"There," she'd said. "Now we shall have some blessed silence from the Twelfth House during the next practice, hm?"

Not likely.

I lost plenty of those matches, but I also got better. I learned from them, whether they meant to teach me or not. I always got back up and would accept another challenge a quad-span or so later, or issue one myself, if only because it irritated the fuck out of some of my fellow Nobles. Even one ill-advised sparring against two House Guards at once didn't see me stop fighting, despite injuries which kept me in my quarters once for eight cycles.

"Prideful Sareci," a Noble sniffed at my birth order. "She needs an elder female to remind her of her place at Court."

That isn't ever going to happen.

I enjoyed sparring whether I won or lost; the effects of each, whether high or low, were as temporary and resistible as any time Jilrina and Kaltra had tormented me in the past. Like sex, the fighting was never truly over; like the Red Sister of several turns ago, I found it became easier to laugh in victory *or* defeat.

My attitude and skill growing together also drew more Noble males to the practice rooms, wanting to watch me do both. Even Micraen and Tohni eventually approached me again, and after a close and well-earned victory, I decided, still sweating and panting, to take both of their young staffs at once in the privacy of my quarters.

"This time," I told them, peeling Micraen's shirt open to caress his nipples, staring each Davrin in the eye, "no potions. All my way. Understand?"

They grinned and cooperated. Word would make it out as the males gossiped, and I would eventually see Reaf again as well. When I next fucked three young poles at once, it was while I was sober and in control.

I liked it better the second time.

I ENJOYED THE NEXT DECADE AT COURT MUCH MORE THAN MY FIRST HALF-a-one. I was ninety-nine turns old, approaching my hundredth birth-cycle with a reputation as a decent fighter with a stubborn streak and an entourage of male admirers at Court.

The first century was a significant marker, one by which most children of the Nobles had found their place and purpose within their family. Unless Mother allowed me to join the Barracks, I doubted I would ever find mine back at House Thalluen.

This would not keep me from searching for a place of my own, limited as those options might be. I would never have to think about providing for children of my own or begging my Matron for help and support; as a lone fighter, I could be hired and live on simple necessities if I was ever ousted from Court.

Perhaps I could even find a service in the city. Or join the Palace Guard.

That last one felt like the path of least resistance, given that they had trained me. I wasn't sure where else to aim, though, and saw no reason they wouldn't take me. Nobles didn't have as many choices as it seemed to those commoners staring up at us in our comforts.

I hadn't been called to participate in a Priestess ritual again, thank the Spider Queen, but it was only a matter of time as I puttered around the royal grounds, pretending I was anything more than a useless Third Daughter.

A Daughter who, sooner or later, will be whispered to be infertile.

I couldn't indulge in buas forever without catching if I claimed to have a working womb. The other females would notice in time. Following the Priestess initiation ritual — where it was widely assumed by now that I'd taken half the males in the chamber up my backside and sucked their dirty cocks afterward — I was still playing that card for what it was worth.

I only took seed in my mouth or my ass now, ostensibly to delay having a child, and I bragged about it. This might give me another few decades rumor-free, but any Noble Daughter who hadn't proven her fertility one way or another by one-hundred-fifty invited comments about what was wrong with her.

I had heard rumors about some Noble females gaining children in secret, trading for robust infants from among the commoners, but that was far from proven. If I did that, of course, then I had to think about how to take care of a baby, which would in time force me to return home.

Maybe I'll figure something else out by then.

One eve after another Nobles' party, I risked standing on one of the Court's balconies alone, looking out over our Deepearth City.

Never much of a view, and I only sensed noise and movement in my bones and along my nerves, distant and immaterial until it came close enough to be a threat in the dark. Clusters of lights flickered here and there; bright points out in the massive Great Cavern, of which I had never made out the ceiling even from up here. Fire torches or magical light waved and blinked along the streets and outskirts, because sometimes the other senses weren't enough.

I often wondered about that. If the Davrin were born and would die in a place with no light if we could see in the dark as well as any creature around us, why did we still insist on indulging our eyes with colors?

Our eyes were part of our overall beauty as Elves, I knew, as we possessed a variety of beautiful faces. Perhaps it was our eyes coupled with our written languages of material and magic which set us apart from and above the other races of the Deepearth. All the others — often squat, moist, and dirty in their own settlements — possessed poorer eyesight in the light of fire or magic; they often could not discern the nuance of color. They struggled to learn how to read, and they archived none of their own histories and spellcraft as we did.

Our mages, our spellcasters, and potion brewers set our race above all others. We studied and used magic more than any other kind. I was not a mage, but I owed much of my convenience and comfort to them. I also owed to them much of my early torment as well, for it was a mage who had created that compulsion potion Jilrina had purchased, dooming me to silence beneath her cruel hands until she died.

My silent suffering could have lasted for much longer than three and a half decades. As aimless as I felt now, I was still free of that, at least. I didn't know what I might do if I should ever find the brewer who had given that potion to Jilrina.

She's probably already dead, I thought.

I had since learned permanent compulsions like what I had been given were forbidden magic. In my mind, it was extremely likely the Sorceress Elder who had questioned me about it had since gone to find the mage making those vials for Nobles to use on each other.

The Valsharess forbids it. The Red Sisters enforce it.

And I could see why. The Noble Davrin often couldn't control our indulgences when there were no rules or, like Jilrina, some thought the rules didn't apply to them.

From where I stood on the balcony, I could see the Web Garden directly below me. The glittering strands of spider silk managed to absorb and reflect the pale blue and green fluorescence of cave lichen growing in tended patches along dressed stone pathways, benches, and sculptures. Spiders specially bred for the Valsharess had made those designs, their tiny minds just magical enough to understand they couldn't make the same web twice. One could become lost studying those intricate patterns.

Engaged as I was, I still heard a boot scrape against the stone behind me and whirled around.

A Red Sister stood there, watching me sternly.

She gave me that warning on purpose.

"Sirana Thalluensareci."

I kept my stomach firmly in place as I curtsied. "I am, Red Sister."

She wasn't the short-haired warrior of before. This one was new to me. She was not quite as tall or as broad in the shoulders, and her face also appeared as though it might crack if she so much as smiled, much less laughed. She did not wear a helm, and her hood was down; her hair was in a tight bun without a strand free to flutter in a draft.

Her features were sharp, her eyes a very dark shade which seemed black in the colorlessness of my Dark Sight. Her cloak was open, and I could see her weapons belt holding two daggers, a hand crossbow, five or six pouches, and a selection of slim, stoppered vials.

"Um, what may I do for you?" I asked, thinking back over the last handful of spans in case there was a misstep which might warrant this attention now. I couldn't think of anything.

"You may come with me."

Shit.

My body recognized where I stood now: as I had on the cusp of the Priestess ritual. My flint-eyed escort had arrived with little warning, and I had an instant to comply with her instructions and step forward. I wasn't part of a larger group this time, but at least I wasn't being asked to swallow an unknown potion.

Not yet, anyway.

I approached the leather-clad warrior in my flimsy evening gown and slippers, breathing normally up until the point she gripped my upper arm in a painful hold and snapped the fingers of her free hand before my eyes.

All fell black. I couldn't see.

Braqth's Tits, she's a mage.

My heart tripped like my feet, and I forgot to breathe as the Red Sister dragged me from the balcony. I couldn't be sure if her spell only affected my eyes, or if we were cloaked together in magical shadow to avoid being seen. Either way I trembled, first expecting a poisoned dagger to enter my back before my mind seized on the possibility that I was being taken to the dungeon instead.

What have I done? It can't be Jilrina's death again. Why wait for fifteen turns to punish me for an accident?

Let it be something else.

Getting my feet under me, I matched the brisk pace of my collector exactly. I counted my footfalls in my head, mapping the hallway to try for a sense of where I was going. Somehow the Red Sister could tell what I was doing, and she didn't like it.

"Stop that," she hissed, drawing something from her belt and striking the back of my head.

I stumbled, swallowing my cry as she hauled me around several times in a circle then forcibly pushed me until I fell. Disoriented, I felt her take my bare ankle in hard fingers and start dragging me. My dining gown went over my legs, nearly past my hips; if the blindness was mine alone, then the Red Sister likely saw I wasn't wearing anything underneath.

That didn't concern me, however; nor did any possibility of my dress tearing or my hairstyle being mussed. I was much more concerned to be skidding and struggling on the polished stone with no indication that she would stop any time soon. The bruises would quickly turn to open cuts and abrasions, and I remained blind and dizzy.

"Let me up!" I blurted. "Please, you've done well, Red Sister, I've lost where we are!"

She released my ankle as she stood over me for a tick before dropping her knee right into my stomach. My breath was hurled to a forceful stop.

"Presume not to command or assuage me, little Noble. I'll sever your calf through and leave you here to bleed out. You'll miss your chance."

Her voice was only a hiss, but in the absolute darkness, it seemed louder, penetrating. I shuddered, sucking hard for breath as I curled up to protect that calf.

Miss my ... chance?

"I apologize, Sister," I gasped. "Please let me walk again."

She hauled me up by one arm, and at first, my other senses were rattled and useless to me; I needed her strict, guiding arm as we continued walking forward, or backward, in darkness. By the time I walked with my escort without support, I had become aware of the door in front of my nose just in time to not hit it.

"Ur'nithel," the Sister murmured in rich, mage's pronunciation, motioning and touching something with her gloved hand.

The door smelled of stone and tasted of magic, hardly making a noise as it moved to the side. I imagined that I might be disappearing into the very walls and may never be seen again.

"Move," she growled, pushing my shoulder.

A first step and I felt the floor drop beneath my slipper-clad foot. My heart pounded in my chest as I counted the stairs downward, and this time the Red Sister didn't seem to care.

I wanted badly to ask where I was being taken, and why. Was it the dungeon? Or an interrogation room? A sacrificial altar? I began to wonder if I should have attempted to run from the balcony, if I'd lost my only chance of escaping to live another cycle. Yet if I had, where would I go? The Red Sisters would find me anywhere in Sivaraus, and I couldn't leave our borders unprepared and expect to survive in the wilderness.

Noble livestock at Court, waiting to be bred and culled.

The urge to flee took deep breathing to get under control. I repeated to myself that I'd done nothing to justify feeling so scared. As back at my Mother's House, if I showed it, it would be a presumption of guilt.

I've done nothing, I thought. *Nothing at all.*

After eighty-three steps the floor leveled, and I sensed the tight walls retreat, and the air became less close. I smelled no blood and no filth, heard no moaning or wailing of prisoners. My right arm hurt where the Red Sister still gripped it; she led me to some mysterious point on the floor, and we stopped.

"Stay."

I stayed. I waited patiently, for all that I tried not to lose my meal in a fit of heaves. I closed my eyes; it made no difference if I could see or not, but it helped with vertigo. I listened as well and realized I could hear breathing. Not just the breath of the Red Sister who'd collected me, but that of several more. Maybe three. A reddish hue had materialized behind my closed eyelids. The spell's effects must have receded, and beyond my lids was true light. I hesitated.

"Open your eyes, Sirana."

CHAPTER 5

My stomach clenched. I knew this voice, though I'd not heard it since this Red Sister had visited House Thalluen.

"Open them. Now."

I obeyed and immediately flinched, tears welling up and dripping down my cheeks. The sting came from too many candles, several scores of them in a large and circular room empty of furnishings. The walls were dressed stone and draped with the Drider's Crest of Braqth, the Shining Web of the Valsharess, and the curved dagger silhouette of the Red Sisters.

Oh, Goddess.

This was a formal room used by the center of power above the Nobles, and I stood here in a dirty, rumpled party gown. The floor beneath my feet had been polished to such a shine as to be able to see my reflection. It was as if I stared down at myself in an underground pond; as if I stood on the surface of black water.

There were two Red Sisters in front of me standing several paces away, and the one who'd brought me here stood on the outside right of them. I recognized the Sorceress Elder in the middle and my collector on the left. The youngest Red Sister on the Elder's right was new to me and closer to my own age. She couldn't be more than a half-century older and was the only one from whom I could glean any emotion in her face.

It was sympathy.

"Your dining gown is unsuitable, Sirana. Please remove it."

I blinked in the abundant candlelight, hesitated a moment too long as the Sorceress frowned in displeasure and stepped forward. I took an involuntary step back when she drew her dagger.

"Stop!" she barked.

I obeyed, frozen in place. She pointed downward, and I followed her gaze. There was a subtle inlay of garnet-colored stone that formed a diamond about a pace and a half wide, and I stood right in the middle of it.

"Step outside that diamond before I tell you, and your blood will be thrown by the cup back into your own face until it's all you see and smell and taste as you drain out."

I centered myself in the diamond and looked warily at the decorated dagger she held as if it were part of her own body, the intensity of her gaze eschewing even a glance at her face.

"You heard my first command, didn't you, Sirana? Or would you like assistance?"

My hands rose instantly to pull the silver straps off my otherwise bare shoulders. My pale gown was thin and flowing, covering me from bust to toe although in this light it took only a squint to see the details of skin and curve beneath. Once it was off my shoulders, it took very little to let it drop and pool around my feet. Without being asked, I also stepped on the heels of my slippers to slide my feet out of them.

The eldest Red Sister nodded in approval and gestured her hand smartly to the side. I kicked the gown and slippers out of the diamond where the youngest Sister collected them into a basket. She circled around me, studying my nudity critically.

"No hidden weapon?" she asked.

I hesitated again but reached up and pulled a long, thin needle from within the white braids of my complicated hairstyle. She held her hand out for it, and I passed it cautiously, trying not to prick her with it. She smiled, and I could see the subtle creases at the corners of her eyes.

Despite the warm color of candlelight, I could also tell there were just a few blonde streaks in her otherwise pure white hair. She sniffed the needle.

"Gauric's ointment," she chuckled, passing the weapon to another Sister who dropped it in the basket along with my clothes. "Enough to send anyone to worshiping their private throne for the better part of the resting cycle." She returned a hard stare at me. "Is that all?"

"Yes, Elder."

"Take down your hair. Undo every braid."

This was almost as meticulous and tedious as when the Palace servants had styled and put up my hair earlier before dinner. I came very close to yanking on the snarls in my anxiety but only had to glance at the Sisters watching me to refocus and tug gently on the strand that would do the most good. They were all poise and self-control, and they were observing my every facial tick and eye blink.

Given enough time, my hair flowed free and covered my shoulder blades, the ties and pins added to the basket. I was then instructed to remove my jewelry; the youngest Red Sister held out the basket so I could drop them among my other effects. The Elder Sorceress stepped behind me and combed her fingers carefully through the white tresses several times; I knew she was searching me, but it felt good in a way. I sighed to ease some of my tension.

Then I felt her gloved hand on the back of my neck, applying pressure. "Take hold of your ankles, Sirana."

I nearly spun around; the muscles in my pelvis flexed protectively as I understood that she had one more search to do. She squeezed my neck hard, prevented me from turning, and roughly forced me to bend over. She kicked at my ankles like a beast of burden to get me to widen my stance so my toes would touch the side points of the diamond. I'd seen plenty of males placed in this position. I'd even ordered it before; it gave such lovely access.

Not so fun when it was me nude in front of the Queen's Enforcers.

"Take hold of your ankles, Sirana. Don't make me say it a third time."

My hands grabbed at their instructed purchase, and I tried explaining,

"There is nothing inside my body, Elder Sister."

She ignored me. I felt the soft leather of her gloved fingers trace my sex; she was gathering what moisture there was. It wasn't a lot; I was too scared. She pressed a finger into me, and I cringed at the discomfort as she felt around inside, satisfying herself that there wasn't any foreign object stored in my feminine hole.

A few moments more allowed me to anticipate that she would check my third orifice as well, so I didn't tighten up at the first probe where it would only hurt. Instead, I relaxed, allowed the digit to penetrate me more easily. It wasn't slick enough and was very uncomfortable, but it also didn't last very long. I breathed a sigh of relief when she withdrew.

"Good, Sirana. Now get on your knees and spread them out. Touch your feet together. Now hands on the stone, bring your palms together, elbows out. Touch your forehead to your hands and keep your eyes down. Make yourself fit the diamond, imagine you are a spider waiting in her web."

Or a slave awaiting her mistress's pleasure.

"Now, continue to wait until we return."

I heard no snickering as I complied, and it did make me wonder. There was no additional pat or fondle; no final insertion to remind me of my submission to her. The Elder just glided away with the others, and I waited.

They left me there like that, the candlelight creating dancing shadows which swirled over the polished floor and teased my sensitive eyes. I don't know where they went, or even *how* they went, but it was soon apparent I was the only living thing in the chamber.

Time drifted, and I had little else to do except look at the candles' reflections and the shadows and shift my knees as they started to complain about the hard floor. I was aware of my nakedness, of my breasts hanging close to the ground and the nipples becoming turgid of their own accord before softening again, of the relatively cool air caressing parts of me still tingling from the cavity search.

Nudity on its own wasn't disturbing; Davrin Elves knew we were beautiful, more so than anything else in the Deepearth. The only time my nakedness had bothered me was when Jilrina wanted me unclothed; then I wanted desperately to cover myself with any armor I could have.

I suppose I wanted some armor right now; the position which I was to hold, and which the Red Sisters' standard was enough to make me obey, was one of supplication I had never needed to perform at Court, even at that Braqth demon-summoning orgy. Being naked only intensified the feeling that I was expected to act the servant, and my fate lay at the whim of the eldest Red Sister who'd commanded me to kneel.

What does she want of me?

My back was getting stiff, and I stretched it first upward, lingering, then arched my back down, trying to rotate my shoulders and hips a bit. Now if I could just give my knees some relief—

The thick, throaty hum behind me and the puff of hot breath on my inner thighs pushed any thought of body aches out of my mind. I froze in mid-arch, unable to move as I realized something was in the chamber with me. I hadn't heard it enter.

How could that be? How could it have gotten so close — ?

A long, rough tongue rasped along the folds of my sex and the cleft of my buttocks, and I gasped in shock, at last able to make my body move. I abandoned my position and spun in place, planting my rear on the ground still within the diamond, and closed my legs, facing the creature that had licked me. A complex mix of revulsion and arousal spread from my chest down to my groin as I recognized what it was.

Sathoet.

A hybrid birth, half-Dark Elf, and half-demon. A magical son born to our Priestesses of Braqth. Occasionally I saw them at executions or sacrificial ceremonies, attending their Mothers. After the orgy a decade ago, I'd put together that mass rut intended to aid in summoning an Abyssal servant to help conceive one of these creatures for the newest Priestess of the Spider Queen. Her Sathoet had been born only eight turns ago. I couldn't imagine it had matured to this size already when a decade-old Elf remained at hip-level to most females. This was a much older one.

Yellow, pupil-less eyes narrowed at me from a black, elongated face.

It had sharp teeth and a snout; very little of the bestial face resembled a Davrin, except for the dark skin and the mane of white hair. It was muscular, taller and stronger than me, with big hands and feet and claws on each digit. Except for the hideous face, it was well-formed, with balanced and sculptured musculature.

As my eyes drifted down, I was reminded of what I'd heard: that all Sathoet are born male. He was undoubtedly a *ready* male, erect, his chest moving deeper and faster as if catching his breath, and he weaved from side-to-side as if waiting for me to do something. He even whined briefly. I wasn't sure he could talk.

I glanced around the chamber; it was still empty. Just me and the Sathoet, both naked, and him with an erection. He breathed in my scent with evident pleasure, even if he dared not do more than lean his head over the garnet border of the diamond without touching it. I did not know what to do, what was expected. I still didn't understand why I was here. Perhaps I was just to be toyed with in some twisted games before being killed for some imagined slight to some bitter crone.

You'll miss your chance.

So my collector had said.

What chance? What did they want to see?

The Sathoet leaned down and licked my ankle, and I flinched, although it hadn't felt unpleasant, just different. When I kept staring and studying him, he hissed and reached with his hand to stroke his erection a few times. I recognized it was to delay some of the aches that would come if he wasn't allowed release soon.

I watched, fascinated to a degree, but still not sure I could become interested in a half-demon scraping at my feet as if begging for a pat on the head. It didn't make me eager to open my legs. There was no banter or clever hunt, no power struggle or reluctant surrender as with my Noble males. Games like this were what made me hot to couple. It would certainly take something more than whining to make me eager to bond with a Sathoet.

I could imagine, though, that if we only sat here staring at each other until the Red Sisters returned, then the Elder wouldn't be pleased with me. I'd be making things worse for myself, yet I couldn't only go through the mechanics of mating just because they stuck a demonic cock in front of my face. The dead feeling between my legs, the resentment, and the distaste for the situation would linger for me and prove nothing to them except that I took the path of least resistance.

I decided, for my best interests, that he must do something to make me want him, and I must give him some hint of what that was. Already he was showing signs of discomfort and impatience, looking balefully at the garnet border he seemed unable to cross. Muscles in his arms and shoulders flexed with tension.

I wondered what he would do if I were outside the border? Perhaps bowing and scraping for sex wasn't his first choice.

I slid my foot toward the edge of the border; the movement caught his attention, and his eyes were pinned to my progress. When I stopped just short of it, his yellow eyes glanced up at me but returned to my foot almost immediately as if he might miss the briefest opportunity of my toe reaching the edge of the border. I felt my heart rate increase as a predator's gaze fixed on my foot.

Not just a dumb beast or a fawning pet.

There was power there, something to give, something to take. He was half-Davrin, after all. Dare I do it? Did I have any understanding of what I tempted? No, I didn't, but I'd learned at Court that fully half of gaining control of any situation was acting like I did. If nothing else, it would be more interesting than just sitting here, and it would be my choice. Risk nothing, gain nothing.

I scooted forward and thrust my entire foot outside of the garnet border. The Sathoet froze for the split-moment it took him to understand that I was his, then he seized my ankle with one hot hand, yanking me out of the diamond with one pull. I was on my back staring up at him, and I kicked with my other free foot, striking him in his chest with my heel. He growled and dragged me the rest of the way out, close enough to him that he could kneel between my legs and lean over me. He bared his knife-sized teeth in a snarling, eager smile.

"*Don't. You. Dare!*" I roared with all the bluster I could bring to bear, rising up like a serpent and swatting him open-handed across the face.

The sound of the slap echoed perfectly in the chamber, and he appeared genuinely dumbfounded for as long as the echo took to fade. His grip loosened on my ankle, and I slipped free, rolling to get to my feet to gain distance before facing and glaring at him. A brief pause, and then his snarl came back as he made eye contact with me.

He charged.

I could have dodged back into the diamond and gloated at him, but that would be a decision I couldn't reverse, and I'd be stuck until — or if — the Red Sisters returned. Instead, I stayed outside the diamond and danced with the demon.

I ran, and he chased me. When he would get close to dragging me down, I dodged and changed direction. This could only go on so long in an open, circular chamber, but it was enough to wind us. Spinning around to charge back at him, I threw myself into his arms. It surprised him utterly, and I had my legs wrapped around his waist and one hand gripping his mane before he could throw me off. I drew back my free arm and slapped him again.

"You want to fuck me, Sathoet?! *Do you?*" I shouted in his face, pouring every drop of venom and fury I could to increase the potency of the next hard slap. "Were you told that I was your reward for being a good bua for the Priestesses? Huh, were you? Because I'll tell you right now, you brutish half-blood, I am *no Priestess's* reward!"

I slapped him again.

The Sathoet could understand what I was saying, and I could read a familiar Davrish expression on his dark face. The essence translated to, "*How did you know that?*" Sometimes I guess very well, or I get lucky. Sometimes I'm inspired during a heated rage as I was now. Perception and intuition were twins I valued immensely.

"I could bargain with you," I said with more calm, almost soothing, and he perked up. To my own surprise, I smiled as I felt his hands slide under my buttocks to support my weight. His erection had softened, but he dug in his claws a little into my flesh.

"*Rrrrm?*" he rumbled.

I was still panting. "Tell me your name. I prefer to have a name to go with a cock."

The Sathoet wasn't pleased and shook his head in refusal, a rough growl leaking from between his teeth along with his saliva.

"You have a name. All demons do," I replied firmly, "and I'm not asking for the one that binds you to the Sanctuary. I want to know what your Mother calls you. Tell me *her* name for you, Sathoet."

He looked away from me; he couldn't help it. The repeated slaps had regressed him. He appeared confused, and I saw his eyes flicker toward a section of the candles. I noted the location. Someone was watching and listening, and I felt encouraged; if he looked now to whoever was behind the wall of candles for support, it meant I'd genuinely shaken him.

A demonblood wasn't kissable on the mouth, but I pressed my lips into the side of his neck and tasted the oddly spicy flesh. I felt the real excitement, now; I liked his reluctance, his need to be persuaded, and the fact that his loyalty to his Mother clashed with his base urges to fuck me. The idea of mating with him in a similar manner to the ritual which had spawned him had real appeal to me. When power flowed between beings, lust rose as part of the high.

I adjusted the way my body held to him, pressed my buttocks into his hands and pressed my hot sex against his softened genitals. There was a small but immediate response.

"Tell me your name, Sathoet," I whispered to him, my eyes half-closed as my breathing hadn't slowed. I kissed his skin, nipping at his collarbones.

My attention and the continued swiveling and squirming of my hips against him brought him back to full erection. His breath heaved, and he quivered a little, standing and holding my weight. Perhaps his muscles strained by now as well, but he didn't want to interrupt what I was doing.

I lined up his erection so that the tip rested at the entrance of my body, and I held it there. He tried to thrust upward, but I lifted myself with him. There was no further penetration, just my warm, wet slit caressing and teasing the sensitive flesh of us both. He tried forcing my buttocks down and onto him, but I drew my hand back, threatening to slap him again. He stopped.

"I told you what I want," I said. "I can stay like this a long time. I can even climax like this. I'll get mine for certain, but you? It's your choice if you get to sink in deep, Good Bua."

He blinked when I called him that.

The teasing went on for a good long while. The Sathoet was in a furious state of arousal and could not be subtle as I stoutly resisted penetration and even struck him again. It fascinated me that he wouldn't hit me back. One unrestrained punch from him could knock me unconscious.

He is very well trained.

Once the Sathoet made a motion as if to kneel us both down on the ground, and I hissed a challenge at him with enough venom to give him pause. He stayed standing. He wasn't easily swayed, not at all. But finally, finally—

"*Kerse,*" he rumbled through a mouthful of teeth.

"You *can* talk." I grinned, pleased. He couldn't be articulate if that one harsh syllable were any indication, but it was good to know a Sathoet could speak."Kerse. Your name?"

"*Ssirranna,*" he hissed back, the corners of his wide mouth rising in response.

Someone had told him my name, or he had been near enough to hear it.

I said, "We have a bargain."

I impaled myself on him and groaned, wet enough by now that it had only taken one thrust to be balls-deep. He howled in relief, and I felt his hands slide up to my back, the claws press in as he gripped me harshly. Kerse kneeled to lay us both down on the reflective floor, placing me with extraordinary care on my back to settle between my legs before he began to pound me with desperate need.

The rough, fast pace was exactly what I wanted; I climaxed within moments, my scream of delight echoing around us. Kerse drove hard into me. I was surprised he'd lasted to my own peak and even more surprised when, his lips pulling back to expose clenched teeth, he suddenly pulled out. I groaned in disappointment.

The Sathoet reached to grip and stroke himself to completion, spraying his seed across my thighs and buttocks to drain in a puddle beneath me on the polished floor. I felt his hot gasps on the skin of my neck and in my hair.

He ... he fucking pulled out?

Did that mean the demonbloods could impregnate a fertile female? If so, had his Mother conditioned this strong *response* from him? It spoke of an unsettling amount of power to the Priestess who owned this Sathoet.

"Up," I panted. "Get off me."

Kerse obeyed, lifting himself up and backward to sit on his haunches, his shoulders drooping with exhaustion.

"You're a good bua, Kerse," I crooned as I sat up and reached out to stroke the side of his face. "I enjoyed that."

He made an unintelligible sound and tried to turn his face from my hand, though he didn't work very hard. The tone reminded me of an adolescent who wanted to shrug off a flattering compliment but responded to it nonetheless.

Whatever just happened, I'd won.

I heard soft footsteps, and the only reason I did was that one set had the quick click of someone agitated. I looked over my shoulder and saw the same Red Sisters returning: the Sorceress Elder, the elder who had collected me from the balcony, and the youngest Red Sister. It was my collector who gave away her emotions in her walk.

I stood up out of the puddle of ejaculate, aware of the cooling wetness that glazed my rear end but turning to face them nonetheless. I stood with my back straight, with greater confidence than when I'd arrived here.

"You're outside the diamond, Sirana," the Elder commented slyly as the three stopped before me.

"Forgive me that I thought it necessary, Elder Sister," I replied.

I thought she smiled, though it was subtle. I wished I knew if that was a good sign or not. My collector, however, scowled at me as she muttered a harsh, foreign word to Kerse. He bowed his head to her, standing up and walking toward the darkness beyond the candlelight.

I noticed when Kerse looked back again, at me. Then he disappeared from sight.

"Becoming bored embarrassing higher Houses with their weaker sons?" my collector commented, her arms crossed as the Elder glanced at her and let her speak. "Now you want to agitate a Priestess?"

Despite hearing a clear confession that the Sisters had been watching me for decades, Jilrina's face flashed before my eyes and my first thought curdled to one promise.

Anything to agitate a Priestess.

"Is it so easy?" I asked instead, an unintended sneer coming to my lips.

She noticed, tilting her head. "A fool would pray to test it."

The Elder Sorceress motioned then for my collector to stand down, and the Red Sister did so willingly, straightening her back and watching me with something like suspicion. Still not even a twitch of a smile from her, for any reason.

I turned toward the eldest. "May I ask, who is Kerse's Mother?"

She shook her head. "You may not ask, Sirana, it is not your place. But you may find out regardless."

The Sorceress stepped around me again, studying me as she had once in my own bedroom. This time the observation did not seem to delve more than skin deep. "I see that Kerse scratched your back."

I shrugged and said nothing. I could feel the sting now, and I might be bleeding. At the time, it had felt good.

"You enjoy rough play with young cocks?"

Behind me, she touched her fingers to the sticky wetness on my backside, tracing the crease at my buttock and upper thigh, thoroughly coating two fingers with Kerse's spending. I tried not to squirm.

"Where appropriate, Elder Sister, yes," I replied cautiously.

"What about with more than one?" She walked around to the front again and popped her fingers into her mouth, tasting the Sathoet's seed.

I shrugged again. "I've done it before."

"Ah, yes. I heard about your participation at that last Priestess initiation ceremony." Her dark red eyes twinkled as she smiled.

I answered the smile. "And more since."

"Indeed. Unusual for one so young. Oh," the Sorceress added casually, "you must clean your mess, Sirana. This chamber is to remain dry and polished."

I looked at the puddle of semen, at the spray and smear of Kerse's release from our coupling, then back at the Elder Sister. She seemed amused waiting for my response.

I considered asking for cloth but discarded it. I trusted my reading of the eldest; it would be a mark against me. So I had two choices: use my hair or my tongue. One would leave a stiff, distasteful mar to my gleaming, white tresses for the rest of this ordeal. The other was a small performance and fleeting mental image for the observers.

"A moment, Elder Sister, I will take care of it."

I dropped to my hands and knees and leaned down, touching my lips to the cooling, bitter liquid. I slurped in loudly as if I supped from a spoon, hummed in theatrical pleasure, then sucked in more. The floor was nearly dry already, only a few more drops. I thought I heard both a giggle from the youngest and scoff from my collector.

"Do you mock us, *Thalluensareci*?" the middle Sister asked.

I lapped up the last bit, licked my lips and straightened up, sitting on my knees with my legs folded under me. I looked up at them, not meeting their eyes but studying at the red leather armor of their chests. "Of course not, Red Sister. Why would I mock you? The floor is clean, as instructed, without Noble sulking. I thought you'd like that."

My collector drew in a breath to say something else, but the eldest raised her hand again, gestured her to be still. Those aged, copper eyes were studying me intently.

"Satisfactory, Sirana. Now take your position in the diamond again. You'll meet your new companions in due time."

A new test, then.

I rose and walked stubbornly calm back to the diamond, where, kneeling down, my knees immediately recognized the hard surface. I glanced up to the three Sisters before putting my forehead on my folded hands, taking the slave's position. I hadn't heard the youngest Red Sister make any noise, but again she had seemed to have an expression of sympathy for me.

Don't waste your pity on me, I thought with indignation, pricked with anxiety I wished to deny. This was nothing so far, whatever the purpose. Court antics and House games using a different tool. Had they expected that I would shriek in disgust at mating a Sathoet? Make me shy away from the eldest Sister's caress or refuse to taste the seed I'd drawn, as the Elder had already done right before my eyes?

This is nothing. Bring those new "companions." I'm ready.

Chapter 6

Time passed while I waited in the candle-filled chamber, the magical light shifting in subtle ways as the candle grew short in predictable fashion. I was tenser this time as I expected someone or something to touch me from behind.

The voice came from directly in front of me. I nearly flinched.

"Look up. Now."

The voice was male. Full Davrin this time, neither hissing nor bestial.

When I looked up, I saw nothing. I could smell him, however, and feel the heat seeping off invisible flesh. Then I felt a hand seize my hair and force me up straight with a painful jerk. I almost opened my mouth, enraged enough to shout at him.

How dare he?!

The familiar, soft texture of an engorged glans pressed against my mouth and I pursed my lips shut, remaining silent.

"Suck me, Noble," the disembodied voice murmured to me, both bitter and lyrical. "Open your privileged mouth."

Briefly, I felt cold. I tried to turn my head, but he made my scalp burn to keep me in place. I locked my jaw but a groan slipped out, and he was excited by the sound; preliminary wetness seeped from the tip of his cock onto my lips.

"Open up. I'm going to fuck your throat whether you wish it or not, Noble. If you bite me, the Elder's punishment to bleed you and make you swallow *that* instead still applies."

Another mage. This one a male claiming the Sorceress's support. He sounded so confident and so very hateful. Worse, he wore an invisibility spell not disrupted by forceful physical contact, which was usually all it took to dispel.

Is he that powerful?

It could have been another mage who cast a spell on him, but my gut told me it was him, his own magic. It was in the surety in his voice, the anger and resentment, and the intent to force me as he wished and get away with it. Borrowing another Davrin's spell wouldn't make it ring so true, would it?

I had to decide in an instant, and I did. I squashed down my pride and arrogance for now. This was another spar, and I needed an opening gambit. Whatever it took to gain the upper hand eventually.

I took a deep breath and opened my mouth willingly to let the invisible flesh pass between my lips. He pressed in with a laugh and jammed my windpipe; it was just as well that I held my breath. I closed my eyes so that sensing everything yet seeing nothing before me in the chamber wouldn't be so distracting. As in any martial challenge, I must detect my opponent's body language; I must not depend on his face.

I swallowed his shaft with an enthusiasm I wanted to surprise him. I swirled my tongue, reached up to massage his scrotum and sucked him as if I could pull his brains out through his penis. His grip on my hair tightened, and he guided my rhythm, moaning and cooing at me.

Every so often he would flick the edges of my pointed ears with his fingers; it was a sharp, disruptive pain that did not damage. I still hated having my ears flicked, and the distraction cost me control of how deep his cock went more than once. I gagged and choked, and he would laugh before I fought back to regain the pace. I would succeed in pleasuring him with all my considerable experience at my disposal.

He gasped, "Good … that's it. Ah, stupid, Noble slit … ah. G-good. Next, you'll turn around. And spread your thighs open for me."

Like the Void, I will.

I hummed in acknowledgment, my throat sore and my mouth full but able to breathe for now. I made a show of slipping my left hand between my legs, putting a finger into my sex still wet from my union with Kerse. The wizard groaned, seeming to stare as he encouraged me to higher speed and energy. I obliged because I didn't want him to mount me.

Suck until he's too close.

I could tell when he tried to convince himself it was time to abandon my mouth and order me to turn around. I heard it in the way his breath would draw in as if to speak. I'd do something different and inventive with my mouth then, and he'd sigh and let me go on for a few more strokes.

And a few more.

He was close.

Now or never.

I pulled my well-lubed finger from my sex and brought one hand up to slide it between the wizard's buttocks, distracting him by groping his sack with the other. It only took a flick to find the ring of flesh I sought.

"Augh — !" he gasped, flinching as I pressed my finger smoothly inside him, much more comfortable than the Eldest Sister had done to me.

Don't complain.

Immediately I found the nut-like gland inside, behind his bladder. I massaged it, and the wizard cried out again, his control faltering. He started spurting down my throat, his knees weakened. He tried to pull me off him using his fistful of hair, but I held tightly to his hips with my free hand and vigorously massaged his gland, swallowing his seed until he was done. He tasted healthy, far less foreign than the Sathoet. Almost like an underground hot spring infused with my favorite spiced mushroom delicacy. His semen warmed my belly.

He's taken something.

I sensed his body flinch when I removed my finger and pulled my mouth off him at last. He was gasping, his member shriveling. He withdrew a step and slapped me in the face.

"You think you're so clever, do you?"

The wounded pride in his voice was palatable; my cheek stung as it never had under a male hand. I was glad I couldn't see his rage. He trembled when I looked up at nothing and kept a calm, straight face.

"Why hide your identity, wizard?" I asked. "Afraid of retribution?"

"Retribution? From you?"

He laughed, his disembodied voice echoing in the chamber. It was louder and angrier than it would have been if he'd been in control, but I knew he must be one of the wizards of the Tower then. He sounded disconnected from Court life and the politics of Houses.

"You're powerless here, Noble. Your body belongs to us until the Red Sisters come to claim you. If they come to claim you."

Us. I recalled there was at least one other, as the Eldest had promised.

"If my body belongs to you," I challenged quietly, "then yours belongs to me."

Another harsh laugh. "Oh? Who is on her knees before me?"

"Who chose your climax?" I smirked.

His voice spat at me. "Try that while flanked on both sides."

Strong arms wrapped around me from behind. They were arms I could see this time, dark with smooth skin, well-formed from hard work and athletics. His hands were rougher and scarred.

Like the hands of a soldier.

Those hands slid from my hips up my belly and cupped my breasts as teeth bit hard into my shoulder. I winced but leaned into him rather than away, wanting a sense of his size and ability as my back and buttocks aligned with his front. He was stronger than the wizard but no taller; I might have been taller than each of them, but I was in between for strength.

Out of my periphery, I caught a glimpse of a reasonably handsome face leering with eagerness. An erection settled comfortably lengthwise in the cleft of my backside, and he pressed hard. I smiled as he pinched my nipples, twisted them roughly.

A wizard and a fighter.

The two didn't mix that well; their methods and training were too different. I chuckled for the first time in this second trial, hissing in excitement as I reached back to dig my fingernails into naked flanks and well-sculpted buttocks.

"Fuck me, soldier," I ordered.

"When I decide, slit-sucker," he growled back, squeezing my breasts hard and grinding into me.

His voice had quavered.

"Now!" I barked, spreading my knees apart wider and thrusting my butt out. "Mount me!"

I couldn't see the wizard's expression, but I hoped he was choking on the insult.

The soldier liked to bite my neck, making me hiss through my teeth. He reached down to grab the tuft of white hair at my crotch, tugging on it almost as hard as the wizard had at my nape, making me whimper. He managed to tease me for a little while, pawing without the best technique, but finally, he just pushed me down flat onto my stomach, forcing my legs wide apart with his own before ramming his phallus inside my sex.

"Oh, Goddess, yes!" I cried.

The soldier held me down with his weight. I struggled against him only to encourage him, reaching out and digging my fingers into the garnet border as if trying to pull myself free of him. He hardly needed the added excitement. He wallowed and slammed between my legs as though he were trying to fit his entire body inside.

"This ... is how you do them, wizard," my soldier gasped, jarring me with every furious lunge, air forced out of me with each one.

"She's biding her time, grunt," my invisible wizard replied sourly. "Sooner or later you have to let her get up. What'll she do, then? What will you do?"

"You think too much."

My fighter pulled out prematurely, just as Kerse had, and I grunted in displeasure. Then I felt him reposition his erection at my other hole and my eyes widened.

The soldier replied, "Just make her too sore to run after you."

He pressed hard, dilating my back sphincter very quickly.

Shit!

I relaxed quickly to allow it rather than be damaged.

"Oh, *Goddess!!*" I shrieked as he rushed to bury his meat inside me, stretching me tight around him. I couldn't tell if it was a cry of pleasure or pain. "Excitable agony" came to mind. Still, I forced myself to refocus and relax the muscles of my pelvis again. I could handle this, and I would get mine in return.

At least he was still slick.

"Do it, ground-pounder!" I shouted at him. "Enough babble with the wizard! You weren't made to talk!"

He snarled, grabbed my hair fiercely and held my head to the floor, my right cheek pressed hard to the polished surface. He drew out part way and thrust back in between my buttocks, increasing his tempo. It didn't take long for the nerves of my clutching ring to numb, then begin to heat up in a way that was actually pleasant. It was only then I could make convincing sounds of pleasure. I was partly acting, but then again, I already knew my will and mind were powerful; I would survive this with ease.

"She's not going to break that way," the wizard commented as he watched the soldier plow into my backside, almost reading my mind.

The thrusting slowed, hesitated, but didn't stop entirely. He still wanted to climax even if the wizard revealed his purpose might be something else.

"Keep going," I whispered, panting. "Don't stop."

The fighter's fucking quickened again.

"You're doing exactly as she says." This time the wizard was mocking.

"Squat on a staff, scroll sniffer. Ungh. She's taking this."

Over the grunting, I heard the mage blow out a breath in frustration. "Fine. Then roll her over, hold her on top of you. You'll still get her ass, and I'll show you how *I* do them."

I flushed with heat. I wasn't sure if it was anger or excitement.

The soldier must have been curious because, after a beat, he obeyed the wizard. With his cock still impaling me, he hooked his forearms at my underarms and locked his fingers together at the nape of my neck, clutching me tight to him and rolling both of us. It was in my best interest to move with him and make sure he didn't slip out; reentry at this point wouldn't be pleasant.

I was layered in sweat where I'd been pressed to the glossy floor, and my skin broke out into pebble-skin as the air of the chamber washed over my front. I couldn't do much with my arms, and at most I could kick at the invisible male.

But I didn't really want to kick at him; I kept my legs open, a mocking, challenging smirk touching my lips. "Think you can control yourself this time, wizard?"

"I love to hear you say that, Sirana," the wizard said contemplatively, and I felt him touch my inner thighs gently with both hands. "Perhaps I should return the favor."

I was surprised; his tone was a lot different than when I'd been kneeling before him. He sounded as eager as I'd been with the fighter, and I knew he had caught on to how I had wanted to play the two against each other. If their mission were to "break" me through rutting misuse, they would have been doomed to fail as they strove to out-do each other.

Now the wizard massaged my thighs and stroked my sex as if he knew what he was doing. I still couldn't see him, not even a vague outline, but I could see the depressions his fingers caused on my flesh. I gasped when what had to be his entire mouth covered my slit, and he began to feast. Warm pleasure contrasting with the heat of my netherhole not only arose inside my abdomen, but I swore there was an external tingle of energy directly off his tongue as he stroked it over me, swirling and slapping at my most sensitive spot.

I had been willing to wager my best sword that this bitter, angry, scholar could *never* show much enthusiasm for this particular chore, and therefore not even much skill. I quickly discovered I would have lost that bet. He had learned an extraordinary technique in his time, and if he pretended to enjoy doing it, he was as convincing as anyone at Court.

Oh ... Goddess ... ! I whimpered inside my head, writhing, unable to get away from either male as the stimulation grew ever more intense.

"By Braqth, keep doing whatever you're doing, wizard!" the soldier exclaimed as he held me immobile. "She's clutching me hard! She likes it."

I did like it; very much, I did. One of the wizard's fingers had slipped inside my sex to press on a similar pressure point inside my cunt, parallel to my stroking his nut gland through his ass. His other hand caressed and teased my crown of fur at the same time, the thumb rubbing in gentle circles, stretching, and stimulating the folds of skin cradling my center of sensation.

Meanwhile, his tingling mouth explored every point in between and around his hands. I could hardly keep track of each touch he made, inside and out; it varied smoothly and infinitely, and it almost felt like magic seeped into me, enhancing every moment. With the fighter's prick up my ass at the same time, holding me open as it was?

Oh, I am in trouble.

I was going to peak, it was coming!

Then he stopped.

Shit, fuck, no!

He began again, and I couldn't keep from squirming, yet when the wizard lifted his mouth off me three separate times, barely preventing me from climaxing, I finally whimpered aloud.

"Just ask me, Sirana," the mage said softly, his breath a puff of hot air in the short, white hairs adorning my mound. He kissed my netherlips softly, and I flinched just as he had with me. "Ask for it. Beg for release."

I wondered if I might beg him to let me over the edge. It was so tempting; the lust was strong enough to make all else seem exceedingly small. No. I'd taken control from him at the start with my finger up his ass; I wouldn't give it back to him so easily!

The soldier got into the rhythm set by the wizard, following the other male's lead, stroking his cock in and out as the other sucked and rubbed and caressed, and stopping when the scholar stopped. By the sixth aborted lead-up, the sixth time I was denied climax, a loud groan of frustrated disappointment slipped out of my mouth. They had ceased being in such a hurry to subjugate me; now they worked together, taking their time humiliating me instead.

The wizard had intense focus; I could imagine him poring over scrolls and books for full marks on end. It was the fighter's impatience that may be my only chance to ruin their plans. He was fascinated with these magic tricks so far, but he was the one who fully penetrated my backside. Sooner or later the tender eggs inside his sack would hurt fiercely from denial; he would pine for release right along with me.

"Just ask, Sirana," my fighter echoed his partner, and I sighed in relief when I heard that same quiver as before. He very well could break before I did.

He has to.

"However you will ... to service me," I murmured. "I can take ... all the attention you're ... willing to give."

At least I hoped so. I floated in a near-altered state of mind, as when my sister would serve me a draught which I didn't know. My tongue was heavy, and it took such effort to form words. It was pure practice that kept the same tremor from my words as my hated sister's voice came back to me in that haze.

You are so stubborn, Sirana. Just let go. Submit.

The ninth time this wizard stopped me from coming, I heard him rise up over me then felt something scalding hot graze my thigh. His hands grabbed my legs to keep them open, and I felt his prick squeeze into my other available hole.

"Ah!"

The cry forced its way out my throat, my eyes widening from their half-lidded stupor. The wizard's breath flowed across my breasts as he gripped my hips and thrust into my sex every bit as hard as the fighter had. At my first serious effort trying to get what I needed to climax, he withdrew and went back to eating me.

Goddess damn it!!

The wizard kept alternating. He would mouth and finger me for a while, then rise up and penetrate me, stroke in tandem with the fighter for several moments, and then withdraw to put his mouth and fingers back on me. He wasn't letting me come, and I was hardly given time to catch my breath. I forced myself to think again, slowly wrenching my attention from between my legs. It was a monumental feat.

"*Know that if you bite me, the Elder's punishment still applies.*"

The wizard had said that at the beginning. The Red Sisters were watching this. He claimed they were attempting to "break" me, yet the Elder Sorceress had told me to expect them. There were many actions they hadn't done that might work faster. No threats to disfigure me, to blind me; they weren't torturing me beyond a rough throat fuck and a rougher rear entry. No broken bones or cuts or severe bites.

They were controlling my climax. The sex seemed the point, the very grounds for the game of control. *Like with the Sathoet. Like at Court.*

There were rules to this game.

My body went limp, exhausted. I leaned my head back against the soldier's shoulder and let my legs and arms relax to the sides, breathing deeply and still feeling them drive into me with two cocks. My sudden passivity took some of the sustained tension out of me, but the stimulation was still there. If anything, the relaxation encouraged the blood to rush between my legs even more. However, the physical signals, the ones my magician had been using to control my reactions, were no longer there.

"Giving up, Sirana?" said the scholar with a chuckle, thrusting harder, then slower. "Do you want us to stop?"

He bit down on one of my nipples; I groaned and gasped, but didn't resist. A groan was acceptable. It could mean anything, and the sounds pleased him. Yet, without the wriggling and straining I'd been doing which communicated everything to him, he began to thrust harder, urging more reaction out of my limp body. The fighter beneath me followed the mage's lead, humping like a Sathoet finally being let off his leash.

It was intense, and it was enough. *Goddess! Finally enough!*

I remained unmoving until, at the last moment, I drew in a breath and cried out as long-delayed thrills racked my body. My fighter was taken off guard and couldn't prevent falling over the edge himself; I could hear him grunt and feel his member throbbing as he spent himself in my bowels. The wizard cursed, feeling my spasms as I climaxed.

"Augh, you slitty ... .! Goddess-damned cold fish!"

Suddenly, I began laughing. I couldn't stop. Shivering and quaking, I laughed at them. *I won again!*

The wizard pulled out and slapped my mound with what had to be the flat of his hand. My slit still buzzed, so that was a shock and my whole body jumped as I blurted another scream.

"Let go of her, grunt, now!" the magic user snapped, and his partner obeyed. "It's my turn. She won't be laughing as I surge off next!"

I panicked at the tone of his voice, my afterglow souring as I made ready to resist with everything I had. The soldier withdrew from my ass, pushed me off him and gripped my arms hard to prevent me from scrambling away. The army grunt had gotten his; now he was at the wizard's beck and call if it was fun helping in what he did to me.

For an instant, it was Kaltra holding me down, and Jilrina standing over me. I imagined a sacrificial blade pulled from discarded robes, preparing to cut me, or stab me. I roared, struggling against the hold.

No!

I looked over my shoulder and paused.

I ... I can see him.

It was not Jilrina. Or Kaltra.

My wizard's spell was wearing off. There was a vague outline of a nude, male Davrin, a bit shorter than me. With short hair. The chances were good that these males' time with me was almost done. That was what I needed to know to hold myself together and accurately read what was happening in the candle chamber, not inside my youth's memory.

I could see hints of my wizard's expression now, like smoke wisps rising off a snuffed candle. He had lost the game, he knew this, and he was frustrated but not murderous. He wasn't going to kill me, and more, he felt no victory. He just wanted satisfaction of *some* sort.

I couldn't really blame him; I would want that, too. If a Red Sister had directed him then anything he'd done in the goal of winning the challenge was, in theory, forgivable. With females, though, whatever was done *after* the game was over and won would never be forgotten.

I did not fight or panic but instead allowed the fighter to roughly set me on my hands and knees. He pushed my shoulders down until my arms collapsed and he held my head down on the floor with the weight of his body, fisting my hair again. When the wizard kneeled behind me and gripped my haunches; between the two of them, I really couldn't move. I felt my muscles flex protectively as I waited for further violation.

I'd already learned that no amount of humiliation was worth dying or breaking. I could survive any position and always get revenge later.

Just ask Jilrina.

I winced as the wizard forced his long-sustained erection into my netherhole, not giving up without spurting where the warrior had gone. He pumped methodically, hard and seemingly without much pleasure. He made sure it hurt me, though I bit my cheek and refused to make a sound for him. I was sore but still elastic from the prolonged thrusts and slick from ejaculate the soldier had given me, not to mention tired from the crashing orgasm I'd had.

I could endure this, even if I could open my eyes and see myself getting fucked in the polished floor by a wispy, semi-invisible form leaning over my haunches.

Finally, the wizard grunted, pressing hard to me and adding his own seed to the mix in my ass. He did not linger before withdrawing quickly and standing up. The fighter released me, and at last, I scrambled to my feet, whirling around to scowl at them, both my face and my asshole burning.

I stared hard, memorizing the soldier's face and studying the outline of the slowly clarifying mage. The magic user took an involuntary step back, realizing then that I could look right at him. I grinned seeing that. The wizard was the smart one; he moved for the shadows immediately, followed by the fighter a few heartbeats later.

The fighter was dead for sure. And I'd damned well look for that wizard.

This time I didn't hear the three Red Sisters approaching, but I expected them; it wasn't as unnerving to turn around and find them there. For the first time, my collector was smiling, looking satisfied, and the face of the youngest was carefully neutral.

I looked to the Elder, trying to read my fate in her eyes. As with

Kerse, I'd played this game with the two Davrin males my way, yet I still didn't really know what this eldest looked for when she studied me as she did.

"Stand in the diamond one last time, Sirana," the Sorceress said quietly. "Retake hold of your ankles."

I sighed to myself and obeyed. That sounded disappointed to me. I had no idea where I'd failed, or maybe there never had been a way *not* to fail.

At least I'd had a few good climaxes before discovering what they truly wanted.

Chapter 7

I moved back to the diamond and bent over again, spreading my legs and holding my ankles in my hands. My twice-fucked orifices were tender and oozing semen, my sex engorged and sensitive, and just like the laughing, short-haired warrior in my rooms a decade ago, this was where the Elder Sorceress focused, with gentle, tactile exploration as she stood behind me.

Her gloved fingers glided effortlessly across my sex now, plenty wet unlike before, before swirling them slowly around the swollen ring of muscle farther back. I sighed and relaxed; if she chose to penetrate me now, it would hurt, but I wasn't about to refuse the eldest Red Sister in the chamber anything.

I had a good understanding of power games despite my youth, and I knew where I stood among these females: precisely as I was, bent over and gripping my ankles in a secret chamber within the Palace, surrounded by assassins in the dark. I realized if she whipped my buttocks and ordered me to do so, I'd say without hesitation, "*Yes, Mistress, may I please have another?*"

Pride is real enough for any Davrin, but it only takes me so far before it will get me killed.

"How do you feel about your visitors, Sirana?" she asked, removing her exploratory hand. She did not penetrate me.

I decided to be honest. "It was fun until the end. None of them gave up the game easily. The two Davrin were poor losers, though."

The eldest chuckled. "You determined quickly they wouldn't do anything permanent to you. Did that spoil the intensity for you?"

"Not at all, Elder Sister. Thank you for the gifts."

I think she nodded, but regardless she paused before speaking again. "So you've proven you will couple with a Sathoet, and you even figured out how to control him to an extent. Did it disgust you?"

"No, Elder. I shall remember the coupling fondly."

She grunted softly. "You can also turn a dominant male situation to your advantage, even if temporarily." Then she laughed, and I was surprised to discover that I liked the musical sound. "If they had been allowed to kill you, I believe the wizard probably would have strangled you himself!"

Perhaps, perhaps not. A smile twitched at the corners of my mouth. "With all due respect, Elder, he would've had to prevent my hands from reaching him first."

Her voice took on a softer, more probing quality. "Yet they both force you to take their seed ... here." She pressed a shallow, teasing finger into my sore and throbbing orifice, and I winced. "Was that the 'end' where it was no longer 'fun'?"

I swallowed as I felt a tremor; I wanted to tighten up. I took a breath and responded forthrightly. "The fighter had a simple understanding of the challenge and no understanding of my signals. I could tell him whatever I wanted, and he had no idea what to do except hump me. It even felt good because that's what I wanted. Yes, it was a base rut unplanned, but I chose to enjoy it."

"Indeed." She removed her finger, and I tried not to sigh audibly. "What about the wizard? He was not so easily lead. What of his final act? I know he caused deliberate pain. You were silent."

I'd been about to say that he had given me the perfect justification to kill him later.

No, no. Wizards take time to train. They're expensive to keep and use costly things.

A competent officer in the army might still bring down a powerful female's wrath, and she could kill him, so the fighter had relatively little protection. Yet a wizard's execution was not taken as lightly.

A Sorceress like her would not appreciate casual threats of killing one.

"Sirana?"

I gave it more thought and realized that I knew why I had allowed the wizard to have his revenge on me for taking the control from him twice in one encounter.

"He couldn't kill me, and if he had conceded after losing the challenge, it would have ended him with the grudge against me. I let him indulge because now he will fear me coming after him. It will make the finding of a faceless wizard easier if he is nervous."

"Oh? And what will you do if you find him, Sirana?"

"I know I cannot kill him, Elder. It is the Word of the Valsharess whether he lives or dies. But I will find him without magic, and I will return the favor. We can continue this game beyond this eve on my terms." I grinned at the floor. "*That* will be fun."

The eldest Sister listened without interrupting then let the silence stretch, having taken her hand away and circling around me until she stood in front. I could see her excellent, red leather boots, making no sound unless she willed it, her red leather leggings and the tip of her sword sheath. I could not see, however, the blood red sash I knew to be at her waist.

Finally, she spoke, but not to me. "Qivni. Clean her."

My collector gasped softly and balked, sounding shocked and a little disbelieving. "Elder D'Shea?"

"I said clean her. She is coming with us."

Qivni stiffly walked over to where I still held my position and kneeled behind me. I felt a very soft tongue start lapping hesitantly at the folds of my sex and I truly felt bewildered as to my reaction. Strictly as a sensation, it was soothing after the rough sex. My emotions, on the other hand, sent me trembling and shrinking away from her in disgust. I struggled to keep images of Jilrina and Kaltra out of my head lest I scream from pure hatred.

"No," I growled, biting down on the slip.

Shit.

The invisible marks were still there, and somehow still fresh.

There was no surprise in Elder D'Shea's voice when she gave her next command, and there was little reason there would be. Instead of disappointment, however, she sounded calculating.

"Qivni, stop. Gaelan, take her place."

My collector stood up and gratefully left her post at my backside, and the youngest Red Sister glided forward and knelt without protest. Gaelan began by tenderly licking my anus, collecting the oozing semen onto her tongue and swallowing it. She also hummed as if in pleasure, though I wasn't sure because memories of my eldest sister still crowded my thoughts. I wanted to spin around and push her away from me, jump on her and strike her with my closed fist repeatedly.

I stiffened and trembled instead; I wasn't ready to die for attacking a Red Sister.

"Sirana."

Elder D'Shea sounded as though she had just discovered a soft spot in an otherwise firm fruit. "Tell me who is in your mind right now."

I hesitated.

"*Now!*"

"My eldest sister, Jilrina," I said through clenched teeth.

Gaelan licked and sucked between my legs. The slurping sounds were distracting, and my internal armor which I had built so painstakingly was crumbling fast.

"Why?"

It was the enormity of the question that made me hesitate this time. How to even explain it? Didn't she know already? Hadn't I already confessed it fifteen turns ago as the First Daughter's body had lay stiff in the barn?

I risked a glance upward, realized how my head pounded from the blood pooling and looked back down. "Because I hate her."

"She's dead." Her leather creaked. "Is she not?"

I nodded. "Yes, Elder."

"Wrong. Perhaps her body is. Your hatred gives her life to you. What did she do to you to earn that immortality?"

"I-I confessed before I came to Court, Elder. I answered your questions."

"And yet there is something more."

I both gasped and flinched when Gaelan stiffened her tongue and pushed it into my netherhole, licking me on the inside, too. Oh, Goddess, it felt good and yet I didn't want her to continue. I felt sick to my stomach at what she was doing.

"Jilrina," Elder D'Shea said again. "First Daughter of House Thalluen. What did she want most?"

I attempted to get my stream of thought back as Gaelan's hands rested on my hips. "She wanted to be a Priestess of the Spider Queen. She practiced since before I was born."

"Interesting. Practiced? Let me guess, she needed an altar, and you became it."

"As soon as I was placed under her care, yes." My head throbbed worse. "Kaltra was already broken by then and played her 'apprentice'."

"And your Matron did not stop it?"

I swallowed. "Jilrina was never caught, and I couldn't speak of it. You know this, Elder, she gave me a magical draft, a compulsion against accusing her."

Elder D'Shea approached me again. I couldn't see her eyes, only her boots. "Where did she get her inspiration?"

These were the questions she had never asked back in my room at my Mother's manor, even as I had been expecting them at the time. The Sorceress was asking now, while I was naked, sticky, exhausted, and with a Red Sister's tongue up my ass.

It seemed appropriate for the Sisterhood's reputation.

"She got her inspiration from the public sacrifices. Younger Priestesses she befriended or slept with to pump them for details. Any book she could find."

"Did anything unusual occur during any of her 'rituals'?"

I shook my head, felt Gaelan close her lips over my pleasure nub and gently start sucking and flicking her tongue. The unexpected spasm of pleasure that resulted surprised me; hers wasn't entirely unlike the wizard's technique.

"Ah … ! Um, not that I-I noticed, Elder Sorceress."

Elder D'Shea ceased questioning me then. She merely watched me, watched Gaelan working me. Qivni stood somewhat behind her, the stance of her legs antsy to me. As the chamber grew quiet except for the sounds of the youngest Red Sister eating me, I found myself drawn inside my head, alone with my resurfacing memories.

I'd been penetrated with an object the first time without being able to defend myself. I didn't understand what my sister was trying to do. I'd bled, and my sister nearly panicked, afraid of being found out by the Matron. I'd been healed though, and I'd long since swallowed the draft which silenced me.

Jilrina taught me to pleasure her with my mouth and tongue, convinced that her climax produced her most robust magical flow; all the rituals ended with it unless I could escape. When she brought in Kaltra, I could never get away. As the living part of the altar, I was always naked.

Jilrina had the new idea that if the Priestess and the Living Altar peaked at the same time, the power released would be incredible. It took a long time and many tries before that happened, with Kaltra's head between my legs and Jilrina squatting over me. The details of the "rituals" always varied, became more or less harsh or trying, depending entirely on her mood and her "inspiration."

But the ending was always the same.

Nothing ever happened. No attention from Braqth whatsoever. My sister was just a foolish wannabe who could never be sated.

Gaelan hummed against my sex again, and I groaned at the vibrations. I had taken so many male lovers since coming to Court, but never a female one. Even at the ritual orgy — a real one — I had only had sex with males. It was considered unusual. For me, the images of the new experiences helped push out the memories of the old ones.

It was much harder now.

"Is Gaelan doing a good job, Sirana?" the Elder asked. "Is she pleasing you?"

I nodded, quivering a little. It was a slow rise because I was fighting it and I didn't think I could — or wanted to — ever climax from a female tongue again. But I wasn't lying to Elder D'Shea, either; Gaelan's lavish attention on my sex made my heart pound harder, caused my breath to shake.

Yet I still felt distressed.

As D'Shea gave me another moment to ponder, I finally heard that underlying thread of steel which had been in her tone.

Is she doing a good job? Is she pleasing you?

I realized the questions were also a warning. Elder D'Shea had given me the easy challenges first, yet this was another. To refuse to climax under such attentive and generous aftercare as I received would be an insult to Gaelan, which was an insult to the Red Sisters. I needed to let go; D'Shea must want that from me. A simple choice now: orgasm or insult them. Regardless of my distaste for the memories of my sisters.

Curse it.

I swiveled my hips a little, helping Gaelan find the right spots with her mouth. I allowed myself to moan more, encouraging her and focusing on the softness of her lips and tongue on my raw and used flesh, on the intense sensations as she closed her mouth over my nub to gently suck me again. The pressure in my head built as I stood bent over and something like a coiled spring was forming in my lower abdomen.

At last.

"Harder," I gasped. "Please, press harder."

Gaelan flattened her tongue on my most sensitive point and pressed as hard as she could, moving it just a little bit back and forth. I cried in relief as the spring uncoiled inside me and my body flushed with heat and pleasure. My vision blurred with red for a moment and my head suddenly hurt quite a lot. My knees buckled, and I fell forward, landing on all fours though still within the diamond. Gaelan followed me down and thrust two fingers inside my sex, causing an aftershock to sweep through me, and I shrieked. My pelvic muscles grasped at her fingers as I rode the wave down, barely braced on my forearms.

Afterward, I stayed where I was, gasping and dizzy enough to fall over if I lost focus. Without being bid, Gaelan got up and moved around in front. She kneeled and took my chin to raise my head, leaning down and letting her lips hover just above mine. I could smell my own scent, see my lubricant glistening around her mouth.

I didn't dare hesitate this time. I kissed her, tasted myself, licked around her mouth to clean her as she'd cleaned me. A slight smile touched Gaelan's young face as she stood up and joined Qivni a few paces away.

Elder D'Shea made a sound of satisfaction, offering me a nod. "Stand up, Sirana, and come with us. You've shown promise. Now we'll see if your demons can be exorcised. Red Sisters have no demons except each other."

Her words echoed over and over in my head as we walked toward the candles. I understood why I was here. I was being considered for recruitment into the Sisterhood.

The Red Sisters. Braqth, help me.

A thrill passed through me, I knew what it was. Goddess, the power I could attain was more than I could ever hope for being born a mere Third Daughter of my House, even had I not been barren. If I entered the Sisterhood, I need not fear any Noble, not even a Matron, and I could laugh whenever I wanted.

Simultaneously, I was terrified. I was not the best fighter at Court. I had never worked as one of the Guard — City, House, or Palace — nor had I experience as a mercenary or assassin. This did not appear to matter, as the first tests were ... what? To me, they tested the basest self-knowledge and willpower, and it wasn't only the elite Swordsvrin they were looking for.

The Sisterhood looks for something else first.

I had never heard even one rumor that a recruit's trials might start with mating a Sathoet, or that angry, Davrin males were turned loose to rape and dominate her as they liked.

Not one whisper.

That really only meant one thing: the ones who failed the trials never lived to tell about them. I hadn't known it, but the moment I had walked off the balcony with Qivni, I would not have had the choice to leave or refuse.

It is all or nothing.

To live, I must become a Red Sister. To become a Red Sister, Jilrina and Kaltra had no room in my head anymore.

Red Sisters have no demons except each other.

Elder D'Shea walked up to the same section of candles where Kerse had flung his desperate glance for direction during our tussle. She stood before them for a few instants, then drew in one breath and blew out at least thirty-five of them. These were magical candles; no smoke or soot arose as the curtain of light withdrew, and slowly my eyes adjusted to make out the additional room beyond the line of standing candles.

I could see no less than thirty figures, all female, all wearing the same uniform. The ages ranged the gamut of able-bodied Davrin, and all of them wore different expressions: of stone, of eagerness, of deceit, of hatred, envy, jeer, disdain, calculation, and contempt. My eyes wanted to stop on the short-haired warrior standing in front.

It's her.

The first Red Sister I'd ever met; the one who'd kissed me in my own quarters after the ritual orgy, only after seeing me bathed and tucked in bed.

She is still alive.

She also chose not to look at me. The warrior stood at attention with her hands folded behind her back, her eyes resting somewhere across the candle chamber behind me, at enviable peace.

Don't draw attention, then.

I pushed myself to keep scanning the front until I found the absolute oldest Red Sister — older than D'Shea by many centuries — and the next-oldest one standing to her left, a tall, calm Red Sister powerfully built, who carried herself like a General in the Valsharess's Army. Neither she nor the ancient one was a sorceress like Elder D'Shea, I was willing to bet just looking at them. Neither held their hands the way a mage did, and both had too many subtle scars in their skin. I studied the lined and wrinkled expression of the most-aged Davrin. She merely looked contemplative. Perhaps a little bored.

"This is your offering, Varessa?" she asked Elder D'Shea, her tone confirming her disinterest.

My apparent benefactress looked at me, a smile touching her lips before looking back. "Yes, Red Sister Prime. She bends, she doesn't break. She will prove it."

The Red Sister Prime nodded, glancing at the tall officer beside her, who suggested the next step. "We need an altar, Prime."

"So be it."

The Prime turned around. The other Red Sisters parted to let her through as she headed for the granite door that appeared in the far wall only as she approached it. The second eldest followed her next, and the other Sisters stepped after them, their boots hardly making any noise.

Fear touched me for the first time. Real fear. I was still naked, disheveled, and sore. I'd seen sacrifices placed on the altar in exactly that state, and my sister had forced me to experience it over and over again. I didn't want to do this, I didn't want to! The mindless, animal terror overrode my better judgment. I balked, pulled against my sponsor when she took my arm.

"No demons but us, Sirana," Varessa D'Shea hissed into my ear. "You will live or die by that truth, so accept it now. Or is my confidence in you misplaced?"

I forced myself to move my feet, to walk and be guided by the Sister Prime and Elder D'Shea. We were followed by every one of the Red Sisters — Qivni and Gaelan directly behind me — through the granite door and an empty, private passageway.

The walls were lit intermittently with candles, so our vision didn't revert to Dark Sight, but this gave me no indication where we were in the Palace if we were still within the Palace. Or beneath it. If we passed any doorways or branching halls on either side, they were masked from my sight. My feet had grown cold walking barefoot upon the stone by the time the Red Sister Prime chose a wall at random and waved her hand across a Ward panel I only assumed was there.

A door opened, and she entered. We all followed her.

My vision maintained full-color thanks to smokeless torches lining the walls, though such colors as there were in this new chamber were somber at best. A high ceiling proved to be black, as black as the walls and the rough-textured stone beneath my feet. No polished, reflective surface on this floor.

Nine grey steps were leading up to a platform with a backdrop of Braqth's Crest in colors of deep purple, red, white, and black. On the platform, there was a marbled stone pedestal of white and blue, large enough for only one body to lie on it.

Not a pedestal, a small, frightened voice sounded in my mind.

I knew it was an altar, one which had been used for rituals by the Spider Queen's Mothers of the Web. The top of it was still stained with dark blood not easily scrubbed out by the Sanctuary's servants and slaves.

Numbly, I placed one foot in front of the other as we walked across the basin floor to the steps, and there we stopped. By some invisible signal, four Red Sisters unknown to me stepped out from the crowd. The rest moved off to kneel on the floor inside a pearly web design inlaid within the stone, each facing the altar. They had all taken on the same expression, reverence, as they looked up at the Banner of Braqth.

Varessa D'Shea kneeled at the front closest to the altar, with the short-haired warrior on her left and Gaelan on her right, both slightly behind her. The oldest officer kneeled with Qivni on her right and behind, but with the Prime standing on the left and in front.

That's interesting.

Meanwhile, the four Red Sisters surrounding me removed their weapons, effects, armor, and clothing until they were stark nude as I was, setting their uniforms neatly off to the side. Their bodies were toned and healthy; to a one, they appeared perfect and capable; intimidating, even naked. Or perhaps mainly because they were naked.

The Red Sister Prime was the only one within the web who stood, watching everything yet seeming disinterested. Her nose wrinkled a bit as she scanned my relatively soft body, and I wanted to quail under her gaze but dared not show more weakness than I already had.

All or nothing. I would become a Red Sister, or I would die in this chamber. Upon that altar. *I can't die that way. I can't.*

We waited. I wasn't sure what we expected until I heard the whisper of a hem trailing along the ground somewhere near the altar. From out behind Braqth's backdrop came a true Priestess, not the wannabe Jilrina had been. This female wore deep violet robes lovingly holding to her curves, and her black spider headpiece framed her beautiful face while holding her long hair back from her eyes. A ceremonial dagger in its jeweled sheath rested at one hip, a black leather pouch at the other.

She was adorned with silver jewelry; fine webbing covered the backs of her hands, and shining rings encircled her elegant fingers. A necklace of Braqth's spider nestled between her breasts, the abdomen filled with a perfectly polished amethyst, and multiple studs and glittering dangles pierced her pointed ears.

This Davrin Priestess held herself with more grace and confidence than any I'd ever seen at the public sacrifices, and it was because of her presence drawing every eye in the room that I finally recognized her. This was the speaking guide present at the orgy of which I'd been a part, the last Abyssal Initiation.

A new Priestess had to complete her own ritual in coupling with and conceiving by the summoned demon, but there must also be a divine guide of considerable power. If control faltered, the sire of a Sathoet would become a dire threat to the entire drugged congregation. I recalled this guide had been the only one not participating in the orgy.

What was her name? Hadn't some of the more experienced Nobles been talking afterward? Hadn't they mentioned her? Yes. I knew her title.

"*Lelinahdara*," I whispered, and the four, naked Red Sisters all glanced at me.

The Kiss of House Lelinh. A favored Daughter, though not the eldest, and she would never rule the Third House as Matron. Simply by merit, for being as influential of a Priestess as she was, she held the title which generally defaulted to the First Daughter.

The Red Sister Prime snapped her fingers, and the four Red Sisters moved up the steps. I was not touched or guided; I was expected to accompany them under my own volition. I climbed the nine steps with them and paused, unsure whether to go forward and lift myself onto the altar or not.

Unsure? I couldn't afford any uncertainty right now. I moved forward toward the marble table at a speed that implied confidence but also allowed me to catch any disapproval from the Priestess.

Lelinahdara held up her hand, and I stopped in an instant with relief. She approached me instead and looked into my eyes. Her mouth curved slightly and her voice embodied the reverence on the faces of the watchers: rich and seductive, a speaker's voice.

"Your eyes are blue. That always denotes an unusual Davrin."

Her eyes were green. Brighter than emerald, and even more unusual. But I made no comment on that.

"What is your name and title, daughter of the Davrin?"

"Sirana Thalluensareci," I answered.

The Priestess nodded and stepped away from me. She reached into her pouch and sprinkled a light dusting of a pale powder atop the blood-stained altar. She'd begun chanting in a tremulous alto as she stepped around to face the congregation of Red Sisters. She nodded again to the four others standing on the platform with us, and they seized me. One Sister grabbed each limb and lifted me up as roughly as if I resisted them. I emitted a cursed shriek and felt my body being drawn out, my arms and legs held taut as they raised me up and set my bare, scratched back on the cold, stained marble.

They didn't let go but held me helpless, spread like a bat as the Priestess came into my view again. Lelinahdara stood beside me and placed her hand on my abdomen. Her flesh was warm and dry; mine was chilled and sticky. Her hand glided up to rest above my pounding heart. She still chanted softly, and I could feel a tingle of magic coming into me from her palm.

No. No, what is she doing?

Jilrina had done this, but I'd never felt any quiver of energy before. Not like this.

Yes, child. Think about your sister.

The tingle trailed up from my chest, through my lungs and neck and into my head. It felt like fingers were cradling my mind inside my skull, probing and squeezing for who knew what. My eyes were tightly shut as my head throbbed beneath even the meager light of the sparse torches on the walls.

Interesting, her voice drifted through me, *your sister must have had a contact inside our temple. One who divulged more than she should have about our rituals. Did you ever know who it was?*

I shook my head, my eyes still closed. *No, Priestess.*

No matter. We'll find her if she still lives. Right now, I want to know the most feared ritual that she did to you. Show me.

My body struggled hard as she searched around inside me, and although it now felt stronger, the Red Sisters held it firm. *Stop! No —!*

I know she couldn't get away with the real sacrifices without your Matron finding out, the Priestess coaxed, her fingernails pressing into my sternum as my heart slammed beneath it. *It cannot be that bad, Sirana, you still have all your limbs and digits, you still have your eyes and all your organs. I know this, I've healed the damage you took from your trials. I know your body. I'll perform the ritual for you, and you'll see what real power is.*

The Priestess placed her other hand beneath my jaw, trying to cup my face. I turned away from her.

NO! Not again!

Shush. Jilrina is nothing to fear.

But she needed to die, I seethed.

Did you kill her, Sirana?

I fucking didn't! It was an accident!

Very well. The timing was interesting. We were about to accept her into apprenticeship before she died.

Jilrina had no magic! She was an imposter!

*Yes, she had magic, Sirana, through her Consort sire. If she continually failed to raise much power using you as her Living Altar, I do not wonder that Varessa D'Shea has selected you to be tested for the Sisterhood. I am here to see if she is *right.*★

Lelinahdara's hands remained over my heart, now clutching my face with a ringed thumb hooked under my jaw.

★*You shall be the Living Altar for a true ritual for the glory of Braqth, Sirana. This will happen, accept it. Survive it with your mind intact, and the Red Sisters will be your new family. But you must give me what I want first, child. Keep resisting, and I will choose the ritual. Unfortunately, the Red Sister Prime will have no use for you, then.*★

All or nothing. I wanted to piss myself, though desecrating the altar was not my intent. Desperate to relax and reign in my panic, I closed my eyes and drew a deep, shaking breath, picturing the calm peace of the laughing, red warrior. It worked. The moment I stopped fighting her, Lelinahdara found the memory.

★*Ah. Vicious. She left you unable to bear children, Sirana.*★

★*So my Matron told me. The Sorceress Sister told her. That's why I'm at Court.*★

★*There could be no other outcome. How could you ever be Matron of House Thalluen?*★

★*Because Jilrina simply would not be, no matter who I had to pray to.*★

★*Careful of such thoughts in the future, Sirana, though it is too late now. Your House is a crippled House which may not last much longer. Kaltra is infirm as a Matron. You are barren.*★

My body struggled of its own accord again, trembling with rage and fear, though I felt oddly separated from it as Lelinahdara's voice filled me and I kept my eyes closed. Someone's mouth and tongue played at the junction of my thighs, teasing and soothing my sex, yet someone else was biting my nipples, causing sharp pain.

★*My sister couldn't get away with what she did! She just couldn't!*★

★*Perhaps she did. But now it has stopped. Now what?*★

★*I-I would have found a way to get an heir,*★ I wept. ★*If my Matron had given me a chance over Kaltra.*★

The Priestess chuckled, low and smooth. ★*You cannot know the irony of that thought, daughter. It seems our Lady of the Web has a most interesting place for you in Her Design.*★

I flinched as something liquid and hot dripped onto my thighs, my belly, my chest, scalding my skin. I knew what it was without opening my eyes. Candle wax.

The first part of Jilrina's ritual.

The drips came too frequently, and the heat became too much. I screamed at the next set of successive, stinging burns. The loud wail seemed to be what they wanted, for no more wax fell. Soft mouths sucked on my toes and fingers instead. What had to be a thick candle pushed between my legs, spreading me open and filling my birth canal. A fist gripped my hair and pulled so that I must squirm and shift my body up farther upon the altar to where my head was no longer supported by the granite.

The second part.

I leaned back, my hair draping and almost touching the floor, and I could smell aroused female petals right in front of me. The Red Sister still gripping my hair forced my mouth on her, demanding I service her with nary a word. I hadn't done this since Jilrina died, yet it would seem one never forgets. My tongue flicked out and up, and I sucked on her, eating her with forced skill and practice.

The fat candle was soon withdrawn from my body, and the Priestess was chanting again. I remembered this third part and writhed desperately, my cry of fear muffled between silky thighs. The Red Sister pressed me to her so hard as to almost suffocate me. Two others still held my ankles and my legs apart, and the fourth draped her weight across my chest to hold me down.

NO! No, no, no, no ... please no!

Though I couldn't see her, I knew the Priestess would be standing between legs with her ceremonial dagger unsheathed, the naked blade shining. I was to take that dagger as I would a phallus; I would feel it thrust up inside me.

Jilrina had almost killed me when she did it. For whole marks of the candle, I suffered, bled, until she — out of sheer fright at being found out a sister-killer by our Matron — had brought me a healing potion from somewhere. I took the chance and drank it, and the flesh had healed and appeared normal on the outside. Inside, I now knew, there was scarring. My womb had not been thoroughly repaired, and if there had been anything else to be done for that, I could not speak to anyone about it.

The cold metal touched my thighs. Its point scraped upward, drawing small pinpoints of blood, I was sure. The tip was nestled between my lips and paused there.

I screamed again; this time the sound was trapped inside my head.

Sirana? Did you ever know what this ritual was for?

I was mindless in my fear. I couldn't answer, even with a thought.

Sirana! Answer me!

Every breath I heaved was steamy, fragrant, a Davrin's intimate scent filling my head and her heat warming my face. Yet I was so cold.

Damn sisters. Braqth curse all sisters ... !

Are you ready to break? the Priestess taunted me. *I shall shove this blade inside you, and you will bleed out on the altar, your body dumped by slaves to feed the Dread Spiders of the Pit. What a pathetic end for a Noble, barren Daughter.*

I screamed in rage, thrashing as I could, unable to break the Red Sisters' hold. *F-fuck you, Priestess! Fuck you all!*

She chuckled inside my head. *I think you shall, Sirana.*

Lelinahdara began pushing the dagger inside, and I expected fully to feel the edge slicing me open again. Instead, I felt the hard, thin shape of the naked blade but not the razor sharpness, as if it was still covered in a protective sheath. I also felt a tingle, then a rush of energy that flooded into my guts and caused me to gasp with the keenest points of pleasure and pain I'd ever felt. My body was straight as a bowstring, and I made wild sounds between another female's thighs, but now I could not comprehend what I was even trying to say.

More? Stop? Don't stop?

The Priestess kept about half its length moving in and out, fucking me gently. Instead of the ripping and shredding I remembered, it was electric and mind-wracking, like being squeezed in the grip of an endless orgasm with every tender stroke.

This is Braqth's Threshold, young daughter, Lelinahdara said with pride.

This was the ritual your sister tried to mimic. It is a fertility ritual to guarantee a child by the next seed of a male chosen. The longer I concentrate on your sensation, the higher the reward and the magic can last for cycles.

"Ah!" I cried aloud, churning my hips clumsily against her refined strokes with that dagger.

If my relic touches the entrance to your womb, Sirana, it heals what was destroyed, she thought. *It makes you fertile again. But I haven't reached your core yet. Can you take more of me without going mad? Can you take it all?*

I writhed. I could barely think. I don't even know if I was breathing. I was hardly aware of who I was anymore.

I ... I ... oh! ... .oh, Goddess!

The Priestess's voice crooned to me. *Yes, Sirana, Braqth's Threshold. True divinity, to be used sparingly. Go ahead and feel it. Do you wish to become whole again? Do you want sisters? All or nothing, Sirana, just as you've realized. You're a smart cait.*

I shuddered, straining against the exalted flood of sensation. I did not understand what the Priestess said through my ecstasy and my agony, yet I twisted my head violently to the side and somehow freed myself from the grip of muscular, feminine thighs. My body undulated, and I scooted down the altar, thrusting myself fully onto the ceremonial dagger, feeling the magic-laden point press hard against the entrance to my womb. I screamed until my voice echoed in the ritual chamber.

Vaguely I knew what I'd done. I'd taken the entire length of the dagger willingly. My eldest sister had asked the same thing of me. A requirement, she said. I would have rather died. I almost did when she lost her patience and forced me to take it.

This energy, however, with the dagger all the way inside me and centered in my core, was intense, hot, and divine. I squirted when my pleasure peaked for the last time, spraying clear fluid over the dagger's handle and the Priestess's hand. Then I collapsed and fell into a paralyzing afterglow, my legs dangling off the altar. I couldn't move, couldn't open my eyes, but I could still hear. Barely. I believed even the Priestess thought me unconscious as she carefully slid the naked blade out of my healthy and whole cunt.

"Well, Priestess?"

It was the Red Sister Prime.

"Will she come out of this with a useful mind?"

"Absolutely," Lelinahdara replied with confidence. "I could sense her to the very end; she was as lucid as any in the past who have survived this ritual."

A wet, sticky hand adorned with metal was placed over my abdomen, and the Priestess continued, "She is also not barren anymore. She will be highly fertile for the next few cycles. Unless you wish her to catch a child, keep males out of her reach. She will be craving them."

"She won't be seeing *males* where she's going, Priestess," the Prime said, a subtle emphasis of disgust on the word. "Not for spans."

The third voice to speak was Varessa D'Shea. "Sirana is accepted for the next trial?"

"She is ours now, Elder," the Prime confirmed. "Inform her Matron after the recruit has been taken outside of the city."

One corner of my mouth twitched as my consciousness faded.

No demons but them.

Chapter 8

I awoke naked and chilled, although my eyes remained closed by life-long habit. My breath was steady as I pretended to asleep. I inhaled, drawing in scents of rock, algae, and moisture but little else. My ears detected regular drips echoing in a cavernous area, and the fingers of my left hand trailed in barely moving water.

Outside.

A low, female voice returned to me.

"Inform her Matron after the recruit has been taken outside of the city."

My eyes flew open, and I jerked my hand out of the water before some creature could begin nibbling on it. I clutched it in my other hand, barely warmer, flexing the feeling back into it, reassuring myself that it still worked. I took a sniff of the moisture on my numb fingers and smelled almost nothing.

Where am I? Be quiet. You already disturbed the surface.

I lay on my side in the dark. The hard stone beneath me was uneven and dank, and my left shoulder and hip had gone numb from lying here unmoving. Swallowing a groan, I shifted carefully onto my back. I looked around as my eyes adjusted to the pitch dark.

Is no one else here?

The cavern was not large; enough floor space to fit quarters for five, perhaps, with a dark pool in the middle. I flexed my wet hand again, disoriented. I touched wet fingers to my tacky lips, licking them.

Freshwater. A pool deep enough to sustain a score of Davrin indefinitely.

I knew this from touching it; not a stagnant pond, but a silent spring being fed by a subaqueous stream. We had one on my Matron's plantation, but even such a valuable pool would not support any type of agriculture or animal husbandry for longer than a few decades. We'd needed more.

I closed my eyes tight against an ache in my head. *Pointless. Still practicing what it takes to be a Matron? A decade and a half at Court and the only change was ...*

My stomach chilled all the way back to my spine as my heart picked up.

The Red Sisters came for me. Fuck. Where am I?

I had used my ears and nose to determine there was no urgent threat, my tongue to confirm a safe drink if I wanted it, but it wasn't as if I was blind. My eyes weren't useless.

Unlike in the city, there was no light here, and I could not see the color spectrum. My eyes could detect heat to a degree, but more than that, it was the other Radiants beyond Light forming shape and depth when I looked around me now.

One of our tutors at the plantation, a mage from the Wizard's Tower named Hortis, had once described this natural ability for our people to see in the dark. I had listened with half an ear most of the time because I wasn't a mage and never would be. The lesson on Dark Sight was one of the few things he'd explained that stuck with me.

"Everything moves, or emits movement," he said, motioning dramatically with his soft, scholar's hands. *"Living creatures, the four elements, everything. Waves of energy radiate out even from stone, from water and air, just as much as fire. If we cannot see color, that energy is a Radiant showing us another view."*

"So?" I asked. *"Other races see that way, too. Maybe in even weirder ways."*

"Ah, but none can use Light and Radiants like we can," Hortis countered, staring at my eyes more than he did Jilrina or Kaltra. Maybe it was the color. *"For example, invisibility spells wrap Light around the caster, creating a chameleon effect where a mage's body does not break those waves of energy as it normally does. That*

spell does not work without fire or some other glow being present."

I remembered thinking then how I would use that to sneak up behind Jilrina. Now only I thought of a specific invisible wizard in a candle-filled chamber.

"Magical darkness also masks energy, both Light and Radiants," my childhood tutor continued. "For a limited time and in a specific location, we can direct both views elsewhere, we can remove enough around us to darken even our sensitive eyes and leave our enemies blind no matter what."

"Send energy elsewhere?" I repeated, confused. "Not just make it vanish?"

Hortis laughed. "Magic can mask energy or direct it, but we cannot destroy it. Energy can be transformed, sometimes explosively, but never ceases to exist. For this reason, it is complex to get the effect you want in spells and requires an affinity to the elements beyond the ability to perceive it. That is why not all Davrin can do it."

"I can't."

"Correct. You, Sirana, are magical enough to use the tools we create for our people, but without any affinity to create your own."

Thanks.

Even without Light, what Radiants remained in the Deepearth cavern were more than enough to give me an entire world of grey shapes and depth. My vision was good enough that I could hit a weaving pincer-worm with my blade if necessary; I'd already practiced. The only real disadvantage, of which the Davrin mages were most aware, was that we were unable to read languages or see sketches on flat surfaces. The reading skill always needed Light; no mage could make due with Radiants, the page just looked blank. Hortis had even mentioned they had tried to develop a "blind-reading" technique using our fingertips.

"It doesn't work the same," he said with a shrug. "It seems Light and its colors are fundamental to Davrin magic, and no texture can match the refined, eye-to-voice instruction provided by a quill and parchment."

All the better reason to not rely wholly on reading and magic, in my opinion.

The cavern where I lay remained quiet. No creature was coming to investigate the noise I'd made thus far, I was sure. Now I only had to figure out why I was here, and what to do next. My body started to relax, and I noticed my abdomen was warm.

Astoundingly warm.

I slid cold fingers gingerly over my belly, mimicking Lelinahdara as she had been touching me at the end of her ritual. She had told the Prime and D'Shea that I was no longer barren. I was fertile.

My womb. My womb is hot.

When I shifted my legs I gasped at the sensitivity of my sex; it was a mistake to reach down and touch it, as all my skin seemed to come alive then and my ability to think left me. Blood engorged the folds between my legs in an instant, and arousal coiled tighter and tighter until it began to hurt. Mental images of sex bombarded me — it didn't matter what flavor, anything that involved splattering semen. My breathing quickened, and I gasped too loud in the still chamber, kept gasping as I grew alarmed through my haze.

What's wrong with me?

I was alone. I didn't know where I was, but I had to find a male. I just had to! I pulled my hand away from myself and rolled to get on all fours, intending to stand up.

I didn't make it.

My groan dampened by a constricted throat, I lowered my head down to my forearms, my hair falling to cover my face. My knees open and my backside high in the air, I prayed that a male gifted with an erection would magically appear behind me and plow my sex hard and fast.

I swear to Braqth, I'll even welcome Kerse! No games this time!

Quivers of uncontrolled lust passed through me, frightening that I could not deny them. How was I to think, to act, or defend in this wilderness if I was paralyzed with this crippling heat? The Red Sisters had known this would happen, hadn't they? I would bet the Priestess had told them, just as she'd told me, taunted me, as I submitted to their ritual.

And they had left me alone like this.

With a growl I reached back between my legs with one hand, my forehead braced on one forearm, to slap my mound sharply. I wanted to squelch this unnerving rush, to make it stop with pain. I flinched at each burst of sensation that was neither pleasure nor pain, but both. Soon the arousal returned, stronger than a few moments ago.

This was not a fire that could be beaten down and smothered.

After another strained look around me, convinced I was alone, I rubbed furiously at my sex, thrusting my fingers inside with urgency. My eyes squeezed shut, and I bared my teeth as my spine tensed and my toes flexed. I just wanted to cum, I just wanted it to happen, to get it over with!

If that stupid Priestess couldn't heal without forcing this on me, too, so be it! I'll, I'll —

"*Nnggh,* " I grunted, suppressing my voice even if the squishing, sloshing sounds from between my legs negated my efforts to be quiet. The wave of pleasure was good.

Oh, very good, ohhhh, that's it.

I came down, but not far enough. I wasn't through. No, I had to go one more time.

Fine, one more. Or maybe another.

By the fourth orgasm, the warm spice of my arousal was all over my hand and seeping from my own body, announcing to the entire Deepearth wilderness that a lone Elf was here, flopping around helpless and exuding her scent to fill the cavern.

Ready to be eaten at their leisure. Fuck, fuck, fuck!

Grouchier than I'd been in my entire life, snarling and frustrated as my slit still throbbed and pleaded for a real cock, not some poor substitute, I rolled and planted myself down to sit, leaning back against a stone.

How long will this last? Will it end?

I snorted a quiet laugh at the irony. Now I would beg that faceless wizard to fuck me, to let me cum, to do as he liked with my body if only he sprayed his seed into my snatch at some point.

I might even thank him for it.

My body already sweated and I flushed both hot and cold at once, biting down on my first knuckle to focus on the pain over the other realization.

I'm terrified. This is real.

Real magic could take my will and reduce me to a gibbering mass. I still clung to my intense distrust of Priestesses and all the divine magics. I had every reason to. Give me a sword or dagger, rope, chain, or poison, I could control that. Give me a secret and a sense of a weak spot, I could exploit it.

I twitched where I sat, started rubbing between my legs again. I was getting sore already, but I couldn't stop. *I can't control this. I can't!*

Could Lelinahdara have prevented this? Was it a plot of the Red Sister Prime, or a punishment? Just an oversight? Simply practicality to keep me away from males so as not to catch?

Had they not realized I'd be like this until it was too late? When they realized it, the Priestess will have doomed me to a unique exile. One where I'd slowly waste away for want of mating. Perhaps not even water and food could interest me.

I ground my teeth. *No.*

I'd not give up that easily.

I leaned forward and crawled on all fours toward the edge of the cavern pool. I made myself drink, to replace what moisture I'd lost already. The temperature was almost tepid. When my lips touched the surface, I sucked in long, satisfying gulps.

At least one thirst could be satisfied.

As soon as my nose lifted from the clean pool, I could smell myself even more. I badly needed to wash. Not only had I just creamed my inner thighs to where they might stick together as I walked to make a rash, but the Red Sisters hadn't done me the favor of bathing me *before* abandoning me. Every mark and substance from their abuse in the secret chambers was still present on my body.

I felt dizzy a moment when I stood up, but I stared down into the water and focused as well as I could below the surface. I watched for any sign of movement, of light, of danger. After longer than I cared to admit, I detected algae glowing dimly far below and small fish cutting silently through the liquid. Knowing there's always a bigger fish, the lack of one now didn't clear the pool as being completely safe to bathe in, but if I was quick?

Hmm.

My attempts to be quiet hadn't made any difference in my safety, now that I thought about it. No doubt I could be scented from two tunnels away. Either I had been fortunate while unconscious or the Red Sisters had chosen this location well.

I grimaced as the magical heat began to rise in my womb again. Soon I'd have to climax again. *Just be quick.*

The pool served to cool me down temporarily, and it was refreshing. Everything from my long, white hair down to my stone-scraped toes I cleaned in the black, underground pool. The swirling water constantly caressed between my legs, and my mind wandered far from the weaker sex and their spurting, creamy seed. The Sisters leaving me here was both the least effort they could make, and the most torture they could inflict.

Or so my cunt kept telling me.

My cunt is a groveling mate-eater.

Curse all mind-altering magic anyway!

I wrung out my hair after climbing out of the pool, shook my hands and let the rest of the water drain down my skin and onto the stone. Without thought, I caressed my netherlips again with one hand, and then grimaced, pulling one hand away with the other. I gripped my hands together and shivered in a way that had nothing to do with being cold.

Should I leave this area? Was I supposed to find my way back to the Great Cavern or find something here? Were the Red Sisters waiting for me elsewhere, or had I simply been left to find my fate in the wilderness?

A note or a sign might've been helpful.

I braced myself against a boulder with arms straight, gripping rock as I was assailed again with overpowering imagery of mating again and again. My legs parted, and my back arched, begging to be mounted and ridden. The emptiness was agony, the lack of willpower maddening.

My ears perked at the sound of tiny, tiny footfalls. I opened my eyes to see the familiar motion of a large spider crawling closer to my hand.

A spider.

Braqth's symbol. Already I could imagine the excitement a Priestess might show for such timing.

I stared hard at the grey arachnid as it crept and stopped, sneaked and stayed. It wasn't heading toward my hand directly; in fact, it tried to avoid me after realizing it had moved too close. I reached out to block its path. It decided to go around my hand, and I blocked again, deftly slipping my fingers beneath its forelegs to lift it onto my fingertips and closer to my scowling face.

I could make out small black eyes in a ghostly face, tiny hairs on a still, hunched body sensing the heat of my skin. Small hooks held tightly so that even if I turned my hand vertical, it would hold on.

A sign from the Spider Queen, am I to take this? Jilrina would have said so. Are You watching, Braqth? Entertained by these rituals shown the Davrin? Do You lose interest when the plaything stops struggling in Your Web?

My sex pulsed again, a frustrating amount of drool anointing my netherlips just now cleaned. I bared my teeth at the spider and slammed my hand down, crushing it then smearing its goo across the rocks.

Well, I haven't stopped yet, so keep laughing, Goddess. Fuck Your Threshold.

The wave of anger passed too quickly, bowing to my craving once again, and I washed my hand of spider guts, preparing to stroke my slit. The Spider Queen's Priestess had left me to face a similar fate. I imagined, enough time spent in the wilderness, and I would be so focused on finding a way to get my cunt stuffed that my senses would fail to recognize a giant threat until I stood next to it.

Squish. The end.

Smooth stone lined the edge of the pool, and slowly I traced the cavern in which I'd been left. I wanted to go before I was so sore I couldn't walk, but I also wanted to be sure I knew what I left behind. It would be just like an assassin at Court to say later, before killing me, *"I'd left something for you. If only you'd looked around and not stumbled off like a witless cock."*

It took longer than I would have liked to check the cavern. Twice in my turn about the place, I sank to my knees, gasping, unable to catch my breath for the sudden waves of want which overtook me. The need was constant, but it also surged and withdrew, allowing me brief respites of relative lucidity where I could climb back to my feet and move again. I knew I would still be in trouble if I ran across something dangerous while in the grips of this … this …

Breeding trance.

For all my recent cursing about magic, there was still that inborn sense a Davrin could develop. It worked to better detect a hidden passage or a magical item nearby; I had that sense, and I did value it. To sense Elven magic was my heritage. Even my straightforward weapons were fashioned through various methods unique to Davrin. If a blade possessed no magical effect in its use, it still held the taste from its blacksmith's skill.

It was because of this I finally found something. I slowed and turned my head toward a small outcropping, partially hanging above my path along the pool's edge. I was on the far side from where I'd awoken, and a silent, familiar vibration beckoned me closer to that outcrop. I found tucked between the stones a dagger in its sheath as long as my forearm. I reached with one hand first to touch it; subtle recognition answered my instinctive inquiry.

Yes.

I used both hands to carefully release it. I felt the curving designs upon the sheath and the hilt with my fingers, so stark and familiar that I could see them in my mind's eye: House Thalluen. I drew it to check its edge; it had an elegant curve made of black metal to reduce reflection. Single edge blade, double fullers on either side running its length. The sheath possessed the crest of my House in the form of inlays, but those were matte black upon black as well. Simple and beautiful, one of the stealth blades.

There was no belt, so I would have to carry the long dagger in my hand. There were no other supplies found as I checked the rest of the area, either; nothing to bring water from the pool, nothing with which to clothe myself, and no food. They had left me a weapon from my own House as my only tool and defense in the wilderness.

Unlike the spider, I could say without a doubt that *this* was my sign and my instruction.

I must find my way back to House Thalluen.

They were testing my previous training, perhaps? How much did I remember of the Palace Guards' survival trials? It wasn't so long ago; I wasn't worried. I also considered that there were two ways in which they could evaluate me. First, wait and see if I ever came back. Or second, have at least one Red Sister stalking and watching me.

My closed smile was as unconscious as the squeezing of my thighs. *Too soon to tell which one, so —*

I gasped and hunched over once more as I was gripped by the divine lust, and I clenched my teeth as I waited for it to recede.

Just make it stop!

When I could straighten again, I tried to get my chain of thought back, but after a moment shrugged to myself.

The point is I must leave.

After one more drink of water, I climbed upward and left through the only opening which would lead me from the cavern above the waterline. It was large enough to walk bent over and only single-file. It occurred to me that I hadn't been left fully exposed while left unconscious.

Only one way in, larger predators won't fit, and the cavern was well off the main travel-way.

I confirmed this as I found myself at the other end of the tunnel, looking down from the lip of an abrupt drop into a broader, barren cavern. There was only one other exit to this one as well. I had to climb down, across the basin, then climb up again and out.

By the time I had navigated the obstacle course to finally reach a real travel-way in the Deepearth, I had become intolerably hungry. I had not eaten since before the Red Sister called Qivni had collected me upon that balcony. Through that entire time — through pure endurance coupling with three different males and the mind-wrenching personal exposure I faced atop Braqth's altar — until I woke to find myself here and climbing through whole valleys to locate a road back to Sivaraus, I had burned more energy than I had in my most intense cycle of martial training.

I stood on the path and waited for my senses to tell me which way to go to return to the Great Cavern. Unfortunately, my grumbling stomach and Braqth's "divine," *fuck-me-now* hangover obstructed my answer completely. I cursed under my shuddering breath and chose a direction — there were only two, I picked the one leading downward — at least to hunt for edible fungus and small creatures.

A pity I wasted that spider from before.

Braqth's creatures tasted unpleasantly bitter, I knew, and some were deadly if one forgot to pinch off the head, but one couldn't be choosy in an area without much growth. Or I could have stayed to fish in the pool; a little late now to be having that thought. Again, I thanked the Priestess for clouding my rational choices.

Dual fits of hunger ate at me for what seemed an eternity as I walked, and this road was empty and quiet. Scuttling flashes of movement were too abrupt for me to think about stalking or pouncing, and I didn't run into anything more substantial than my palm in any case. My reflexes and instincts were not at their best, to say the least.

Fortunately, even had I been throttling myself between my legs right then, I'd have heard that pickaxe when I rounded a curve. Dwarves could never be silent. Whether from their endless array of tools and armor or from their simple plodding on wide feet with dense bodies, they were not made for stealth. But which kind of Dwarf would I see, a Tragar or a Ketro?

And why do I hear only a single pick jabbing at the stone? They're always seen in clumps.

Praying my next mating clutch wouldn't hit me while I reconnoitered the scene ahead of me, I bent lower and padded very soft, watching for loose pebbles or slick moss, testing the ground beneath my bare toes. The focus on a tangible threat helped push my lust back into its proper place, and I crouched behind a convenient stone. I hoped, when I peeked over it, the Dwarf would be within my Dark Sight's range, but I would not be within his.

That was another reasonable expectation: the Dwarf would be near-sighted, and he'd be male. Female squatters seemed to appear only if forcibly dragged out of their holes like a queen insect, and Davrin could see farther than the short stone-diggers. I had the advantage if the Priestess spell didn't fuck it up for me.

The Dwarf proved just on the edge of my vision when I looked. He even seemed to flicker, to swim in and out of focus as he moved here and there. Nonetheless, I could hear his every step, scrape and *tink* with his tools as he shifted around, studying a lay of stone and working at it as if to release something.

I squinted to take in detail. Darker skin, not light grey. A bald head but a short, white beard. Somewhat sinewy but still very strong, with endurance enough to work without end. I knew what it was.

Tragar.

Not a harmless Pyte or an easily intimidated Ketro, but a full-sized Grey Dwarf.

Fuck you, Braqth.

CHAPTER 9

THE TRAGAR WERE THE MOST DANGEROUS RACE OF SQUATTERS, ALMOST NEVER kept as working slaves like the Ketro, unless they were truly crippled. Ironically, if there was a race known to care *less* about enjoying life than even the dourest mid-Dwarf, it was the Tragar. There was a jest that to see one smile meant only that he had trouble passing gas.

They were said to be grim, bitter, and jealous of other's wealth. Their only pleasures were to push around those weaker than them and to work their captives to death. Meanwhile, they never ceased toiling themselves; they expected it. They made sure just being alive was a difficult task, and their measure of strength depended upon how much rock one could move in their lifetime.

Work. Dominate. Punish. Work more. Die.

The Davrin respected nothing about them except their notable viciousness and that an unknown fraction of them had distinct talents never to be underestimated.

Tragar did not make good slaves for one excellent reason: All it took was one in a group with those mental powers similar to the mind flaying Ornilleth, and the bald, dark Dwarves acted like one Abyssal Beast with multiple arms.

One of the more recent cautionary stories at Court had been about a

Trade Mistress rejecting an offer made by a Tragar and foolishly turning her back on him. A fist-sized stone flew straight from the ground to the back of her head while the stern Dwarf moved not a muscle. No warning, for no one had tasted the magic in the air. It hadn't been magic as the Davrin knew it.

Word had it that these abilities in Tragar were thanks to the Ornilleth, an entire race of mind-talent mages that even the Davrin had cause to fear. The tentacle-faces had enslaved more races than even my own kind. The rumors of their experiments, of changing and creating new and warped forms of the natural races as they exercised a telepathic grip on their victims.

This certainly lent itself to suggest the source of a Tragar's eternally bad temper.

So, does this one has mental talents? Why is he working alone?

I had been sitting for long enough that if any others were working in the surrounding caverns, I'd have heard them. I knew Tragar sometimes scouted into our territory looking for gems, and, like a social insect having found a new food source, they would return to bring reinforcements. Listening to a Palace Guard talk about contacts in the Valsharess's Army, it was endlessly irritating keeping the pilferers out.

I pondered whether to take out this scout before such a thing could happen, then grimaced, looking down at my turgid nipples and lack of any armor or poison or weapon with any range.

I'm not stupid.

For being so short, these Dwarves were still quick, muscular, and did not hesitate to kill. Charging him now and hoping to get the drop on him was not an option.

I could smell his sweat after a time as I sat there, and I was aware of the increase in heat in the area. His last bath was far less recent than mine, and Dwarves in general always had an oily heft to their musk, layered with soot and ash, grit and mineral. Dwarves smelled to me like bags of grease and earth, and this one was no different. I remained behind the boulder and stewed, then bit down on my lip and squeezed my thighs together.

Goddess damn it!

Another wave of arousal claimed me. It lasted for too long, far too long as I trembled, and I chose to hold my breath and let it out rather than struggle with the husky gasps that tried to escape. Sweat popped out on my forehead, and I gripped my dagger in its sheath, in serious consideration right then to pump it into my slick slit regardless of how dirty it was or how it scraped me inside.

No! Fucking shit, no!

Quivers of fear mixed with the lust. These episodes were not lessening in strength. If this were a permanent affliction, I would not live much longer, inside or outside Sivaraus. Depending on who discovered this weakness first — the closest one being that Tragar — my death could be a singularly creative one.

I bit down on the sheath of the dagger as I waited for the fit to pass. If this is permanent, I refused to die yet. Not until I got the Priestess who'd done this.

The Tragar paused; he was still as my mind cleared partway, while I tried to catch my breath as quiet as I could be. If I'd thought to take him unaware, it was too late now. He sensed another presence, though I would wager he would not have seen me even had I stood straight up. He'd hear me, perhaps even smell me, but he'd not see me.

I peeked back over the stone, tensing as my body flooded with sensation. The Tragar had gathered up what I was sure were raw gems just harvested, and he moved over to his pack a few paces away. He added the stones to a pouch tied to the outside of the bag, reached to lift and don a simple, steel helmet that had been near his feet. The headpiece didn't have a nose or mouth guard and barely protected his cheekbones.

He stood perfectly still, listening, far quieter than I'd have believed a Dwarf could manage.

I focused on the pack and saw there was a swollen water skin tied to it, slightly damp with condensation. It was a reasonable leap of logic to suppose there would be food inside that pack as well. Now I had a personal reason to confront him. Pilfering in Davrin territory, I could infer, but I wasn't the Border Guard, and it wasn't my responsibility, especially naked with only a blade.

However, the temptation was great to try to take that food and water from him. I wanted it more than he did. If he was a scout, he could hike back and get more. I, on the other hand, was on my own. My only resources would be what I could find, or what I could claim.

I would have to get closer somehow. In other circumstances, maybe I'd consider bargaining with him, but I honestly had nothing to barter away. I would not give up my House's blade, and I hadn't anything else on me.

I imagined an obvious jest, made by anyone at Court, to suggest killing two salamanders with one stone: to bargain sex for food and take care of my intense need at the same time. I would gut someone for even suggesting it. At least a Sathoet was half-Davrin. I'd not fuck a Dwarf, and any Squat would not consider slaking his occasional lust with an Elf.

We would kill each other first.

The Tragar inhaled through his big nose, filling his barrel chest. He let it out. Neither of us moved for long, stretching moments. He scowled in my direction but was not looking right at me. I saw his eyes; they had no pupils. The blank, milk-white eyes resembled those of an Ornilleth, at least as I'd seen in colored drawings.

"*Wrundeg, Davrin,*" the Dwarf muttered, deep and aggressive. "*Ichen blikrow.*"

So guttural. It sounded like Dwarves were hacking and spitting up their own language. Nonetheless, I got the gist. He knew I was here, and he didn't like it.

He's as wary as I am. He doesn't know I'm alone.

If I wanted the food and water, it was time to take control. Or run away.

"Surely you speak Trade, Tragar," I said, standing up slow and steady. He seemed to look right at me but, as I had predicted, he couldn't see this far. He squinted but didn't hold my location for long before his gaze wavered. He was estimating the distance.

The Tragar nodded once, a short, gruff gesture. "I do. Quit hiding, Elf. Come out."

"Mmm, no," I replied with a playful lilt to my voice.

If Dwarven brutishness could intimidate me, then Elven theatrics could unnerve him.

My answer and the silence which followed baffled him, and his face grimaced in a hideous shadow of anger as he gestured with his pickaxe. "Frolicking whores. Try to slave me, I wrench you *all* open from crotch to neck."

That was a pretty good threat, and I believed he would.

"Leave your pack, then," I said, projecting command to my voice as it bounced off the rock. "Those gems aren't yours. Leave everything here, we give you a chance to run."

The Tragar glanced at his pack, his face hardened further, and he shook his head. "You lie. You chase when run. I not outrun you."

"Try," I bluffed. "Leave your pack, and we are even."

He had a very firm grip on his pack as he scowled even more deeply, and I frowned, feeling my first twinge of frustration. Surely, he didn't have anything in there for which he wanted to die or become enslaved for? Was he a fool?

"Leave our territory, scout!" I repeated as my stomach rumbled impatiently. "This is your only chance!"

The bald Dwarf kept quiet, and I saw the doubt cross his face. Damn my hunger; I'd pushed too hard, too quickly and squandered the chance to bluff him and avoid a fight.

"Davrin don't give chance," he said quietly, hefting his pickaxe and his pack, biceps bulging. "They attack when strong, or they trick when they not win by strength."

Fuck me. Bluff called.

He grinned, showing full, blunt teeth as he closed his white, blank eyes. He started to vanish before my gaze.

How the fuck?

"No, you don't," I growled, drawing my blade and sprinting toward his fading outline. Just before I lost him, I stopped, braced my legs, and pitched the naked blade in a lethal spin.

No holding back.

Sparks flew when the blade struck and careened off his helmet. There was a loud clang of metal, and the Tragar stumbled, becoming visible to me again as I also noted where my dagger landed.

"*ULKHEIN!*" he bellowed in rage — I was sure it was an insult — and a stone the size of his fist hurdled itself from the ground toward my chest at incredible speed.

It had my full and undivided attention.

Fuck!!

The stone clipped my shoulder as I dodged to the side, but I stayed in motion as the rock ricocheted against the wall of the cavern behind me and did not return. My shoulder was going numb, and I had to end this quickly. I was not in a position to toy with anyone and expect to come out on top.

A charge, a successful feint to tempt his swing of the pickaxe, followed by a jumping kick to the face. My heel struck flesh, but my ankle hit hard metal.

Ow!

I rolled away and dove for my dagger.

"*Shuz reg!*" he barked, spinning around to follow me, his arms drawn up, prepared to pin me to the floor with his pickaxe. Only that heavy pack slowed him down.

Chink!

Goddess, that was close!

I launched myself up like a serpent with fangs poised, yet even my second dagger strike did not kill him as it should have. He twisted, I missed his vitals, and the sharp edge drew a long line up from his hairy pit. I heard the pickaxe drop, and he staggered back clutching his arm.

"*Fluqsie!*" he exclaimed, perhaps like me, cursing his own deity.

I shoved the handle of the pickaxe farther away from him with my bare foot and brandished my weapon. There wasn't an easy opening to get him through his armor, and although he'd just realized I was naked, it didn't seem to move him beyond a sneer. Maybe he expected Dark Elves to show up naked and crazy.

"Give me your pack," I said again in Trade, not sure what I expected to happen.

The Tragar stood weaponless and bleeding dark fluid from a deep wound. He glared at me as he said nothing, made no sound after that first cry, just gnashed his teeth.

"Give me your pack, thief," I demanded. "Enough games."

He growled, a bit of froth at the corner of his pale-bearded mouth. "No. Will see you speared."

The Tragar blinked his eyes, looked away from me, and I heard the pickaxe shifting closer as if it had a will of its own.

Uh-oh.

The grey Dwarf's head was just the right height, so I attacked as he looked away. I turned, spun, and kicked him with the heel of my foot, connecting with the bridge of his nose this time and sending him back onto the bulky pack still strapped to his back. Blood spurted across his face, and the pickaxe stopped moving. I panted, realizing I must pull what I sought out from under him.

Hmph. Stupid Squat, what's in that pack worth a slash and two kicks to the face?

I listened as the quiet returned after the scuffle. Had we drawn unwelcome attention? Were his own kind coming to investigate? I shouldn't waste time. I kneeled to roll him partly onto his side and to work, yank, and shift his heavy pack from his body. It was quite a chore and took more energy than it should have.

Tragar are so dense, in mind and body.

I fumbled to get the water pack untied as soon as I was able, sniffing the spout and huffing a laugh. It was water alright, but it was mixed with mushroom ale. Or rather, it was mushroom ale heavily diluted with water, enough to replenish oneself but not prevent a dull buzz and soothe sore muscles. This *would* be the drink an ever-working Dwarf would carry.

He might have been buzzed when I found him.

"Better than nothing," I muttered as I looped the strap across my shoulder to let it rest at my waist. Then I started unlacing the leather ties securing his pack.

As I pulled out items looking for anything edible, I ran across a variety of small, nicked tools that, even if I didn't know what they were for, seemed like the essentials for any scout. They were each wrapped in oiled cloths that repelled moisture and were flecked with rock, earth, and dust; obviously well-used and — where applicable — repeatedly sharpened.

He must have been using this same set for decades.

That or he was not the only one to have used them. I set them aside. They were heavy, and I had no interest in excavation tools.

About a dozen raw, unpolished gems were inside as well. Despite what I'd told him about them not belonging to him, I really didn't care about those, either; I set them aside and continued my search. Stuffed in an inner pocket was a package which gave under my touch, and I lifted that out. Enclosed in an oiled leather wrap this time, I smelled what I'd bet was animal fat and tugged at the string tying it closed.

Inside was a dense, pressed block of something that I presumed was the Tragar's dinner. I could smell deep nuts, mushrooms, salted fish, cave fruit, and oil of unknown source. It had all been ground up and smashed together into a compact, portable meal. It was very crude and nothing you'd ever see on the dining plates of the Court, but I wasn't choosy now. Adequately rationed, this one block filling my entire hand from heel to fingertip could last me two cycles of marching.

I took a bite, chewing slowly to taste it first then swallowing more hastily. It wasn't to my liking, far too musky and heavy, but I could live off it.

My first food in more than a cycle.

I took another few bites, and then a swallow of the ale, careful to not start guzzling that. Slowly my hollow middle ceased its incessant demands and quieted.

I found nothing else of interest to me after I emptied the pack. He had no weapon equal to my House blade, and I could not wear his boots nor any of his clothes or armor, which consisted mostly of studded leather braces, heavy shin guards, and a thick chest piece that would take a magical blade to stab through it. His single blanket was shabby, coarse, and smelled unbearable. Overall, he was poor in matters of wealth when compared to the Noble Houses. He possessed what he most used as a laborer.

There were only two other things I considered taking with the food and water: his cloak and his belt. The grey cloak would be short on me but would obscure part of my form and provide warmth. The belt would also give me something from which to hang the sheath of my dagger to free my hands.

I decided to kill him after stripping those things from him. A simple cut across the throat or blow on the head with the pickaxe. I did not want him tracking me, and we could do with one less Tragar hacking at our tunnels. I removed his helmet.

Cloak and belt first, then dispatch the Dwarf.

The cloak also took some doing to get it out from under him, the massive beast that he was. I panted and muttered obscenities as I somehow yanked it free without tearing a hole in it. It smelled of smoke and grease and made me wrinkle my nose, but it was also of durable weave and wasn't as rough as the blanket. I draped it around my bare shoulders, and it fell to my lower thighs. I could picture Elder D'Shea now, pitched over laughing if she saw me like this.

Bah!

I shook my head free of the distraction and kneeled again to roll the Tragar full onto his back and take hold of his belt buckle. It took some figuring out; it wasn't just the clip I was used to, but something that threaded through a wide metal ring and folded back on itself.

You must make it so complicated, Dwarf?

Just as I succeeded in undoing his belt, I felt the rapid rise of another lust-grip sweeping up to take me.

"No!" I groaned in dread, my hands clasping the loosened belt in a grip which hurt my hands. "No, not now!"

My knees were braced for balance and far enough apart to allow for easy mounting. My cunt shrieked at me as if claimed by Braqth Herself, demanding I make it happen right now, right here. *Straddle ... straddle him.*

Are you fucking insane?!

I gasped for breath and trembled, trying to regain my self-control, wrenching my eyes away from where they'd drifted: the Tragar's loose pants and bulging crotch. I looked back at his face.

I froze.

The Tragar's eyes were open, entirely white and subtly glowing, his dark face and white beard stained with blood from his nose. He stared at me, seemed to catch me in a trap somehow as I couldn't move, couldn't look away from him. I felt a sharp pain inside my skull which forced a hoarse scream from my throat. Maddeningly, this did not squelch my need to mate, but the pain only seemed to enhance it.

I'm dead. Oh, Goddess, I'm dead.

And all my body wanted to do was fuck.

The glaring Dwarf opened his mouth as if to speak or snarl, but then his eyes flew wide, and he suddenly sucked in his breath and went rigid. We stared at each other; I still had hold of his belt. I felt a power I didn't understand connecting us — *no* — swamping us, crushing like a flood, entwining and swirling together with the leftover Priestess magic inside me.

It robbed us of our right minds.

I couldn't blink or unlock our gaze, but I knew his cock grew hard as granite within his worker's pants. Not only was the stout club brushing my hands, but I could *feel* his own arousal pulsing through my veins, answering the open call put out by my insatiable slit. It made my belly clench up.

Oh, Goddess.

~Ichfren gow. Fretizga kohr!~

I'd heard that inside my own mind, like the ritual link with Lelinah-dara, and I understood the meaning, saw the image in his mind's eye. It was disgusting, horrifying, and thrilling because it was what I wanted to do.

Oh, Goddess!

I tore his shabby trousers getting them open, but before I could strad-dle him, he grabbed me by both long ears and pulled my face down to his crotch. I gagged at the pungent, oily smell as he rubbed a dark and stubby, but very thick, male member across my nose and cheeks, touching his testicles to my lips. My tongue flicked out to lick at his sack, tasting its salt and bitterness using my full width.

Why did I do that?!

"*Ichfren,*" the Tragar grunted, clenching his muscular buttocks to grind his erection harder."*Ichfren!*"

One thick-fingered hand held my left ear while the right gripped my hair; he was strong enough to pull my mouth over the crown of his cock like putting on a stocking, and for some unfathomable reason I opened my mouth wider and did not bite him.

~*Make it good and wet, stick-legs!*~ Kain said. ~*We'll see if I split you in half with this massive tool when I do you at the other end!*~

Kain. His name was Kain, and he jammed the thickest cock I'd ever taken in my mouth, all the way to the back, making me gag once again. My tongue tried to caress him, tasting his unbathed, odorous shaft. Oh, Goddess, he was foul.

But my cunt wanted it so badly that, for four or five lunges, I held still and let Kain fuck my throat, stretching it in a way I'd never experienced before. I felt his pleasure taken from my mouth, knew it as if it was my own; in return, he felt what it was like to swallow a whole scepter like this, with one's nose pressed into a crisp, dirty-white thatch of Dwarf hair.

Yes. In my cunt next, Kain. It wants it. Needs it.

~*I know you do, trickster. Nothing but cowards and tricks, what Elves are.*~

Fuck my cunt, Kain! Fuck me!

His very thoughts growled like an animal caught in a snare. ~*This is wrong! How dare you corrupt me like this, Abyssal whore! I don't know how you did this, spider-slut, but I ... can't ... stop this!*~

The Tragar pulled me off his soggy prick and pushed me away; I coughed as I nearly collapsed but caught myself. I just got to my hands and knees when Kain stripped his cloak and waterskin off me, and he kicked my dagger away.

My dagger, which had been beside me this entire time, was now next to his pickaxe.

Out of reach.

The soreness in my throat reminded me what I'd just done, and still, I remained on my knees waiting. Some juice from my slit leaked out, and I felt it slowly dripping, cooling, on one inner thigh.

~*Whore!*~ Kain bellowed, sharing that same sensation as he sloughed off his boots and pants completely. ~*How dare you!*~

His broad hands took firm hold of my naked hips, pulled me up into position. Squatting powerful thighs, his big feet just outside my knees, he was in perfect stance to breed me.

Yes!

I shook my head feebly, braced on my elbows and incredulous that this was happening.

"No ... Don't — !"

The Dwarf pushed his cock into my slit; it was sucked in so easily yet opened me so widely that my eyes bugged. My body yielded with sick glee, it was nauseating! I moaned aloud to feel myself spread around his pole, to *see* it through his eyes. The penetration wasn't deep, but I stretched wider to take him than I had any Davrin.

Kain sucked on his thumb and pushed that into my netherhole.

"Uh! Goddess!" I cried out, lifting my head up and staring at nothing, watching my own pucker squeeze eagerly around his digit, feeling my hot, full cunt pulse and engorge further.

I want your seed, Kain. Breed me! Now!

~*Diseased, twisted Elf.*~

He held his fat thumb inside me to his first knuckle as he clutched my ass cheeks and spread them open in his grip, watching his member disappear inside the scalding hole of a racial enemy.

~*Feel this, flat-chested faerie! Feel this!*~

My hanging tits — because I *did* have them, I wasn't flat — shook and jerked as he pounded my hole, reaming it as resentfully as the invisible wizard had taken my netherhole. I was ashamed to hear the sounds escaping between my lips; I wanted another male to stuff my mouth and muffle them so they wouldn't echo around me like this!

Blessedly it didn't take long the first time. The underside of his cock tingled and tightened; I could feel it. Kain threw himself into his thrusts, his fingers bruising my flesh. He would *not* pull out before he had seeded my womb. Before … he planted—

No! No, it's impossible! It can't happen!

My cunt clenched down on him, milking and stroking him when I climaxed, when he groaned and slammed in one more time before holding still, cramming his coarse, filthy body hair up in my crevice, rubbing it along my backside and the backs of my thighs. He spurted inside me, five or six deep pulses as my traitorous slit gulped it down.

That extraordinary, pleasurable release paralyzed him — paralyzed us — as no force could make him withdraw from the warm, wet sheath. I could feel his wide prick flexing and a throb inside me. I screamed at the pleasure of it, the loudest noise yet in the deep caverns, aware of nothing until I felt a softened member withdraw.

My forehead was on the stone as I saw him in my mind's eye. Kain had leaned back, watching with intense disgust and pride as his cream ooze out of a hard-stretched, Elven hole.

"*Noch,*" he murmured.

~*No.*~

"*Kwernish toug?*"

~*Why are you doing this?*~

Resting my head on my arms now, I reached between my legs and caressed my folds, played with his semen. The fire in my belly had calmed down at last, as though the male offering was the missing component.

This is what the spell needs, I thought.

He heard me. ~*Abyssal sickness. Release me.*~

"You can go," I murmured in my native tongue. "Just go."

~***Release** me, whore.*~

It struck me that I was tired of showing him my backside, of kneeling like this. I pushed myself up and whirled on him, looking him in the eye as I snarled, "What do you mean, *release* you?"

Making eye contact again was a mistake.

I gasped, and so did the Dwarf, staring into my blue eyes. He couldn't tell they were blue, he only *knew* they were.

The link.

Still there. Still strong.

The moment one of us had the thought to rut a second time — I wasn't sure which of us it was — the shared heat between us strengthened and began again. I reached to pinch my own nipples, horrified and hoping the sharp pain would quell the surging arousal.

It only made it stronger.

~*Trickster! Release me!*~

Kain pushed me by my shoulders so hard that I struck the back of my head against the pathway. I felt his fat prick pushing between my legs before I even realized he had climbed on top of me, gripping my wrists and pinning them down. When I focused on the broad shoulders and bald head above me, grunting as he rutted me, our eyes locked again. In moments, it was as if the last orgasm hadn't happened.

~*No ...* ~

I squealed beneath the Dwarf like a helpless Noble violated by bandits. Kain crammed himself between my legs while my bare feet kicked toward the ceiling as if I could do nothing else — *wanted* to do nothing else. He slobbered over my tits, insulting the size of them, but also bit my purple nipples, praising their sensitivity. He jabbed into me again and again, and I was going to come.

He was going to come.

The swell of ecstasy would be every bit as powerful as the first.

Yes! Yes!

I tossed my head from side-to-side, sharing the climax as he held me down. I took the Tragar's cream again in the same hole, collecting his offering like a thirsty addict even as my slit was too stretched out to hold much of it when he finally let me up.

"Oh, Braqth, fucking go!" I cried, swiping at him. "Get away from me!"

"*Kwernish toug, Davrin!*" he yelled back, infuriated as the heat of his rage mixed with that in my womb. ~*Stronger. Your Goddess's magic is stronger than me! Stop!*~

It didn't stop. When the lust rose up to claim us both again, Kain attacked.

He gripped my arms in an iron grasp and hauled me atop him. I could feel the stout erection returning already, pressing into my stomach, his naked legs tangled with mine. My nipples scraped across the leather chest piece, and he breathed heavily in my face, at once exhausted and excited. My legs parted to brace my knees on either side of his thighs, and my hips jerked as if to squat down on him myself.

"Let me go!" I yelled in Davrin, but I didn't pull away from him.

My hips moved lewdly trying to impale myself on him. He laughed and snarled at the same time, holding still just long enough that I could take him into my sloppy hole, and then in pure frustration he bit me hard on the shoulder, breaking the skin.

"Ah, fuck!" I cried.

I jabbed him in the eye, kept fucking him as my hips rolled.

"Ulkhein!" he snarled.

We thrashed violently across the ground, and his squat staff popped out of my loose cunt as we fumbled off the edge of a boulder.

"Short snot-sucker!" I bellowed, at last making a sincere effort to get away.

Get out! Now!

I nearly slipped free, but Kain pounced on me, pushing me belly-down to the ground with more than enough weight to pin me. With one of his palms on the back of my head and the other ignoring his terror, he aimed the broad, mushroom head in between my ass cheeks, pressing hard against my netherhole.

"No! Oh, Goddess!"

~*Slut! Don't spread your legs! Don't lift your — !*~

That was precisely what I did. I raised my ass for him, tilted my hips just right, and relaxed. In an instant, that massive, slippery head stretched my puckered barrier, popping inside, and the thick shaft inexorably passed behind it.

"No!" I blurted, jerking with both nausea and ecstatic thrill; my eyes grew wide as the blunt weapon probed deeper. My thoughts escaped me as I froze in place.

Kain, you're big! Oh, Goddess, you are enormous!

He could neither resist nor bear the praise.

Please, Goddess, I beg you, give me your offering!

~Rraagh! Demoness!!~

The bald Tragar lunged three more times, forcing grunts from us both as he squeezed all the way inside me. He held still after he was hilted, enjoying the way my hole resisted such a stretch; I could feel it quivering under strain. I knew what to do.

Relax. Wait. Even with a broader cock, the rule proved the same. Eventually, I loosened up; it was more comfortable for Kain to move and so he did, rutting my dirt hole slowly at first, then faster as I moaned encouragement.

~Trickster ... want to kill you. Need to kill you to make it stop.~

Cream in my netherhole first. Do it. Spurt, Tragar, spurt in my Abyssal pit!

He obeyed, pinning me, holding me helpless as he wallowed in my ass. He drooled on my back when we climaxed; I could feel every moment, every flex and pulse of his ejaculation. We were both scared when we didn't seem to come down from this, but leveled off in a pool of pleasure that swirled around us and kept us spinning. He kept rutting the same hole without softening, going for a fourth time now that my ass was stretched and slick like my cunt.

Oh Braqth, no, we can't! Can't think!

I tried to get away from him, gasping in pleasure and rage, wriggling and scrambling as he held on tight to me as though he was Drowning. He continued plowing into me. I felt his pleasure and pain in my mind; he felt my sore body, my raw knees and elbows and all its holes roughly used. It made no difference; I took that next offering between my cheeks regardless, moisture oozing and squishing out.

~Again ... ~ he thought in a mantic stupor, still gripping me, humping me with half an erection. ~Again, Davrin, take me again. Again, again, again ... ~

Somehow his chant aided a separate thought of my own. In one instant, I saw my situation through this Goddess-damned haze. Kain had given in to the ritual magic, but his mind-talent still powered it like a chained slave pushing a milling wheel. Kain was going to fuck us to death, which could be very soon if something found us. Or, it could be a prolonged death of thirst and exhaustion.

And I was tempted to let it happen. To give in, as he had.

I heard a familiar, female voice laughing in delight inside my head, praising the unexpected boon to the Spider Queen's power.

This is the true version of how I almost killed you! Jilrina said.

Desperate, I tried to toss her image out of my head. I grasped for the feeling, the memory of Elder D'Shea holding my arm, guiding me forward, sponsoring me where I'd never go otherwise.

The reason I was here.

Look at you, Jilrina shrieked in laughter. *Crawling with a Dwarf stuck on your back plugging up your netherhole!*

"*Rragh,*" I growled, vaguely aware that Kain's cock was rising up again. I grasped both for a stone to grip and any thought higher than my waist.

D'Shea said, to the Red Sister Prime herself, that I could bend.

I didn't have to break.

No demons but her now, and she could help make sure I was never on an altar again.

I had to make it back first.

I won't die like this! I will stop this!

I had my chance before Kain recovered his breath after the fifth time I climaxed, my teeth clenched as I struggled to retain any scrap of my own willpower while my slit whimpered for more of what my netherhole was getting. I pushed up and rolled us, finally pushing his cock out of my gaping back hole and twisting to face him.

Straddle ... straddle him!

My free hand sought the first thing behind his head that I could reach. I found it.

~Fuck me!~

Staring at his blank eyes, I said nothing, thought nothing, until the moment before I stabbed the sharp edge of broken stone into his unprotected temple.

The mindlink shattered like crystal. Cold awareness rushed in through the heat. The pain became a real pain, something to avoid not yearn for.

I sobbed, pulled myself free from his muscular arms as they went slack. I did not check to see if the Tragar was already dead before scrambling to retrieve my House's blade from the ground. I returned swiftly to slit his throat.

As you should have done at the start! So what if the cloak got bloody?!

Part of me answered back. *Bloody clothing attracts predators.*

That had been my justification. Now semen leaked down my legs instead, enough of it to reach my feet in an unbroken trail.

Even this will probably attract something which eats Dwarves.

I gripped my stained blade, my arms and back stiff. Slowly, I realized the clarity of thought and the calmness now was like nothing I'd ever felt. My body seemed quenched of the thirsts put upon it by Braqth's ritual, and I could *think* again. It appeared at first my senses were sharper than they had ever been, though that may be relative to the blindness a moment before.

Perfectly still, I listened, scented the heavy air, looked both ways down the dark tunnel. Was anyone watching us? Was any race, any creature coming down the road?

Not yet. I must leave. Now.

I did not act on my first impulse, which was to find something to wipe the gooey stains from between my legs. I left it smeared on my skin as I first scattered the contents of Kain's pack about and pulled on the grey dwarf's pants. I spent a decent bit of time piling dirt and rocks on top of the body to ruin physical evidence.

No one will be able to reconstruct what happened here.

In addition to the waterskin, food, cloak, belt, and my own blade, I also picked up the raw gems and the toolkit containing the most pieces and took those with me as well. I intended to dump them later, far from here. I only wanted to further obscure the reason for the attack on the Dwarf should one of the sentient races find the body before a hungry scavenger did.

My head was numb and my eyes unblinking as I finished up and moved some distance away from the body. There I stood still, listening for a different tune now.

For the first time since I woke alone beside that pool, I could at last "hear" the deep pulses of my City, the call of home that only Davrin could sense. For the first time, I knew which was the right direction.

I took a swig of the ale water to numb some of the soreness and left the semen on my thighs until I could find another water source. I wouldn't spend too much time searching for that, though, because I wanted to make as much progress toward home as I could before I found out whether this mental clarity was a temporary reprieve or not. Both mind and body felt too numb to know for sure.

I ran without another sound from the site of my first kill.

CHAPTER 10

I TOOK MY FIRST OPPORTUNITY TO WASH. BY THEN, MY FEET ACHED FROM sprinting along the naked stone. Rock worn smooth in many places helped me avoid unnecessary cuts and scrapes, but the fact was I had not trained my feet to be this tough. An oversight I'd have to correct if I survived.

The small canal I found next was enticing; it smelled cooling, appeared cleansing. I wanted little else at the moment than to jump in. My skin had an unpleasant smell; my sweat and blood mixed with Kain's aging essence on my legs and in my crevices. This free-flowing river, however, still took an observation to make sure washing was safe. Only a fool recklessly leaped into a moving body of water in the Deepearth without sensing its depths first.

Be quick.

I believed I had found a reasonably safe place but my long dagger within reach. If any tentacle tried to loop my ankle as I stood submerged up to my thighs, it would be instantly severed. I began to wash both my body and the Dwarf-scented cloak, and I had the chance to check my injuries more closely.

A few muscles had been pulled or strained, and I'd jammed one finger on my off hand. A variety of bruises, scrapes, and cuts proved that I'd been in a close-contact fight, but the bite on my shoulder was the deepest mark. For that, I was both fortunate, and unfortunate.

No single injury I'd sustained crippled or posed a serious threat, but the bite mark was identifiable as a sentient with flat teeth. There weren't too many of those type down here. I'd done what I could to cover up the scene I'd left behind, or at least disrupt its reconstruction. My own body, on the other hand, would be a perfect map, whether or not I washed away the evidence between my legs. My kind watched for these injuries; we speculated and gossiped and probed. We couldn't help it. If I made it back, the Red Sisters would know.

I could handle being watched rutting with a Sathoet; I could engage other Davrin, male or female. I had proven it and came out stronger for it, I thought, but I would be fighting an uphill battle if others knew about the Tragar. I hated that this necessitated another secret of my own, but what could I do? I imagined so many derisive thoughts of my own, meeting another Davrin who was known to have been forcefully fucked, multiple times, by a Dwarf.

It occurred to me for the first time to wonder how I might fare on my own if I chose not to return home. No one said I had to go back. For all they might know, I was killed by something, my remains lost or eaten, a lesser Daughter to be struck off the list of potential troublemakers or usurpers.

I climbed, clean as I could be, out of the water and set upon a rise to watch the movement of the water. I wrapped Kain's wrung-out cloak around me, clutched my naked blade in my hand. The river glittered subtly with iridescent life, flickered from the shadows passing over its sources. I sat for a long time, feeling my sore muscles stiffening up but slipping into light Reverie. I needed the rest anyway.

It wasn't in my nature to hide shamed forever, I didn't think. Whether it was my cowardice or my methods for gaining a goal, sometimes I couldn't distinguish them at the time some harm happened. I had always chosen to live and run away, to resist or fight another cycle. I'd learned that at my House, with my sisters. If I ran away now, not to fight at all, how did that suit me?

It doesn't. Should a chance encounter with a poaching Dwarf dictate whether I become a Red Sister? Whether or not I even live with my head up?

It was clear such a thing right now would be cowardice. Not only this but the more I thought about it, the more I realized I had learned.

How many Davrin know firsthand that a Tragar connects mind-to-mind, and can be affected so strongly by our divine magic?

It couldn't be many, and most of them would be of high status: The Sisters or the Priestesses, certainly the Valsharess. I was one of a few who may have witnessed both kinds of psionic strikes, that of flying stone and stabbing ether. I was afraid to remember too much now, but also felt I'd known briefly, intimately, so much about him, about those he'd known, and I'd still been the one to live at the end of it.

I learned far less about my invisible wizard in that time.

I had benefited, I decided. The craving was under control for the moment, and the Tragar couldn't tell the tale. The additional knowledge I'd gained had value, regardless of how I got it. I had thoughts how to use it as a shield, a deflector, should it become a concern in the future.

Wouldn't that be something a Red Sister would do?

Different methods for gaining information, learning weaknesses, exploiting them, or setting a trap. Wouldn't a Red Sister go farther than any Davrin at Court to get it? It hadn't been intentional on my part, but opportunism was often the jewel and cream in our society.

It happened, so make the most of it.

I smiled in the dark without showing teeth. Carving out a solitary life in the Deepearth wilderness and trying to defend it by myself wasn't for me. I could handle my fellow sisters; I already knew the basics. I'd been doing it for most of my life. I looked forward to my return now, I realized, as I partook of my stolen supplies, chewing slowly as I thought further.

The outer farms. The Fringe. Those smaller dwellings might contain a way to heal my wounds.

Who said the Red Sisters had to see the bitemark at all? I could hoard the knowledge and the secret, keep them both until the right time.

Yes.

My feet and limbs were not ready for use when I stood up, but some time spent stretching made it bearable. I took it slow and cautious, wanting most of all to avoid any more confrontations and to conserve my energy. The howling drive to run as far as possible from the dead Tragar had run its course some time ago.

For most of the journey, I didn't so much recognize landmarks or rock formations but could sense when the rhythm of the Deepearth's thrum seemed off. I changed paths and entered other tunnels several times, trying to keep on track with the magical pulse of my birthplace. I didn't avoid all dead ends, unfortunately, but it was good practice in maintaining a reign on my impatience. Scowling at uncaring rock would hardly cause it to part for me.

Act. Don't react.

In addition to the mysterious Elder D'Shea, my thoughts also wandered to the youngest Red Sister at my first two trials, Gaelan. She had touched all three of my used openings with her tongue and mouth, cleaning Davrin semen out of me before kissing me. She had not only been skilled but had seemed to genuinely enjoy it — unlike Qivni, who had reacted with such distaste when ordered to do the same.

I wondered why Elder D'Shea had switched their places. I understood that it forced me to confess and to face my own "soft spot," but that had been with the comparably meek and pliable Gaelan. Why start with Qivni, who openly resented the order? Had Elder D'Shea been punishing her for something, perhaps? Or intended to make it a lesson for Qivni before I drew her attention with my own flaw? That was what my gut said had been happening, but I would have to watch and learn to know for sure.

To learn this, I must enter the Sisterhood.

I could never run away from Sivaraus. How could I have considered it even for a moment because of a single Tragar? I belonged there, as sure as spiders belonged in their web. That was where we hunted for what we desired, and where we caught it.

Not outside of it.

My spirit lightened, and my memories of Gaelan became somewhat clearer. I felt a pleasant warming in my body and in my middle. It was surprising to become aroused at the memory of another female servicing *me* for once.

That never happened before, but so be it.

The arousal grew startlingly fast when my thoughts naturally drifted to the reason Gaelan had had something to clean in the first place: the leavings left in or on my body by the two male Davrin and the demonic offspring of a Priestess, and the tools by which they were born able to offer it. There was no changing that. I remained fully enamored of those fascinating members. The very reason for their existence was to please my hunger. My memories of my trials were already becoming fodder to relive in my mind how they had pierced and stretched me, stroked me so hard, their need not so different from my own.

I had to stop.

Trembling, I set my hand against the rock to steady myself as the wave built without my desire for it. My dismay showed on my face even in solitude.

Oh, no, not again.

The magic was still there; it wasn't quenched. It seemed I should bring myself to climax then without fighting it, conveniently forgetting that this had not worked where I first awoke back in the remote cave. It was even less effective here, as I was no longer alone.

Someone is coming.

I removed my sodden hand from its task and slipped down into a cracked gutter of stone which ran parallel to my current path, a tiny creek running at the very bottom of it, littered with the refuse of the traveling path. I crouched small and still beneath an overhang but above the trash and water, my blade drawn. I was biting my lip, fiercely denying the temptation to look and see whether any in the passing convoy were Davrin I might be able to fuck.

Too reckless. I was lucky to survive the last time.

The squeak and clank of rolling, metal wheels stabbed at my sensitive ears; I even felt the vibrations. One lumbering cart, the padding of many feet, likely lizard mounts. I imagined the Deepearth Pyte were responsible for the construction, even if none were present. I was almost sure that trading on the outskirts of Sivaraus was their purpose for treading this path, and I had no intention of obstructing them. It was a necessary function within the city; it was not in my plans to disrupt that.

Just pass. Leave. Let me be.

Despite my tremors and increasingly lurid thoughts, I remained as I was, and none of those above me got the sudden inclination to investigate the gutter. The sound vanished far ahead of me, and I bit back a whine of need. I climbed back out onto the path, jumpy lest I either catch up to the group ahead or another should come behind me. I had to get off this path!

Farther ahead, I recognized the thrum calling me and knew I would see one of the official gates into the deep, vast cavern which contained my home. It would gradually widen until the ceiling disappeared and broader areas of underground farming would reveal themselves long before the lights of the city did. Sentries were set at that post, waiting, guarding a metal, and magically imbued, blockage.

I would not get past them unquestioned as I was. It would be a bad idea to risk it; I couldn't trust my own actions or words around other Davrin; I certainly couldn't explain where I had come from or why I was naked wearing a Dwarf cloak and satchel. Soon, there would be a patrol to keep the approach clear.

I looked for side tunnels or crawl spaces. I found a few; two were dens I wouldn't enter, another only led to a pit and a dead end, and a fourth turned into a crevasse far too tight to continue. I began to think there was no way into the Great Cavern except through the sentries and our own gate. Then, as the lust receded for the moment and I stared at the pool I'd found in a fifth passageway, I startled a small, white amphibian, which jumped into it and swam down to the bottom.

Not very deep. I could still see its blurry outline.

There was current as well; it seemed to beckon me. The frog's shadow disappeared underneath the rock, and my sensitive eyes could detect movement caused not only by the animal's exit but its entrance into a more extensive body of water.

Or am I hallucinating from want? Just swim through? Follow the frog?

Was it big enough for a Davrin and short enough not to run out of air? Was it small enough to keep larger predators from making their den there, yet wouldn't grow so little it would trap me? Was it already blocked intentionally by our patrol having found it ages ago?

Hard to tell based on one little creature.

This was simply a risk I had to try. I removed the cloak which would only snag and weigh me down underwater. The remaining Tragar food probably wouldn't survive either, but it tasted like offal mixed with grease and ash anyway. The naked blade would come with me. And the water-skin and belt? I wanted something to refill, and I also wanted something to keep my hands free. But now I was entering the territory of Davrin. Did I really want any Tragar possession on me? It would lead to questions and suspicion.

The cloak, belt, skin pouch, and food were smashed into as tiny of a crack as I could force them, using a stone to mash and wedge them in; removing them — if they were ever found by something walking on two legs — would be a chore.

I settled down into the pool, tepid water creeping up to my middle. Dipping under the surface of the water, the hand not holding my blade found the rock opening I sought. I felt around. I would fit, but it would be close. Backing out if the way closed to tight for me to get through would be the only option. I thought this was one of the phobias I knew about in another female at Court: to get stuck in a water-filled underground tunnel and drown there, one's lifeless body floating, swelling with water, and rotting. A real possibility here, but not a fear of mine.

Not yet, anyway.

I waited for a while, became too aroused, and began stroking myself underwater to climax once more. As I delayed, I wondered if the frog had to breathe. Did it have to come up for air? Would I see it come back out if that was the case? Which was it? I didn't know. There was no certainty for me that I could pass through regardless if the white frog returned.

I clenched my teeth, kept quiet as the water swirled around my frantic fingers, as I felt release sweep through me. It did not help any more than

I'd expected, but it felt good, and the frog had not reappeared by the time I caught my breath. I drew ever deeper breaths, filling my blood and my lungs with air before submerging.

Dark Sight underwater does not work quite as well; depth perception was the first thing torn asunder by the ever-shifting liquid which also disrupted the energy of the rock shaping and containing it. There were no real shapes to see unless it was big, solid, and close. I kept my eyes open for the instance of that sudden, detectable movement but used my hands to feel and pull my way through the tunnel. Kicking my feet helped a little but not as much when my heel would knock against the wall, or my knee would get scraped.

I thought that had been the most annoying part about it until I had to squeeze through a section so reduced that it scraped my nipples, and the point of my House dagger was caught between rocks. For a paralyzing moment, I thought I would have to choose between leaving it here or drowning as I tried to get it loose. Fortunately, it came loose a moment after my panicked thought. The rush of blood through me livened the caress of the chilly water on my netherlips, and I became distracted.

So much fun.

I squeezed through that choke point, and my lungs were burning by now, but I kept my focus forward, starting to pump my legs despite the tight quarters. It was too late to back up, and my sensitive eyes detected light and energy ahead. I could see it even as my vision darkened from lack of air.

Faster. Faster!

I was blind as my head broke the water at last, and I sucked in the most painful breath I could remember. I made it! Immediately I looked around me. I had not been subtle to come out from beneath the pool like that, and I should expect something or someone to investigate soon. Around me, I saw deliberate construction forming the boundaries for this pool. It was a reservoir, a smaller version of the type I'd seen in the agriculture districts.

No one stood on its banks.

I was here; I was inside the Great Cavern and on the far outskirts of the city, not yet seen by sentries or anyone else — except for the white frog, which sat like a skipping stone on the bank and again leaped into the water when I spied it. I smiled, watching it swim clear of me before I crawled on my belly up the bank to see what was over it.

As I expected, it was a relatively flat parcel of space, cultivating various mushrooms, softly glowing lichens, and the agriculture that supported Davrin, our animals, and slaves. My eyes skimmed over the few bodies who worked the field. They were not Davrin Elves but the diminutive and ugly Pyte as well as the Ketro, a weaker, greyer version of the Tragar. Then my heart seized when I saw one of my own.

I felt no fear of discovery now. The shock to my system was like a throaty, primal demand; a call for indulgence, not avoidance.

He's so beautiful.

Oh, Braqth, I wanted him so badly. He wasn't a soldier or warrior, and I didn't care to whom he belonged. My cunt began to ache right then and there as I lay on the muddy bank of the pool, demanding his seed. Far better than the Tragar, far cleaner and more natural, this was what my body needed.

This was what would break the spell on me!

The lone Davrin was dressed in simple, rough silk made of two pieces, one which covered his torso, cinched with a belt, and the other a wrap tied at his hips which fell to his knees. His calves were lovely, and his feet were elegantly wrapped in light-colored leather. He wore a few choice pieces of jewelry, nothing much, but I could see metal at one ear and a circlet around his throat, a band around one bare arm — even at this distance I could see them shine. As I traced my eyes back up, I noted beautiful hands and smooth, lean arms, long, white hair drawn back and plaited, and an attractive, refined face.

Goddess.

I would have him. More than once. I would welcome the feeling of his cum filling my body, then glazing my sex before running down my legs, cleansing me of my last coupling. The tremors grew out of my control.

Goddess. Ohh, Goddess!

The fingers of my free hand dug into the mud, jamming the grime beneath my fingernails. I clung to the ground, barely able to wait until he'd gone inside a small, outside structure apart from the main house. A grey haze flowed in front of my eyes as I lay poised and aching, the raunchy images of all I would do to that delicious body dominating my thoughts.

Get him!

I moved in a full sprint as soon as the door to the tiny barn was closed for three full flicks. At the very least, I could capture him coming out and force him back inside. Or, better yet, I could surprise him. A few four-legged and furry chattel looked at me disinterestedly as I passed, and I had my hand on the door latch almost before I knew it. I let myself inside and closed the door behind me, panting hard, my teeth showing in a very wide smile.

He heard me, of course, even as I'd not been an utter clove-footed oaf, and he spun around. His eyes widened in stark alarm. He didn't speak or ask me anything but dove for a farm tool he could use in his defense. He drew down a sickle from the wall.

The farmer wants to protect his virtue. How cute.

My long dagger blocked his weapon when he clumsily turned it on me, and with a flick of my wrist, it flipped out of his hand, landing out of reach. I snatched the wrist of that offending hand and gave it a twist, making him cry out. With another twist, he fell to his knees in front of me, grimacing.

"Do not do this," he groaned.

"Quiet," I growled. "Better if you don't fight."

"Pray, listen, Mistress, you do not underst — "

"Also better if you don't speak."

A pity, that. He had a lovely voice.

"Please!" he said, his expression frightened about something that might or might not have been me. Maybe I cared a little bit about that distinction, but my cunt certainly didn't.

"Shut up." I flicked his ear to see him flinch. "Take down your hair."

When he hesitated, I reached to pull the band from the tail of his braid, running my fingers through silky hair as the plaiting began to unravel. He kept his free hand clamped to his thigh as I held his wrist, and with a growl, I grabbed hold of his hair by the roots as well and gave it a jerk.

"Finish it. Take down your hair."

He winced and slowly reached up with one hand to comb out the rest of the braiding until his hair flowed freely down his back. I was staring at his face while he did this. I'd never seen a Davrin with his face before. Nowhere, not my House, the Court, the Palace.

Who's been hiding you away from all of us?

"Beautiful."

I pulled his head back to tilt up his chin so I could take his mouth. He didn't fight me, but he did not respond in kind. Still, he tasted clean and fragrant, felt smooth, smelled healthy. He kept his lips closed, but I saw his nostril twitch when I finished. It seemed my own scent was offensive.

Too bad. I will have you.

I looked around the shack and didn't see much room or comfort among the tools and stables. I did see braided leather thongs that would be useful. I released his wrist to reach for two of the coils, looping them on one shoulder as I kept a tight hold on his hair. He cradled one hand in the other and waited.

"Is there anyone back at the house?" I asked.

He stayed silent, glancing at me with a glimmer of defiance but didn't hold it. I kneeled to caress what interested me most through his silk, gathering his genitals and squeezing gently but not without an unspoken threat. Those gorgeous eyes widened, and he looked nervous and fearful.

I smiled. "Is that a 'no?' "

"No," he said ambiguously.

I couldn't tell if an answer so unhelpful had been on purpose or not. It annoyed me that I couldn't say.

Fuck it.

My grip on his hair renewed, I dragged him up and out of the shed, toward the principal dwelling farther away from the reservoir where I had entered the Cavern. He tried once to break free, and I rewarded his insolence with a fast punch to his gut, which left him on the ground and unable to breathe. Immediately I was shocked I'd gone to striking him so quickly. He couldn't fight a female; it shouldn't be necessary.

I knew my control was fast crumbling.

If he doesn't cooperate, he's going to get hurt.

I asked him again, "Is there anyone at the house?"

"N-no," he answered again, but this time it sounded like an answer.

He could be an excellent liar, of course, but I seized that needed focus to peer around. This was also one of the smallest and quietest outposts of agriculture I'd ever witnessed. Even if the lack of lanterns or light-stones hadn't precluded seeing to the border of the farm, I was willing to bet it was some distance to the next neighbor. The three slaves present were still out in the fields, still working and not intervening in Davrin business if they even saw us.

In my state, I went on nothing more than gut instinct on this was the only Davrin here. One Davrin, even a male one, would be able to control the few other living beings here. It was not a big place. That he was alone in this outpost likely meant he'd been assigned or banished here.

We continued to the house once he could breathe again. He was just docile enough to keep my lust in check as we approached, following the elaborate, cobbled walkway which protected his pretty feet from the dirt. I knew he hadn't wholly given in yet; he was still looking for a way to escape. I was glad. Something in me would have been disappointed if he had given up so easily.

I needed to mate, and I needed *him*. I'd ride him into exhaustion one way or another, but like at Court, I wanted to enjoy the challenge of earning his surrender. Having spirit was preferred against the alternative. I always thought those who favored the cold fish were only uncertain of themselves, an ego that couldn't survive true rejection.

"Disarm any and all Wards," I instructed. "Open the door."

My capture obeyed, needing both hands to do it. I was satisfied there would be no alarms to anyone crossing that threshold, especially when he tried to reason with me.

"I can tell you are no commoner, Mistress. Please *think* about what you are doing. There will be consequences —"

Kain's face stabbed at my vision, and I flinched. Then all the sound and sensation of being held on that Altar by the Red Sisters, Lelinahdara's proud, elegant face above me.

Keep males out of her reach. She will be craving them.

She's ours now, Elder. Take the recruit outside of the city.

The high laugh which escaped my mouth sounded off-kilter even to me, and it unnerved us both as I dragged him inside. I leaned closer to inhale the wonderful scent at his neck to banish those memories for now. He trembled but didn't outright shrink away.

Consequences.

"There always are," I said, closing the door.

Chapter 11

The dwelling was lit by a few, very soft candles yet even that made my eyes ache as I adjusted to proper color again. The place was furnished with the basics I'd expect of a tiny plantation, but a few quality furniture pieces accented with objects of art caught my eye, as did the handful of paintings and mirrors lining the hall which led from the kitchen, where we'd just entered. These were very nice gifts from someone. A Matron, no doubt.

He must serve her well.

From where we stood, I could see us in one of the farther mirrors at an angle. I looked exactly as I was: a muddy, disheveled, nude warrior half-mad with lust. My damp hair was stringy and lay flat to my head, dull with dirt, contrasting with my hand gripping the glossy, white hair of a beautiful, reluctant companion. It pricked at my pride but might not have made a difference if my eyes hadn't landed on the Dwarf's bite mark on my shoulder.

The Davrin must have noticed, but he hadn't made it obvious. It was then I remembered, I sought healing draughts to cover it up. I could hold off, couldn't I? I could be clear of the taint from my body, especially that bite, and even be clean and beautiful as well when I took this irresistible farmer. Indeed, aching though I was, my pride won, keeping me from becoming an animal again. As I'd been with Kain.

I can clean up for this one.

Setting my House dagger on one counter, I brought my captive to the polished granite table and tried to bend him over it. He panicked and fought me fiercely even though I'd set down my weapon.

"No. No!" he said as he struggled. "Please, Mistress, do not!"

"Stay!" I barked.

Getting him under control again took a firm hold before kicking one ankle hard enough to make it slip on the polish stone floor. I pinned him to the table, but he still strained and thrashed. It was only when I pressed a nerve point in his shoulder that he stopped moving, unable to scream for the pain as I kept the pressure on.

"Will you behave?" I asked.

He managed a faltering nod, eyes wide and focused on the granite underneath.

"*Will* you?"

Again a nod, this one urgent. When I eased the pressure, he sucked in a breath and moaned loudly, blinking out the tears which had formed in his eyes.

"Answer me this," I said, trembling as he did, our bodies touching as I smeared mud on his light silk. "Do you have any healing potion in this house?"

He nodded and mumbled. "Within the cabinet. F-far left, top shelf. In a drop bottle."

I used one of the leather thongs to lash his wrists together in front of him, then tethered him tightly to the sturdy legs of the table; his arms were stretched tight and straight. I kept the spare for later. He could kick, but he wouldn't hit anything if I stayed to the side.

Inside the cabinet was a bottle shaped like a teardrop, exactly as he said. I took it down and picked up my blade again, standing next to the table with his arms in front of me. He twisted his head to look at me, and I smiled grimly at him.

"Pray you aren't lying."

I drew a small cut across his forearm, and he blurted a cry more of disbelief and dread than pain. He stared at the blood like he couldn't believe it was there. I took the stopper between my teeth and tugged it out, holding the open mouth of the bottle above his open wound. I watched him. He dared to scowl but stayed very still, protesting nothing, not a speck of fear or uncertainty in his face should I dribble the contents on that blood.

It told me what I wanted to know.

I let some of the potion meet his wound, and he flinched. We watched the cut close, healing entirely and leaving only a small streak of blood behind. No scarring.

"Potent," I commented, taking the stopper from my mouth. "What's the dose for fatigue and surface injuries?"

"Two spoons," he said grudgingly.

I swallowed a small mouthful straight from the bottle, made a face as it was bitter, but soon felt the glow of magic inside. Warmth diffused through me in soothing tendrils, easing all my sore muscles and mending my flesh. My skin itched as it erased the evidence of my altercations, my sex remained swollen only in arousal and not hard, repeated use.

Excellent.

I returned the bottle to the cupboard and set both my blade and the spare thong on a counter. A small tub of water waited for some sort of wash at the deep sink, and I found a kitchen rag to wipe the mud from my body as well. I felt *much* better, and I was more than ready for him. Moisture collected in my slit already, dampening my inner thighs as I closed them, despite having just wiped them down.

"What injured you, Mistress?" he asked.

If he'd been trying to distract me or to make a connection to converse, it was the wrong tactic to work. I wanted to *forget* that while I was here!

My mouth was a hard line as I picked up a round root from a basket in the corner. I tested its firmness and size and nodded. My captive started breathing quickly again as I approached him.

"No, please listen to me, Mistre —" he began just before I stuffed the root into his mouth, forcing his jaws wider and filling his mouth so he couldn't talk.

"I said it would be better if you don't speak."

I tore a strip of silk from his waist wrap to tie around the root and behind his head, holding it in place so he couldn't spit it out. He made muffled, desperate sounds, shaking his head as I stood behind him and lifted his stained, silk wrap to bunch it at his hips.

Goddess. Perfect.

I squatted and stroked his legs and bare buttocks, admiring their shape. I reached between his thighs to test his member, not surprised to find it flaccid. Not a problem; this was why males had nut glands. In my invisible wizard, touching it had set him off at my command. In a reluctant partner, it could at least prepare him for use.

The lovely farmer only hurt himself trying to deny my fingers entrance, however, and he did manage a glancing kick at my knee. I growled at the pain, shot to my feet and took hold of his hair again to jerk his head toward me. His back bowed tight as an archer's pull. I hissed in his ear.

"Alright, you've fought against me. Now *think*, lovely bua. How much of this do you want visible to the next female to visit you?"

His breathing was still too fast, and he kept his eyes closed, threaded his fingers together as if he was praying. When I caressed his ass again, he didn't protest; when I eventually dipped once more into his crevasse, he tensed but didn't thrash or kick. I took it that he didn't want to be marked up.

I can oblige that, lovely. I only need to fuck you, not hurt you.

He was dry, of course, but so was my mouth, and sucking my finger wasn't enough. I found a handy bottle of cooking oil and used that, now slipping one finger through his tight ring with ease. He writhed and squirmed as I worked his gland, his hair spread over his back and shifting with him as he hid his eyes against his arm. I combed his hair and caressed his back, spoke soft and encouraging words as I inserted a second finger into his netherhole, stretching him.

"That's it. Relax." My voice quavered in need. "I don't want to hurt you, bua."

I twisted my wrist a little, and he moaned through the root in his mouth. His breath was ragged though he still shook his head in denial as

I withdrew and entered him again and again with my fingers. His hips rolled like a slut, the moans got louder, more despairing, when I reached around with my other hand and stroked him. He was hard, and slick droplets leaked out of the tip. I spread them around the head.

Goddess, I can't wait any longer!

I withdrew both hands and forcibly flipped him over from his stomach onto his back, which twisted his arms above his head. Then I lifted him so that his backside rested fully on the table. I climbed up as well, blocking his attempt to curl up and get his knees in the way, shoving them down. I pull his wrap up, all the way, exposing a generous gift, and finally straddled him.

I shuddered and gasped, hardly in control of myself as his cock poked at me, teasing me, and I reached between us to aim him at my pulsing slit. I squeezed him right into my hungry channel without pause. A wordless, hoarse sound escaped us both. His scarlet eyes were wide open, staring up at me as I took him.

Bright lights flashed behind my eyes merely sitting on him. The pleasure gripped me like a constrictor, then I regained a breath and screamed at the ceiling.

Oh, Goddess!!

My body was wracked by spasms as I grunted in pleasure over the farmer, humping him though even half-strokes seemed too intense to bear! I experienced the strongest peak I could remember with barely any movement, and my gorgeous farmer kicked and turned his head to one side, squeezing his eyes tight and sucking air through his nose.

He feels this, too. I'm sure of it!

Braqth's Threshold, fulfilled.

Yes! I need one like you!

I stroked him with my cunt in an eager grip, managed a few at full length, and climaxed again. I was very loud in my throes, yipping, and weeping in holy pleasure, gripping his ribs to keep hold of my prize. Magic and strength rushed through me, through us, in a circle as it had with Kain, but this felt so pure! I babbled nonsense as I fucked him to a third peak not a moment later. My mouth didn't work. I couldn't speak, but I heard myself.

~*Give me your seed! Give me your child!*~

I couldn't understand how my bua had resisted so far. My womb was ready and waiting, craving his essence, so thirsty to use it and begin the transition from Daughter to Mother at last! I fucked him, felt his inherent magic seep beneath my skin and bond with what the Priestess had done to me. He resisted me, struggled not to erupt as he bit deeply into the raw vegetable in his mouth. It was torture for him to hold back. It was torture for *me*.

~*Why do you deny me, beautiful? Come! Give me an heir! I'm ready!*~

I didn't recognize the sound behind me at first, but I knew the instant after, when something looped around my neck, that it had been the door opening.

Oh, Braqth damn it.

A strap tightened, and the hard pull backward choked me, forced me to straighten up. Pain in my throat briefly overtook the pleasure between my legs. A flick later I couldn't breathe, even as I clutched hard and wouldn't let my chosen sire go.

Mine!

Another loop of rope came around to add to the strap, and a strong arm kept the line taut as she pulled herself in close enough to grab me in a melee lock. Blood-red boots planted themselves on either side of us on the table as she climbed up. With a giant heave, my body was yanked up and off my conquest and then tossed onto the floor.

The violence of my reaction would have shocked me if I'd been in my right mind. I screamed unintelligibly and in pure rage as I vaulted up again off the ground, aiming for the Red Sister standing between me and my chance to break the ritual's spell. She had already jumped off the table and still held the other end of the rope which was around my neck.

Though I struck out in ways so practiced I didn't have to think, she blocked most of them and the fact that my House dagger was still on the counter may have saved my life.

The first opening I gave her, she swept my feet out from under me, and I fell again. My vision turned pure red; I was blind, my mind blank as I rolled, got my feet, and charged back. My opponent was ready for me; she turned and connected a well-placed kick to my head, and I went down, stunned.

In that time, she rolled me, tied my hands behind my back and my ankles to my hands with the other leather thong I'd set aside, taking back the lasso she'd used at the start. My throat was sore, my neck burned; I coughed and drooled a little. I made a sound halfway between a moan and a growl, blinking blearily toward the table and its movement.

Two sets of feet and legs, and she had removed the root from my farmer's mouth because I heard him moaning in relief and gasping for air.

"Did you release inside her? Even one time?"

"N-no, Red Sister," he panted, his relief at being able to claim this palatable. "No, what you see on me is … my only release."

"Looks like it. Impressive."

She sounded amused at the quantity that implied. Meanwhile, my womb, no, my entire gut, felt like a bed of smoldering coals threatening to flare up again. I pulled at the restraints. They were too tight.

"Let me go!" I demanded in a deadly voice. "Get away from him!"

The farmer still lashed to the table flinched, but the Red Sister didn't even acknowledge me. Instead, she cut him free, and he rolled off the table, pulling down his wrap to cover himself. Falling to his knees, trembling, he kept his eyes on the floor. I could see the damp stains all over his clothes. He hadn't lasted two instants after I'd been pulled off before spurting his load.

What a waste, I thought viciously.

"You will tell your Matron nothing of this," the Red Sister commanded him. "You will clean yourself up and never speak of it."

"Nothing happened, Red Sister," he answered. "This cycle was as uneventful as the last."

He sounded like he believed it.

"I need your clothes," she said. "I will burn them while you watch."

He didn't hesitate to strip nude in front of her, and I groaned in abject misery at what had been taken away. But for rope burns I saw around his wrists, he was flawless.

The Red Sister did as she promised, lighting a cooking fire and disposing of his ruined clothing. I wasted time on useless threats as my lust seized me again, and the Red Sister gagged me. Meanwhile, my stolen prize grabbed a blanket from another room to cover his body.

The lone male watched in silence as the red warrior collected my dagger from the counter, attached it to her belt, and then collected me from the floor in her arms. I thrashed and struggled indignantly, gnashing my teeth and snarling in frustration, her fine, leather armor a clashing sensation with the tools against my bare skin as she carried me outside.

A mount waited in full tack and bridle, the Davrin-bred reptilians kept only by the elite and wealthy. The Queen's Sister threw me belly-down just in front of the saddle before mounting up behind me. Her arm pressed me down firmly when I arched my back, preventing me from squirming my way off.

Next, it sank into my addled mind that my ankles were still tied to my wrists, and toppling off for spite might break my neck, or if it didn't, how would I run?

Covered in sweat, I quivered for some time, but the distance from the Davrin male helped to clear my head a little. The lizard carried us away, and I was given quiet enough to replay what had just happened. Everything from the moment I broke the surface of the water in the reservoir. What was that total and terrifying loss of control? How could I rape him like that? Was I mad?

I didn't even know his name.

Soon I focused on the ridge of the mount's back pressing into me; it was difficult to breathe. I tried to look over my shoulder, but the Sister would just turn my head back toward the passing ground. I could see her long, red boots, though, and wondered at my urge to rub my cheek against them.

Don't be ridiculous.

"You remember you're fertile now, don't you?" she asked.

I resisted spewing expletives at her. How could I forget? These Abyssal surges of mating heats had been everything about my life for cycles!

"You can't catch right now," she added.

"And if I do?" I asked caustically.

"Well, for one, you would force a decision not in your hands which you might not like. Do you want details?"

I scowled at the ground but was silent. This was new territory. I'd never had to be concerned before. Although I blamed my infertility from a botched ritual for my banishment to Court, I didn't want to blame my fertility from a successful one for ending my life before ever having my chance at the Sisterhood.

The realization came back around for me in full. *I'm fertile.*

"For another," the Sister continued, "the particular stud you attacked was a poor choice."

I sneered. "He was the *best* choice."

"I agree, one of the best. In fact, had you been of clear mind, would you have wondered why there was a circlet around his neck? One with a crest on it?"

I was quiet. I had noticed the circlet as part of his jewelry. I hadn't seen any crest, even being right on top of him.

"Which House?" I asked warily. My cunt was buzzing but talking with another helped me think of something besides that.

"Not just the House, Sirana. The crest. D'Verin's standard, but with the round belly silhouette."

My stomach went cold.

"*Ffuuuck*," I hissed with the abrupt pounding of my heart.

I can tell you are no commoner, Mistress. Please think about what you are doing.

He'd been trying to tell me. How could I have expected that?

You didn't have to, because he wore the goddess-damned circlet, you cunthead.

I blurted, "What the fuck was a Royal Consort doing way out there all alone?!"

The Red Sister chuckled. "The land plot is D'Verin, and I hear Bred Consorts sometimes ask for odd rewards in their service to a Matron. It seemed he asked for some solitude, and it was granted."

"What?!" I barked. "That's the stupidest thing to do with a Consort!"

"Shh, Sirana. The next stupidest, maybe," she teased me. "There *were* protections in place. I know you must have bullied him into releasing the Wards in the house, but the ones around the plot's borders weren't tripped. I think Elder D'Shea will find that very interesting."

When I said nothing, the Red Sister continued to poke at me. "You could have carried a sought-after line. Elder D'Shea would probably lose you to the fangs of the Driders after you gave birth. No telling whether D'Verin would get the child or whether she would be raised by the Priestesses."

Never. I ground my teeth, too furious with the very idea to think about being fed to monsters. "Are you saying you saved my life?"

"We both know I did, Sirana."

"And how did you just happen to be in the right spot to interrupt?" I asked with very little grace.

She laughed softly. "I was far too late, as far as I'm concerned. We've been watching you. My Elder will have to check you over, just to be sure you didn't catch just now."

My stomach heated up a little in anxiety, but not from a thought of pregnancy. "Watching me. For how long?"

She was silent a moment, but answered, "You'll figure that out. You're smart."

Damn it.

"Where are you taking me?"

"Somewhere more comfortable."

"Why?"

"No demons but us, Sirana."

I didn't like the sound of that. This had all been some test, I knew, but I didn't know how I'd fared. Fortunately, this Red Sister granted me one small mercy there.

"While you're in heat like this, you'd best stick to the Sisters. We can fuck you three ways from the Abyss until the effects of the ritual wear off."

*Meaning that it **will** wear off. Oh, Goddess, thank you!*

Such relief at that moment, before the rest of it sank in.

"Wait, what?" I turned my head to look at her again, and this time she let me see her face inside her red hood. My eyes widened. "Gaelan?"

The youngest Red Sister I'd seen thus far grinned at me and caressed my naked backside, then gave me a sharp slap which made me jerk on the saddle. It sparked and fanned my arousal in an instant, just that one smack, and I groaned. Her gloved hand caressed me some more and slipped between my thighs, stroking my tacky netherlips; I garbled an encouragement before she withdrew quickly and slapped my other cheek.

"Slit." My nipples tightened and brushed against the saddle as I gasped for breath. "Don't tease me."

"Why not?"

Her hand slid down my back and over my bottom, making my skin tingle and come alive. Her fingers returned to my netherlips, slipping right between them and into my soggy sex. I stiffened and found myself trying to hump against them, but she withdrew her hand again, leaving me empty, my hands able to grab at nothing.

"Oh, Braqth," I moaned in agony.

"Will you repay me in kind, Sirana? I think you owe me."

My teeth gritted. I wanted to say yes. "In kind, meaning?"

"Well." Her hand returned to my crotch. "You know what *my* mouth feels like here."

She flicked my clitoris, and I cried out.

"And you know what it feels like … here." She plunged two fingers into my slit, and I thrashed very much like the Consort had before she withdrew. "And, most especially, here."

She pressed a finger straight into my anus and held it there as I strained, unable to be still. That she wouldn't move it was torturous; I was very, very close to climaxing.

"I want to know how your mouth feels."

"Please, please," I begged.

Even if this had been the wizard and not Gaelan, I still would have begged. *No fooling myself.*

"Will you repay me in kind, Sirana?"

"Yes," I gasped. "Yes."

"If we have the means to satisfy your every craving, would you submit to anything we told you?"

"Yes!" I cried, angry for losing my climax, for falling back from the edge. "What d-do you want?"

"We want quite a lot."

Gaelan urged the lizard mount to climb at one point, and I tensed as I waited to roll off, but she held me tightly against her, one arm clasped about my waist as I was pressed into her warm belly and thighs. Discomfort started to overtake my arousal as Gaelan stopped playing with me; the position in which I was tied with my head hanging down for the last quarter mark took its toll, and I moaned softly in pain when jostled.

I became aware of us riding into a cave. It was just big enough for Gaelan to lean down, covering me crossways with her chin close to the body of the lizard. It was deep; I lost track of time before Gaelan could sit up straight again, but finally, she stopped the mount and got off, tethering the lazy-eyed animal to a post near the exit.

I heard her drawing a blade and tensed before realizing she had severed my bonds. She gave me plenty of time to unfold my legs and try to bring my arms forward. I would have fallen off if she hadn't caught me and set me to the ground.

I looked at her. She was familiar, I thought. Maybe from somewhere before the trials in the candle chamber, but I couldn't place it. Around Court, perhaps? The Red Sisters might not always wear their uniforms when they were watching us. She began rubbing the circulation back into my limbs, which hurt almost as much as just before they had gone numb.

"Shh, not too loud," she said as I made my discomfort known.

I made no reply, but I studied her face as pins and needles swept through my calves, to focus on something other than pain. Gaelan was fine boned compared to some, her large eyes tilted slightly upward, her cheeks high and her nose on the short side but broader at the nostril. Her lips were fuller than mine, her chin strong enough, and I saw a swollen spot where I'd managed to strike her jaw, though I barely remembered connecting. Her hair was tied up in a tight braid and coiled at her nape.

After she finished, I sighed, relaxing a moment, and Gaelan ran her hand up my thigh, cupping my mound and I flinched, gulping down a cry as my sex flared to life again. She chuckled and pointed farther back into the cavern.

"Go to the chaise."

I blinked and turned my head. She was correct, there was a chaise back there, plus a few other seats against the stone wall. The chamber also contained a small fountain built into the stone, I realized, smelling a bit of fresh water though hearing no burble or trickle.

The simple furniture looked to be set up as a place from which to watch whatever might be happening in the middle, which was a clear space but with a few convenient chains hanging down, bolted into the rock above. It was then that I recognized several familiar devices and contraptions pushed along the opposite side from the furniture.

"This is an interrogation room," I murmured.

"Still more comfortable than bare stone or farmers' mud, wouldn't you say? And private." She paused before repeating, "Go to the chaise."

She hadn't said how to get there, though, so I made an actual effort to stand and walk there as she removed her gloves. She took the opportunity to touch me as I first rolled stiffly to all fours, tugging on my fur a second before dipping a bare finger inside my sex and I gasped and lost track of what I was doing for a moment. I stayed on all fours, waiting for more.

With a firm pat to my rump leaving a wet fingerprint, she encouraged me to move forward. "Go on."

I had to crawl for the first little ways but regained unsteady feet. She didn't obstruct my efforts further, only paced me, standing behind where I could not see her without turning — though I didn't dare turn. When I reached the lounge, I stood there looking at it.

Gaelan came into my view at the head of the chaise, and she gestured. "On your hands and knees, facing me."

That would mean I should take to the foot of the chaise. I got down slowly on all fours with my knees not quite at the edge and positioned myself. The velvety material was cool and a bit dusty, but soft; infinitely preferable to the hard stone. My sex pulsed in anticipation, as if I could expect someone — or more than one — to step up and satisfy me from behind, as during the ritual orgy from a decade ago.

Not impossible.

A Red Sister, maybe this one, *could* have the tool I craved most, even being female. I'd seen enough executions by them, I knew they used false phalli in painful and terrifying ways. From the sound of her voice so far, Gaelan did not sound as though she intended to cause me pain. Not if I obeyed.

I watched the Red Sister disarm and undress. I should have been paying better attention to every detail, memorizing every piece she removed.

Cloak, satchel, gloves, bracers, a belt of pouches, weapons, small vials —

When she tugged off her leather boots, slow and sensual, to reveal long legs and red-stocking feet, I surprised myself. The reveal of her bare, wiggling toes was startlingly arousing. She stood again, unbuckling the red leather armor, peeling off pieces to reveal either more skin or dark, soft, form-fitting underclothes against chafing. Those were also removed.

I stared, my mind muddled. With the air on my empty sex alongside my insatiate appetite, I did not have the focus as I wished, and I kept waiting to see something like the black toys they strapped to themselves before someone was going to die. But even looking for a distinctly male trait, part of me was embarrassed to admit that this naked Red Sister, with *all* her female characteristics, was as alluring and attractive in her way as the bound Consort had been.

Gaelan took down her hair, too, removed it from the severe braid as I'd demanded of the pretty bua only marks earlier. It was much longer than it had looked. It flowed white and soft, matching the tuft between her legs. She was beautiful, standing with a poised grace that mimicked the very Spider Lady we worshiped: light on one's feet, defined muscles coiled, ready for action.

She smiled at my expression. "Shall I show you more?"

It took me a moment.

"All you can," I forced out, figuring she would anyway. I didn't know which to expect, if I might recognize pure female lust and techniques all too well, or if she really would, somehow, satisfy my "every" craving.

She leaned down to pluck up a small leather satchel from her pile of belongings. My eyes widened, tightly focused on that bag. What she pulled from it caused me to exhale. An erect, black phallus of right size. It flopped and waved with a realistic weight to it, so it wasn't made of glass or marble. It was the right color for Davrin flesh as well. I swallowed, an unfortunate thought and disgust showing on my face.

Gaelan laughed, sitting on the edge of the chaise facing me, her legs wide apart where I could see all of her. "No, Sirana. It's not a body part."

"Why does it look so real?"

"It's a magical device. Fine craftsmanship, no?"

I pursed my lips. I supposed it was, but it was unwieldy. "Want me to use it on myself?"

"No, I'm going to fuck you with it. And get off on it, too."

I almost snorted my disbelief in her face, even as my sex complained of asking questions when there was a penetrating toy so near. "Oh? Where's your harness?"

"Don't need one. Here, watch."

I watched with wide eyes as she parted her netherlips with one hand and fit one end of the phallus into her sex with a pleasured sigh. Then she stroked and molded the very realistic erection to conform to her body. She murmured a soft word, and a spell was fulfilled, magic plucking at the very edge of my senses.

A shimmer, like in an illusion, and the phallus connected to her and anchored itself in what appeared a solid hold. It didn't look to me as though she was suddenly male; there were no testicles, and I could still trace the ridge back to the part that was lodged inside her body, her cunt visibly wrapped around it and holding it close. She needed no strap or halter to keep it in place, just as she said. She lifted both hands in the air with flare and grinned, sporting a proud and satisfactory cock.

I was at once unbearably excited and scared out of my mind.

Was this what they were using ... during ... ?

I had never been near enough to an execution to see what had been holding the phallus in place while a Red Sister brutalized the condemned — male or female — nor had I wanted to be. I knew from Court talk that the female wearing a contraption like this was *usually* submissive to the leader, who often rode it to her peak. The cait with the false cock rarely received her own satisfaction; she was the "servant," like Kaltra had been to Jilrina.

But the Red Sisters upended that role, subverted it; one reason they unnerved Nobles especially.

As at an execution, I felt that strange dynamic here, close, and unavoidable. That "magical device" seemed to pleasure Gaelan just being inside her, and her posture clearly indicated that she was not the bottom one between us, even being the one to wear the cock. I recalled agreeing to submit to anything, too, as long as the Sisters could satisfy me.

What in the goddess-hating-fuck have I agreed to?

My body didn't care; my scalp prickled as my cunt anticipated yet more fucking. Like the two males dominating my body in the candle chamber, I imagined I would take that piece in whatever way pleased her most and not have much say about it. I felt the flip in the roles keenly; I felt the confusion and the urge to resist, to defend my "standing" and the usual sexual positions, but my body quivered and froze up. My slit flexed to what I saw before my eyes.

"Seeing as how your mouth is already open, Sirana," Gaelan snickered as she braced herself and slid toward me along the lounge, settling on her knees and placing her hand on the back of my head.

I didn't need the explicit command. Even up close her erection looked quite real, and I turned my head slightly before letting her slip the crafted cock between my lips. The texture was accurate, though the taste remained sterile as I swirled my tongue around it. I was shocked to hear Gaelan moan in response, to feel her toy shudder in my mouth like it was real. I paused but sucked on just the tip.

"Ohhh, yes, like that," she whispered, stroking my hair, letting me suckle her like a baby. She moaned again, moving her hips to rub the round, squishy head along my tongue.

She can't possibly feel it? But that also means that ...

It suggested that the other Red Sisters I'd seen probably felt this, too. Every bit of it.

It explained a lot.

NO DEMONS BUT US

I shuddered, tightening my lips and bobbing my head to suck her and get rid of those unpleasant mental images. Still, my eyes were open in my disbelief. I'd never heard of such a device as this. Phallic toys were known, even common, but always fell short of the real thing. The wearer could *never* feel the tip of the damned thing!

Who made this? I thought, running my tongue along the underside as if I might find the signature of the mage scratched in. It was smooth and textured like skin. It had real body heat from the wearer. I could almost imagine I sucked on that Bred Consort instead of Gaelan's "device."

She reached to caress both my breasts and I moaned in response. She humped her hips to fuck harder between my lips, nudging the back of my throat with her pole. For some insane reason, I let her push past my gag flex, lodged her there and swallowed around her. She felt that, too, and shivered.

"Damned Braqth," she murmured, trapping both my nipples between her fingers and squeezing as tiny bumps broke out on my skin. "First time? Lead is going to prize you."

Who?

I coughed when Gaelan dragged the black, magical prick from my throat. I blinked tears back, but my cunt was in a loud trill of demand that my tits and tongue do not get all the fun. I rolled my hips in need, and she noticed.

"You want me, Sirana? How I'm shaped?"

"Yes," I admitted.

"Fast learner."

I remained still as she slid off the chaise to step behind me. I trembled as she got close enough that I could feel her heat and fairly shuddered as her hands touched my haunches. My breath shook, and I ached for her to penetrate me, in spite of how this usually worked between two females. So what if the one who wore the cock was the dominant one? That's how Red Sisters were different.

"Show me, Sirana."

I arched my back in answer, presenting myself, even widened my legs for her. The Red Sister gripped my hips, aimed, and pushed; I yielded, my newly fertile body sucking her in, and my heart tripped to hear her moan. I rolled my hips and pushed back against her, encouraging natural movement, and she fucked me with delicious thrusts.

Maybe it was the lasting effects of the ritual, but no feeling of threat hovered over my back with her. She may as well have been a Noble Son interested only in pleasing me while she pleased herself. I called and cried again as I climaxed twice; Gaelan slammed in and moaned the second time, peaking alongside me as her toy flexed and throbbed like a real cock. Then she stroked gently, in and out, coasting and coaxing out a few more, little groans for herself.

I was stunned. *She came.*

The haze in my mind left me curious if I'd find some kind of fluid afterward.

"Okay. Too fucking hot to keep standing here."

Startled by the new arrival, my cunt clenched the tool working it. Gaelan bottomed out and seized my shoulders to hold me in place and impaled. Her toy did not soften one bit.

"Don't move," she instructed.

My heart slammed against my chest bone, and my face became exceedingly hot.

I knew this voice, which was lower in timbre than Gaelan's; she had spoken to me twice before. I knew her scent and the texture of her lips. I'd recognized her at the candle chamber, and saw her as she watched my fourth trial on the Altar of Braqth.

Here she is again.

The first Red Sister who had stood in my bedroom at House Thalluen.

She had brought a few others, from the number of boots I heard on the stone.

CHAPTER 12

"A little anxious to get off the bottom rung, aren't you, Gaelan?" said a higher voice than the short-haired one in the lead.

"A little," she replied as if being coy. The tone sounded off.

They surrounded us. I was nervous, trapped on all fours upon the chaise with my knees wide and a hard pole lodged up inside me; held like an Uroan needing gelding.

"Is the novice broken in yet?" the third asked, sounding too eager as her eyes scanned the various methods for torment in the chamber.

"Not doing it here, remember?" the short-haired warrior said with an air of command, even as her eyes trailed over me from head to foot. She rubbed herself through the crotch of her leathers, an obvious whetting of a healthy appetite. "Only sent to bring them back."

"But Lead, we're *right* here," the high-voiced one protested. "Can't we have first claim on her before the others?"

The "Lead" lifted a red-gloved fist without taking her eyes off Gaelan and me, and the subordinate shut up.

"Elder's waiting, Gaelan," she said. "Pull out, clean up, get dressed. In that order."

"Yes, Lead."

The youngest Sister withdrew her phallus out of my sex with a wet suck and gained her feet while I quickly sat my ass down on the chaise, my heart still beating rapidly.

What does she mean, "before the others"?

Although Gaelan glanced down at her pile of equipment as if to collect it and take it with her, her Lead stepped over until I thought she was going to step on them. The older warrior crossed her arms.

"Get to it."

I didn't hear Gaelan's feet as she slipped over to the fountain to remove her magic tool; she was silent until I listened to the splashing water on her crotch. The Lead's body blocked the other two from getting near Gaelan's stuff, but that didn't stop them from curiously approaching me, flanking me alongside their superior. One of them, whom I was sure had been a commoner, leaned down to take a sniff even as I leaned back from her.

"Phew!" she exclaimed with a grin. "Smells like wilderness and sex."

The Lead grinned as well. "A favorite." She addressed me directly as all three loomed above. "You aren't as cut up as I would have expected traveling naked for two cycles."

I swallowed, uncertain what to say. Whether to say anything at all.

"She found healing in an outer dwelling," Gaelan supplied, nearly finished and joining us to dress. She was as efficient as her summary of my return. "She also managed to both find and keep her House dagger. I have it, now."

The Lead nodded, still watching me. "Healing, but no clothes before leaving? Not a bath?"

"She never left. She was distracted."

"By?"

Gaelan had donned all her under layers and her boots, now slipping on her leathers, armor, and bracers. "The Priestess effects. There was a male present."

The Lead's expression changed from anticipation to disappointment and annoyance. She glanced at my middle and looked resentful while I held perfectly still.

"I got there in time," Gaelan hurried to explain on my behalf, finishing up with belt and weapons and cloak. "Elder can confirm."

"Hope so," her superior replied, looking the younger Sister up and down, seeing her ready. "Any female witnesses?"

"None."

A nod. "Good enough for now. Let's go. Kiren. Lawret."

With two matching giggles, one pulled out a black bag from her belt and the other stepped behind me and seized my hair, gathering it up to secure inside as the bag went over my head.

Shit!

The two lifted and handled me roughly as they brought me to the lizard mount again. Their questing fingers invaded my two, unprotected holes as they boosted me up; they laughed as I squirmed. Soon tied to the saddle, I at least sat astride it this time. With my wrists and ankles tied to the body of the animal, however, it proved more comfortable to lean against the long neck than to try to sit up. I attempted to hold still. All my senses except the one tuned to the deep thrum of Sivaraus were muddled by the bag, anyway.

I could not help but be concerned. What did the Sisters not want me to see or know? Was I to be tested further without pause? Or maybe they didn't want onlookers peering too closely at me? This was one of their secret initiations, wasn't it? I was convinced that was the case when I overheard public comments as we finally, after a long ride with minimal talking, entered populated areas. I was presumed to be a prisoner, and once they even affirmed it for one curious wannabe-Matron.

"I'm sure she deserves the Wrath of the Valsharess's elite, Sister," the onlooker said imperiously. "Give her three lashes for me!"

I felt markedly better when I heard the lead Red Sister chuckle and mutter, "Boot-licking fool," after we passed.

For their part, even though Kiren and Lawret had continued to poke at my vulnerable backside just to watch me become aroused against my will — I supposed because they were bored — they only did it when we were in the outskirts. Once within Sivaraus proper, they and Gaelan kept others from coming near me.

No one could touch me or throw anything at me, even though some apprehended fugitives were known to suffer at public hands. Each one who tried was soundly dissuaded, and our Red Sister Lead merely said it was for the Valsharess to judge and decide. No one questioned her.

I reflected that none of them had called me by name except for Gaelan, who apparently was "the bottom rung." I was still not on the inside of the Red Sisters yet, but I was being protected if only to save me for themselves.

It finally occurred to me to wonder if failed recruits remained slaves to the Red Sisters, used such as they obviously wanted to use me. Regardless, she would be unable to be released after seeing so many secrets. Or did they save themselves the trouble or potential rebellion and just kill them after having their fun?

I won't find out, I promised myself in the darkness of the bag. As far as I knew, I hadn't failed yet.

Eventually, I was unlashed from the lizard mount and dragged off. The two carried me indoors somewhere, disheveled even worse than when they'd carried me out some time ago. Several doors opened and closed; I counted those and the turns but wasn't sure what good it might do me. Boots clapped loudly on the dressed basalt, I thought because now they wanted to make noise. Finally, someone tapped a rhythm on a hollow stone, and I sensed a Ward released.

"Enter."

The door opened, and I was shoved forcefully forward such that I could do nothing but fall hard to the ground with a grunt. I heard a pack and a weapon set down on a wooden table to the left, then the door closed a moment later. I stayed right where I was and said nothing.

The silence continued for a very uncomfortable time; from straining my senses, I knew there was only one other Davrin breathing in this smaller chamber, and a few candles emitted heat. She would be watching me. But who, and why?

I was determined to wait her out, and I stayed as I lay, curled on my side on the floor.

At long last, I heard a soft laugh. "Did they cut your tongue out beneath that bag?"

My heart surged, and heat diffused through me to hear Elder D'Shea's voice. I squeezed my thighs together; I remained sensitive, and my body's cravings took me at random with no apparent source of relief despite no longer being alone.

"No, Elder," I said.

"Good. Take it off and let me see you."

Gingerly I tugged at the drawstring beneath my jaw, loosening it, and took a clean breath of air as I lifted the bag off my head. I blinked hard, my eyes protesting the candles after such a long time out in the wilderness. I focused on her.

Elder D'Shea was dressed not in her Red Sister uniform but in a comfortable and soft-looking robe that showed her form well. It was deep purple in color but decorated with silver and red threads which formed interlocking webs in a curve that doubled back on itself. She wore sandals not much different from the Royal Consort on the farm of solitude, and she had a golden toe ring looped around her left, little toe.

When I looked at her elegant face, the Elder Sorceress was expressionless, sitting in observance with her hair piled atop her head in fashionable disarray, delicate, gold chains accenting her white locks. I knew she had to be around my own Matron's age; mature at five or six hundred turns, and at that stage where presence and grace came as natural as breathing. Her force of will was potent, almost tangible when we locked gazes. She smiled with a benevolence I wasn't sure whether to believe or not.

"Did you enjoy your first time outside the Great Cavern, Blue Eyes?"

I thought of the Consort here. Better to purse one's lips closed and not answer than to say what I was honestly thinking. *Why leave me out there alone? I could have died from sheer **want**.*

In the candle chamber, I'd at least been some version of myself I recognized. Now, after the Tragar, the Consort, and Gaelan — and still craving cock — my confidence, or arrogance, was not so steadfast. I'd lost a great deal of control, if not all of it, and I was not happy about it.

"Say something, Sirana," she said quietly. "Anything you wish to say."

I paused for a heartbeat. "What mistakes must I avoid to become a

Red Sister?"

Her white brows raised in mild amusement, but she seemed pleased with the question. "First tell me how you came to be here, in my room, from drifting off on Braqth's Altar. Then I will answer your question."

My eyes shifted as I considered what to say, and how. Lying was second nature, but I had to know whether it would do any good here. She would get nearly the whole story from the others at any time she wanted; for certain the Bred Consort, but hopefully not the Tragar. I wasn't used to making entirely truthful reports; no one at Court was. D'Shea would know that.

"I made my way back from where I'd been deposited," I began neutrally. "It was slow travel, as the side-effects of Braqth's Threshold were distracting."

She nodded, propping her chin lightly on her palm, her fingers relaxed against her smooth cheek. "Go on."

"I did not want to face the sentries. I-I thought I would attack them, in my need. I wished to see how close I could get to the Palace without discovery. Without meeting anyone."

"Ambitious." She looked skeptical about the attainability of that goal. "Dangerous, too. The same as being drugged at a dinner party without a place to sleep it off."

That seemed a well-chosen detail to me, but she was also right. No telling who might have taken advantage of my state had I continued past the first farm I found. "I found a pool which revealed a passage through the rock. I swam through it and reached a farm without having to confront the sentries." My heart sped up and doubt caused my skin to flush hot as I hesitated here.

"Go on," she said quietly. "Do not lie to me, Sirana, or I can't answer your question, and I can't help you."

"I … discovered an isolated, Davrin bua there," I admitted. "As I feared … I … lost control of myself and captured him."

Her head tilted a bit, her brows drawing down. She was displeased. "And?"

My heart continued beating in my ears. "I tied him down. Got his cock inside me, but not for long enough for him to give me his seed."

"You're absolutely sure?"

"Ask Gaelan. She was the one who dragged me off. He spurted all over himself."

D'Shea's full mouth twitched slightly. "I would have paid to see the fight that followed."

I felt my face heating; I clearly recalled being the loser.

"Continue," she commanded softly.

"Gaelan tied me up and took me to a cave. She used a ... a magical device to give herself a phallus, and, well." I paused, unsure how to say it.

"She did as I told her to do," D'Shea finished.

"Which was what?" I challenged.

She was pleased enough to answer. "To find you first. To make the first time reasonably pleasant, given your condition."

The older Davrin chuckled when I opened then closed my mouth.

"I can see how it worries you, Sirana. Don't let it. The lust will lessen over the next few cycles, and your energy will return to normal. A little faster if you indulge, though the only way to stop it instantly is to become pregnant. I can see that hasn't happened."

I swallowed.

She spoke with a voice of command. "Offer your body to any of the Red Sisters, no one *but* the Sisters. This order goes forward until I say otherwise. No males, no matter how submissive, understand? On pain of death, Sirana."

I felt myself deflate with regret. "Yes, Elder."

She noticed; her mouth quirked. "So then Jaunda found you both and brought you back, is that so?"

Jaunda. That's her name. I nodded. "Yes, Elder."

"Did anyone else use you?"

"No. Lead Jaunda wouldn't let them. Kiren and Lawret."

D'Shea was pleased I was paying attention despite the magical weakness, I could tell. "You have very few marks."

"I stole a healing potion."

"Yes, I can see some magical residue. As I could before."

My eyes narrowed then. Once again on purpose, the Elder recalled for me a well-chosen detail. The first time we ever met, just after Jilrina fell to her death. I almost asked how long she'd been watching me, but that wasn't as important as the question of my future.

"So, your answer?" I prompted. "To help me?"

D'Shea tilted her head in thought. "What mistakes to avoid? Becoming pregnant, for one. For another, the Prime. Although you probably won't be able to avoid that. Just remember that as in the trials, you cannot be permanently crippled."

She didn't even pause to give me an opportunity to react to that.

"Let's see. Avoid offending the Valsharess or the Priesthood, deserting the Sisterhood, being more trouble than you're worth, and failing to obey your superiors. There are too many pitfalls to name, Sirana, but trust your instincts, and you'll do well enough."

All common sense. And vague. Although I hadn't been specific myself.

"Alright. What is the very next thing I must do to become a Red Sister?" I asked.

D'Shea chuckled deeply, reaching to take a sip from a half-full glass of dark wine. "Stay inside this complex. Submit to be tested. Don't try to escape. Each of the Sisters will test you in her own way. If they don't find you lacking, you'll earn a uniform. Then we'll train you on more specifics."

"And who will you be to me?"

"Your primary superior. My word goes above all others for you, except for Elder Rausery, the Red Sister Prime, and the Valsharess. Although if an order does not conflict directly with my instructions, do not defy another of a higher rank. It will take time to rise in the Sisterhood, Sirana, but all who survive do rise."

I extrapolated quickly from that. "Is Rausery your superior?"

D'Shea sipped her wine again, smiling small and elegant. "In age, yes. Not rank. Our specialties are different. The Red Sisters have 'teams,' for lack of a better word. As in our army, there are units within the larger body. It is more efficient than if the pecking order was determined straight down from the Prime Sister.

"Our primary objective is to serve and protect the Valsharess. The Priesthood holds little authority over us. They can direct us toward known subversives and heretics, but we are the balancing power which prevents the Priesthood from dominating the Chosen on our Throne. Checks and balances, a needed anchor, or you might imagine how the power structure would change every two-span with Braqth's Priestesses in charge."

I nodded, shuddered even to think it. Then I had to ask. "If I should somehow fail to earn the uniform?"

My superior's gaze settled on me as if determining whether I was having doubts. I maintained that gaze. I was not; I simply didn't want to be kept guessing.

"It would depend on the 'how' of the failure, but if you weren't executed, you would become either a slave stripped of her will or given to the Priestesses to be transformed into a Dread Spider, which amounts to the same thing. The dungeon isn't an option."

The cold chill and dread flooding me were welcome, in a way. I'd guessed correctly, and it was all in line with what made the most sense to me. I could understand this group, it was within my ability. They could become much less of a mystery, as I would join it. I wanted to explore all aspects of it, I wanted to see, and I wanted to know; I wanted to become. It was my new purpose in living. It was the reason I'd come back despite what happened with Kain.

D'Shea stood up smoothly, setting down her wine glass and turned her back on me. Those would be all the answers I'd receive for now, and she'd been generous. She stepped over to a textured bathing tub, turning polished metal knobs that opened a broad-mouthed spout, and water began to flow, filling the vessel at a quick rate.

I was amazed that I could detect humid heat in my nose. A water system like this was known in the Noble Houses, but the source of the heat — if there was one — ranged anywhere from a complicated connection to a deep thermal spring to laborious fires to magically-imbued heating stones. I could not know how this was heated, but I was suddenly hungry for a warm bath all the same. I knew I stank.

I sat, however, as D'Shea disrobed, the purple cloth sliding down her skin as she kept her back to me. My eyes drifted in the direction I'd heard a weapon be placed upon my arrival and saw my House dagger laying there. It was within reasonable reach; D'Shea was too far away to stop me from reclaiming it. Was she was testing me? Almost certain. No Davrin stayed facing away from another so long if they weren't.

I remained as I was on the floor as she removed her sandals and added some ground crystal to the water. D'Shea was naked, taking down her hair as she turned, and she smiled at me, amusement glinting in her eyes, red as her wine.

"Bathe me, Sirana."

Very well. I got to my feet for the first time in a while, very stiff and sore from top to bottom. Still, I would play the servant to my superior as I wanted the hot bath for certain, but I also expected this was D'Shea's excuse to take her turn with me before all the others did. Did she have a tool like Gaelan's? Would she use it?

The water was almost too hot as we settled down. The heat seeped into my muscle down to my bone, setting our skins bright with Radiants despite the candles interfering with Dark Sight. I groaned inwardly. Whatever the Sorceress had added to the water was working to soothe my nether regions.

At a look from her, I took the bottle of scented soap and a large, plush cloth and began to soap her up above the waist. She was well-formed and muscled as I was, perhaps more so, although not unusually bulky. A very few, subtle silver lines marked her black skin, and I was inwardly shocked to see those scars.

One scar ran about finger-length along her ribcage beneath her left breast, another crossing her spine between her shoulder blades, and — when she stood up for me to scrub below her waist, I saw another drawn with the direction of the muscle on her abdomen on the right side. That scar would be parallel to her womb. They were small and easily erased, one would think.

Why had she kept them?

After she'd spread her legs for me to wash between, which I did and rinsed in good time, I fully expected her to order me to put my mouth on her then. I waited for the order.

She didn't give it.

The Elder sat down in the water and turned around again, telling me to wash her hair next, which I did, lingering a bit massaging her scalp and letting the wet, soapy hair run through my fingers before rinsing. After we'd finished, she languished in hot water and watched me as I cleaned myself head-to-toe.

When that was complete, we just sat to feel it slowly cool. She silenced me each time I tried to ask a question, and I stopped when she looked vaguely annoyed. It was quiet in her chamber as it had been in the wilderness cave where I'd woken up.

Eventually, the water was no longer pleasant, and we got out. I was instructed to pull the drainer. I dried the Elder before I dried myself, and I still awaited the order to either start my oral service or to present myself for inspection. Instead, I was told to plait her lightly damp hair for her, and then do my own.

"It is late," she said, her voice low after I'd tied off my own braid.

She gestured toward a simple but comfortable bed with white sheets, barely large enough for two bodies, and I appraised it with ambivalence. I was exhausted enough to fall into reverie shortly after climbing into a bed like that; would she command me to perform for a mark or so upon it before I could sleep?

At my hesitation, she gestured again with a frown. "Get in."

I settled in, waiting, expectant as the candles went out, but D'Shea had only lain down and relaxed. Within a short but dragging time of me fighting to keep myself awake despite the soft bed sucking the very will out of me, despite expecting something to happen, I was almost certain Elder D'Shea was deep in Reverie.

Asleep.

I'd never lain next to a female who was unconscious while I was awake. Though we were both nude, D'Shea didn't touch me or reach for me. We lay close but apart. She smelled good, but I dared not reach to touch her although I had the impulse. I *had* been tired, but my confusion seized me long enough for the soft sheets to brush my skin and awaken it, for my hand to reach thoughtlessly between my thighs. My nerves sizzled; there was no way I was following her into such an enviable state now.

Goddess damn it! I just want a rest from this fucking need!

At the very least in all this, I knew I wasn't pregnant. Looking back, it had been so narrowly avoided — and not through my own efforts but that of the Consort and my new Sister.

Biting my lip, holding in my whimpers, I tried to bring myself off in silence. My Elder had said this urge would lessen in time, but indulgence was part of the process. I could be satisfied, I had to be, even for a little while. Despite my best attempt, I must have been shaking the bed. Elder D'Shea turned her head toward me, and her eyes opened. She smiled. I froze.

"Here, I shall help." Her voice was husky with sleep. "Just this once."

She reached down, moved my hand out of the way and cupped my slobbering mound. I sucked in my breath as the heel of her hand pressed to me, and her middle finger slipped inside my slit. She did not stroke me, however. She said something I didn't understand.

Then her hand shocked me.

"Godd — !" I strangled a squeak, then I was cumming. My chirps and yips sounded ridiculous to my own ears as I humped against her hand, but my body loved every stroke. Sensation shot high in an instant took a long time to come back down, and I was panting by the end.

She brushed a damp thread of hair from my brow. "Rest. While you can."

I nodded, my eyes dropping. The next moment my Reverie took hold of me while it could.

CHAPTER 13

ELDER D'SHEA DRESSED AND DONNED HER UNIFORM, GROOMING HERSELF. I was not required to help, and I was offered no clothes although was allowed to brush my hair. I braided it as well to keep it out of my eyes. When it was time to leave this small, warm place and walk out that door, for an instant I wished I had never even gotten out of her bed.

I didn't know what, or who, was on the other side of the door, but Kiren's blurt in the interrogation cave about getting me before the others collided with the Sorceress's confession of sending Gaelan with explicit orders to make the first time "reasonably pleasant."

The war inside was fierce between my head and my crotch, and the thought came to me that other recruits from the Nobility wouldn't have Priestess magic making them *want* the blunt crudity the Red Sisters had to offer. Not in that way. Was that fortunate or not?

Offer your body to Red Sisters only, D'Shea had said. *No males. This order goes forward until I say otherwise.*

I had only seen two extremes so far with these magic cocks: intimidating torture of strangers, and Gaelan being "pleasant" under D'Shea's direction, or so she said. Similarly, I was certain Lead Jaunda had wanted to do something with me in my state; the desire on her face as she admired my position, impaled by Gaelan, had burned bright even in the dark. Yet she had prevented two others from claiming more than opportunistic molestation.

Lastly, Elder D'Shea had kept her hands off me at first; she had me touch her instead, and in practical terms only, until the moment I just couldn't sleep. Then she got me off in a few flicks and nothing for herself.

And now?

My gut told me I was about to find out why Elder D'Shea assumed that she — and those undoubtedly loyal to her — would be favorable to me by comparison. It implied that she wanted me to trust her, to pledge my loyalty to her as well. It was obvious manipulation, granting some respect and boundaries when not required.

But, in these circumstances, what options did I have? No one had ever courted my favor before, even if it was asking my willing servitude. What else could I think to demand? Red Sisters had rank, and the longer one survived, the higher the rank.

She answered when I asked, in trade for recounting my journey. She could have demanded my story for nothing. A threat would have worked.

I could choose my loyalty, perhaps, or refuse to grant it, but that was it. I might even be considered lucky that D'Shea gave me solid reasons why it should be to her I chose. The other two elder females hadn't even spoken to me.

"Follow," she commanded.

I could sense we were below the Great Cavern itself, though not far. This place had the same feeling as our cellars and cisterns at House Thalluen, but I walked in an interconnected, complete compound. The hallways were narrow and extremely bare. No decoration of any sort, no rugs or padding, no mirrors.

There *were* heatless torches near the low ceiling, but even those were spaced far enough apart that the place remained dim, colors muted while my Dark Sight struggled to decide whether to engage or not. It gave the area a surreal quality; this was one of those conditions where space itself played tricks on Davrin eyes.

Someone was coming around the next bend. *Two.*

These Red Sisters were younger, and a bit louder — though that may have only been because I was barefoot. They were aware of us by the time we spotted each other. In unison, they stopped and lifted their fists to rest near their temples in a salute to Elder D'Shea. It was a motion I hadn't seen before, but I noted how it offered a clear opening to jam a dagger anywhere from armpit to abdomen.

Must be the significance.

As soon as the Elder acknowledged them with a nod of her chin — she did not raise her arm in any similar fashion, nor did she stop walking — the two grinned at me. Hungry predator looks.

"The 'cruit made it," one commented to the other.

"Carry on, Corpora," the Elder said without pausing.

One reached out as I passed, but I slithered by her, skimming the wall, and kept close to D'Shea's back. While I hated them being behind me and watching us, I was glad they didn't follow.

"Nice ass," the other said as they continued on their way.

We took another few curves, and I noticed there were no hard corners in this place as in the Palace and Sanctuary and no stairs. That was not to say some bends weren't extreme enough to be called a turn, but the pathways up and down were ramps, and overall the floor plan mimicked the natural tunnels of the Deepearth far more than most of our city's other constructed shelters. I wasn't sure if that was the point, but I could not mistake this place — wherever I was — for any other.

We took one true decline to another level and came to an oversized door at an apparent dead-end. It was rune-marked, and even I could feel the warning of Wards. Elder D'Shea suspended them with ease and, in the same motion, gave some command which caused the doors to slide open part way, enough for the two of us but no more.

"At last, D'Shea. Kept me waiting. Let's just push through this."

The speaker was the eldest Red Sister, the Prime, and she didn't look up from the stout table bearing maps, rolls of scrolls, and scores of notes. All of this rested on a platform with space around to present to an audience in an otherwise bare, black-stone room. There was not one decoration, and even the candles and torches by which we could see were unremarkable.

The Red Sisters do not demand things of vanity for their headquarters. Maybe they don't loot much when fighting, not like the army.

I was distracting myself on purpose. I did not know what "push through this" meant, but the Prime made it clear I was a disruption in her cycle. She may not have noticed if I had never returned from the wilderness. Her indifference was so blatant that I might have thought it for show if I didn't see her dead, resentful eyes as she came around the table and down the ramp to our level, her red cloak flowing behind her.

Such a stark contrast to the two Sisters who had drooled as if presented with a fresh plate of meat, or Gaelan and Jaunda, who used my name and knew who I was. Or Elder D'Shea, talking to me, washing and resting with me. Deigning to express even modest approval in anything I said or did. Would the Prime's interest in me ever change? What did I have to do to prove myself? Did I even want her attention?

I followed the Elder's lead and kept my feet firmly planted, although the Prime tested my resolve. She got too close, showed me she was taller and stronger. Her leathers did not creak; they were well worn and silent. I kept my chin and eyes down, staring at her chest. She sniffed me like a scavenger vaguely interested if there was a meal buried underneath a pile of trash.

"Still reeks of magic," the Prime said, and D'Shea answered.

"Yes, Prime. The ritual's effects will wear off, but it may take a few more cycles without a bua to sate her."

The mention of young males, even as a general description, brought out the same tone of distaste as when I'd been on the Altar. "Priestesses. Hmph. Still usable?"

"Yes, Prime, she is. Quite useable."

Useable. I remembered the Consort being useable, writhing beneath me, his cock up inside me. My face and my gut flushed alarmingly fast, and the Prime noticed me squirming. Whether she knew I was thinking about males or not, she still might have wanted to spit.

"We'll see what Rausery thinks."

A rough, gloved hand took my jaw, gripping hard as she forced me to look up. I squeezed my thighs in unconscious want, my desires clashing as I met eyes like scratched rubies or Kain's unpolished gems. I saw raw centuries there. I'd never been this close to a Davrin this old.

"Blue eyes," she muttered without blinking. "New Consort seed, eh?""

"No, Prime, she is not their seed," Elder D'Shea corrected. "Her older sisters were. Sirana is a simple mix of the Eleventh and Twelfth Houses. These eyes are a fluke from either Thalluen or Bovritz."

The Prime squinted at me, and I held still even when she pressed on a nerve by my teeth. She could see my pain; she seemed to like it, and her calm awareness of my presence strengthened on that account.

"Throwback?"

D'Shea tilted her head. "Clarification, Prime?"

"Bah." The old Davrin tossed the comment aside as if she'd already lost interest. "She needs training, D'Shea. She *looks* like a Goddess-damned Noble. Soft as unfired batshit."

The Elder Sorceress sounded as elegant as a Noble in her reply. "It shall be done, Prime."

Our superior released my aching jaw as I blinked back tears which I did not want to flow out onto her glove. I could barely move it at first, but that was just as well; it was clear I should only speak when spoken to. The Prime turned her back on me and returned to her platform, several awkward moments passing as we waited, I presumed, for the other Elder.

When the Wards were suspended again behind me, and that third female walked in, I had the impression she had not been in a hurry to get here. The Prime did not grouse about the wait as she had to the Sorceress.

"Plenty to do, Elder," she said briskly.

"Prime."

Favoritism came to my mind. The Prime did not seem to cherish mages all that much, and Elder Rausery was a warrior like her. Perhaps they each saw the sorceresses and wizards only as a necessity and not the basis of our refinement compared to the rest of the Deepearth.

Or maybe they don't give two fucks about 'refinement' at all.

Elder Rausery came to stand next to Elder D'Shea while I stood on the Sorceress' other side. I kept my eyes and lashes down although my chin up and back straight as Rausery nodded to my sponsor without any derision I could detect.

"Elder D'Shea."

"Elder Rausery."

The Sorceress allowed an appropriate pause, and our eldest spoke without looking around.

"D'Shea, report."

"Sirana crossed back into our borders with House dagger in hand eight marks ago. Her stated intent was to return to the Palace. She reasoned that she did not know where to find us."

The other chuckled. "Yeah, that *would* be a problem."

I was surprised to hear the humor in the second Elder's voice. It was the rare kind that didn't drip with spite.

"The Priestess ritual adversely affected Sirana's efforts, however," D'Shea continued, "and she attacked the D'Verin Consort on the outskirts. Fortunately, no Davrin except Gaelan bore witness."

"Pregnant?" Rausery asked.

"No. Gaelan caught her in time."

A pause. Then, "I wasn't aware the D'Verin Consort was alone to be attacked. Why would the Matron risk the wrath of the Palace and Sanctuary if he was taken or killed?"

I saw Elder D'Shea nod out of my periphery as she expected the question. "I will be looking into this. However, he *was* protected. My Sisters found the place riddled with Wards. Sirana found a way around them and forced him to dispel the rest."

"Well, that's … impressive. I guess." Her head turned to look at me. "Must have been dying for some cock."

Rausery sounded amused again, but she couldn't know how accurate that had seemed at the time. I *had* thought I might die. I ground my teeth as my memories were replaying with this "report." My breathing deepened, I quivered a little, and both were noticeable.

"What next?" Elder Rausery prompted.

"Lead Jaunda and her team brought Sirana back here. She's had one rest period with a meal, and my understanding is it's the only one she's had since the ritual."

"Okay." Rausery moved in front of me, tapped at my foot with her boot. "Eyes up, recruit."

I obeyed, glad she wasn't grabbing my jaw to make it happen. We watched each other a few moments. I saw deep umber eyes which were bright and alive in every way the Prime's were not. This one was cunning as D'Shea, I would wager, and not indifferent to my being here. Elder Rausery held her mouth with amused interest; like Jaunda, it wasn't hard to see her laughing freely. I felt small in front of her and aroused as I imagined her wearing a magic cock like Gaelan's.

"Wanna be one of the Sisterhood?" she asked.

"Yes, Elder," I answered without hesitation. My nipples chose this moment to become pebbled and turgid as if she'd offered to suck them instead. My fists clenched in embarrassment.

Rausery tilted her head curiously at me and didn't even glance below my chin. "What do you imagine being a Red Sister would be like?"

I weighed my response despite the tremors. Freedom from a House where I had no place, freedom from the centuries of petty drudgery and politics facing me at Court. This, against the brutal terrorization of others for which the Queen's Enforcers were known, and likely a shorter life ended by violence. Bold action under powerful, intelligent females who could easily get me killed versus caution and more time to watch drift by with full dependence on petty Matrons.

I asked myself just why I would want to live a long time anywhere else? I also asked myself, could I do what I'd seen the Red Sisters do? How soon would I be tested? What would happen if I hesitated? Did I have to enjoy it? What constituted failure in their eyes?

"Difficult," I answered, my heart pounding in my ears. "Challenging."

"Scared?" Rausery asked.

"Yes, Elder. But awake. And glad about it."

Her eyes stared into mine. "What do you mean?"

"I was haze-walking at Court. Nothing to do but drink, breathe incense, and fuck in between plots for revenge."

"Why would you think that would be any different here with us?"

That response put me off balance for a flick; she seemed serious.

"Maybe it's not," I retracted. "But I already respect the Prime and the Elders more than the Matron of the First House. More than the Priestesses."

Saying that aloud before now would have made the entire Court table gasp in alarm and I could expect horrible backlash. Here, the Prime didn't give a shit, and Rausery only smirked at me, her hands on her hips.

"You respect us? Why? Because we had you used and humiliated a few times and dumped you naked to find your way back alone?"

"You chose my final trial upon the Altar, Elder," I returned as I learned her method. "You called the moment it would happen. I've never been so afraid, yet I made it out the other side with someplace I can use my ambition. The Sisterhood's been watching me, I know. You want something, and I want to be strong. The Sisterhood can offer me this. The Matrons and the Priestesses can't."

Rausery looked at Elder D'Shea, then. Out of my periphery, I saw the Sorceress show her beautiful teeth, straightening her shoulders as if she was proud or proven right in what she'd said about me. The commanding warrior grunted, looking back at me.

"It's gonna hurt, recruit, falling and getting back up till you stay on your feet. The candle chamber wasn't the worst of it."

My arousal blended with fear, and I stood there heaving like a fool on ecstatic spirits. "Yes, Elder. That's *still* better than centuries at Court."

"I hear the Priestess made you fertile again," she countered quickly, never blinking as she verbally shoved me off balance again. "Wouldn't you rather go back to Matron Thalluen and challenge Kaltra as the Heir Apparent? If things got too hard here, would that be your backup plan? Just offer your Matron your new fertility. I'm sure she would take you back."

My quivers passed into trembling as the Prime stood up straight and turned to face us. The look on her face was like nothing I'd seen; I might imagine staring into the face of a Drider after being cocooned in its silk. I knew I didn't have that choice despite Rausery bringing it up as a temptation. I'd already seen too much.

"No," I said. "My Matron and Kaltra deserve each other. I don't want them. I want the Sisterhood."

Elder Rausery chuckled, nodded once, and turned her head to share eye contact with the Prime. "She's worth a test, Prime. Give this cait the two-span here. See if she can take it."

"So be it," the Prime rumbled. "Give the Sisters their orders, Elders, then both of you come back here. We have many tasks beyond coddling the recruit."

THERE WOULD NEVER BE AN APOLOGY FOR WHAT HAD HAPPENED SO FAR, NOR for what happened next. After the Elders had gathered what members were in the compound with us — not nearly as many as had been in the candle chamber, and perhaps that was lucky for me — they kept it short.

"This is Sirana," the Elder Sorceress said, her hand laid with some possession on the back of my neck. "Get to know her."

Lead Jaunda was there. She had been grinning from the moment we walked in. As soon as D'Shea released my neck, Jaunda threw the first punch against another Red Sister, and the room erupted into a brawl as the two Elders left and sealed the door, making sure I couldn't follow them out.

I backed up against a wall as several caits in red uniforms lunged for me while being tackled and dragged back by others. I sprinted the perimeter of the room as pursuit became clear, as some bloody noses and abraded cheeks showed how determined they were about getting to me first.

Holy Braqth.

Gaelan was there but far at the rear not engaged in the brawl; she was trying to meet my eyes. I couldn't tell what she was trying to say but spotted her casting something which made most of the others sluggish and fighting a yawn just as Jaunda broke out from the rest and avoided the effects.

"Cheater!" someone groused.

"No such thing," Jaunda replied with a boisterous laugh, and she drove me into a corner. "C'mere, sweetmeat."

I didn't fight her but let myself be grabbed and tossed over her shoulder like a sack of roots. I didn't know who else among these hard fighters I might want to catch me anyway, so I curled up like an auf's cub on her muscular back and accepted without protest the hard slaps she landed on each buttock as she crowed her delight in seizing the prize. I felt my sex respond to the strikes and begin to ache.

I hoped this Lead had a magic toy like Gaelan.

Jaunda moved fast like she expected others to follow, weaving through the curving hallways and passing down a ramp or two. Gaelan wasn't behind us, but I did hear noise fading from the room in which I'd been fought over. I made no motion which would slow Jaunda down or throw off her balance, and after we slipped into a void-black room. As she got the door closed and secured, the Lead commented on my cooperation, whispering in my ear as she pressed me to a cold, stone wall with her hard and hot body.

"You're making this easy, recruit."

She nipped the tip of my ear. She was breathing hard, and she smelled like she had just been in a fight.

"W-want me to resist, Lead?" I asked as she ran her hands over my hips, waist, and back before gripping my ass in fighter's hands.

"Only if it's real."

Jaunda kissed me as hard as before, forcing her tongue into my mouth as she had in my quarters at Court. I didn't scream this time; I felt no need. She yanked off a glove, tossed it aside, and pushed two fingers into my sopping slit, and I moaned in pleasure. She wrenched her mouth off mine, and I complained in a different tone.

"Braqth's Tits," she cursed, and I could see her shape better now in the pure dark as my sex squeezed around her fingers. She curled them, and my knees nearly collapsed as my eyes rolled up. "You're ready to go, aren't you, Sirana?"

She had mistaken my shakes for fear. They weren't. Not at all.

"D-do you have … what Gaelan had?" I asked. "The phallus?"

She chuckled. "Fuck, yeah. Gonna use it, too."

"Good."

We shared another kiss, one I initiated, and my cunt squelched with moisture as she explored me deeper.

"Fuck me," I begged her.

I WASN'T FULLY AWARE OF EVERY MARK DURING THAT FIRST SPAN IN THE RED Sisters' Cloister, as different groups came in and out in between missions. I recollected the most intense pleasure alone with Jaunda in her dark room, and a few more brawls and pursuits ensued which woke me up temporarily from the haze of lust. When some Red Sisters grabbed me and used my body in groups, it became a blur — mostly pleasurable, thanks to the Priestess ritual, but not always.

They didn't all have their own Feldeu — that magical attachment through which they felt so much arousal and sensation — but some would share the tool and others would make do without, grinding my face and various parts of my body with their furry mounds. They all marked me in their way, and there was no part of my body which remained unexplored or unsampled.

I learned quickly to submit and not to think about Jilrina at all, no matter how many slits I was made to suck and lick. This was a test, and I wouldn't fail; I wouldn't be released from the Cloister regardless, so best learn to be accepted by these others.

I even had an edge that most recruits didn't, with Braqth's Threshold keeping me receptive despite the soreness. With the seemingly endless variation and lack of boundaries in what was acceptable for females to do to one another, it didn't feel the same as a wannabe-Priestess' rigid rituals with an inappropriately aged sacrifice, anyway.

I knew a lot of Red Sisters before I saw Gaelan again. Kiren's comment about her wanting off the "bottom rung" rang true as she was one of the last to take me into her arms. She tried to get me alone as Jaunda had, and I was willing, but I learned that a Red Sister also needed to defend one's territory from bigger, meaner ones.

"You've already had her, Thena!" Gaelan growled after a scuffle with Suna and Panagan in her own quarters where she was knocked down. Meanwhile, Moria grabbed me in a headlock.

"Go lap D'Shea's dirt hole, conduit."

"*Elder* D'Shea! Sirana, say n —"

Suna punched Gaelan in the gut while Panagan bound and gagged her.

"Yeah, yeah." Thena grinned unpleasantly at me. I hadn't seen her in about four cycles and wished she wasn't here now. "Ready, Sirana? Been dreaming about you in the field and we got some pressure to blow off. You make such delicious sounds hope you haven't forgotten how."

I had some martial training from Court, but it wasn't enough to take on four Red Sisters and expect to stay here alone with Gaelan as I wanted. Gaelan didn't even have that, and they'd made sure the mage couldn't cast behind their backs.

I smirked at Thena while Moria squeezed my neck with her arm. "I haven't. And you make such funny faces, Thena. I need a good laugh."

"Cute, cait."

She grabbed my hair, Moria let go, and they hauled me to their barracks on the other side of the Cloister. Unfortunately for me, the effects of Braqth's Threshold were wearing off. Thena and her group didn't seem to notice or have a concern, and they were rougher than before unless it was only my perception.

Either way, this was different. This was a punishment of something more than making a snide remark. I maintained the banter and stubborn smirk at first, but they kept me awake and without rest for a long time, wearing me down, taking turns themselves to rest. I wasn't sure how long, but Thena only seemed satisfied when I was finally thinking about Jilrina far more than was good for my survival.

When I contemplated a Red Sister's murder for the first time.

"She's gonna bite it off, Corpora," Suna said to Thena, a mock at me and a warning to her.

Their leader just laughed. "Goddess, look at her eyes! She's livid! I wanna make her gag while she looks up at me like that!"

Something snapped when Thena approached me again, brandishing her phallus. I growled. My fingers curled into claws. I moved first, trying to gouge her eyes out without thinking.

"NO!" I roared as the other three pounced on me, as I ripped bloody lines open in Thena's left cheek but narrowly missed her eye. "No! Get off me!"

I yelled at the top of my voice, surging up, butting my head into Suna's nose, and elbowing Panagan somewhere that made her grunt. Moria hooked my thigh with an arm, her cheek pressed to my dirty, naked ass, and pulled me off balance and back onto Thena, who grabbed my hips, trying to make me sit on her Feldeu for the third time while facing her.

"Gotta tear you up a bit more to play right, 'cruit? Fine. Suna, mount up behind her. We'll go together."

Thena twisted my wrist, perhaps broke it. I screamed full-throated and didn't hold back any sound that came after.

"Eat my shit, Corpora!"

I bellowed, struggled, and resisted more than I had any Red Sister so far as Suna got behind me, pressing her own cock into the crack of my ass.

"Let me go! I'll kill you! I'll fucking kill you!"

The Ward on the door shattered and it opened behind us. Panagan and Moria were startled, jumping back, and the next thing I knew, I heard a clunk and a grunt from Suna before she flopped to the side. Someone grabbed hold of me with both arms, around the waist and across my chest, hauling me up and off Thena the same way Gaelan had wrenched me off the D'Verin Consort. This time, however, I wasn't tossed onto the floor but instead passed securely into the mage's arms.

"Enough, Corpora," Lead Jaunda ordered as she stepped in front of Gaelan and me. "Time's done. She said no, I heard it."

Thena had scrambled to her feet while Panagan and Moria positioned behind her, but Suna was still coming awake on the floor. I shook so badly I would have fallen had not Gaelan pulled my good arm across her shoulders and supported my weight. My throat felt worse after all the screaming, and I pressed my aching wrist to my middle, glaring at them all without blinking. Even then, I hoped in private desperation that this rescue wasn't another game, not a slight of hand to trick me into giving something away.

I wanted it to be what it appeared to be. I wanted to go with Jaunda and Gaelan and be safe. I didn't want to stay here.

Thena spat, her face still bleeding. "Makes sense little Gael would have to get *you* to help feed her some scraps, Lead. Take the novice. After this long, she's all loose and used up, anyway."

Jaunda heard Thena acquiesce as I did; I was relieved when she took no umbrage and briskly nodded her acceptance. She motioned Gaelan and me toward the door while she guarded our backs against the grumbling predators. The short-haired Davrin didn't bother with any verbal shot to the Corpora, but she did close the door in the middle of Thena's parting remark. I didn't care whatever it was that Thena said, either.

I limped with them to the wing where I'd been some time ago. Jaunda and Gaelan's barracks were not too far from each other, and I wondered at first if we'd go to the Lead's room for extra protection, but we returned to Gaelan's room. There, she placed me down on her pallet where I curled on up on my side, crossing my arms over my chest.

Jaunda dragged the single chair over to sit at the door after it was closed and secured. The Lead then sat and leaned back, pulling a blade to hone while Gaelan stripped down and settled behind me, spooning my body and putting her clean arms around me despite the dirt, saliva, and sweat covering me.

"I don't … want to," I murmured to her, even aware she wasn't wearing her Feldeu.

"Won't force you," the young mage returned softly, combing some hair at my temple.

I snorted. "Everyone else has been."

"That so?" Jaunda asked curiously, her blade touched up enough to return to its sheath. "You seemed willing most of this span, Sirana, up until now. For what it's worth, I've never seen any novice take us all on for this long before cracking. What I understand, that was the first time you said no and, no matter what, you made an impression among the Sisters."

She might have been right about most of that, but a lot was just mist in my mind. I shrugged, arms still crossed, feeling Gaelan's warmth and soft skin as she cradled me. I exhaled and tried to ease my tense muscles.

"I didn't have a choice. I make it here, or my life is over."

"True for the most part," Jaunda said. "But there's a limit for those who've held on strong as you have. Thena and her crew just hit it. But if you'd crippled or killed one of them? Yeah, the Prime alone would decide whether to keep you or not. We wouldn't see you until she declared that to us, and you'd only see her in between."

I struggled with my bladder for a few moments. *Fuck.* "That why you barged in?"

Jaunda grunted. "Yeah. The Prime's killed the last three recruits handed over to her for going feral on a Sister. If she's kept *any*, it was before my time. But then, she thinks we're getting soft."

"While our Elders constantly remind her," Gaelan added, her breath soft on my neck, "that we need to keep *some* to *have* a Sisterhood. There must be some standard to pass."

Jaunda nodded in agreement, her smile dry when she and I made eye contact. She still looked at me like she had at Court, like I was worth something, even after being stripped of both clothes and all control.

"We'll teach you how to get out from under a Sister's Feldeu if you really don't want to take it, Sirana. There are ways, and you don't have to take everybody who asks or demands it."

I blinked, my heart surging. "I don't?"

She grinned and shook her head. "Nope. Though take my advice and pick at least five to make part of your regular appetite, once you're back to normal. It's never gone well for a novice who tried to snub everybody, and no one here is exclusive. One or two is too few. Five seems enough to build the bonds you need to survive."

Given her estimated age, I thought Jaunda had some room to talk about that. I wondered about her five. Or ten. I wondered if I could be another one added to her "regular appetite."

Which seems substantial. I nodded. "Got it, Lead."

"Good. Better see to her wrist, Gaelan."

Jaunda tilted her head at me, her boots crossed at the ankles and her hands folded over her middle, cloak draping along the floor as Gaelan got up to get something from her chest.

"So," the Lead said, "has the ritual worn off? Finally? That why you erupted like a hotspot on Thena?"

Cautiously, I reached down with my good hand, lightly caressing my netherlips. I did not feel the instant sizzle as I had for the last eight or ten cycles. It was so strange, both lacking but also as if I'd just come down from a high fever and rounded the bend, coming out of a lengthy illness. I felt weak but hungry for food, water, and a chance to walk around and do something other than fuck in bed. Preferably something that allowed wearing clothes. I'd worn nothing at all since handing over my dinner gown and slippers in the candle chamber.

Once you're back to normal.

"I think so," I said. "Probably."

Gaelan lay back down behind me, offering a small vial over my shoulder. She had a smile in her voice. "Here, drink this. Elder D'Shea will be pleased, although you have one more Sister to get to know before we take you to her."

"Who?"

"Lead Qivni," Jaunda replied, watching me with a devious grin, and I swigged the bitter tonic. "She wasn't gonna be anywhere near you stuffed full of Priestess juice. You're off it at last. You take a Reverie, bounce back from Thena and her gang. By the time you wake up, she'll know it's her turn."

I let that sink in alongside the healing potion, recalling how Qivni had commanded the Sathoet, how she'd spoken that grinding language with ease. How she seemed to know the lines I was tempted to cross with the Priestesses and gave me dire warnings. How she'd resentfully tickled my anus with the tip of her tongue, for a reason known only to D'Shea.

Out in the wilderness, I had been curious to discover more about that. About her. Now I wasn't sure if I had the strength to make it worthwhile.

My Collector. Joy.

CHAPTER 14

ONE LEAD PASSED ME OFF DIRECTLY TO THE OTHER WHEN WE MET IN THE HALL-way. I was still naked and barefoot but bathed. Qivni sighed, standing at the door to her room, not having entered it herself since coming back.

"Now?"

"Now," Jaunda replied, smiling at the grim expression on her peer's face. "Sirana's sobered up. She's clean and everything. Almost done. Unless she tries to kill you," my Lead winked at me, "or you find some terrible flaw, I think we'll have a new Sister soon."

I thought it was clear that Qivni would rather skip this part; perhaps she would give Jaunda her way than touch me. This was an obligation or tradition; even though a crowd of Sisters wasn't watching her right now, there was still pressure for her to perform. With a slight curl to her mouth, Qivni took my arm. Her grip was not nearly as harsh as on the balcony, on my last eve as a Noble.

"I'll be back for her after your Reverie, Qiv," Jaunda said and excused herself without waiting for dismissal.

Like the Elders, there were only two Leads in the Sisterhood: Jaunda and Qivni. One was a warrior, the other a mage, and they were swapped in their apparent loyalty: Jaunda with the Sorceress, and Qivni with the General. I wasn't sure if that was as the Prime and Elders had wanted it or if, like me with Qivni now, they were required to accept the assignment.

I knew as well that there were four Lunents — two each under a Lead — but would have to recount Corporas now that I was "sober." I thought I had known eight, being passed from one to another, and except for the Prime, the rankings seemed to prefer even numbers and multiples of four. All others beneath the Corpora were simply "Sisters," ranked according to seniority and divided up four to eight per Corpora.

Meanwhile, a recruit changed to "novice" before she became a Red Sister. Still, even some higher-ranked females were still called "Sister" by their peers, if more casually. Probably not formally. Everyone started as a novice, then a Sister; from all their talk above my head, my ass, or my slit, I had already gathered that there wasn't a way to buy or bribe oneself up a few ranks.

Everyone starts at the bottom. Even Elders Rausery and D'Shea, centuries ago.

The door closed behind me, and Lead Qivni disarmed herself, putting all things in their place before carefully removing each piece of armor. If she had wanted to command me to serve her, she didn't show it, and she probably didn't trust me to competently remove her gear without damaging it. Her tight bun looked disheveled, and I wondered what she'd been doing before she got here to have me thrust into her space.

I sniffed the room and realized hers was the only room so far that held a lingering scent of incense which reminded me of the Sanctuary.

"Can't remember the last time we had to rut a needy cait for so long before making a decision," she muttered, now removing her boots and shirt.

"That wasn't my doing, Lead," I said. "I'd have fought the Priestess harder if I'd known how long it would last."

"Then you'd be dead now," she stated, turning her head sharply to glare at me. "And did I tell you to justify it to me? No. Be silent while I dress down and relax."

I was not in the mood for this attitude, and neither was she in the mood for me, but I held close what Jaunda said: one more Sister, and I was in. I managed to wrap one lip over the other and keep my thoughts to myself for the time it took Qivni to strip down. This wasn't going to be as easy without the breeding urge from the ritual, but I hoped it wasn't a slog.

"May I ask a question, Lead?" I ventured, looking at the simple dresser with the full-length mirror beside it, both comb and brush resting on the mirror's side of the dresser's top.

Qivni exhaled in sufferance. "Ask."

"Lead Jaunda said you wouldn't accept me while I was still under the Priestess's ritual effects. Is that true? If so, why?"

The Lead pulled a few pins and a tie from her hair, letting it down, and I stared to see it was longer than it had seemed, falling just below her shoulder blades. She was nude and brushing out the very minor tangles without looking in the mirror. Her face was set either in a scowl, or that was her thinking expression.

"True, and I'm sensitive to divine magic," she said. "I wouldn't be able to evaluate you properly on my terms."

Why, for Pit's sake, would they place a mage-adapt like that in the Sisterhood, not the Sanctuary?

"Were you a novice Priestess before you were a Sister?" I guessed.

Wrong tactic, I could see.

Jaunda would have punched me. D'Shea would have silenced me with a look. Qivni did a mixture of both as she stalked forward, probably in favor of casting something under temper. I was glad that she'd taken off her boots when her bare heel swept up and hit me on the side of my head. My ears were ringing as I pushed back up to sit, but I didn't feel much of a bump rising yet.

"You may ask no more questions about me, Sirana. Ever. Understand?"

"Yes, Lead."

Qivni looked down at me while I looked up. Our eyes locked, stress and emotion powered by the resistance we both felt. We could be equally stubborn, I was sure, but I wasn't in a position to challenge her. I looked down for my own good, but if she had wanted to make it so that I promised myself right there on her floor I would find answers even if I asked no questions—

"You're too curious," she remarked as if reading my mind. The Lead mage returned to her stand, tying up her hair again after smoothing it down. "You can't resist, can you? That tendency shall get you killed too soon."

I scowled at her back, and she might have seen me in her mirror. *Better than being stupid like Kaltra. As if the only way to think is like you?*

By the Void, this Davrin could remind me of everything I hated about the Sanctuary watching them up close for fifteen turns of everything my sisters had admired about them from afar. The Sanctuary link in Qivni was evident to me, and I'd be a fool to dismiss it, but I'd been an idiot in following up the hunch without patience.

I also couldn't forget there were only three Red Sisters above her; I knew she was barely older than Jaunda. Former Priestess or not, Qivni already had the skills I wanted and further talents I could never claim.

Yet she was so *sour*. How was I to even eat her, much less learn from her? I breathed out, closed my eyes. *No demons but us. Home is here, or nowhere. Jilrina has no power to drag me down or hold me back, ever again.*

"If you don't want me, Lead," I said, allowing a small smile, "why are we required to do this, again?"

"Everyone learns the new Sister in some way," she replied, sounding dutiful.

"It seems you've already learned what you want to know about me, and I'm not to ask about you."

"Quiet."

Her bun was perfect again.

"Could I ask about me?"

"What?"

I felt my mood lighten. "Could I ask about me? You seem like you'd know the most about what happened to me on the Altar."

She glanced my way and arched an elegant brow. Qivni was stern, but she wasn't ugly; she had the air that she could have been at ease wearing the Sanctuary robes.

So why aren't you wearing them?

"It is always about you, isn't it, Sirana?" she said, and it wasn't really a question.

I shook my head. "None of us survive older siblings if it isn't, somewhere in our heads."

She went still for a moment, but despite my expecting another coy suggestion that I'd killed Jilrina and had gotten away with it, Qivni asked me nothing about my House.

Maybe she doesn't understand, I thought. Perhaps she was either an eldest or an only child from somewhere.

Qivni snapped her fingers at me. "On the pallet. I want to check you over."

I crawled over to the bedding and thick mat, glad to be off the bare stone. Only Elder D'Shea had an actual bed risen off the floor that I knew about, although I hadn't seen Elder Rausery's quarters and didn't want to see the Prime's. Taken as a whole, the Cloister was austere to an extreme compared to the Palace.

This was one area where Qivni suited the Sisterhood to perfection; the incense I detected wasn't a luxury, I wagered, but necessary to perform her function.

Elder D'Shea fit far better among the decorative trappings of the Palace, wearing that silk robe, and drinking a glass of wine when I had kneeled on *her* bare floor. The Sorceress was also the only one so far with a generous collection of scrolls and books, boxes, potions, and gems on several shelves. Even this Lead, claiming to be "sensitive" to the divine magic of the Priestesses, didn't have more than a few written pieces, far above the floor and near her weapons.

"On your stomach," Qivni commanded.

Bah.

I settled down, rested my chin on my arms, and kept my legs together; I consciously resisted turning to look at her and kept my eyes forward. We were both nude as she touched me, but her fingers and hands across my back weren't sensual or massaging. She prodded and traced my muscle and bone as if trying to see under the skin; she studied me though I knew not for what. Not long ago, even this might have aroused me, particularly when she reached my buttocks, but now it didn't.

She didn't demand I open my legs.

"Turn over."

Pursing my lips to hold in the sigh, I did. Qivni studied me with only her eyes at first, forehead to toes; she wasn't interested in my breasts or fur or netherlips. She whispered something quiet, and I wasn't too surprised when she focused on my womb; her hands covered that spot first.

"First a Sathoet, then a Consort," she said, disapproving although I wasn't sure of what.

"And a wizard and a fighter, Lead," I added. "And almost every Red Sister here."

Qivni huffed with a shake of her head. "Are you tired of sex, yet?"

"Almost. But only because no one can fuck forever."

"Oh? You haven't found some limits to your tastes?"

"Seems better for a Red Sister, my Lead, if there are as few limits as possible."

She didn't disagree, although I wondered how she had made it where she was now with a few of her own limits in place. Or maybe those had developed as she gained status and her tastes hadn't started out that way.

She asked, "Did the Royal Consort say anything to you?"

"He tried to tell me who his Mistress was. I stuffed a root in his mouth."

"You didn't see his circlet?"

"No, Lead. I was fuck-blind."

"Indeed. Well said." Qivni was pleased with that admission; she actually smirked a bit. It was smug. "Did you enjoy him?"

"What I got to do on him, yes. We were interrupted."

"Fortunate for you."

"So I've been told, Lead, many times."

Her hand still covered my womb. Her red-brown eyes were unfocused. I wasn't sure if I felt any magic or not, but I was sure nothing intangible lingered from that conflict, such as D'Shea could see when I first got here.

"Did it feel at any point as though he got beneath your skin?" she asked.

I hesitated. "I don't understand the question, Lead."

Her other hand covered my heart. "You're not mage-born, so I'm not surprised. But I think you'd recognize the sensation all the same."

Maybe.

"Are you saying it isn't just the Priestess ritual to which you were sensitive?" I asked. "Was it the Consort, too?"

Qivni frowned at me but didn't speak. Perhaps only her focus on something I couldn't see or hear kept her from striking me again.

Fuck, now I was *really* curious.

"Answer," she commanded, finally removing her hand.

I didn't pretend I'd forgotten the question. "Yes, Lead, it did feel sort of like that. But it's hard to describe, and it's been gone for the last span."

"What about the cycle before you found him?" she asked. "How did you fare alone in the wild tunnels?"

I shook my head. "I don't remember much except fucking myself, Lead, and it didn't help. The magic drove me insane enough to attack the first Davrin I met."

She found that believable and might have continued interrogating me except that I could see she had had a long cycle already. I was her final "duty" before she could rest. Jaunda had even implied that I had to stay here for Reverie as well.

Qivni exhaled, poured us both some water from the same pitcher inside a locked cabinet. She handed me the small, metal cup and drank hers while I cautiously sniffed mine and hesitated, watching her.

"There's nothing in it," she said with impatience. "Drink it, or I will."

I downed the water. I hadn't always gotten enough to drink while being passed around the Cloister, and my slit was dry now that the magic had worn off. There was a blanket folded neatly at the foot of the pallet, but Qivni didn't pull it up but lay on her back and opened her legs, resting her toes on it as she combed her fingers through her white fur. She showed me purple netherlips which were only modestly flushed.

"Serve me," she demanded.

No Feldeu? I wasn't disappointed about this given my own lack of moisture, but it might have been the easier way to make her climax. I doubted I could with my mouth. I hadn't been as out of sync with another cait as I was now since Jilrina, although I knew it was because I'd been *avoiding* them until the Sisterhood gave me no option but to accept their attention.

At least Jaunda was fun. She laughs and jests, and she wanted me.

I licked and sucked Qivni's snatch for a while, lightly holding her hips or her thigh, pushing past the strong scent of hard exercise at her crotch. I knew my part was mindless movement; I wasn't listening to her signals. There was no magical drive to do so, and I hadn't found my own yet.

Like a back massage, my service on her wasn't objectionable, but it wasn't going to get her off. We didn't even rise off the starting point. I waited to see if Qivni was one who tied her feminine power into whether or not she climaxed. It was easy to threaten the one serving, to blame it on her if she failed.

In the end, she just pushed me away, bored, and frustrated.

"Enough, I want to sleep," she growled, intending to enter Reverie with that tight bun still in place. "You do the same. Don't touch me, take no stupid action to mess it up, novice, and touch *nothing* in my quarters. Obey, and you will be a Sister come the next cycle. I'll make the recommendation to Elder Rausery."

I nodded. That was a good deal. "Yes, Lead."

"Go to Reverie, then."

Gold.

Searing, golden light.

I knew that it should hurt, I should be screaming in pain. Not knowing its source, I felt it beat down from above, and the ground beneath my feet wasn't stone.

It was soft and constantly shifted. My feet sank.

I watched the light burn everything, slowly and over time. Red cloaks sur-

rounding me disintegrated, turning to grey tatters. Our black skin scorched under the onslaught, becoming painful, sensitive to the touch until thin layers peeled away in dark, ashen flakes.

Our eyes would not stop leaking water, losing that precious moisture, and we would be blind forever if we stared straight at it. Darkness within impossible heat, like the center of the world and yet everything I knew felt turned inside-out.

I should be on my knees right now.

Screaming.

"GODDESS' WEBS, SIRANA, *shut up!*"

Someone shook me, slapped me, and I woke up trembling. I stared up at Qivni, my eyes wide as when I'd come aware with my older sisters standing over me. The Lead was furious.

"What did you dream?" she hissed. "I'd think you were being dissected alive upon the Altar!"

"L-Lead," I stuttered, gasping. "Apologize … for waking you."

My heart pounded; my muscles were frozen.

Qivni narrowed her eyes at me. "Your dream?"

"Burned alive," I answered. "Too much light. Gold. Gold light."

Her mouth had formed a straight line. I knew nothing of her thoughts before she shook her head. "I cannot sleep with you here. I need you out."

"I-I apologize, Lead! Please," I said again, abruptly terrified that I had come so close but would be rejected by the Sisterhood. That I was facing my death or my will's destruction. The lingering dream didn't help. "I don't have Reverie like that ordinarily. I've never screamed like that."

Naked, Qivni got to her feet. She trembled, too. She went over to her hanging uniform, to the belt, and retrieved something from a pouch. It was a small pellet that she broke between her fingers while murmuring a word.

"Lead Jaunda will come to get you," she said.

I felt sick. "H-have I failed?"

My Collector scowled at me. "No. I'll make the recommendation you stay. Elder D'Shea wants you, Goddess knows why. She can deal with your quirks; I don't have to. I suggest not using such fearful dreams as a method to grab undue attention, Sirana. It'll get tiresome quickly, even for Elder D'Shea."

That isn't what happened.

Still, that was more lenience and advice than I'd received from some, and she wasn't having me thrown into a holding cell. I kept my mouth shut until Jaunda arrived and took me from the other Lead's quarters.

"She's in," Qivni said, motioning her hand with a disinterest that belied her discomfort, as she looked elsewhere. "Take her away, I want to rest alone."

Jaunda nodded. After the door closed behind us, the warrior signed for me to be silent until we got to her room instead.

"What the fuck happened?" Jaunda asked, squinting at me. "Qiv doesn't get jumpy around novices any more than I do."

I heard my Lead's familiarity with and acceptance of her peer; I knew to tread carefully. "I intended no harm. She checked over my body but wasn't in the mood for sex. She asked me about the Consort 'getting under my skin,' and I said yes. B-but I don't know what she concluded. She kept it to herself, and we fell asleep. I woke up from a bad reverie about burning light, I-I woke her, I was loud, and she ... uh ... "

"Got up and called me?"

I nodded.

Jaunda thought about this. "I will need to pass you on to Gaelan soon but keep this quiet. Tell *only* Elder D'Shea what you just told me, next time you see her. Clear?"

"Yes, Lead."

"Good. Looks like you're in, then."

The first Red Sister who had ever spoken to me offered that infectious grin and patted my backside, pinching one cheek, and I jumped for her amusement.

She chuckled. "I'm going to like having this ass around."

I LAY ON MY BACK ON GAELAN'S PALLET, ARMS AROUND THE MAGE'S THIGHS, MY head buried between them, eating her as I'd promised. I did so with much more enthusiasm than I'd shown Qivni, and none of it was driven either by ritual magic or the Feldeu.

"G-Goddess, Sirana, you're ... " she gasped, trembling as she braced above me, her knees wide and her palm resting on the top of my head. "Ah! Oh! Oh, there ... "

I felt no rush, and she had all my focus. If we were interrupted, so be it, but I wanted to get her off this way, and I knew I could do it. It didn't feel wrong; at last, this wasn't disgusting or degrading. Gaelan's hips jerked, and she ground against my mouth and chin, fragrant and clean. No sickly aroma as I'd always detected in my sisters or had convinced myself was there.

Gaelan and Jaunda tasted good, smelled arousing, as did other Red Sisters who hadn't infuriated me the way Corpora Thena and her crew had. I was still a novice, but now the youngest Sister. I relaxed for the first time in spans, and I took my time with Gaelan.

"Yes!" she cried, her peak rushing up to envelop her, and I moaned against her, encouraging, aiding her coast downward.

When she flopped down next to me to catch her breath, I laid there without seeking a cloth to wipe my face. There was no need to talk, and I almost drifted off still breathing in her scent.

"I'm glad you made it this far," Gaelan said, hushed as if she didn't want anyone else to hear. As if they could.

One corner of my mouth rose. "When do I get clothes?"

"Soon, I expect. The Elders will need to see you again."

I hadn't seen them at all since D'Shea left me amid that first brawl. "How long has it been?"

Gaelan paused, reaching to brush strands of white hair from my forehead. "Eleven cycles. Almost span and a half."

Elder Rausery had said she would give me a two-span to prove I could handle it here; I was five cycles away. By then, it would have been almost three spans since I'd last been dressed in a gown and leaving yet another Noble dinner party to stand on a balcony.

It already seemed that time was much longer ago.

"Can we start those tips on escaping an unwanted Feldeu?" I asked.

"Sure," Gaelan said. "I know some. Lead knows more."

And all the ways to negate them, no doubt. I couldn't imagine anyone taking Jaunda's holes if she didn't want them but could well imagine her overriding the defenses of one she'd tutored.

I guessed, "She knows some wrestling moves?"

Gaelan nodded. "If it gets to that point. Your best defense is not landing on the ground in the first place."

Cunning before strength was already my leaning, but it hadn't always worked. I lacked the skill to go with both, and I knew it. I sat up on the pallet and looked down at the second-youngest Red Sister.

"Ready when you are," I said.

Elder Rausery strolled around me, appraising my nudity for a second time. Her red cloak moved with her, quiet but very distracting.

"You've toned up some," she commented, and a wry smile lightened her face. "That was a lot of sex."

My face warmed. "Yes, Elder."

The Prime snorted audibly but made no comment. This time, we were in a smaller meeting room with a table and chairs, and the eldest sat at the head with her seat pushed back, her knees wide apart as she occasionally drank from a large, plain goblet.

I smelled something different from wine, but no doubt fermented. It appeared she'd only made time for this meeting when she might have been drinking like this anyway. She was the only one sitting.

Elder D'Shea stood across the table from me, observing the other Elder and me while keeping a fragment of her attention always on the Prime. She seemed to be waiting, more than anything, and hadn't been required to defend me much. It could only be good for me that I satisfied Elder Rausery and the Prime on my own merit rather than needing this Sorceress to persuade and convince them.

Because she wants me, Qivni said. 'Goddess knows why.'

"Lead Qivni reported trainability and a curious mind," Elder Rausery said to the Prime, "and Lunent Agalia confirmed resourcefulness under pressure. Lead Jaunda's already established rank, and the rest said things which confirm Elder D'Shea's claims of lasting resilience under magical influence. A natural outcome of her upbringing."

Jilrina wasn't magical, I thought again, but then the Priestess' words came back.

★Your sister had magic, Sirana. If she failed to raise much power using you as her Altar, I do not wonder that Varessa D'Shea has selected you to be tested for the Sisterhood.★

What does that mean? I'm not a mage.

I glanced at Elder D'Shea but looked back when the Prime grunted again, and I watched her take a drink. A drop escaped out of the corner of her mouth, got trapped in the fine creases there before she licked it away.

"Not a hunter or a leader," the Prime said, seeming to add to my thoughts the qualities I lacked. "Always one of the hunted."

I clenched my teeth as Rausery nodded. "Correct, Prime. But high intelligence, a potential for spying and assassination. Self-motivated and self-directed, if need be, but could learn to work in a team."

The Prime sighed. "Another one." She looked at Elder D'Shea with hard eyes. "Can't pick anyone bolder from the start, Sorceress? Gotta be these sneaky caits who just prove they can take a beating and not whine about it?"

D'Shea smiled. "That is Elder Rausery's expertise, Prime. Mine is finding those who can serve the Sisterhood at any level of Sivaraus above 'Fringe'." Her eyes shifted to her peer, her voice teasing. "I note that more of my choices from the last century are still alive, and they tend not to do brash things which result in their deaths within their first five turns in the Cloister."

The other Elder grinned at her rather than take umbrage. "Yeah, but I found Jaunda for you, and you're still paying me back for that. Test of the streets, D'Shea. I won't pretend I get what you look for but grant you got the numbers so far."

No one had talked around me, or about me, in this way before. It was ... generous, I thought. These three leaders could have already had this conversation before I was brought in, or perhaps they had and were even better pretenders than at Court, but I didn't think so. Elder D'Shea could act, probably, but the other two?

No. Rausery smiles, laughs. Like Jaunda. And she 'found' her. The Prime never smiles. Neither does Qivni. They show what they really are.

I wanted to believe this was real in a way the Matrons and their Daughters weren't.

Not even me.

"So. Are we right about you, recruit?" Elder Rausery asked me, stepping closer again. "Still want to be a Red Sister?"

She did not protest when I looked up at her eyes. I was still naked, and I felt a shiver pass through me. Unless I was under some magical influence, it seemed they had just laid it out for me, what my use was, what my place would be, and they had done it in a way I would be incompetent to fail to meet those basic expectations.

The three did not talk through the thin veil of polite arrogance; they spoke plain. This did make me wonder how this differed from the Priesthood's leadership.

"Yes, Elder, you are," I said. "And yes, I do."

A surge of excitement flooded my gut as I spoke and saw only approval and satisfaction. The Sisterhood made sense to me in a way I'd never expected to find once moving to Court. Right now, these leaders could show all their doubts in me they wish, and I didn't care.

I was in.

I could prove myself.

CHAPTER 15

MY LEAD NUDGED MY SHOULDER, AND I TURNED MY EYES AWAY FROM THE CLIFF to read her hand.

★Whom do you watch?★

Jaunda showed her teeth in a smile; I could detect the dull gleam from the torchlight far below us. She was confident those below were too far to see it.

★Well?★ she prompted.

★The army,★ I replied, gesturing in kind. The torchlight affected our Dark Sight, blurring our expressions slightly, but we could see each other's outlines just fine.

She gestured smartly back. ★Didn't ask what. Asked who.★

★No one specific.★

She smirked, and the tilt to her head told me she waited for more.

I looked back to the drills. This was the closest I'd ever been to a more substantial part of our fighting force. Not only kept away from the Palace and the city center in general but also away from the higher Houses, including mine.

We were close to House Aurenthin, the twenty-fourth in rank and at the bottom, and the Matron couldn't really refuse to allow the drills going on now, spilling into her field. They weren't a significant agricultural producer anyway, so the wan crop they managed just to feed their own residents wasn't threatened too much.

The unit of sixty below us was all-male. Jaunda watched me a little longer then tapped my shoulder to gain my attention again.

★You are searching for someone.★

I smiled without showing my teeth. ★I am.★

★You won't find him here.★

★Find who?★

★The soldier from your trials.★

I offered her a smirk as well, confirming her guess. ★Why is that?★

★Because he couldn't keep his silence.★

I considered that, the different, less educated way the fighter had spoken to the wizard about me. Maybe the bua had already known he was dead, and that made it easier to do whatever he wanted to a Noble. I didn't want to be in his place.

★And the wizard?★ I signed. ★He wouldn't be executed.★

Jaunda smiled wider and made no reply.

I shook my head, leaned closer, and whispered aloud, "You're all spider-bitten sluts."

The Lead Red Sister laughed loud in a sudden burst, projecting her voice and causing it to bounce off the ceiling of the cavern. I jumped, and so did all the males below me. The sudden tension and lack of focus in the unit below were apparent as a lot of them looked up and saw us. One of them pointed up just as a rod cracked down on his hand.

"You most of any of us," she purred, brushing my cheek with knuckles covered in leather. She nipped my ear then bit my neck, and I felt a genuine stab of pleasure when she did. "Follow."

I did as we crawled off the cliff to show ourselves to the unit. The commanding officer was female, and she kept all expression from her face as she scanned us head to foot coming out of deep shadow.

My Lead was taller and powerfully built, wearing red to stand out, and she was the only one. I was the clear subordinate, and perhaps not even a Red Sister to them; the leathers I wore were black. I wore similar weapons and a useful belt of pouches and small tools, but I could have been a mere messenger. Still, the officer picked up on my novice status; she gestured a salute of high respect for Jaunda and offered a formal one to me that counted at least as the Commander's peer.

I dared not show surprise; this was something to which to become accustomed, and quickly.

The male unit before me all wore black as well. There were traces of color here and there to signify rank in visible light. Purple and gold, the Valsharess's colors, but the patterns forged into the helms and armor itself — the same in either visible light or Dark Sight — served better to differentiate them at a glance than any colorful decoration useless in the dark.

This was both consistent and subtle compared to the multitude of ways that each Matron chose to show the pecking order among her House Guard. Each of the twenty-four Houses was different and difficult to keep straight. It wasn't uncommon for a new Matron to change the appearance of the House Guard after her Mother died.

"Commander Beyn," my Lead acknowledged. "How are the buas?"

The Commander offered a terse nod. "Passable, Red Sister. Not stupid enough to be found in a corner licking up cobwebs."

"Always a perk."

"Do you need another altar-piece, my grand?" she asked. "I caught two more cocking each other. They're in chains. Welcome to take them both."

Jaunda shook her head. "Not why I'm here, but I'll let my Elders know. Don't kill 'em yet."

Every male in front of me heard that; the collective shiver was subtle. I could only shake my head and sigh to myself. I didn't really understand it. My Matron hadn't been on a flute-hunt for buas mating each other since I was born, and I didn't know if she had any time before that, although I'd witnessed that particular cruelty at Court.

It was fine for the female Davrin to flirt and rut with each other at any time; just caits being caits, they said, and it helped establish ourselves wherever we were on the social ladder. It was entertaining for buas to perform for us, and some females liked watching two males sucking or fucking each other, as long as she was involved and gave permission.

Whenever males thought to entertain only between themselves, out of female viewing or approval, the reaction was vindictive and violent. I wondered now if the fighter from my trials might have been from this unit if perhaps he had wanted my netherhole because of a punishment he couldn't escape. Payback before he died.

"Let us go to my tent, Red Sister," Commander Beyn offered, and Jaunda nodded acceptance.

"Stand guard outside the tent, Sister," she instructed me as the officer gave her unit their following duties.

I nodded. Still not a peer to the Commander in practice, even if the other female's salute suggested it. I felt no resentment; I'd have doubted the Sisterhood's true effectiveness if a novice with little field experience was treated higher than a Commander centuries older, and one undoubtedly in control of a whole mass of Davrin. There was status, and there was a reputation; they weren't the same thing.

I did as I was told, felt the sound-dampening Ward take effect behind me, and observed around the camp. The buas ignored me and worked hard on chores, keeping their eyes down and away. Perhaps they hoped I wouldn't become bored enough to call over the first who made eye contact. Jaunda had already warned me, but I enjoyed watching them anyway. I even wished I *could* fuck one of them until his prick throbbed inside me. I wanted to hold him down and see his unguarded face as he grimaced and chirped in pleasure, as he writhed beneath me.

I breathed out slowly as my middle warmed, thankfully without the ritual power behind it. It was just me thinking raunchy thoughts.

You're fertile, Sirana. Can't jump on buas like that anymore.

I'd survived my first quad-span in the Sisterhood wearing the black uniform; multiple Red Sisters had trained me, and I was stronger, faster, and had more skill in weaponry and hand-to-hand than at Court. I had it together in my mind, too, and could boast self-discipline, but even four spans later Elder D'Shea hadn't said whether I'd ever fuck a bua again.

At least I didn't yearn for phallus in general. A large handful of Red Sisters were ready and eager to don that magic tool and bend me over to fill me up if I but winked at them.

This was the first opportunity I'd had to think about the two male Davrin in the candle chamber with me, and my Lead had been able to tell. The fighter would be dead; I agreed with her this was likely even if there was no proof. The wizard would be alive and likely in the Wizard's Tower, smirking over his scrolls with ink staining his fingertips.

What will you do if you find him, Sirana?

Elder D'Shea had asked me that while my netherhole was still sore from his use. That soreness was gone now, and I knew no one was going to help me with this, but I hadn't been forbidden from looking, either. The question had long since changed in my mind.

How will you find him, Sirana?

Get invited to the Wizard's Tower, somehow. Look and ask around.

Then what?

My plan needed work. I didn't even know the extent I'd be allowed to push him, but at the least, I wanted to see the look on his face when I cornered him. I'd never met a bua who could show such disrespect to females and be allowed to leave the room.

Maybe he's been punished already. But who is he? What is he to the Red Sisters?

That wizard had such spirit compared to the Noble Sons at Court; he had teased and controlled me for so long, he had *wanted* to win the game of wills, and he truly had thought that he *could*.

Was that common for mage-born sons sent to the Tower? Had he needed to be born a Noble to sound so condescending and arrogant? Or was it the resentment of someone born very low and brought up to a refined cage?

I shouldn't be so curious, perhaps, but as Qivni had said, I couldn't help it. I knew he was still out there in the Great Cavern somewhere, and he was exceptional compared to every cock I'd known before. He was the first bua I felt truly deserved me punching him in the nose.

I'll find you, wizard. In time. It's a small world down here.

The Palace and Sanctuary were positioned upon a rise to look down on the rest of Sivaraus. This was both symbolism and practicality.

Grand, lovely architecture of smooth stone rose up to mimic the massive stalagmites of the Deepearth, built with sweat and magic, glorified with decorated balconies and molded windows. The dwellings possessed graceful curves, organic in nature despite the polished and mildly enchanted finish to the outside that made it difficult for anyone to scale up from the outside either efficiently or unnoticed.

Within the multi-spired Palace and centered in clusters of smaller Court residence wings were spider gardens and semi-private groves, each decorated to the taste of their Mistress. I'd suspected the Sisterhood had been watching at various times from within these very walls, from viewpoints I never spotted.

I'd gone looking for secret passages before, and it amazed me how little I'd found, but then I hadn't known what to look for. I had not understood how to see past the subtle spells set to "encourage" someone to pass over a suspiciously clean wall or to ignore the slight draft at their ankles.

I knew now that I should be grateful Braqth hadn't been maliciously playful and allowed me to "find" one.

Several types of spells protected the doors to hidden passages, and I had been shown one so far: the easiest, I was told, those leading to secret passages, and where I had only to stare as though seeing in my periphery and mutter a banal word for the switch to reveal itself.

"Remember to neutralize it," Jaunda had said, almost in passing, as she demonstrated.

Even taking time to spot the way in and get past the trap, the passageways saved us time getting from point to point, and they allowed me to see scenes I never would have as a Noble without powerful allies. Spy-slits were ubiquitous in this first network, and not at all unknown, I learned. I'd already been through it once, down the wider, straighter passages of dressed stone from the chamber of candles to the hidden, sacrificial altar.

Most used by the Nobles or servants of Sanctuary, Jaunda signed.

I hadn't known that much but was not surprised to learn there was also a second maze the Red Sisters used. The nausea I felt passing into them, even being given the method to protect myself, left a sober taste on my tongue for how bad it would be for the uninvited.

The Priestesses allow this? I signed.

Most don't know. A couple do, and trade ritual confession to the Queen and Prime for their use.

I crawled into the dark, and Jaunda waited for the feeling of sickness to pass.

I gestured again. *The Sisterhood is higher than the Priesthood?*

Not publicly, Jaunda answered. *We have checks to watch them. We protect the Queen, Sirana. Top mission.*

I felt my mouth rise on one side. Not even the Valshraress fully trusted a Priestess. I could relate to that.

We planned to explore for a while; she said I would become familiar with them, in time. These tunnels were small, and the smell was close and oddly sterile. Just enough height to stand and turn around, but most fighting moves would be restricted. I found intersections but no interior rooms or direct doorways except at each end: the Red Sister Cloister and the Valshraress's Palace wing.

One could easily get lost in this labyrinth long before reaching either point if they weren't supposed to be there.

Most of our spy-slits looked down into a room from a high vantage point. One didn't have to glance in every time, but I had found the temptation compelling. Yet for each time I slowed us down, Jaunda would take the opportunity to molest me, churning my uniform askew. She also required me to correct it before we continued, and sometimes I needed to use her vial of mending to seal rips before she was satisfied.

Jaunda warned me with glee, *If we run out of potion before we exit, Sirana, you're walking back naked and stretched.*

I thought that went without signing.

Looking again, more than once, I tried to glance in. Magical glyphs near each slit dampened sound, so even if the Lead pinched my ass too hard and I uttered a cry, it would still be swallowed up in thick darkness.

The redundancy of this disruption seemed to be the point; I couldn't concentrate and do anything on my own, so I soon found it in me to ignore the spy-slits unless she stopped first.

Hold, Jaunda gestured, leaning to peer down into a slit, squinting and then nodding satisfaction. She motioned for me to come closer. *As I've shown you.*

What she'd taught me was either standing or kneeling before the spy slit with bare hands. I pulled off my gloves, tucked them at my belt, and chose to stand with my feet comfortably apart and my hands lower, covering the glyphs. The hair at my nape rose as I felt the magic slither over my hands and bond with them, connecting securely until the release word was uttered.

I had refused to touch the glyphs the first time ordered, taking what abuse came. I wouldn't until Jaunda had explained more *and* told me the release word. She'd laughed but seemed pleased with my forethought. I didn't know much magic, but pure survival had taught me to be cautious about touching runes which sparkled in darkness.

I knew now that those imbued carvings amplified my hearing and sight. I would be able to hear a whisper in the room below; I would be able to see as if I stood only a few paces away or if I concentrated as if peering over a shoulder. I might be able to read a missive being written or a map held at the right angle; I could study expressions in detail.

My first glimpse into this room revealed three individuals down below, and one drew my attention first. My mouth opened in a silent gasp as my heart seized hot before the sensation spread through the rest of me.

Kerse.

The Sathoet with whom I'd sparred and coupled upon the glossy floor surrounded by candles. Now I understood why Jaunda had stopped at this spy-slit.

Had she been looking for this room? Did she know in advance?

I sought more information. There were two female Davrin in the room with him. The door was closed and probably Warded. I studied the ranking female's face, for I did not know her. She was a Priestess and; an older one who sat dignified, her back straight, albeit in a grey, fiberstalk chair more useful for its portability than its grandeur.

Next to her was a small table, again made of fiberstalk, round and decorated with ritual props familiar to me thanks to a blood sister hoping to become a Priestess, but the quality here was much better than Jilrina's had been. One item already in use was the black candle with the red dots, counting each mark and providing enough light to see color. The room itself was rather small and sparse, like an interrogation room with minimum furnishing.

The Priestess herself was ornate, wearing a fashionable headpiece of a stylized black spider which both framed her face with elegance and held her blonde-streaked hair in place. Her gown shifted colors between garnet and amethyst, cut in a classic design that I had seen before, but her silver belt was unique. The decorative end was made up of many tiny chains looped and draped around each other, expansive enough to cradle her left hip in ornate, shining metal against a dark backdrop.

If that belt weren't an heirloom or a status symbol, I'd swallow Tragar piss.

This must be Kerse's Mother.

Qivni had thought I would agitate the Priestess by seducing her son the way I had. Elder D'Shea wouldn't tell me her name but had said I might find out regardless. I'd wondered once or twice before if the Sathoet had been punished for the trade he had made with me, giving me his pet name in exchange for my cunt and giving up the fight, but I could not see anything changed about him.

Even crouching by his Mother, Kerse was taller than her, powerful and monstrous. Same black skin, yellow eyes, and white, shaggy mane of hair that sprouted along his spine to his middle back. Still the ugly, toothy muzzle, bestial face, and intimidating talons on his large hands.

Unlike the first time I'd seen him, a simple, dark green wrap circled his groin and hid his endowment. Somehow, I was sorry about that.

I became aware of Jaunda standing very close behind me. With one hand she swept my cloak to one side and slid the other between my legs, reaching from the back to take a tight grip of my sex through my leathers.

The stiff leather covering her chest pressed into my back, and her mouth was right next to my ear.

"Still and silent," she breathed. "Watch, no matter what. Be prepared to report to our Elder."

I couldn't hand sign with my hands pressed to the glyphs, so whispered, "Yes, Lead."

I had figured this was her intent as soon as she touched me. Remain as I was with my hands pressed to the glyphs, watch the room and focus, even as Jaunda began massaging my crotch through the black leather. I studied the third Davrin.

She was on her knees before the Priestess. She was young, with shorter hair, though not as cropped as Jaunda. She wore a Noble's dress, cut to be loose and teasing around the torso, long to the floor from the waist, with slits on both sides from ankle to mid-thigh. One did not do any hard work wearing such a dress. It was a brilliant blue, and all her jewelry was gold and platinum, accenting her wealth.

I searched for an insignia or something to tell me to which House she belonged, or for her to raise her face off the floor. Perhaps I knew her.

"Rise, Curgia," said the Priestess in a surprisingly low voice, the deepness exceeded only by the Red Sister Prime's hoarse rumble. "As much as I condone prostrating for the glory of Braqth, this is thinly veiled self-indulgence. You try to appeal to my vanity, not to my connection with our Goddess."

Curgia was indeed known to me from Court, and I'd never respected her much. She was greedy and not terribly subtle. She was the Second Daughter of House Itlaun — currently the Tenth — and the merchant had done her share of insulting my Matron of the Twelfth, even as only House Bovritz was between us, and our tasks worked in similar spheres.

The Noble now rose straight but remained on her knees, perhaps thinking more about the grit getting into the quality fabric as her copper eyes flicked downward. From the strands of hair stuck to her temples, I guessed getting on her knees hadn't been the first attempt to persuade the Priestess to give her whatever it was that she sought.

"That is not true, Priestess! I ask in all earnestness. Your recommendation of House Itlaun for the next Worship ball would allow us our first opportunity in four scores of turns to tithe to Braqth well beyond our normal means. We only wish a chance to prove it."

"In exchange for the full term of a Royal Consort."

Jaunda breathed out on my neck and pressed harder on my sex as she massaged me. Sensation and pleasure increased, but I paid very close attention to the conversation.

The young cait tucked a lock of hair behind her ear. "If our offering does not buy us a decade, then we would gladly accept him for only a turn if it pleases you."

"The Valsharess decides the terms, not me. She speaks on your offering."

"Yes, but She speaks through the Priesthood," Curgia replied in a testy tone. "Is there anything I could offer in advance of the auction to persuade you to recommend us to the Queen?"

Kerse's Mother looked briefly offended, and I could guess why; Curgia pushed a blatant transaction that had little veiling of faith. While I did not think other Houses favored with Royal Consorts had claimed them in a procedure much different from this, some theatrics was required.

I imagined the Nobles who gained one were not so clumsy in their presentation to the clergy. My opinion of those "faith auctions" might match Curgia's, but even I knew it wasn't a good idea to show one's impatience and desperation to a Priestess, no matter how many marks I'd been made to stand or kneel before her.

What had I missed thus far? Not only did Kerse's Mother now smile, but she relaxed her previously stiff posture. Eerily similar to the stance a spider takes when it knows its prey can't leave its web and merely waits for mealtime.

"Perhaps there is," the Priestess said. "I require a show of faith, young Curgia. Your distinctly secular vocabulary disturbs me, but perhaps the only problem is that your merchant-bred family has gotten too used to each other, and your manners require only a bit of polish. You do have faith in your Goddess's choices, in Her Valsharess and Her Priestesses, am I right?"

Curgia nodded earnestly. "Of course, I have faith, Wilsira Tachnathon, Chosen of Braqth. That is why I come to you, to help place our House in the path of change. We have seen recent fortune, and it's a sign from the Spider Queen that we must pursue with aggression to get our name out there again!"

I almost winced at more merchant-speak, but at least I knew the Priestess' title, name, and House. She was Wilsira of the Second House Tachna, and she had forgone her birthright, with the Valsharess's approval. Unlike Lelinahdara, who was a favored Daughter but not first-born, Kerse's Mother was First Daughter of her House and would have been acting Matron if she had not had a higher calling. The Second Daughter would be the Matron, but the influence of Wilsira on the House's rule was unavoidable if she wished it to be so.

No wonder Qivni had shaken her head at my taunting this particular Sathoet.

"Will you prove it to me, young Noble, right now beneath the Eight Eyes of Braqth?"

I saw Kerse shift then, raising his head to look at his Mother with interest in his eyes. Curgia didn't notice, or perhaps she merely refused to look at the Sathoet as so many others did, but I felt a shudder go through me as Jaunda's lips closed on my earlobe, and her strokes on my sex grew slower.

"Yes, I will, Priestess. Anything."

Jaunda chuckled lowly, and I realized how hot my crotch had become from her attention, how hot my entire body felt. Between Kerse's suddenly intense eyes, imagining "anything" Curgia might do, and knowing without a doubt what Jaunda *would* do, I shuddered in arousal.

"That's it, novice," Jaunda whispered, unbuckling my belt. "Keep watching."

She let it fall, the sound muffled to the softest *paff* in the passageway and unlaced the leather thongs at my hips to loosen my pants. She slid her hand down my naked flank to my nest of white fur, and I opened my mouth when her finger slipped inside me.

My Lead found me wet, and she sighed with contentment; the sound made me smile, and I pressed my backside against her. A murmur of approval as she thrust her hips forward in return. When she did nothing more than keeping her fingers in my twat, I took the hint to return my attention to the room.

Wilsira let Curgia's last words hang in the air a long time until the Noble began to fidget again. Kerse looked at the young female, leering — a shocking display of insolence if we were in public — but she still did not acknowledge him. I knew how his uneven prick felt inside me, and my own arousal spiked when I imagined him humping her as he had me.

Curgia would dislike it far more than I had.

"Remain on your knees," the Priestess said now, "and place your elbows on the ground. Let us take a moment of reverence for our Lady of the Web."

Curgia hesitated a little but slowly lowered herself to rest on her elbows, still trying to look up at the Priestess. The young Noble's hips were higher up than anything else, so it was easy to imagine Wilsira walking behind her, lifting her dress up, and inviting Kerse to mount her. Curgia wasn't a warrior; I wondered if she would fight or just protest?

"Place your forehead on the ground."

Nothing was quick about this; I heard murmured prayers for several ticks, first spoken by Wilsira and required repeating by Curgia. The Noble kept her eyes down and subtly brought her legs together while she prayed, as Kerse weaved slowly to his Mother's voice.

Finally, the elder Priestess stood up from her chair and walked toward the worshipping trader, circling around her as I had imagined, although Kerse stayed where he was. Wilsira tapped her own cheek with a bejeweled finger, her expression thoughtful and self-satisfied. I glanced at Kerse again; he had an erection beneath that cloth.

"Is it you?" Wilsira asked.

"Priestess?" the younger replied in confusion.

"Who is to conceive first, should your House be favored with a Consort? Is it you?"

I saw Curgia swallow; I wasn't sure why. If she was the one negotiating, then why shouldn't she enjoy the fruits first?

"The Ball is mere cycles away, a cluster of marks," the Priestess continued. "Do you purify yourself?"

"Uh —"

Wilsira lifted Curgia's dress to expose her backside, smirking as she looked. Like most who were well-off at Court, Curgia had no underclothes. The young Noble's legs squeezed together, making it hard to see her sex even if I hadn't been at a side-view. But her dark skin was smooth, her curves softer and fleshier than mine for being mercantile over military. Curgia moved to push up on her arms, a knee shifting forward as she opened her mouth to say something.

"Stay as you are!" Wilsira barked.

It echoed through the glyphs and hurt my ears. Jaunda hissed in discomfort, and her frigging stopped for a moment.

We all waited as Curgia stiffened then reluctantly settled again. The Priestess leaned down and took a dignified whiff of her scent, not thrusting her nose into the Noble's crotch at all but inhaling the warm air near her skin. Wilsira stroked and patted the young Davrin's haunches before straightening herself, leaving the dress resting on her hips. I saw a spread of tiny bumps arise on Curgia's flesh and knew she felt vulnerable.

"I can smell it," the Priestess said, walking around to the front again. "The fertility potions, their essence seeping through your skin. You *have* been preparing, I daresay bathing your insides with them. So certain of your success, are you?"

"Hopeful," the young one murmured. "Why not give it the best chance? It is my Matron's goal, I will do whatever I can to make it so."

"Indeed. Not aging well, is she? That she'd want you as the broodmare."

"I was chosen, and I am loyal to my House."

"And the status means nothing to you?"

"Status means everything. That's why I'm here."

"But you have been saying you're not here primarily for yourself," the Priestess continued. "If your House were favored with a Consort, could you see another sister or cousin conceive first, ahead of you?"

Curgia was silent.

"I've given you much of my time, Noble, and you've said many things. I want to know if you will back them up, in the name of Braqth. If your House is worthy of my support."

The young Noble's body language showed signs of nerves and dread; I could see her toes flex in her sandals; her chest expanded, and her bottom lip trembled. "How?"

"Give up your own plans to conceive first, and I will grant my recommendation to House Itlaun at the Ball."

Curgia tentatively raised her head, and when she wasn't shouted at again, she looked up. Her expression seemed to ask, *That's all?*

I thought she was right to be suspicious. How would that benefit Wilsira? Why would she even care who conceived first at House Itlaun?

"You'll notice I added 'first'." Wilsira smiled encouragingly, still without the sadism I had expected to see. "You may still conceive. Doesn't that speak well for the length of the term that your House might keep a Consort?"

Curgia nodded carefully. "Yes, Priestess."

"So? Can you give up the first claim, young merchant?"

The air was heavy with expectation, and the merchant had trouble coming to terms with the deal. She wanted to make a counteroffer, but she wasn't in the position — literally and socially — to do so. All her usual tactics were useless, and she was at a loss. She could only agree or refuse and leave, and House Itlaun would not have another chance at a Consort for another generation.

Jaunda and I waited in near stillness for her answer. I'd been watching Kerse, too, and his interest in the exchange had not wavered. He was attentive, listening to everything.

"Very well," Curgia said, the bitterness loaded in her throat. "I will … give up the first claim if you will recommend my House for Braqth's Blessing at this Worship Ball."

The elder Priestess nodded in satisfaction. "I still require a guarantee, a show of faith. I know merchants find ways to go back on a deal or get around it."

"It is a sacred agreement, Priestess, I would not dare!"

Braqth's Chosen finally chuckled; she showed me what I'd been waiting to see. What I always figured I'd seen in a Priestess.

"And you know how well our own Lady-Goddess changes her mind."

The young Noble's mouth hung open as she tried to work out the Priestess' faith yet acknowledged how fickle the Goddess really was, especially compared to a merchant. There was no answer of which I knew.

In that hesitation, Wilsira gestured to Kerse, who came forward eagerly, crouching again beside his Mother. She stroked his mane and reached casually to untuck his groin wrap and pull it away, displaying the first sight I'd ever had of the Sathoet, his member turgid and ready to breed.

Curgia's eyes widened considerably. She shook her head in denial.

"Where is that guarantee, Curgia?" the Priestess asked, and I could hear the threat in her deep voice. "Show me the faith in our agreement."

The younger Davrin trembled. "What guarantee do you want?"

"See to my son's needs."

Kerse scooted forward on all fours and crawled partly over Curgia's prone body, his erection aimed at her flushed, purple lips as the white crown of her head brushed against his dark belly.

"This is interesting," Jaunda said. She started to grind herself against my backside as her fingers fucked me.

I agreed. I couldn't tear my eyes away.

"Do not deny him, Curgia. Or you deny Braqth and me."

Curgia shivered again as Kerse snuffled her backside, rumbling low in his chest as his Mother watched with blazing eyes. The young female was desperate to find justification for letting the rigid, demonic rod slip past her teeth.

Come on, merchant, what else can you do? I thought. *With all those fertility potions in your blood, just be glad he isn't plundering your slit.*

Kneeling Curgia must have had the same thought because she suddenly opened her mouth and took him as far as she could, actually making an effort to please him. I saw a flash of a pink tongue as she tilted her head, licking and swirling on his cock, and Kerse rumbled louder, his muscles tightening as he stretched his throat and lifted his head upward, a drop of spit falling onto her exposed buttocks.

"Good," Wilsira said. "Sign that you agree. You shall draw out his seed."

I watched Curgia hand sign that with her mouth full. I had been where she was now many times already, in the Cloister. Watching her brought back so many recent memories, not the least of which was my rut with this same Sathoet. The way he humped at the Noble's throat now, with some restraint as he glanced twice at his Priestess, reminded me that he could be tamed. That I had tamed him.

I looked at his Mother, tried picking up subtle signals from her, and Wilsira gave him a smile of adoration when he made Curgia gag. Jaunda dry humped my ass, going harder, and it was getting distracting.

"Just fuck me, Lead!" I hissed.

She licked my ear and pinched my clit, pleasure-pain streaking up my front. "Drooling cunt wants it, huh?"

"B-badly. Please, Lead."

"Gimme a flick."

I wasn't the only one drooling as Kerse used his huge hands to maul Curgia, first fumbling underneath for her breasts, pawing at her sides, and then moving to squeeze and knead her exposed haunches. It didn't take long before he licked and slobbered in her crack. I heard Curgia squeak and squeal a few times, writhing along his underbelly, adding to his pleasure. I remembered the way Kerse had licked me from nub to pucker as well, and even surprised, I had enjoyed it.

Jaunda had eased off me; her hands drew back to prepare her Feldeu. My wet slit pulsed once in desire, aching for penetration as I watched Kerse have his fun thrusting into a Noble's mouth. I couldn't remove my hands from the wall to push down my own pants; I had to wait for Jaunda's strong hands to shove them down. She did so impatiently, kicking my ankles apart before aiming the head of her toy between my legs.

She pressed in, spearing inside me with one stroke.

"Fuck!" my Lead gasped happily as I choked on a groan. "Such a hot cunt!"

And hers was a hot cock. She could feel my body heat through the phallus, and I could feel hers.

My Lead knew the moment I squeezed her with my muscle, and the force of Jaunda's answering thrusts pushed me closer to the stone. It wasn't hard to imagine Jaunda and Kerse experiencing similar sensations, though my Lead would climax without the messy spurting that I secretly still craved.

I wondered if Curgia would take demonic cream in her mouth or somewhere else. I could feel my own lubricant cooling on my thighs as I repositioned my head to look back through the slit, as Jaunda serviced herself and me. Kerse thrust harder down Curgia's throat, and she was gagged often.

I heard something, the barest whisper. Unfortunately, with Jaunda gasping in my ear, I couldn't tell what was said, but Kerse lifted his head to look at his Mother and withdrew smoothly from the Noble's mouth as she coughed and sputtered, tears staining her cheeks. He moved to the side, and Wilsira came closer as Curgia lifted her strained gaze, her own spittle glistening on her chin.

"That is enough, then?" she gasped, and the Priestess frowned in displeasure.

Short memory, I thought. *You didn't draw his seed.*

"I promise to conceive second —"

Curgia's eyes bugged out as the Sathoet moved behind and quickly mounted her. Although her legs were still together, his member was slick enough to drive straight into her sex whether she was open or not, and Curgia shouted in outrage. Jaunda fucked me harder against the wall as she groaned.

"Stop him!" the Noble shouted, trying to twist out of the half-demon's grip. "Please, he feels disgusting! Deformed!"

Wilsira stiffened in anger, her bejeweled fingers tightening. She spoke coolly. "I will have that guarantee, Curgia."

"But I promised, Priestess! I will let my older sister conceive of the Consort first!"

"Of course, you will. You shall have no choice."

With no further explanation, Curgia tried to scramble away, unwisely kicking at Kerse, thus widening her legs and giving the Sathoet opportunity to strengthen his hold on the struggling merchant. He thrust in deeper.

"Oh, Priestess, I can't … Don't do this — "

I gritted my teeth as my Sister rammed into me, harder than Kerse was into Curgia, as the Lead came with a growl. Then Jaunda reached around to brush my wildly buzzing clit as I watched the Sathoet open his mouth, showing sharp teeth as he snarled.

He's going to do it …

Kerse's thighs and buttocks flexed as he stopped thrusting but pressed in hard, his claws pressing against her flesh without drawing blood. The demonblood roared, and abruptly I hit my peak as well, imagining his seed spraying deep into her fertile core. Curgia wailed.

"No," the Noble swallowed a sob before looking to the Mother of the creature pulling out of her. "Why?"

Wilsira smiled. There was the sadism of a Priestess. "Can you not see his aura, Curgia? *That* is power. He is of Davrin blood, Noble, conceived through ritual. Part of me. He is my own. You would think this a more divine gift than a stupid, pretty toy of weaker magic, would you not?"

The young Davrin shuddered in disgust, shaking her head, her shorter hair hiding part of her face. "I don't … I wanted —"

"I know what you wanted."

The Priestess nodded at the Sathoet, and he began to rub himself stiff again. He looked hungry enough that I didn't think it a problem to go for a second breeding.

"You must earn what you want, merchant, as do we all."

"Please, if there's anything I can do that will … If you will help me end it, Priestess, if I should catch …"

Wilsira sighed in disappointment. Jaunda bit my neck and pulled her Feldeu out just as Kerse shuffled up to mount Curgia, who glanced back and gasped in horror. She tried to move forward, but the Priestess stood in the way.

Wilsira caressed herself from breast to mound in one smooth gesture through her luxurious gown before petting Kerse's mane. His cock was seated in Curgia again by then, and he moved as enthusiastically as he had the first time.

My Lead was watching over my shoulder, catching her breath. "Well played. Wilsira has her in her pocket."

I nodded, breathing deep as she wiped us both down with a pouch cloth, laced up her pants and had begun to pull up mine — all the while my hands still firm on the wall. By that time Kerse roared again, leaving Curgia's snatch as stretched and soggy as mine had been with Kain.

Shit. I stopped breathing, kept my mouth closed. *Shit! Don't think about that.*

We stayed to see if there was any further discussion, but Wilsira made no such offer, and Curgia could barely pick herself up off the floor as she wiped the tears from her cheeks. Her dress and hair were mussed but, overall, she didn't look too different from when she'd walked in, merely as though she'd been in a small room for a long time and was frazzled.

"I shall escort you out myself," Wilsira said, reattaching Kerse's green groin cloth and petting him again. He was panting and looked a little sweaty.

Curgia said nothing, but her back straightened when the door opened, and the Noble tried her best to pretend that her puffy eyes wouldn't give her away. Jaunda had stepped away from the spy slit then while I had just murmured the release word and lifted my hand from one glyph. Kerse moved to follow the two females out.

I froze when the Sathoet slowed for a moment and looked behind him. He looked directly at the wall which contained the slit, though I knew it was camouflaged with magic. He smiled. Almost as if his blank, yellow eyes looked right at me.

Then he left, the door closing behind him.

I stayed still for an extra moment, my heart delayed in its return to normal as I considered the possibility that Kerse had sensed us somehow. He couldn't have heard us. Had he just been looking back into the room with fondness at what had just occurred? I couldn't know for sure unless I saw him face-to-face again.

Not a good idea.

Most of my Sisters had teased me at one point or another about my first challenge against the Sathoet, about him giving up his name to me. All of them had so much as said that it would be stupid to be purposefully in the same room with Kerse and his Mother, and now I had seen one reason why. Should I tell Jaunda about the glance, or should I keep another secret? What would she even do about it?

Jaunda tapped my shoulder and signed, ★What're you waiting for?★

I hurried to don my belt and correct my uniform for the ninth time that cycle, focusing on my body to shore up my disconcerted mind.

★Nothing,★ I signed back, face placid. ★Good show.★

Chapter 16

Elder D'Shea was in the process of dressing up her uniform when we were bid to enter. She had set out a few pieces which would enhance the beauty of it, transforming it from the practical into the formal. She was heading out soon, likely to the Palace and something to do with the Valsharess. While she was calm, the thought raised the hairs on the back of my neck.

"Report," she ordered after the door closed on its own.

"We found them, Elder," said Jaunda. "Removed from the common space, and they'd been there a while before we saw them."

The Sorceress nodded once, her face set in a frown as she considered the pieces of her rank. She spoke without looking at us. "What did you witness, Lead?"

"Priestess Wilsira breaking another young Noble. Toeing the line, as usual. Sirana saw the details."

"Oh?" My sponsor glanced over her shoulder at me with a small smile, fitting a bracer just right. "Thank you, Jaunda. I believe Elder Rausery was looking for additional hands for a border excursion. Present yourself and yours, see if she has need of your team."

Jaunda smirked and nodded. "Yes, Elder."

"But first find Gaelan and send her to me."

"Yes, Elder." Jaunda made a respectful bow to D'Shea, winked at me, and strode out, all power and confidence as she went to fulfill her Elder's commands.

"How goes the training, Sirana?"

I blinked away from the door just closed. The Sorceress gestured me forward, making it clear she wanted me to assist in putting on her decorations. I had to split my focus between noting her hand signals on how to dress her and answering her question.

"I've improved my endurance and patience, Elder," I answered, "to keep up as your Lead and Lunents run me through courses. I've laid eyes on political figures before, but this was the first of personal connection to me."

"You've met Wilsira before?"

I frowned; I wagered she knew I hadn't. "No, Elder. Kerse, the Sathoet. He was with her. You and Lead Qivni warned me about his Mother after how I chose to handle him during my trials."

She merely smiled, waiting as I floundered to pick up the next piece. I chose a blue-ribbon brooch.

"That piece goes on after this one." She swapped it with another small bracket of pure silver. "Now give me your report, Sirana. All of it."

I slowly attached the bracket before accepting the ribbon bar, working to get it level on her chest. "Lead showed me many of the tunnels and spy-slits we use through the Palace and Sanctuary."

"Showed them again."

"Yes, Elder. This time we were in them long enough I have a rough map in my head."

"Excellent. Continue."

"I looked in some of the spy-slits, but without touching the glyphs, I only sensed impressions of residents doing mundane tasks, and Lead wasn't for loitering much. She found the small meeting room as if she'd been looking for it, or something like it. I know it was on purpose. She put me on the glyphs to witness, and I recognized the Sathoet."

Elder D'Shea nodded without acknowledging this, lining up the next three bits for me and indicating their order and placement. "Go over the entire scene once. I want objective detail first. Your impressions may be invited after."

I described it once all the way through first without "impressions," also trying to minimize how often Jaunda distracted me.

"Interesting," my Elder said without much reaction. "What are your thoughts on this?"

"Anything specific, Elder?"

"Just talk, Sirana."

"Curgia didn't pander to Braqth enough, in the Priestess' view," I commented. "Or she had early on, and Wilsira wore her down enough, so the Noble revealed a weak mask."

The Sorceress nodded once. We finished decorating her uniform, and she was now doing her own hair to make sure it was perfect. As she lifted her tresses up, we could meet eyes in the mirror.

I continued, "Kerse seemed to expect being included in the 'negotiation.' He watched his Mother, became erect almost on command. Like he was trained. I was not surprised that Wilsira used him to humiliate the Noble by rutting her, but the Priestess' confidence that Curgia would catch seemed misplaced." I thought about Jaunda's comment, of Curgia being in Wilsira's pocket. "Maybe it was only the merchant's belief it would happen that Wilsira will use to torment her for a while."

"Oh? Why do you think so, Sirana?"

I shrugged. "I've never seen or heard of any female bearing a baby sired by a Sathoet. Most Nobles I knew assumed they are sterile."

"The Priestesses' half-breed sons are not sterile," Elder D'Shea said soberly. "But they are not allowed to breed. It's the Priestesses who are sterile, from birthing those very sons."

I blinked in shock. "But ... the Royal Consorts. They're Priestess sons, too, aren't they?"

D'Shea smiled unpleasantly. "They are, yes. And quite fertile, allowed to breed by order of the Valsharess. As a Red Sister, Sirana, you'll not make this known."

I nodded. "Yes, Elder. But how do the Priestesses have Consorts? Is it before they have the Sathoet?"

"Another time, perhaps, after you've witnessed more." The Sorceress had her hair pulled off her neck in an elegant sweep. "For now, focus on what you saw this cycle."

I thought over this yet again. "I think I understand Lead saying Wilsira was 'toeing the line.'"

"She always does because she can. Curgia won't bear that creature, but she will be tortured with it for a while. Her will tested for usefulness. We'll watch House Itlaun, as it's not clear to me why Wilsira wants the Second Daughter, but it's not the first time Wilsira seeks to make another bargain in exchange for aborting something the Queen has forbidden anyway."

I pondered this as well. "Wilsira commented Kerse was part of her, that his gift of offspring was more powerful than the Consorts, who are just 'stupid, pretty toys.' She prefers her demonblood son to any breeder."

D'Shea chuckled. "Yes. That is telling. In some ways, she's right. The Consorts are beautiful and make beautiful children. Most have the magical strength to offer a lineage, but they aren't trained to use it themselves. They are not taught to read or to cast. They are show-studs rented out to the pious bidder. Their ability to carry a conversation of any interest varies remarkably, but most Matrons don't care."

Indeed, my Mother hadn't.

While Elder D'Shea wrapped a black sash around her waist, my thoughts wandered to the Consort I'd attacked. He had been pretty and delicate, performed no casting, yet he had not seemed vapid to me.

Those eyes.

Sometimes I still dreamed about him. Writhing under me, equally desperate to contain his release as I was to bring it out. And he had tasted of strong magic.

I dared to ask. "Did you ever learn why that one Consort was alone and unprotected where I could find him, Elder?"

D'Shea turned around, stepping to retrieve her cloak from the wall hook. "That is not your concern, Sirana. Your thoughts should be on Wilsira and her son. They may become dangerous to you."

So, she spoke it plainly at last. Very well.

"What have you seen of a Sathoet's abilities, Elder?" I asked instead. "Can they be trained to detect other presences the way a mage can?"

My superior stared straight at my eyes then, held them, and when I didn't move but waited, she slowly smiled. "What have *you* seen, Sirana?"

"I don't know, Elder."

"Unacceptable. What do you *think* you've seen?"

I was quiet for a moment. "How powerful are those glyphs at the spy-slits?"

"Very," she answered, never blinking. "You know it's impossible for your hands to slip by accident once activated, and no Davrin has natural senses strong enough to detect what we don't want them to detect."

"Who made the glyphs?" I countered. "How do we know that there isn't some weakness? The Sisterhood doesn't use as much magic as the P —"

D'Shea slapped me, and the echo faded as we stayed still for a few moments. When she didn't admonish me further, her expression strangely peaceful, I took it that she didn't forbid me to think along those lines. She was warning me about grappling the wrong topics out loud, and too soon. It was not the first time she had done this. In her own way, she trained me as much as Jaunda.

"What did you see Kerse do, Sirana?" she asked with an unspoken promise. There would be consequences worse than a stinging cheek if I deflected the question again.

"He was the last to leave the room," I said, my chin down. "He stopped and smiled behind him at the empty space. He seemed to look straight at me. I don't know for sure that he knew I was there."

"Given what I've told you, why do you think he would?"

My chin was still down. "I had whispered the release word and removed one hand from the glyphs before he exited the door."

"Mistake," she said. "Don't repeat it. Always wait until they have all left." A pause. "Right hand or left removed?"

"Left."

She frowned. "You're sure. And the other was still in place."

I nodded. "Yes, Elder."

"Had you moved your feet?"

"No."

"And where was Jaunda?"

"Five steps to my right, facing the wall."

She was quiet before she stepped past me to check her room before we left, as was her habit. I resigned myself not to be privy to her thoughts; I so often wasn't anyway. My cheek still stung, and I decided I wouldn't have another.

Elder D'Shea paused in front of me. She was awe-inspiring in her dress uniform; the balance of red and black meant she would match a backing of Sisters, but the blue and gold accents made her stand out as one of our leaders. This was not something to do on a mission or in battle, but it was something to do at Court and the Palace.

"He couldn't have heard or smelled you," D'Shea said now, and I was stunned that she'd given me that. "The only glyph you deactivated was to enhance your own senses. All other wards were still in place. Unless you slipped your other hand without realizing?"

She raised an eyebrow as I shook my head, eye contact not wavering. "My hand did not move, Elder. I remember the grit beneath all five fingers and the magic in my palm."

Slowly she nodded; she looked to believe me.

"This isn't an ability you know of the Sathoet?" I asked cautiously.

My superior half-smiled. "Each one has a different sire. Only their mothers know what they might expect from their heritage as they grow, but the Valsharess, the Prime, and I keep them in check. Meanwhile, we watch, learn, and catalog. It is disturbing that he might be able to sense through powerful wards. We'll work on determining that for sure. He *is* one of the oldest Sathoet sons."

My white brows lifted with interest. "How old, Elder?"

"Nearly five hundred."

Sobering. I wasn't yet one hundred. I had also never seen a full-blooded Davrin male who was that old. Only females. Maybe it was easier to understand why the Priestess preferred his company to the young, pretty Consorts if the two had been together that long. And I'd teased that ancient son; I'd fucked him the same as I had my previous conquests. No wonder Qivni rolled her eyes.

"Would Wilsira know if he developed this strength?" I asked.

"Of course," D'Shea answered. "That's what is disturbing. She dotes on him more than most Priestesses do, and he is loyal to her. She controls him, and she has been using every aspect of him to her advantage for the past three centuries."

"And yet he told me his name," I commented.

She gave me a sharp look. "Nothing to be smug about, Sirana. Coaxing a Sathoet to stray from his Priestess is dangerous. Do not think one coupling somehow gives you real sway over a creature conditioned to do what she tells him."

"But I did just that," I countered. "If his conditioning were absolute, I would never have gotten his name. He would have broken my body and done as his mother said."

My Elder's face hardened. "Meaning what exactly?"

"He has freer will than she knows. She's underestimating him. He could even be hiding that new ability from her. He waited until she'd left the room to look behind him like that, she never saw it."

D'Shea's mouth twitched. "Perhaps that was accidental. He knows what benefits him."

"Are you underestimating his intelligence, Elder?"

"Are you overestimating it?" she shot back. "I've been watching him and his kind for my whole life. Perhaps his conditioning isn't ironclad, perhaps he can be clever now and then, but he is still not capable of intricate, lasting plots, Sirana. Sathoet appetites are immediate, and they are easily distracted by opportunity. If Kerse can sense beyond the glyphs and if Wilsira doesn't know now, then assume she will in the near future. Distraction followed by renewed loyalty to his Mother is one thing the Sathoet sons all have in common, and it has never changed."

I was surprised my other cheek wasn't stinging by now, as much as I'd been debating even in the privacy of her quarters.

"That boldness spoke well for you in the trials, Sirana," she said, "but

I tell you now, don't pursue him for pride. You do not have the experience to take on Wilsira and *not* end up like Curgia."

I stood, uncertain. "Was that what you wanted me to learn? To be wary and afraid of a Priestess? After handling her son. After what you said about Jilrina's memory holding me back?"

Elder D'Shea didn't answer that. "I have plans for you that don't include that Priestess, Sirana. As your knowledge grows, so will your reach. I promise you that if you obey me and pay attention. Until then," she patted my sore cheek like I was a child, "don't be reckless and get on the wrong side of Braqth's Chosen. Avoid her offspring where you can. He'll forget you if he hasn't already."

D'Shea had longevity and experience I could not discount, and perhaps it was paranoia more than curiosity which made me think Kerse was lying in wait for something, withholding abilities his mother didn't know he possessed. Maybe I thought this only because my own sister had underestimated me in the same way.

She hadn't seen it coming.

He smiled at me. I am ... almost certain he did.

"Yes, Elder. I will obey. And pay attention."

GAELAN AND I FLANKED D'SHEA AS WE EXITED A BACK PASSAGE INTO A CAN-dlelit hallway. We were three distinct Sisters; the one in the dress uniform of red and black, the pure red one, and the solid black one. There in the hall, for all to see.

I wondered if I stood out as much as my superior except as the trainee rather than the commander, or did the mixture of black into the Sisterhood's dress confuse those who knew little of our inner workings? It soothed my ego to think so as we passed cautious Nobles, Palace Guards, and servants. I wouldn't act like a novice.

D'Shea had only said one thing to us before we left, her eyes conveying unspoken punishment if we embarrassed her. "Do not speak and do only what I tell you."

Gaelan had let me go in front of her, and she pinched my ass before we left. I had jumped but made no sound.

"Too tense, Sister," my superior said without looking behind at us.

I shot a glare at Gaelan; she just winked in response. Her lips drew my attention as she smiled, and I recalled them pressed soft and hot on my sex. I decided to relax and let my irritation go.

This young Red Sister was a defender for me. I'd never had any defenders before but knew Gaelan, Jaunda, and Elder D'Shea were real. Excessive taunting or harassment in the Cloister had lessened lately as I seemed to get over an unseen hump. Since the beginning, Jaunda's laugh and Gaelan's sexy smile were rewards which improved the experience of just staying alive.

They accept me. They enjoy me, I enjoy them.

Elder D'Shea's authority and leadership were real as well, and hard-earned, and I felt like an apprentice even without any mage talent. My sullen, childish Court attitude had taken so many beatings since this began in the wilderness that I wasn't sure what was genuine in me when I compared myself to them. I was still figuring out what they saw.

Perhaps Gaelan pinched my bottom as a reminder. *Bend, don't break. You can be that confident, you can laugh like Jaunda.*

Later. Not on the way to stand before the Valsharess.

I wondered when the next potential recruit might come into our midst. Would it take a few turns, or decades? How long had Gaelan waited for me to arrive? How much did that change D'Shea's focus? I had yet to ask my closest Sister; our Elder kept Gaelan busy, and there had been barely enough time for me to submit to a quick fuck to relieve stress, spreading my legs to her Feldeu.

We had yet to trade places; I wasn't sure if it was allowed yet, or if she wanted to. I wanted to. I wanted to try fucking my closest Sister with that magic tool.

D'Shea paused outside a chamber, the immense, ornate double-door empty of the Palace Guard. With a motion of pure grace from the Sorceress, the door swung inward as if by an invisible hand. We entered a chamber filled to the brim with decoration and banner, the walls lit by just enough smokeless torchlight to display the vibrant purples, golds, and reds, accented by blue and black.

The theme of the decorations could not be missed: webs and spiders, wands and potions, swords and daggers and arrows. Everything and everywhere that we were strong. My mouth twitched when I noted the lack of many shields.

Maybe they're just not those you can see.

Expression left my face when I saw the formidable, aged Davrin sitting straight-backed on the onyx and basalt throne. The crown woven into her blonde hair was elegant gold laced with diamond and amethyst, integrated with a few rubies. Her robes wound about her body in shimmering, bright bands of gold and purple; her long neck, shoulders, and a hint of cleavage exposed but otherwise, all skin from Her wrists to Her black-slipper feet were covered.

She was much older than the Red Sister Prime, with similar wrinkles at her eyes and the corners of her mouth. At the moment, She looked as stern. Unlike the Red Sister Prime, however, I could tell the Queen had been a beauty in her prime. Even now Her presence filled the room, drawing all eyes to Her.

I had been instructed on how to bow to Her fifteen turns ago upon coming to Court, though I hadn't needed to very often. It had been at large balls or congregations where She made an appearance, and the Court or the public would bow together in a massive wave of white-haired heads and colorful fabric. With only three Red Sisters directly before Her, I was much more self-conscious. I must have been passable because nobody seemed to notice me specifically.

After that all-encompassing moment, I glanced at movement in my peripheral right. A group of robed attendants stood nearby with two Priestesses I didn't know, one with her Sathoet, and several non-Davrin slaves were face down on the ground and averting their gaze.

"Our Greetings, Elder D'Shea." The Valsharess's rich voice filled the chamber, though I'd have almost thought it distracted.

The Sorceress bowed deeply again and gave a more extended greeting, acknowledging our Queen's power, titles, and a prayer of continued longevity. I had a hard time focusing on the exact words, for when prayers lasted longer than three flicks and could be interchanged with pandering, I thought about something else. Old habit.

I nearly missed my cue when the Valsharess gestured, and we stepped to the side opposite of the small entourage. D'Shea remained beautifully still, and I was not sure how she did it. Gaelan and I could only flank her like rigid statues.

We waited long enough that the Valsharess audibly sighed just before the door opened again and a larger group of Red Sisters came through: Elder Rausery, Lead Qivni, Lunent Agalia, and three others I did meet once but needed a prompt. Forty-something naked caits all look alike from below.

Elder Rausery bowed with her five as well, gave a similar greeting as D'Shea had, and at the Queen's acceptance, stepped to the side to join us while a few Priestesses arrived just behind her. The Elders mostly ignored the Sanctuary females, and Rausery was close enough for me to hear her say out of the corner of her mouth, "Only the two starters, D'Shea?"

My superior smirked, looking straight ahead as the Priestesses gave their own dance before the Valsharess. "Spry enough to hit their mark on time. Were you napping?"

Rausery snorted softly. "Finding errands for your ass-scratchers. I hope you don't need them any time soon."

A delicate shrug. "Jaunda likes it outside of the city. It was her turn."

I wasn't sure whether this was good news or not. I'd heard D'Shea instruct Jaunda to go find Rausery to "help." Perhaps the intent had been to delay Rausery so D'Shea would reach the throne room first? But then Jaunda would be gone for longer than this meeting. Maybe Rausery being late would have happened anyway, given the first time I'd met the Elder inside the Cloister.

It did tell me something interesting, at least. Rausery took her leadership seriously enough to task all Red Sisters who came to her, even D'Shea's most loyal and even as far as being late for a royal meeting. Politics and appearances didn't drive her the way it did a Matron or perhaps

245

my own superior. And she had mentioned something about "the test of the streets."

Plus, she must be able to get away with it.

I supposed all that mattered was how the Valsharess interpreted it. She had sighed with impatience but said nothing. What followed was an overview of the upcoming Worship Ball, and for which the entourage on the right had been preparing for as long as I had been scrambling to make it back to civilization. I had missed a lot of what was going on in Court being fucked and tested in the Red Sisters' secret Cloister.

Doesn't matter. You're not a Noble anymore. You have no House.

It would be a formal ball, and there would be a feast and dance with fertility rituals at which all those present would gawk. The season's Royal Consorts would be exchanged or re-gifted, with the introduction of any new ones coming out into society. Those "virgins" would be premium; new blood and beauty traits not yet introduced to the Houses; young buas ready to quicken Noble wombs and trained to attain multiple erections in one session.

Aside from imagining the altar sex, I found the details excruciating in their fastidiousness. A lot went into these events but thank goddess it wasn't my responsibility. I had been to only one ball at Court, for these happened every five to ten turns, but had sneaked off quickly enough with some Noble sons willing to play.

What I hadn't realized then was that the Red Sisters had been present but invisible, except for a handful. The visible ones were to assist the Priestesses and keep the peace, to remind the Nobles of their manners. Elders D'Shea and Rausery had brought the next handful from which the Valsharess would select the visible red uniforms at this new ball.

Understanding this, Rausery's objection when she first walked in made more sense. Why would D'Shea have only brought the two of us, the two youngest, with one still in black leathers, no less? Weren't we called the Red Sisters for a reason?

The Queen won't choose me. I won't match the decorations.

Our Valsharess rose to her feet when She had finished with the entourage to the right of the throne. She approached us, and we stood at attention and silent.

"Volunteers, step forward," the Queen said, and we all did except for D'Shea and Rausery.

She scrutinized each of us in turn, face impassive as She inspected the six in red with a pause in between. She said nothing, gave no indication whether they were selected or not. Then She reached me and paused again. I was looking straight ahead and over her shoulder. I heard only the murmuring of the celebration planners in the chamber; the Queen said nothing, and yet I felt an unrelenting urge to look up at Her face.

I resisted.

"Look at Us, Red Sister."

My heart skipped, and my eyes flicked to the most consequential Davrin face in Sivaraus. I stopped breathing. The Valsharess' eyes were strange. A pale, tawny yellow, as if they should have been bright copper but had become faded with Her immense age. Somehow still those eyes were enhanced by Her blonde hair and golden crown. Her gaze was glassy and eerie, however, her thoughts unreadable, and I was not pleased that She paid particular attention to me. I was sure it was because of my eye color.

To the Abyss with blue eyes.

The Valsharess reached up to touch my chin. I couldn't believe it. For an instant, I wanted to break away and run. I felt a quiver pass through me and remained at attention. The barest touch of spun silk brushed my jaw, breathy in its contact yet with a spark of magic. I froze, pure fear surging as I struggled to swallow my heart back down out of my throat. Sweat popped out at my temples, the pounding in my chest making my balance seem wobbly.

Goddess, so powerful.

I thought of Elder D'Shea, of her confidence in me.

I will not break.

The corner of the Queen's mouth twitched once. The age lines were noticeable this close.

"Hm," She grunted and turned away, taking that suffocating presence with her. I was grateful. She didn't speak until She was seated and, even then, we had to wait.

"All of them are selected," She announced. "Acceptable, Elders. You are dismissed."

We bowed as one — myself slightly behind — and left the audience hall. My knees felt like water, and I relearned how to breathe in measured draws. It was not until we'd reached a different passageway and entered through a new hidden door that either of our superiors spoke. It was Rausery who spoke first.

"Eight spans, D'Shea," she whispered, growling even then. "Blue Eyes isn't in her reds yet."

"She is acceptable, our Queen said so," the other replied. I was curious why she sounded smug about it. "This is not a difficult duty for a novice. Why did you bring your Lead and Lunent if you did not expect Her to select them, too?"

"You didn't bring enough selection," the warrior rumbled. "That's why She took the black, too."

Both leaders fell silent as they realized how hard we were listening to their whispers. I wasn't quite following, but it was interesting to me all the same. I shared a curious look with Gaelan, who only smiled. She couldn't see my anxiety, but Qivni could sense it and spoke up.

"Sirana does not know enough about these Balls, Elders," the Lead said. "What are the consequences if she embarrasses us?"

"Are you volunteering to cram that education in two cycles, Lead?" Rausery tossed over her shoulder, and while Qivni hesitated, it was barely noticeable.

"If you command me, Elder, I will."

"Noted. Might be a good idea."

D'Shea's reply was smooth. "It would be my decision, Rausery, not yours."

"And what would you 'decide,' D'Shea? Not to unroll the scroll, but do you *have* the time to squeeze the novice in?"

Someone behind Qivni snorted, and the Lead darted a look at the Sister, who fell silent. Meanwhile, the challenge had risen to a real debate.

"You were late," D'Shea replied. "What do you care how Sirana makes us look? The Prime wasn't even there, why should you be? You both prefer being on the rough grounds and leaving me to the goings-on of the Sanctuary and the Palace."

Rausery shook her head once. "It's your talent, but I'm also not stupid. I know the Palace duties count as much as anything else. I was only late because you sent Jaunda to me at just the right time."

"Oh, yes," the irony was audible. "I planned that perfectly, didn't I?"

"You sure as fuck did. What game are you playing?"

"Nothing. It was my Lead's request for all she's done. You and the Prime approved, and *you* selected the time. You could have waited until after the Ball, Rausery."

The older Davrin narrowed her eyes. "Right. I know you well enough by now, Sorceress."

D'Shea huffed a breath as a laugh. "Think of it this way. Most present at the Worship Ball will be yours. You will have more eyes and ears there than me."

I could have sworn Elder Rausery had rolled her eyes, even as I stared at her back while we walked. "Those reports are boring as fuck."

"Then trade them to me when you need what Jaunda brings back."

Rausery considered that all of two flicks. "Slippery Sorceress."

We'd reached the Cloister through the maze when Rausery stopped and stared hard at D'Shea as if trying to pierce her with her eyes. My superior calmly looked back, and all of us lowbies were enjoying the frank back-and-forth even as we also knew the two talked about plans outside our imminent scope. I stood at the Sorceress' left shoulder while Gaelan was on her right, and it was only as I glanced at the two of them that Rausery moved.

I knew the eldest warrior was fast, but I still wasn't used to it. Her hand closed tight around my forearm, holding me when I tried to pull away. Next D'Shea's hand caught my opposite elbow, gripping not quite as hard, but I was still pulled between them.

"Rausery," my Elder warned.

"We will prepare her," Rausery said. "I can make the time to do some Palace work. 'Bout time I got to know the new blood, anyway. You will get her back in two cycles with a clue how to act at these things."

"No. I have need of her."

"You may have two of mine for the interim. Any of them have more experience than this one."

Suddenly the Sorceress looked sly. "You've sent my best team on duty I know not where. What if I said I think you owe me more than two?"

"What?" Rausery chortled. "That was *your* suggestion to give them to me."

"Was it? Maybe you should ask the Prime."

The contradiction and delivery were perfect to stop the momentum. Rausery didn't seem interested in the suggestion. She went direct.

"How many you want?"

D'Shea smiled. "Thirteen should suffice. For Jaunda and her team, adding Sirana, specifically to be trained for the Worship Ball. They'll give their reports to you as well when I release them, whether you offer any reports to me."

I stared at them in disbelief, and Qivni's mouth opened before she snapped it shut again. Even my ego couldn't think D'Shea was concerned about getting a high price for me. She *was* playing a game. On top of this, Qivni and I both saw Rausery was considering the trade despite knowing that.

The Elder nodded. "Done."

My lips parted without sound as I felt my elbow released.

"I want these five," D'Shea indicated Qivni and the others chosen for the Ball, "plus your teams Three and Four."

After another moment of stern-faced observance, Rausery nodded again. She turned and jerked her head at Qivni. "Find them."

Qivni's expression was complex. She hated being traded away from Rausery to D'Shea for me, and she was baffled why her superior wanted to train me at all when D'Shea could do so. At the same time, if Qivni was genuinely worried about me embarrassing them at the Ball, which seemed the case, then it wasn't to be D'Shea who prepared me, but her own Elder whom she obeyed and trusted.

If the job was done right, how could the Lead complain?

My Collector bowed briefly to them both and left with one other Sister. Rausery dragged me down another hall, and D'Shea, Gaelan, and the rest moved in the direction of her quarters. Gaelan and I glanced at each other, and maybe we both thought the same thing.

Still no time to take turns with the Feldeu.

I'd had more sex and play those first two spans after Gaelan dragged me away from the Consort than I'd ever had before or since.

Once all the others were out of sight, I focused on keeping up with the stubborn, fast pace of the older female. Rausery's gloved hand was tight enough that my fingertips tingled as we weaved through the Cloister.

"What is D'Shea up to?" Rausery asked me. "She likes to make things complicated."

"I don't know, Elder," I answered, knowing that wouldn't be good enough, even though it was the truth.

"You know more than that, you just don't know it," she said flatly.

"No, Elder. I don't."

"We'll see."

CHAPTER 17

THE ELDER RED SISTER TOOK ME FOR A RUN OUTSIDE. JUST HER AND ME, PANT-ing and sweating. Before too long, I realized this was a natural obsta-cle course; not only running, but climbing, crawling, swimming, and jumping through grit, water, silt, mud, and rubble.

Come on, novice, move your ass! she signed in our silent tongue.

Elder Rausery didn't make me do anything she did not demonstrate herself first. Her dexterity and strength were incredible, and I gaped at her sometimes. I knew this didn't prepare me for the Ball specifically, but she put my mind where she wanted it.

I was holding her back. She was capable of so much more but was waiting for me. She protected me in the outskirts of Sivaraus, keeping her eyes out for threats as I showed her how much I could handle, where I stood in my training. By the time we made it back to the Cloister, I felt small and appropriately pliable, submissive, and even admiring, without audible word or a rough hand from her.

As with D'Shea, I wanted to believe this was real, but if it was, I still didn't grasp all that it told me. The Sisterhood was different between ourselves than how I'd viewed them as a Noble, and yet anticipating what that meant lay beyond my experience.

I had to keep going to find out.

We reentered the Cloister, just Rausery and me. I was trying to breathe a stitch out of my side when the Prime came around the bend. Adding to my discomfort, she seemed to notice me as much as the Elder. The thought crossed my mind that I'd been nude but bathed the last time the Prime looked at me and wondered if being dressed, ripe, and filthy was what gave her pause.

"Rausery," she said, motioning with her hand.

The Elder strode up to her, stopping an arm's length away. I didn't have to be told to stay close and just behind her. "Prime."

The gaze of the oldest Red Sister drifted to me again as I ignored the ache and looked only at the wall behind her.

"Where's Lead Qivni?" she asked.

"With Elder D'Shea, Prime."

The Prime sounded annoyed and maybe surprised. "Doing what?"

"You'd have to ask her, Prime. I don't expect to see them for at least two cycles. Although D'Shea gave me Jaunda and her team in exchange, and for much longer. I sent them where you said."

There was little interest in those old eyes, such that I wondered if who actually "said" might have been the Valsharess and the Prime the mouthpiece. She grunted. "D'Shea gave her over, huh? No whining?"

"I didn't speak directly with her, Jaunda came to me."

"*Pff*. Sulking. But at least she did it."

The other warrior's face was placid. "You could have informed me you wanted Jaunda to lead this one alone, Prime."

"I could have," the older female said. "I didn't. More interested in seeing what the Sorceress did. Not surprised she snatched *your* Lead as a crutch."

"She's got more wits than that, Prime. Don't forget."

Another grunt and the Prime seemed to recall I was there, glancing my way before looking back. "And you have this one? Not really a fair trade, Raus."

The Elder nodded. "Nothing more pressing than the Worship Ball, though."

The old female's mouth tightened as she contemplated my shape.

"How is this one against other Sisters?"

Rausery shook her head once. "Beginner. Lead Jaunda had been guiding her training, but right now we prepare her for the Ball."

The disbelief was evident; the Prime hadn't made the connection. "You're jesting me."

"No, Prime. The Valsharess selected her. I witnessed it."

"You're *fucking* jesting me."

"I don't understand it, either, but that's the way it is. We give her two cycles and a set of reds. Push her out where the Nobles can see her."

The Prime glared at me, taking a deep draw of air as if she sampled my scent. That wasn't good. "What in the ice pit did D'Shea do?"

"I'd say she accelerated some frontend training, but not much more," Rausery said, unruffled. "Been a while since we've had a recruit who could be a new face for the Sisterhood. Might ask D'Shea if that's what she's aiming for."

The Prime shook her head in disgust. "Manipulative cunt. She'll have us serving taze as we watch the Nobles piss their time away at the table with crackjilts. Bah!"

My stomach trembled with nerves. If the Prime hadn't shown up for the Worship Ball meeting despite the Valsharess being here, and if the older female wasn't aware of any plans Elder D'Shea might have for me, it didn't speak well for the information gap between them. Rausery was the bridge for now; I'd be a fool to anger her.

"I wanna see this slutty soft-bait fight before she struts around in any goddess-damned reds," the Prime said, scowling directly at me; I could feel it even avoiding her gaze. "Where are Corpora Thena and her team?"

I could have sworn Rausery started to smile before she reined herself in. "Also with Elder D'Shea."

"What?"

"We traded full teams, Prime. She has my Three and Four."

"Suck a Drider's ass … Who've you got right now?"

"Panagan and Moria," the Elder replied without much pause.

A roll of the eyes. "Fine. Get 'em together. Meet you there in a quarter mark."

The Prime bulled through between us, brushing Rausery perhaps but thoroughly knocking me to the side on her way past. I remained against the wall as I grappled with my fear. Elder Rausery watched the Prime leave, her hands relaxed on her hips.

When our ultimate superior was out of sight, the Elder smiled at me and hand-signed the lifeline I needed.

★Prime knows about Jaunda interfering with you and Thena. She wants to see if you do it again. Entertain her, novice, and keep your temper. She'll get herself off, then we'll move on.★

RAUSERY HAD JUST RUN ME RAGGED, AND NOW I WAS EXPECTED TO FIGHT. I didn't complain but worried about going up against two fresh Red Sisters. Without a word, the Elder led me to a stock room and collected a few things, handing me one I could identify by the three red dots on the black, wax seal.

A rejuvenator.

I drank it, felt the warm influx of mild but accelerated healing of my hot, aching muscles; it would keep working for a while yet. I nodded my head to Rausery, indicating I was ready but didn't draw attention to the gesture. The most it confirmed was that, whatever Rausery had had in mind for me following that long wilderness run, the Prime had thrown us off-path.

Now she brought eight healing potions of greater strength before summoning the two other Sisters with a message pellet. We met them in the hall on our way to one of several sparring rooms, this one lit by two torches.

Panagan and Moria looked me over in the new light, took a whiff of the air around me, and smirked. Their red eyes showed the memory of their part in our last confrontation — when I'd been even sweatier and wrung out to my very limit — but made no comment otherwise. I was just glad it wasn't Thena and Suna, as their appetites for torment were harder to fill than these two.

The Prime came in and took the only fiberstalk chair. She said nothing but watched us with hard, faded eyes and an ugly scowl which gave no hint whether she might gain any enjoyment by watching this. I knew not whether Rausery had meant the Prime would "get off" on this physically or merely symbolically, but I was to "entertain" her. Somehow.

"We don't have a lot of time," Elder Rausery said to us. "The Ball starts less than two cycles from now." She looked at me. "I trust you'll keep up."

I nodded. "Yes, Elder. For the Sisterhood."

Rausery looked at the other two. "Your goal will be to capture, immobilize, and penetrate her. Hers will be to prevent it."

They nodded as well, although Panagan signed to be acknowledged, which was granted. "Elder Rausery, didn't we already do this?"

The Prime grunted in displeasure, and Rausery smiled without showing her teeth. "No." She looked at me. "First, I want to see what you know, novice. Begin."

Right.

Moria blinked as I charged her and swept a hard kick at her knee.

I couldn't believe it when I connected solidly or that she'd been so slow. Maybe it had been the potion. Regardless, she wailed hoarsely in pain and Panagan cursed, moving to attack me. I didn't have time to grab the Feldeu at Moria's belt; I backpedaled to avoid either of them seizing me and dragging me to the bare, stone ground.

I'd learned a lot from Jaunda, and I wasn't as ineffectual as I'd been before. My Lead and Gaelan knew my personal attacks and could anticipate them, but these two didn't.

I stayed away from Moria, who was reaching for her belt and led Panagan around the room, drawing her in and attacking and drawing in again. She bared her teeth and watched me with fierce eyes, unable to catch me yet but waiting for an opening.

"Not as easy when there isn't six of you, is it?" The hatred in my belly flared to a boil fast, but I kept a tight leash on it. I must keep my temper; I had to focus.

She sneered. "You *wanted* it that long, altar-bait."

My lip curled. "Eat Dwarf dung."

I heard Rausery chuckle as I landed a punch to Panagan's cheekbone and she backed up, looking shocked. Then something small cracked open at my feet, and a burst of fumes rose up into the air, and both of us began coughing uncontrollably.

We fell apart from each other, unable to breathe, when Moria crashed clumsily into me, shoving me to the far side of the room and out of the fumes.

I tripped, still coughing, landed, and felt her haul me up only to slam me against the wall and let me fall again. I heard her gasping in pain as she did so, her boot scraping with a heavy limp. Moria was growling as she landed on me, yanking and ripping at my pants. I felt a hard erection smashed against my thigh and realized she'd had ample time to get her Feldeu in place. On the ground, it was harder to fight her off, but she still had that knee injury.

As we struggled, she pressed a nerve point at my elbow just as I landed another blow on her knee; she screamed and gripped me hard, and I went rigid in pain, unable to make any sound. She left off her attempt at stripping me in favor of hitting me in the face and hissing rambling insults at me. I can't say that I was impressed with the repetition.

As soon as I could feel my fingers again, I grabbed her cock down near my hips and pulled. Hard.

"Cunt!" she shrieked and punched hard into my gut to knock the wind from me. It almost worked but the hardened leather absorbed the worst, and I got another twist on her member before she squirmed free, mewling.

I rolled but was not able to scramble to my feet before Panagan fell on me next, also ready with her pants open and raging, hard staff jutting out. She pressed me to my belly, and I cursed luridly, struggling to find a way to get her off me as her black pole pressed lengthwise between my buttocks.

"Get over here," Panagan growled at Moira, who crawled over on three limbs. She didn't need to be told to pull my pants down while

Panagan held me.

I never stopped fighting but cried out when, as soon as my leathers were down around my thighs, the Red Sister atop me crammed half her Feldeu into my sex. It was dry and not the least comfortable. It took repeated lunges, but eventually, she got it all the way in, dragged it halfway out, and rammed in again. It stung, and I gritted my teeth; I was in for a very rough grudge fuck.

The Prime hummed.

"A win, Panagan," Rausery said. "At attention."

The body atop me went stiff, trembling in rage and lust. Panagan's voice was incredulous, clear she didn't want to stop. "E-Elder?"

"Now."

"But —"

Rausery started to walk across the room, and Panagan fumbled off me, her slithering cock vacating my body with a reverse suck. I took the opportunity to surge to my feet, resetting and closing my pants and backing away, facing all of them.

My lungs still itched from the gas pellet Moria had thrown down, and I could tell the other two were affected as well when Panagan heaved a panicked cough as she retreated from her approaching superior.

"Stand still!" Rausery barked, closing the distance in a blink and grabbing her subordinate's erection to keep her in place.

Watching answered a lingering question of mine: the Feldeu didn't go soft. It did not even waver even though Panagan was terrified and had lost her fire staring into Rausery's eyes. It remained turgid and at attention, though its wearer grimaced at the tight grip and did not look aroused anymore.

"Don't hesitate again," our Elder murmured low and deadly, though we could all hear her. "Your purpose here is this," she jerked on the magical cock, "for our use. Nothing else. Understand?"

Panagan gasped at the tug and nodded. "Yes, Elder. I understand."

Rausery glanced at Moria, still favoring her leg and who piped up, "I understand, Elder."

She nodded, pausing before releasing Panagan's cock, and turned her attention to me next. I stayed quiet as she stepped up to me since I really had no idea whether I'd done anything wrong or not. I almost looked away to judge the Prime's mood, but that would have been a mistake like taking my hand off the glyphs before a Sathoet had left the room.

"Your first choice was to crack her knee?" she asked.

After a flick's hesitation, I answered, "Yes, Elder."

"Why?"

I thought it was obvious. "To put her out of the fight and take her Feldeu."

"Mm-hm. Didn't work. Moria was still effective."

Between the gas pellet and her determined brawling, yes, she was. Now that I thought about it, Moria shouldn't have been able to slam me into the wall as she had; she shouldn't have been able to stand up at all.

Was she that tough? She didn't look it. She did have more tools on her belt, though, and I didn't know what they all did. She'd probably taken something when Panagan was chasing me around.

"No plan if you failed to get the Feldeu," Rausery stated, watching me. "Just reacted to what Panagan was doing."

"Correct, Elder," I admitted.

"Escalation like that is either stupidity or revenge," the Prime commented.

"Or both," Rausery remarked, smiling as she glanced at the superior in the chair before she looked back at me.

I smiled back. "I admit both, Prime, Elder."

The Prime snorted, but I thought Rausery's eyelashes twitched in a wink. I heard Moria call me a filthy name under her breath, and Rausery chuckled as she looked at her next. She removed a small bottle from her belt and held it out to her subordinate.

"Drink this, Moria. You and Panagan go into the next room and wait till I call you."

Moria limped forward and took the bottle with quiet but polite gratitude, drinking it then and there. She grimaced — perhaps it was bitter — before limping with Panagan toward the door, their rigid cocks still bobbing in front of them. Moria's gait slowly got smoother, and I knew she would be fully healed in a very short while, even as she made sounds as if the process hurt her.

Rausery waited until the stone door had slid shut before speaking again. "Was the retribution enough for you, Sirana?"

The Prime's nostrils wrinkled, and I knew this wasn't entertaining her, but I also didn't know what either of them wanted to hear. My attention was fractured before I pulled it together to answer with an impulse.

"No, Elder."

Rausery tilted her head. "You'll continue until all four have cracked knees or worse?"

I knew that wouldn't reward myself in the long term, as great as it might feel for a moment. "No, Elder. I could be satisfied with their keeping their distance from me off-duty. After showing them I'm not an easy mark."

Rausery hadn't blinked. "You mean you want it different than it was with your deceased sister?"

I didn't want to compare them like that. "My Sisters are here. Panagan and Moria are my Sisters. I'll work it out, as I did Jaunda and Gaelan."

The Prime rolled her eyes. "Don't think they wouldn't take an opportunity to see you lurch to your own death for being stupid, lowbie."

"So be it, Prime."

"You sound like a wizard."

This baffled me. I kept quiet. Rausery seemed more entertained than either of us.

"Tell me one thing you've observed about Elder D'Shea, novice," she said, and the Prime actually sat up. "Your choice, Sirana, but I must find useful."

Fucking Abyss. I grappled for something to say that wouldn't put the Sorceress at a disadvantage because of me.

"Has she fucked you, yet?" the Prime asked.

Rausery's mouth tightened at the direction. Maybe that wasn't her first choice of information, but the Prime did override the Elder.

"Elder D'Shea has not fucked me, Prime," I answered.

"You haven't taken her Feldeu?"

I had never confirmed she even had one. "No, Prime."

"Eaten her?"

"No, Prime."

"Tell me what you *have* done."

Why does that matter? I swallowed. "I've bathed her three times. I've slept in her bed as often. Only once, she made me cum with her fingers in my cunt and a shock of magic from a spell."

The Prime looked disgusted. "That's it? You don't even know what her pussy tastes like?"

I had just said that I didn't. The tension against my Elder was rising, and I didn't want to be here. "No, Prime."

"And she has all her parts? Is she deformed?"

Where in Braqth's Web did that come from?

"Why would she be, Prime?"

Her face shifted dangerously. "Answer the fucking question."

"No, Prime," I obeyed quickly, "Elder D'Shea is well-formed and has all her parts."

Although nervous, I omitted the scars I'd seen below D'Shea's breast and low on her abdomen. Let either be more specific in their impromptu interrogation about my Elder before I'd mention those. This smelled like fishing, anyway; if they knew something already and only wanted to confirm, they were doing it wrong.

Elder Rausery's mouth had tensed at one corner, and she looked away at the far wall, frowning as if her concentration lay on something else. She didn't seem fixated on my answers about D'Shea as the Prime was. It occurred to me that the Prime probably had the power to demand D'Shea strip for her. If the older female had such basic questions about the Sorceress's body, why hadn't she?

"Let me show you a few moves before we call Panagan and Moria back in," Elder Rausery said, backing off on her own question which had sparked the Prime's interest. She even took a step back until we were within sparring distance, her body language warning me to get ready. This felt like a wasted opportunity, and we still had the Worship Ball to prepare for after "entertaining" the Prime with this.

At least I'd have something to report to D'Shea instead.

"When Panagan and Moria come back, you'll have some tools to fend them off without cracking bones." After a pause, Rausery added, "But don't let that stop you with anyone outside the Cloister."

Anyone, huh? Including these same Red Sisters?

I didn't ask aloud. It seemed clear enough. The instruction began.

I came to understand the "soft touch" Rausery was teaching to complement Jaunda's efforts, and her demonstrations on me were very effective. No strikes, no bruises, but I blacked out in moments if she got hold of me. After I stood up the third time, I marveled at the skill.

The other Nobles and I had been taught strikes, weaponry, and footwork, and Jaunda had built on that, and yet Rausery could subdue me, entirely and unharmed, between the end of one breath and the start of the next. My neck wasn't even sore. It seemed odd for the reputation of the Sisterhood but, at the same time, having more tools to refine a response to different targets excited me more.

This made a warrior like her less predictable.

"Decent," Rausery remarked. "For a beginner."

Understood, Elder.

Rausery allowed me to practice my arm and hand placements on her so I could be sure of my technique, but she also had a thumb on a nerve point just in case I tried to get cute and knock her out in front of the Prime. The thought made me smile but at no time would I volunteer to be standing alone in a room with the Eldest, much less arrange it with a bite on the hand that protected me.

After teaching me four such techniques, all for various shapes of neck and angle of attack, Rausery called Panagan and Moria back in. They looked no less disgruntled for having had the break, but they did look like they might've been sucking each other's cocks while they waited.

The first engagement was not successful for me. I failed to hold my grip even a few flicks on the first, genuinely furious Red Sister, and eventually found my face smashed against the wall, my backside abruptly exposed.

"In her ass," the Prime instructed in a grunt.

Panagan's Feldeu thrust in as directed and Rausery did not stop her. Not that I expected her to override the Prime, but my attacker laughed and rutted me harder when she realized it.

Eventually, she forced me on all fours and Moria jammed her own erection into my mouth, gleefully blocking my air as they double ended me, just how it had been with Thena and her team before, not stopping until they'd climaxed.

Somehow, I didn't bite down; I kept my temper.

"A win, Panagan, Moria. Stand down."

Glowing with success and satisfaction, they withdrew without hesitation this time. The Prime herself offered each a healing potion as Rausery walked over to me. I glanced to see the Prime inspecting their soiled erection, nodding with a cruel sneer and instructing the both of them to clean each other off.

"With your mouths," she added, touching herself through her pants as she watched.

At least it isn't me.

Yet.

I pulled up my torn pants, my jaw clenched tight, and I couldn't look at Rausery's eyes as she stood next to me. She offered me a draught as well and leaned to whisper.

"Mix the messages," she suggested.

I took the bottle then gulped down the potion, feeling the sharp stabs of pain in my ass first get worse for several moments and then finally start to fade and feel normal.

"Take 'em out," I heard the Prime said. "Let's put the tonic on them for the next loss."

The two Sisters obeyed, each whispering different words of release to remove the bulb of her phallus from her twat.

I scowled, and I nodded to Rausery. "I want to try again. Now."

"Good," the Elder said abruptly as she stepped away.

She waited until the Prime acknowledged her after smearing something from a bottle on her own belt on the tips of each phallus, whispering a magic word of her own, and Panagan and Moria only just realized something had changed.

"Begin," Rausery commanded, and I sprinted forward.

The two Red Sisters blinked, looked at their Feldeus, and moved swiftly to reattach them. I jumped Panagan before she could speak the command word, wrenching it out of her cunt and flinging it far across the room where it landed with a heavy slap.

Moria shrieked a threat, but I already had the proper grip around Panagan's neck, holding for those moments I needed to make her sink to her knees. When Moria lunged, I used Panagan's body as a shield to knock her sideways, noting Moria's cock was fully attached by the time I dropped her Sister unconscious to the ground.

"I'm not going to stop with your mouth this time," she growled, eyes narrowing and white teeth gleaming in the torchlight. "You'll be gagging on your own filth."

"How? You've forgotten how to get it on your own," I mocked. "Always need one bolder than you, slug."

The fight was short but furious. Moria injured me as I needed to sacrifice one wrist to get close enough to hold her — a sprain, not a break. We went to the ground again, but this time it was my groin against her backside. Her squealing in denial and rage ended quickly as I cut off the blood to her head and her eyes closed. By that time, however, Panagan was waking up, groggily shaking her head as she got to her knees.

Damn.

I released the pliant body and sprinted for Panagan's Feldeu on the ground, clutching it in my strong hand. I couldn't use it myself; I didn't know the command word to which it responded. For that same reason, I couldn't remove Moria's cock, either. Nonetheless, I wanted an available weapon in *my* hand, not theirs.

Panagan's bitter gaze found me holding her Feldeu soon enough, and she ground her teeth but didn't charge me as I half-expected her to do. "You can't wear that. What are you going to do with it?"

"Probably stuff it in Moria's mouth. Or yours."

Whatever the Prime had smeared on the thing worried her, I could see it. "You think you're the only one who knows the sleeper holds?"

I shrugged, feeling a large, Jaunda-inspired smile spread over my face in spite of my sprained, throbbing wrist. Having put two Sisters down with minimal effort and fuss plus brandishing a smeared phallus in my hand, I had all the time in the Deepearth and a bit of the power back.

Panagan watched me warily as I kept a focus on the edges of her shape should she reach to toss something explosive or distracting the way Moria had. Over a quiet moment where both elder females said nothing, Moria groaned softly and began to wake up. I was aware that two awake were harder to fight off than one, but if they wanted me, they'd have to come to me. They understood that I intended to wait them out.

I dared not look away from them to glance at Rausery, who was so quiet and still in the room I could almost think she'd slipped out. She was still here, and from the contemplative look on the Prime's face, they both just wanted to see how this ended.

Entertain her, Rausery had said.

The two Sisters tried taunting me with derisive names, but it really had little effect. They avoided the weapon the Prime had made.

"If you two only stand there, at least perform for us," I suggested with smirking insubordination. "Panagan, since you lost your cock, how about you kneel and start suckling Moria? Give me a preview of what I can expect shoving this into her ring?"

"You'll be sorry you healed yours tight again," Panagan remarked.

"Tough threat for someone who lost her prick."

The Prime's face finally cracked upward; this was mildly amusing to her. I tried chuckling aloud, and I liked the sound of it. I laughed louder for no discernable reason. The two hesitating to spar looked at me like I was unbalanced. Rausery leaned against the wall, arms crossed.

"Che'nara," the Prime said mid-laugh, and the torches went out. The room was black.

Move.

With eyes closed, listening, I moved toward Rausery. A crack of air sounded where I'd been standing as Panagan tossed something. I held my breath and swiftly moved through the plume, feeling the lining of my nose tingle although my mouth and eyes were tightly closed. Panagan had retreated far enough backward by the time I got there that my blind-fighting wouldn't help me.

Fortunately, Moria remained where she had been, unwilling to move into the fouled space. My arm drew back to full strength, and I slapped her across the face with the anointed phallus. Her cry of surprise was a song to my ears, ended with my second foot strike on her. Not just luck that I hit her in the gut, and she crumpled this time, unable to breathe.

Panagan was close enough to lunge for a tackle, but I turned into and spun through it, a move I hadn't known a mark ago. She growled and managed to grab my wrist to haul me away from Moria, but she couldn't get that lock on my body, so I went willingly down with her to the ground, wrapping my legs around her hips and squeezing hard. She tried to snatch my sprained wrist but wasn't fast enough as I leaned up to kiss her full on the mouth, my tongue licking her lips before I bit her.

"Augh!"

Her howl of rage left her mouth open long enough for me to yank my wrist free and thrust the head of her own Feldeu past her lips to the back of her throat. She gagged, but I kept it in place, tightening my legs to hold her to me and using my forearm to apply pressure to the back of her head.

Panagan was unable to dislodge the soiled cock though she tried, and the sounds she made could have made me cum had I been more like Jilrina. By the time she'd spit it out and screamed at me, Rausery was laughing as loud as Jaunda might have, the rich voice laced with delight, filling the chamber alongside the torchlight.

"A win, Sirana," she said. "Disengage."

I released Panagan and stood up, taking the phallus with me a pace or two from the sputtering Sister. Moria was on the ground with gloved hands hovering above her face without touching it; she was beginning to mewl as Panagan started coughing and moaning hoarsely, her voice quickly disappearing.

The Prime watched them suffer, holding out her hand when Rausery might have acted.

I understood from watching them that touching the stuff on their

Feldeus would only make it worse. Worth noting that, sensations aside, substances that burned on real skin didn't burn through the Feldeu. A quality I hadn't known.

Again, better them than me. The Prime would have liked to see that stuff shoved deep into my body; I had no doubt.

Rausery stepped forward and held out her hand to me for Panagan's Feldeu. I placed it in her gloved palm, and Rausery moved next to Moria. She spoke quietly but over the mewling. "Moria, remove your Feldeu and give it to me."

The second Sister was distressed but obeyed, whispering her command word to release the item's magical grip on her flesh and slowly slipping it out of her sex. She handed it to her Elder, her eyes still closed and her face grimacing.

"Dismissed," the Prime said, apparently intending to have them seek an antidote for whatever venom had been on their cocks themselves. She sounded disappointed. I wondered but also shivered what the outcome might have been if she'd had her choice of Red Sisters to test me.

"I have a few more techniques to show you," Rausery said, slipping each soiled Feldeu into its pouch and setting it on one of the few small tables set along the wall. "This time you will be fending off *me*."

I made a small show of swallowing in consternation, and the Prime smiled, straightening up. She looked only now to be enjoying herself. I anticipated my orifices to be yielding several more times, although I could have been more dismayed than I was.

I didn't mind spreading for Rausery, as this part was probably to satisfy her own superior. I wasn't sure how much hand-to-hand combat I'd get to practice, but I was determined to learn anything at this point.

"I'm ready, Elder."

CHAPTER 18

SEVERAL MARKS LATER, ELDER RAUSERY LAID ME ON THE FLOOR IN HER QUAR-
ters, and I curled up. I couldn't stand if a herd of Ornilleth thralls were
bearing down on me.

"You okay?" she asked.

"M'okay, Elder ..."

I sounded pathetic as I whispered that response.

"No, you're not. Give me a moment."

Goddess, I was sore. Everywhere. And filthy, and I ended up with
the burning cunt and ass that the Prime had planned for me anyway, only
it came directly from *her*. If *that* was what it took for the Prime to get
herself off, I should have "thrown" the fight and let Panagan and Moria
win. Letting those two fuck me by proxy would have been preferable.

Fortunately, I'd survived to learn for next time.

"She'll leave you alone now, Sirana," the Elder said as if reading my
mind. She sorted her things and rummaged through a few travel bags on
her walls. "You didn't panic or fight her, so you impressed me. No one
your age interests her for long, and you won't change that. I could read
her. As your Elder, I'd say let the anger go. It won't help you."

I wondered then how many of those scenes the Elder had watched in
her time to sound so nonchalant, and if all Red Sisters had to see it that

way to gain in the ranks. For the first time, I gauged whether Rausery was speaking from experience, and D'Shea might have that in common with her. Maybe they had more, being centuries older.

Or perhaps she was saying the Prime might be interested again once I got older? I hoped not. I'd do all I could to avoid her interest in the future.

"Novice?"

"Hear you, Elder. I understand."

"Good. You showed enough pain. She keeps harassing a recruit if there's a hint of defiance until that's gone and the will's broken. But you bent without breaking, just like D'Shea said you would."

I wondered how she could tell I wasn't broken. What even counted as "broken"?

"Like I said, you impressed me. You can make it as a Red Sister." Rausery kneeled at my back, and I heard glass on glass as she opened something. "Pull down your pants."

I didn't have the strength to be paranoid or alert. I obeyed, settling the leather around my thighs, and she patted my leg to prompt my curling back up to give her access to both my holes at once. A shockingly cooling, soothing sensation spread over my chapped and burning netherlips as Rausery rubbed three fingers over them, and I groaned aloud in relief, unable to prevent it.

The Elder chuckled, gently slipping first one, then two of those fingers inside my slit, spreading the ointment where it needed to go. Everywhere she touched, the fire went out instantly.

"Better?" she asked.

"Th-thank you, Elder."

"Mind if I prod at your shitter next, Blue Eyes?"

The tone of the remark drew a bit of a smile. So different from the Nobles. "Not at all, Magic Fingers."

"That's D'Shea. Mine's all skill."

My eyes rolled up as she spread a generous amount of goop around my netherhole and carefully worked that inside as well. Not only was the venom from the Prime's cock being neutralized but it was a topical healer as well. The swelling went down, and the pain faded. A tangential thought came to me as the sharpness of it all receded.

"Will you still train me for the Worship Ball, Elder?"

"Yeah. Even less time than I'd hoped thanks to catching the Prime's eye. There's enough left if we focus. After a rest. Undress, novice. Put your things in order over there and let's get cleaned up."

Rausery didn't have a private bath like D'Shea, but she did have a basic sluicer at the back corner. There was a drain in the floor and a similar spout for water, although it was placed toward the ceiling so that we stood underneath the spatter while we scrubbed down.

This set-up was intended for cleaning many Davrin at once, fighters and servants, in the fastest and most efficient way, shedding the worse of the Deepearth and conserving water. It was quick, but far from relaxing, given how many fights, traps, and forced sex started in the sluicing rooms.

Private baths for the Nobles were luxurious and safe, meant to get naked and lounge until the water cooled, but at this smaller scale, I thought it almost as nice as the Sorceress' bath, somehow reassuring and soothing. It highlighted the difference in origin between the two Elders, too, and showed me where each was most comfortable.

Soon I felt better. Clean, healed, cold as the water wasn't heated, but safe. Even with Elder Rausery looking down at me, watching every tick of expression I made.

"So D'Shea really hasn't taught you much," she observed.

"Depends what about, Elder," I replied, watching the water stream down her dark, hard body.

This warrior's scars were from previous injuries, for sure. D'Shea *was* physically softer by comparison, with far fewer blemishes, but that wasn't a tick against her. To me, she was the perfect balance between magic and melee, Noble and commoner, with wit enough between her ears to remain out of the ruts and habits of either.

Compared to the Prime and Elder Rausery, the Sorceress was a form of pure grace who, perhaps, had more in common with the Valshatess. In contrast, no doubt in my mind Elder Rausery was built to run the entire army, if necessary.

"Hey, Blue Eyes," she said, tapping a finger on my damp head, and I looked up. "What are you thinking?"

Elder D'Shea had asked me that, too. The Prime didn't.

"I was thinking about scars," I said, shivering from the chill, and Rausery stopped the water, grabbing something to towel off. There was only the one, and I wrung out my hair while she ran it over herself first. "You have them. The Prime. Even D'Shea has a couple. I had a lot of them ... inside. Until recently. Or so I'm told."

"Yeah? So?"

"Nobles avoid getting hurt where possible, pay a lot for potions to erase them. Having them implies you're a commoner or a servant of an altar."

Rausery grinned, handing me her damp towel to blot my skin. "Still don't get your point, novice."

"Do you keep them intentionally? Like a record of accomplishment?"

Rausery laughed, walking over to the box-pallet on the floor and tossing a single blanket back. She crouched and sat, elbows on her knees, watching me as I finished drying. I could see her sex clearly.

"It's more I don't give a shit, novice. Did you know your peers waste their wealth on those potions, and the merchants know it? If the Nobility could fucking wait, those scars would disappear on their own. What you see on me are only the worst from the last fifty turns. Same with any commoner who doesn't spend a coin at the brewers' shops."

If that was true, Elder Rausery surely didn't stand back from the danger.

"What about the Prime's scars? They looked old. Different from yours. Why aren't they gone?"

The Elder shrugged. "Don't know how she got them, but I'm betting they're Abyssal scars. Those *don't* fade over time. Given she works closely with the Palace and Sanctuary, I wouldn't be surprised."

That could even explain her tastes, I thought. Not far from what Jilrina might have become, had she lived to become a Priestess of Braqth. D'Shea's warning about the Priestesses being barren after birthing a Sathoet returned to me as well. *Abyssal scars. That might make sense. But then, how are they birthing the Royal Consorts?*

I hung her towel to dry, and Rausery gestured me closer. I obeyed. Without speaking, I knelt on the floor where she sat on the edge of the bed.

"Not what I meant," she commented wryly, and I shrugged.

"May I taste you, Elder?" I asked, my face warming to hear myself. It was another impulse, not without genuine gratitude.

She eyed me, deciding my motive for herself. "Hm. Alright."

Rausery braced herself on her arms, tilted her hips back to give me access, but her muscular thighs didn't open fully until I used my hands to part them. She sighed softly as I began suckling on her netherlips, and I went slow, tired as I was. Her breathing changed in time; she was letting herself feel what I was doing. She allowed herself to enjoy it.

"Mmm, heh," she murmured, taking a deep draw. "The caits were right. You are good at this."

She put her hands in my hair. Her fingers felt good stroking my scalp as my tongue darted inside her, around and out and in again. By the time she heaved a shuddering exhale, her back straight as a rod, I had two fingers inside her, was flicking my tongue and using all my many tricks to service her. Her hips thrust up and she growled short and low on occasion, but she didn't make much sound or talk.

I kept going.

Her legs began to tremble as she pushed against the floor and held her tense, hard ass slightly off the mattress. Her head tilted back as she got closer to climax. I decided to take a risk and do to her as I had with the wizard. I lubed up the middle finger of my other hand between my own legs and slipped it between her buttocks, penetrating her ring, quick and with force, just as it seemed she was ready to orgasm.

"*Rraughh!*" she roared.

And she squirted.

Shocked as my chin and chest were drenched with a hot, clear spray, I stayed with her. I could feel her body spasm around my fingers in her ass and cunt; I could smell the musk and feel the heat pressed to my face.

"Fuck!" she gasped, coming down enough to speak.

I removed all my fingers from her body as her backside touched the mattress again and straightened up. She stared down at me with bright but unreadable eyes as she caught her breath. I stared back and did not quail, remaining on my knees and in place. I did not even attempt to wipe the moisture from my lower face and chest, a vain effort without some sort of cloth. Maybe she wanted to see it. Admire her own efforts.

When she didn't say anything for several moments, I let a small smile show on my puffy lips. "Seemed like a good one, Elder."

One side of her mouth tugged upward, and she shrugged. "Hm. No wonder they all want a piece of you."

"Thank you for your training," I replied. "It shall make me a rarer commodity."

She chuckled, leaning down to touch my own sex. I obediently opened wider for her, and her fingers slipped in to test its readiness. She soon withdrew and lifted her fingers just beneath her nose to take in the scent. "I'm sure it will. Stay where you are."

She stood up to retrieve something from a locked drawer in her desk, and I knew what it would be. Rausery strode lazily back over, handed me a cloth to wipe my face and chest. While I did so, she lifted one leg to insert her personal Feldeu into herself and whispered the magic word.

As I'd seen with many others, the phallus glowed subtly, and the shape changed to conform perfectly with Rausery's body, becoming part of her until she uttered the release word. She made a sound of pleasure and stroked her black member a few times as I finished wiping down before gesturing to me. "Stand up."

I did, not sure how she wanted it but eager to replace the memory of the Prime's scorching Feldeu with something more pleasant. I was genuinely aroused by eating her, by her cumming so loudly and spraying on me like a bua might. My healed holes were receptive to this Elder.

"Get my chair," she instructed. "Set it out from the desk."

I looked behind me and saw the hefty fiberstalk chair with four legs but no arms. I had to lift it carefully to avoid pulling a muscle, carrying it over slowly and putting it down, too aware of my vulnerable toes.

"Good." Rausery moved to sit on that chair, getting comfortable and looking up at me with a half-smile. She looked down at her erection and back up again. "Well? You want to get off, too?"

I hesitated. "You … want me to mount you?"

No one with a Feldeu had invited me to do it this way. If Rausery had been a bua, I'd be taking control of her, fucking her like I was the dominant one. A laughable thought.

"I know it's one of your favorite positions with the young buas," she said.

I stared at her.

"What?" she asked. "Am I wrong?"

My voice betrayed my nervousness. "N-no, Elder, but I can go without. I don't need —"

"Ohhh no, you don't." She shook her head, her dark red eyes gleaming and her teeth showing like a playful predator. "Get on my lap and get this thing up your twat now. Fuck me, recruit."

Damn it.

With the chances of offending a powerful female rising, I moved to obey, placing my feet wide apart on either side of Rausery's thighs, hovering over her lap and her Feldeu. For the first time in my life, I didn't feel in control while I voluntarily straddled a cock from above. I held one of her shoulders as I reached between us to aim her erection at my slit, then I slowly squatted down on it. Rausery sucked in a slow breath as my sheath engulfed her rod.

Oh, Goddess, yes …

This felt good. So familiar. I hadn't done it this way since before Qivni escorted me off the balcony.

Or since I claimed that beautiful Consort.

I lifted back up, using my thighs with both hands on her strong shoulders, and lowered myself back down. She hissed in pleasure again and reached around to squeeze my buttocks.

"Come on," she growled in an odd mix of delight and irritation, "show me how you fuck a cock."

My face was hot. My first strokes must've seemed meek because my Elder opened her eyes and scowled at me.

"I've already seen how you take a cock, Sirana. You'll do fine if you're ever on the Surface. Now show me how you fuck one."

I felt a white-hot flash of shock go through me at her words, and my mouth dropped open. Would I be going to the Surface at some point? Had *she* ever been — ?

Rausery parted my cheeks and filled my other hole just as I'd done hers, and I jumped. Then she leaned forward and claimed my open mouth in a hard, wet kiss, thrusting the Feldeu into me as she kept her finger in my netherhole. Whatever just happened, my arousal surged.

I groaned against her mouth before catching a rhythm of my own, burying my nose in her neck as I did buas, and she let me. She smelled like she never wore any perfume or delicate scent; she bathed with water, but her scent was pure earth and musk. She removed her finger from me and kept her arms loosely around my waist while I used her shoulders for leverage to fuck her cock harder and harder.

Oh, Braqth, it felt so good; I was in control enough to let loose. My partner beneath me was neither limp-fish nor tooth-and-nail fighting, and the shared heat kept the wetness on our skin from cooling.

"Oh, *yeah!*" I ground out, climbing quickly as I worked her like a hard and ready bua.

I was going to come soon, and my cries grew louder than Rausery had been; they grew higher and higher in pitch. She used those cries to gauge just when she should thrust her finger back inside my puckered ring, returning the favor. When she did, something huge exploded in my head, and I screamed in delight. My body clenched hard and I uttered successive, breathy groans as I came back down, immense stress bleeding out of me until I lay lax and gasping against her, my head resting on her shoulder. I realized I had my arms around Rausery's shoulders and our breasts were pressed together.

And her arms were around me.

Shit. Too casual.

I straightened up, still sitting on her lap with the Feldeu inside me, and removed my arms, laying my palms on my thighs. I saw her grinning face. She was panting.

"So, was I anyone in particular?" she asked, white eyebrow quirking.

I shook my head, understanding what she asked and having no energy to pretend otherwise. "No … no. A blend of several."

She nodded. "Looked like fun. You lost yourself in it, didn't even notice when I came again, right?"

My face stayed hot. "Uhm. Correct, Elder."

"If I were a bua, you'd have my cream bubbling in your womb now. You risk catching."

Since we are on the topic.

"If? Will I … ever have anyone outside the Sisterhood? Elder D'Shea said, going forward — "

"Yep, you will. Just don't know when."

She patted my ass to encourage me off her. Her firm, black phallus glistened after I drew my body off and lifted one leg to dismount.

"But if you get stupid," the Elder added, "and get yourself pregnant in your first decade, I'll send you to the Sanctuary with your backside so tender, you can't sit down. Get on the bed now. Time to rest."

She stood up, and I wiped down again as she took care of her toy. I might have been drowsy a moment ago, but now my mind was wide awake, hurling toward the Priestesses again.

Send me to the Sanctuary if I catch?

"What do you mean?" I asked. I knew I sounded scared.

Elder Rausery frowned but said nothing as she joined me on the pallet, laying the blanket over both of us. She propped herself on her elbow, and I felt small compared to her. "D'Shea didn't tell you?"

"She only forbid sex outside the Sisterhood, until she said otherwise."

"Helpful." Rausery exhaled. "Red Sisters who catch on duty can't purge the unborn, or if they do and are caught, the punishment is execution on the altar or becoming a Dread Spider. Per the Valsharess, our Red Sisters are to be sent to the Sanctuary to have the baby. The Priestesses keep it, and the Sister is sent back to us for retraining, if possible. It's the one, unyielding power the Priesthood has over the Sisterhood."

I clutched the blanket hard, my eyes wide as I listened. The Elder was smirking.

"You never had to worry about it before," she stated. "You do, now."

Just imagining it horrified me. I may not have paid as much attention before, but I knew a pregnancy took two full turns to complete. Twenty-four quad-spans — one for every Noble House we had named — and I couldn't even think how many spans that was.

That whole time, trapped in the Sanctuary with the Priestesses, away from the Sisters?

"Th-the Priestess made me fertile again on purpose?"

Rausery nodded. "One of the things that had to be 'fixed' about you before we could accept you."

"I-Is it required to have a baby? For service?"

"No. We've gone two centuries now without losing a Sister to them, thanks to some internal rules of our own. Some like Jaunda simply don't play with bua cocks inside her at all. Never a risk."

Instant dismay. I already knew I couldn't be like Jaunda. Not that way.

Even if it was probably smarter.

"I-I don't know how catching really works, Elder," I admitted. "I don't know how to be sure, aside from abstaining."

Rausery quirked an eyebrow at me; she wasn't impressed, but she shrugged. "I get why, after what your sister did to you. More pressing matters now, but I'll make sure you get some tutoring. For now, rest. Then we focus on the Worship Ball."

Elder D'Shea sent Lead Qivni back to Elder Rausery as it approached the end of the next cycle, signaling that it was time to trade back again. I was almost glad; I had a cracking headache from everything which had been thrown at me, and I was regularly tamping down panic at the thought of not being ready and embarrassing the Sisterhood in front of the Priesthood and the Nobility.

Too late to worry now. We've done what we can. Sink or swim.

"Here," Rausery instructed, handing me a small stone colored dark green with veins of red. "Give this to your Elder. You can head back now."

I took the stone, bowed my head, and wordlessly left by myself. I didn't acknowledge the look Qivni had given me as she studied the borrowed, red uniform and shook her head. My mind still whirled, visualizing things I could do differently, would *need* to do differently. I crossed the Cloister, reaching D'Shea's quarters where I knocked and waited to be bid entry.

I observed my superior's face as she first saw me. She was at her desk, dressed in her lovely robes again with a crystal glass containing a faint green liquid, and seemed to have been writing something. She granted me raised brows and a slowly growing smile.

"Mm. You do the uniform justice, Sirana."

A surprised rush of heat passed through me. "Thank you, Elder."

"I expect you have much to tell me."

"Yes. Elder Rausery gave me strict instruction, and I am ready for the Ball, Elder. I shan't embarrass you."

She nodded. "I believe you, novice. Is that how you spent all of your time with her?"

"No, Elder."

She waited. I chose my words.

"Did you expect the Prime to be interested in whatever Elder Rausery was doing with me?" I asked.

The Sorceress raised a graceful eyebrow but smiled. "Eventual and inevitable, perhaps. The Prime has patterns, but I don't track her where-abouts or moods at all times. Why? Did she show interest in you?"

I narrowed my eyes a little. "You didn't hear anything, Elder? Weren't curious at all, just turned a blind eye?"

"I was busy with Rausery's three teams," she said coolly with warning. "You brought it up, novice. Explain it to me."

"We met the Prime after Elder Rausery took me on an exhausting run," I reported. "She was pleased you had turned over Jaunda to Rausery for wherever she went, but she *wasn't* happy Rausery was filling her time with just me. She didn't like the idea of me wearing red at the Worship Ball. She demanded that I spar with other Sisters first, and Rausery signed to me that it had to be 'entertaining.'"

Elder D'Shea smiled. "Indeed. Who did you fight?"

"Sisters Panagan and Moria."

"Is that who she asked for?"

"No, Elder. She wanted Corpora Thena."

"Predictable." D'Shea smirked with satisfaction.

Manipulative cunt, the Prime said.

I said now, "I think both she and Rausery realized what you'd done to protect me from Thena this time."

A graceful shrug of her shoulders. "Not my goal, but a side effect. The Prime is satisfied with what I've accomplished while Elder Rausery tutored you, that is all you need to know."

A sudden bloom of anger rose in my gut, but I was wary of letting it show. "Panagan and Moria were disappointing, I think. The Prime decided to test me herself after Elder Rausery provided some instruction."

D'Shea's dark red eyes focused on me for a few intense flicks. "Hm. And you stand before me right now, wearing red. You must have bent, and Elder Rausery helped you afterward."

I swallowed. She pinned it. "She did, Elder. She said I impressed her."

Elder D'Shea gave me that proud smile of before. "I am glad she sees it now, as I do."

The anger cooled somewhat. "She thinks the Prime lost interest in me."

"I trust Rausery's judgment in that."

I felt relief; I hoped both Elders were right. Fiddling with a pouch at my new belt, I said, "She gave me a bloodstone to give to you, Elder. I apologize for not mentioning it sooner."

The Sorceress chuckled softly and nodded, holding out her hand as I stepped forward to put it in her naked palm. She set it down on the desk without studying it; she focused on me. "Did Rausery seem interested in you, Sirana? Where the Prime was not."

I recalled my coupling in the chair with the warrior Elder. Offering to serve her with my mouth. Sharing the same sluicer to get clean. The free and even tone of her voice, encouraging me. Telling me stuff I needed to know to survive.

"I ... seemed to amuse her, Elder D'Shea."

D'Shea could tell my words didn't match my tone. "Is that a yes? She likes you?"

"Yes, Elder." I felt some heat come to my face for reasons I didn't fathom. "But I would never expect it to grant me any special favors."

"Of course not. But if I loaned you to her from time-to-time, would you resent it?"

The conversation, such as it was, seemed to be speeding up. I was still trying to determine how likely it was that D'Shea might have orchestrated some of this or all of it? Did she know enough of Rausery and of me to predict the outcome of the last two cycles? Or was she just taking advantage of an opportunity?

"Ah. No, Elder, I wouldn't be opposed."

She kept staring at me. I was not stupid.

"I take it you would have goals for me other than serving her, Elder. You are still my superior, your orders supersede hers."

Her smile really was one of the more beautiful ones when she chose to use it. "I enjoy that you can keep up in our conversations, Sirana."

It didn't feel like it. And since when was this a "conversation," not a report or even an interrogation?

"Rausery might think that I'm spying on her for you," I ventured. "She's not thick."

D'Shea nodded. "Of course. We both expect it when we swap teams." She tapped a few delicate fingers against her glass before taking a sip. "It's one way we get caught up."

Before I had a chance to follow her thought, she added, "You are dismissed. Find Gaelan, she has your next duty. Take your Reverie, and within eight marks, you both head to the Palace."

I had not chosen my own barracks room yet even as some were available. Nothing except a physical lock kept the door closed, and I'd been too tired and lacking in skills to innovate something new.

The magic locks were for those with rank or magic of their own, while the rest were trained in a bit of trap-setting, and Gaelan knew a bit of both. I was still learning from her and even preferred resting with either her or Jaunda if the timing worked out.

This was a change from my House when I'd never closed my eyes in the same room with another female. Not even my Mother.

This time our Reverie allowance coincided by order of our Elder, and Gaelan and I each stripped, wiped down, and lay upon the same pallet. My eyes drooped immediately, and Gaelan watched me with a small smile. She asked me a few test questions about the Worship Ball, and I was able to mumble an answer or two, which seemed to satisfy her, and then I slipped away from consciousness.

This Reverie was one of the deepest I'd known. In it, I saw the tawny paleness of the Valsharess's eyes hovering above me. Not a face or an expression, just the eyes, and the glassy focus soon drifted from me, forgetting me as Her gaze was drawn to the left. I followed the general direction just as the Queen's Eyes disintegrated in a haze.

Now I saw another silhouette, solid black, and hard to make out against an enormous background dotted with motes of light, the expanse such that I couldn't tell if it was a cave or not. Then his eyes opened; milky-white without pupils, a white beard, bald head and skin almost as dark as mine. The body was shorter than me but stocky and very strong.

I backed up quickly, holding my empty palm out in front of me. ~Kain.~

~Sirana.~

He held a dagger.

The ground beneath my bare feet wasn't hard rock but soft grains of infinite number, dry enough to continually shift and slide beneath even my slight weight, never mind the deep, shushing imprints left by the Tragar.

~*Get away,*~ I demanded, plainly afraid.

~*We can't.*~

That was when light rose up behind him. Golden, searing light.

This was no cavern.

Behind him was a curved line of some vast expanse of space. I realized, somehow, I wasn't underground. I was exposed, body, mind, and essence, and there was nowhere to hide.

The light should have blinded me, yet I watched the backlit silhouette of the Dwarf I'd killed now stalking toward me. He lifted his fisted hand, grains of red and yellow sediment flowing from the point of that dagger blade. The dagger itself was black with scarlet runes etched along both sides. They glowed hungrily.

The weapon was offered, and it was brandished.

~*It's a gift, and a curse,*~ Kain thought.

I drew breath to scream. Before I could, the dagger flashed and bit deep into my gut, moving and angling itself independent of Kain's wrist. I doubled over as I clutched them, my mouth wide open but my voice silent. The blade was eating me from the inside out, dissolving my life, my strength, like a spider's venom liquified the guts of its prey.

Now I was on my knees, and finally ...

I started screaming.

"Sirana. *Sirana!*"

I opened my eyes sucking in a lungful of air. My joints were locked, my chest hurting from some creeping pressure. I stared up at Gaelan, who lay on the same pallet with me. She looked concerned and was gripping my shoulder; she'd been shaking me.

"Are you awake?" she asked.

I nodded.

"How many fingers?" She held them up, and I counted.

"Three."

"Alright. What did you dream? You've thrashed some before, but ... Was it the altar again?"

I let out my breath, drew in again, willing my heart to slow down.

What I thought I'd seen made no sense, so I nodded. "Yes. The one with Lelinahdara."

Gaelan nodded, looking thoughtful. "Any of that mixing with the failed one Jilrina did? Or is it just the true one?"

I made a face, unprepared for that line of questioning and baffled why she would care. "I don't know. I can't ... I don't ..."

"Never mind," she said.

Then I remembered.

"Elder Rausery told me my womb was healed on purpose," I blurted, and Gaelan looked startled. "Because every Red Sister must be fertile. And we go to the Priestesses if we are stupid enough to get pregnant."

She bolted upright as if evading a pincer worm, holding her head and shuddering. I sat upright as well, both of us naked from the waist with only a blanket covering as I stared at her. That was a much stronger reaction than I expected if I'd considered any at all.

"What did I say?" I asked. "Did you have to give a baby to the P — ?"

"No!" she barked, her anger clear as she glanced at me. "I've never caught."

Her voice was clipped, and she was looking away from me.

"Then what in the Abyss was that?" I demanded.

She waved her hand. "I thought Elder D'Shea told you."

"Well, it was Rausery who did. And are you lying to me?"

Gaelan shook her head, breathing deep and glancing tentatively at me. "I've only been here five turns, Sirana. Compared to some, I'm as new as you. Think about it, me spending two of those five turns in the Sanctuary wouldn't see me as Elder D'Shea's Right Hand now."

I eyed her. "That's still a fast climb because they haven't chosen many mages for the Sisterhood. You can actually *make* those tools I've seen Jaunda use."

She shrugged, plain in her scowl. "I'm sure I was just a needed replacement for another Sister who died."

"Who?"

"I don't know."

"Did you make potions and things before the Sisterhood? Where are you from?"

Gaelan stared straight ahead and into space; a subtle shiver passed through her, and she swallowed a few times. "That doesn't matter. I don't have a family anymore, same as you."

I was irritated by that blatant block. "Why did you ask about Jilrina in my dreams, then? What does *that* fucking matter to you if we have no family but us?"

Gaelan shook her head, squeezing her eyes as she pressed the heels of her palms against her forehead as if trying to compress it down. "I'm sorry I asked, Sirana. Really. I won't ask about your former House anymore."

"Why not? Everyone else does," I said. "They are still asking if I killed her. Even Elder Rausery has."

"Well, your sister *was* a First Daughter sired by the first Royal Consorts," Gaelan said, taking some deep breaths. "The gossip was widespread even outside the Palace Court, in case you didn't know."

I blinked. "The commoners? Why would they talk?"

A shrug. "Why not? Supposedly Noble breeding matters more. A lot of merchants and guards keep track of the drama."

I paused. Gaelan had been a Red Sister for only five turns, while Jilrina had died twenty turns ago. "You were a commoner? And you heard about me?"

She pursed her lips and nodded, still seeming angry. "But I don't ... really care, Sirana. And now that you're gone from Court, no one else will, either. Just forget it."

Impossible.

"But I'm going to be back at Court in less than six marks!" I said. "Wearing red!"

Somehow that eased the tension in her face, and her white eyebrows lifted as she glanced at me. I was surprised by the small smile. "You look good in it, you know. Even if it is borrowed. It won't be long before D'Shea sees one custom-made for you to fit right."

That almost worked, but I wasn't quite distracted enough. "Why would Elder D'Shea put me under the Nobles' nose again so soon if I was just supposed to vanish when the Sisterhood came for me?"

Gaelan shrugged. "I'm not privy to her plans, Sirana. Maybe she just wants to see how much you cling to your past. What will you do with it, given you have no choice?"

Given half a tick to think about it, I realized Mother and Kaltra would probably be there; they might be at the Palace right now, staying in my old rooms. Where I'd spent a decade and a half living alone except for whatever buas I could draw into my bed.

My chest ached again. Not good. I had been so focused on the training and decorum and ritual of it all that I hadn't thought about who I might see there.

I might see the Consort, too. Shit.

Abruptly, I considered whether my invisible wizard might attend as well. How could I be so unprepared? Had I lost what Court edge I'd worked so long for already?

Maybe this was exactly what my Elder wanted to see, and Gaelan would be there to report on me. Rausery and the Prime would hear about it, too, if I embarrassed them. But how could the Sorceress have known that the Valsharess would find me "acceptable" in the first place?

Shit, I thought again. *This is a personal test, whether it was planned or not.*

"Let's get ready," Gaelan suggested.

CHAPTER 19

THE GRAND HALL OF THE PALACE COULD FIT TWO THOUSAND DAVRIN SNUGLY, which was probably a third of our population, if one didn't count the Sathoet breeds and all non-Elf slaves, servants, traders, crafters, and miscreants which crawled over Sivaraus.

At this festival there would be only a fraction of that capacity: several representatives from the Priesthood and their attendants, select Nobles from each of the current twenty-four Houses along with their Davrin-only attendants and adding a handful of wizards from the Tower.

The purpose of the male mages was the maintenance of various cantrips in the Grand Hall — involving lighting, decoration, and aural control — and generally being available to our Queen and Priestesses should they need them. One never did really know when they would need a mage for necessary things, and the female sorceresses would be handling the more important aspects such as testing for tampering of food and drink, managing and tracking the comings and goings of the guests.

I hoped to approach the wizards at some point this eve, merely to see if I got lucky to find one of them familiar, while I contemplated how I would handle possibly seeing Mother and Kaltra again.

Ignore them, probably. I'm not of House Thalluen anymore.

Meanwhile, the Royal Consorts would either be attending their current Matrons or brought out to be presented by the Priestesses when the time came. Their total number was only twenty, less than half that of the Red Sisters; there were not enough to give each House even one, and it was not uncommon that the top five Houses have two.

A virgin Consort meant only that he had not served a Matron for an official term yet. The Priestesses would never present an untested, untrained male, but virgin or not, each was still required to prove his ability and virility atop Braqth's altar before being sent with his new Mistress at the end of the ball.

Going through twenty of these couplings will take some time.

The last thing for me to bear in mind was that it was for this ritual that Curgia had prepared herself, anticipating she would be the one from her House to test a Consort before the eyes of all present. It would not be her, of course; Wilsira had made her agree it would be another of her sisters instead. I wondered if Curgia would even show her face at the Ball?

Artisans, performers, soldiers, and servants abounded, swelling the number of Noble and Sancta bodies present four-fold, although only seven Red Sisters would be visible to ensure the peace. The four most experienced — Qivni, Agalia, and the two ranking Sisters — would remain unseen, with the clear priority to protect the Valsharess and Priestesses should any threat make itself known.

A quarter of the Sisterhood attended this Ball, which did demonstrate its importance even as it was not a difficult assignment. Any disruption might see us directed to make a public example of a troublemaker. In that instance, I had no Feldeu, and all I knew was that I would do as I was told.

Gaelan and I also wouldn't be able to stand near each other often or take any cooperative activities because we had few overlapping stations to watch and be seen. The visible Sisters would switch areas every half mark, red uniforms vanishing in and out of sight with deliberation.

In position, Qivni's voice came through a message cantrip, a generic sound intended for all of us. *At attention. Follow your path but keep it fluid. Use your tools if you see any threat and inform Agalia and me immediately.*

287

I took my first position to the side and closest to the door as the guests and representatives arrived in due fashion wearing their beautiful, flowing dress and artful decorations, hairstyles, and headdresses. Their choices took advantage of candle and torchlight or cultivated, glowing lichen, and only at a time and place such as this had I ever seen so many vibrant colors all in one place, drenching everything.

As the Grand Hall filled, it returned to me once again how I'd found the social rituals to be excruciatingly dull unless I either became engrossed in a plot or managed to seduce an attractive bua from another House. The only exception had been that mass ritual to help conceive a demon-child, about which I had both wet dreams and terror sweats ever since. Leaving the Ball early wasn't an option; I was here until the end, but at least I wasn't required to be involved in the gossip and chatter.

Ironically, as I made my assigned rounds, I observed more gestures and leans to whisper than I ever had before, blatantly watching them and taking mental notes for anything possibly significant. I saw faces I recognized, but they would quickly avert their gaze if I came near them. Three caits who had taunted me along with two older governesses who disliked my laugh betrayed their shock at recognizing me then quickly covered it up. I had to admit that was satisfying, even as I knew it was all due to the uniform.

I wonder what they imagine I've been through since they last saw me?

Probably stories more insane than it actually was, even though there were several tests I'd rather not repeat.

I spotted Curgia after a time; she had indeed shown up to the Worship Ball. Knowing what I knew, I could detect the strained corners of her smiling mouth and saw the misery in her eyes as she made her own kind of rounds, bartering and hinting with various members, indirectly comparing agendas.

More than once her hand touched her abdomen, but it wasn't in proud anticipation. From the way she was drinking the fermented spirits, no one would expect her to be carrying. Of course, it had only been a few cycles; everything she felt had to be the wisp of possibility in her anxious mind.

When I spotted the next Davrin I knew, she also rested a hand over her abdomen. My gait hesitated and stuttered, and I cursed myself, stepping behind a dark grey column, decorated with the banner of the Second House, to regather my wits.

Fuck. What the fuck?

My Mother was here. I hadn't seen her in almost a decade, and although I counted myself lucky that Kaltra didn't stand beside her, I hadn't expected to see the Matron pregnant.

Already. At least a full turn, to be that size. I never even heard about it, I didn't know she planned to …

The red leather of my glove softened the tips of my fingers as they dug into my palm. To think I could walk up to her now and tell her I wasn't barren. And I'd be telling the truth. It was an action I would never take, *could* never choose and expect to live beyond the Prime finding out.

Daughters are easily replaced, I suppose. And the Sisterhood needs them, too.

After my heart slowed, I considered what this also said about Mother's faith in Kaltra as the uncontested Heir. Matron Thalluen would have been informed of what happened to me; the Prime had ordered it, and there was no way to get me back regardless. I could grant perhaps Mother was showing good sense about the future of House Thalluen under Kaltra the Incompetent.

At least she's still capable. She must be praying for a fourth female. Will she get it, I wonder? What are the chances of that?

I shook myself out of my doubts and refocused, coming out from behind the column and continuing my rounds. I made no deliberate effort to be visible to the Matron of Thalluen, but it was inevitable that she might see me in the Grand Hall, with the light and the bright red of my leathers. I must not have been looking at her when she first caught sight of me because when our eyes did meet, she did not blink.

She had the chance to cover any honest response.

Just as I had.

Matron Thalluen watched me steadily as I strolled around two other groups of subtly shifting Nobles, and she smiled slightly, showing what could be a guarded measure of pride in her scarlet eyes.

Then she looked away like all the rest.

I hesitated, knowing this was a test even if Mother might not be aware of it. I could ignore her — or pretend to — and evade her all eve. I could show my Sisters here, evaluating me, that I'd severed all links to those outside the Cloister. Except I hadn't, yet. And my Elder's both encouraging me to confront my fears and my anger while at the same time avoiding a certain Priestess still rankled me.

I approached Rohenvi of House Thalluen directly, getting within several paces as Nobles around her became aware of me and stiffened. They parted for me or took a deliberate step away from her. None gave away whether they caught the likeness between us, though I'd have thought only the blind would miss it.

"You honor this festival of fertility with your presence, Matron," I said, glancing pointedly at her swollen belly.

She bowed gracefully before me, perfect and elegant as if she really had spent decades at Court before I was born. I was taken aback but kept my face like stone.

"My humble thanks, Red Sister," she replied and, somehow, I sensed the hand on her belly had turned protective. "That is my most faithful wish to honor our Queen."

She wants that baby. She's afraid of me.

I hadn't thought ahead when I decided to speak to her. I didn't know what to say next because, somehow, I hadn't anticipated that she would yield so fast.

Idiot.

"Do you know the sex yet?" I asked, and I could tell she wasn't eager to say, but she wasn't going to refuse. She probably wasn't even going to lie.

"Yes, Red Sister. She's female."

In another turn, I'd have a younger sister. That was four caits in a row, no buas. How could a Matron have it so well and still be struggling?

Because the Consort-bred Daughters were insane or stupid.

I nodded, working to keep my back straight and my chin raised. I had the higher status here, but it didn't feel like it. And none of this should matter.

My Mother curtsied again, giving me an out. "Bless and keep the Valsharess, Defender."

I left, having nothing else to say. I wondered if Qivni had been watching, or Gaelan. I wondered what they'd say to their Elders, and whether I'd failed.

Fuck.

Brooding while the early dining and drinking happened, prior to the Priestesses coming out with the new buas, I had plenty of time to watch everyone three times over and the freedom to move among them without obstruction or delays.

I noticed the Noble male counterparts on the arms of the named guests, saw their simpler desires. Some of them I knew what they looked like naked, and a quiet pang of longing entered my lower gut.

I had adapted to the Feldeu quickly, and I was learning to enjoy sex with caits, which was a feat after my sister, but they all smelled like females.

Buas smell like males. It's different.

I enjoyed their smell, had grown to savor their taste and have fun with their offerings. It still thrilled me to recall the faces my buas made as their stiff rods flexed and spurted either over my skin, down my throat, or deep inside me.

Goddess, I'd enjoy some real cock right now.

Although now there was a real chance I could end up like Mother, and that wouldn't be good for me the way it was for her.

Being unable to pursue them in any way put the Noble Sons in a new light to me that eve. It seemed to have been so long since I'd been around buas that, now being surrounded by them, they moved differently, smiled differently than before.

My plainest thought was I noticed which males had more will and sway over their Matrons or Mistresses. Not all of them stood by handsomely, with interest only for what gifts and compliments could be offered them. Some seemed to have plots of their own, acting to persuade the dominant female protecting them.

What sort of plots interest them, I wonder?

I hadn't really paid attention. I had made a reputation for just wanting their bodies, and those buas who wanted the same gave me signals to pursue them. Any complication came from their sisters and female cousins and governesses. None of these here, whispering in their Matrons' ear, had ever thought I might be worth lying under; I'd had no real connections at Court.

Fortunate for me.

Before Qivni had come for me, I would have laughed at the thought of playing some lasting game of political intrigue with a male, but there were the signs, right before my eyes, I was quite sure. More so, I was reminded of Kerse. Of my doubt in whether Kerse had made eye contact with me or not through the spy wall. I recalled his Mother, not really knowing how much control she had over him.

At that moment, my eyes landed on a trio of wizards talking with each other, near the musicians playing their strings and air pipes. As one they saw me, and two looked away immediately while I could have sworn the third gave me a very familiar, inviting look.

Hello.

I didn't break stride as I changed course to approach them. The two cautious ones did not look happy, but the one with playful, rust-colored eyes was surprised. I supposed this mage expected I'd ignore that bedroom gaze.

No, handsome. Perfect excuse to find out which of you might have plowed my asshole and got away with it.

Yet the mental image of this welcoming wizard disrobing for me and stretching out underneath me, offering me his cock at full attention—

I groaned inwardly.

I took a moment to note the modest, full robes they wore. The material was uncharacteristically thick for most Davrin of status, and it obscured their shape. They favored the darker shades of blue, though I didn't miss the not-just-decorative threads of purple and gold mixed in at the hems. These buas were ultimately owned and directed by the Valsharess and the Priestesses, same as the Consorts and the Sathoet.

The flirting wizard had a subtle swath of brown draped over one shoulder as well; I knew it meant he was connected to the army, and therefore probably a battle mage. The other two had no such marks and so were perhaps Tower researchers or some such.

I reflected that my invisible wizard had been naked at the time his spell was wearing; I had no idea what his specialty was if he had one. I was sure the battle mage was not the one I sought, although my nose would confirm once I got close enough.

"Red Sister, you honor us," he said, betraying no nervousness. "Is there some urgent service for which you need one of us? We will assist and gladly."

His tone withheld any suggestion, and he was not leering; he could have been legitimately asking if I needed a scribe to pen and deliver a message, or someone to relight one of the magic candles that had gone out in the chandelier above. Still, I wagered I could have asked that he take my arm to go somewhere more private instead, and he'd have done it without a blink.

A sure way to get my ass beaten and my holes fucked raw back in the Cloister, too.

If the Prime was in a good mood.

The other two males looked a little green around the edges, desperate to hope that the offer by the battlemage was not accepted. I wavered whether to take the direct method of asking my question, which hadn't gone so well with my own Mother, and which might give my wizard warning if none of these three were who I sought.

I knew they gossiped between themselves as much as any cluster of Nobles, but it would also depend on how many within the Tower knew the details of Red Sister initiation, and whether my wizard was paranoid enough to have let others know one of the Sisters might try to find him.

My guess was "not likely" on both counts.

I decided I could do a mix of direct with indirect, and I took a step closer to the battle mage who had given me the opening.

"Don't move," I warned in a low purr, leaning in with my nose and mouth to brush both lightly against his smooth throat. I heard him draw in air, excited, I concentrated on his scent. New to me; fragrant and attractive but not one I'd smelled before.

I moved back and took a step to sample the second one immediately after; his scent was slightly bitter, tinged with fear, but had sweet undertones. He likely drank a lot of the hot, sweetened taze at the serving tables. Also, one I had never smelled before. The other two shuffled just a little bit as the third one went stiff for his turn; also bitter, but this time savory And new.

None of them were "my" wizard.

I straightened up and stepped back, smiling without showing my teeth; only the battle mage would meet my eyes. "Very nice, I'll wager you can think under pressure."

I gestured to his brown sash. It worked beautifully. He beamed.

"Three skirmishes, no casualties, thanks to me, Red Sister."

I nodded, surveying the room again periodically as we spoke. I was still on assignment. "Against what?"

He had the grace to clear his throat in playful humility; he wasn't going to overplay his worth at first meeting. "Small bands of raiders with a few troublesome Yutogul blocking a river route, Red Sister. But I will be ready for more challenging work when the time comes."

I nodded. "And your name, mage?"

"Callitro, Red Sister," he answered, and did not ask for mine.

"You talk to many Red Sisters, Callitro?"

"No, Red Sister."

I quirked my brow and my smile. "Do you 'not talk' with many Red Sisters, Callitro?"

He laughed, understanding my meaning. "Alas. Only admiration thus far, Red Sister."

"Indeed."

I really wondered about the stories he'd heard. Either he hadn't witnessed an execution performed by the Sisters, or he just had some sweet-and-rotting tastes. It was a bit hard to tell, but I doubted he would fight very much.

Still, the possibility must have been shining in his mind just as it was in mine. Mutually beneficial relationships had their place, even if I was always wary of them.

It came down to total knowledge; if he knew more of Red Sisters than I knew of wizards, it would ultimately work in his favor, not mine. On the other hand, if he knew very little and I learned more about the Tower, then he would be worth the risk of getting closer sometime.

I needed that tutoring Rausery had promised on not getting pregnant first.

I scanned the room as I stood near the wizards, knowing my Sister would note me in the swirling crowd and probably understood my motivation. A few Nobles would have noticed, too, but they couldn't say why. The Priestesses weren't yet present with the Consorts, and the Valsharess was sitting as She had been, receiving one bow after another. Who knew everything She saw?

"Only admiration thus far," I echoed the wizard's words with a suggestion in the eyes as I kept my expression placid.

Callitro maintained eye contact for three full flicks before looking down, a perfectly timed and proper signal of interest, despite the primal desire I knew was there; I could sense the heat coming off his skin.

Damn the Abyss. He smells good.

Noble Sirana would have found an empty chamber or secluded bit of garden right now; Red Sister Sirana could not abandon her post. Nor did I know enough yet whether I could meet him after the Worship Ball.

I reached up to touch his upper arm. "Come."

Callitro seemed to forget his gaping companions as he took a few steps to the side with me. Now it was not so easy to hear casual conversation standing closer to the music.

"Do you receive visitors?" I asked in his ear, and he shivered slightly before leaning back.

The burnt-orange of the battlemage's eyes locked on mine again for longer than would be proper between Nobles. It finally occurred to me that he was fascinated by the blue of my eyes, but he was also not slow in the head, and he understood me.

"No. No casual visitors allowed, but … make an order for me by name," he murmured. "Something you need. A potion, a tool, an enchanted weapon. Send it through Phaelous, my Headmaster. I've seen him talk with the Sisterhood. You may check my progress as you see fit. I have my own small quarters."

Just like that, he had given me everything I needed to find him again on my own schedule. The way he spoke, his lips would have been tough to read as well. Maybe none of my Sisters even knew what was said.

Bravo, young mage. I wanted to smile widely at him but refrained, nodding once. "Return to your duties."

Callitro nodded, bowed and obeyed, stepping away as I began my rounds again.

Two marks on a candle passed; everyone had eaten and drank their fill, had even digested most of it and nothing of interest happened until the Priestesses finally entered. They announced, at last, the most anticipated part of the Ball: the demonstration and awarding of the Royal Consorts.

The Valsharess stood slowly then, raising both hands into the air, the shimmering purple and gold fabric of her gown set off well, even across the hall from me.

"Let all Royal Consorts return to Us."

I witnessed an odd, surreal moment of anxiety as fifteen, beautiful, Elven buas tentatively took their first step to separate from their Matron to walk, alone and untouched, through the crowd toward their Queen.

Each one kneeled and waited as the Valsharess removed the identifying, round-belly circlet from around their throats. While She did this, I marveled and almost laughed at some of the Matron's expressions. They were all determined to get him — or if not him, then another — back by the end of the Ball and, I imagined, to put a new collar on him as quickly as possible.

Something about their naked throats makes them feel threatened.

Being able to see all of them all at once was rare, and I had a harder time keeping my vigilance on the Grand Hall rather than gazing contentedly at such a display of male perfection for as long as I could.

Some had unusual features; a pair of dark ears a little longer than the rest; a few had blue eyes like mine, but one also green, and another purple. One had golden hair granted by birth; he was far too young to have earned it with age. Another displayed bluish-white hair, like some of the cave luminescence I'd seen in the wilderness. Still another had the white-hair/red-eye classic combination, but his hair was oddly curly, even worn long.

The Consorts were mostly the same height; their heads reached no higher than an average Matron's ear. All of them had healthy and trim bodies, and their endowments could be nothing less than satisfying. I could make the educated guess that they were bred to be somewhat larger in girth or length beneath their small clothes than their overall size would indicate.

As the Consorts all returned to the platform with the Valsharess, I searched for and finally picked out the one I thought of as "mine," but more accurately the one that I had poached from House D'Verin for a very brief time. I was plainly curious to whom this Consort would go next. He did not have any of the exotic colors to his hair or eyes, but his features were overall strange to Nobles and commoners alike, though lovely and perfectly balanced. Perhaps if he had some odd coloring to him, I might've known to stay away from him.

But probably not. Not even the circlet had made a difference.

The decisions on who would be favored were already decided, as far as I knew; what happened here this eve were the "signs" from Braqth saying which Consort to gift to which deserving House. I'd always been so skeptical of this part. I thought the Priestesses just wanted to watch the Consorts get fucked and enjoy the stumbling antics of eager Nobles trying to outperform each other in public.

Perhaps, as I recalled this happening at least once, a step more also gave the Sanctuary breeding slave a last-moment possibility to avoid serving a particular Mistress. One bua had been so scared — I guessed — that he'd gone limp when his previous Matron touched him on the altar. The Priestess had called it "a clear Sign from Braqth" that the pairing would not be a fertile one if repeated, there was to be variety, and the Consort had gone to another.

The ritual would be repetitive but very titillating, at least the first few times. Each Consort would be presented to at least three members from three different Houses. The Nobles would touch him, maybe talk to him, and wait for the sign which among them was chosen by the Spider Queen before claiming him.

The chosen one would mount him immediately, so we could all see he still had value as a virile Consort. The ritual required a seeded sex to be presented afterward, one of the few times Nobles showed their privileged slits to public eyes in something less than a perfect state of grooming.

Keeping guard would be easy while everyone placed their plots on hold until after the show. I could smell the rise in excitement and heat around me, and Gaelan appeared in my line of sight. She was standing just behind a purple banner that nearly touched the floor and gestured so briefly that I almost missed it.

Out of view now.

Hm? Oh yes, I forgot …

I slipped past the distracted clusters of Dark Elves, climbed a few polished steps and slipped behind the banner to meet my Sister. We were farther back and deep in shadow, now out of the chandelier light and within the outer walkway which ringed the Grand Hall. Gaelan didn't speak but continued with hand sign. Some gestures were unique in meaning to the Red Sisters, as I expected there were in every closed group in Sivaraus, but I was still learning them, so she went slow.

Prowling is discouraged during altar rituals. Priestesses say it interrupts the magic flow.

I nodded and signed, *Understood.*

Gaelan smirked. *Distracted by the wizard or the Consort?*

I smiled fully and answered, *The Consort.*

Gaelan's stomach moved in silent laughter before she leaned out by the banner to look out. She was still for a time and then gestured, *There. I recognize him.*

A pause.

Still beautiful.

I nodded in agreement and waited until it was his turn. To my surprise, I didn't have to wait long. He was the third to be brought up on the altar, and that gave me an idea of his relative age among his temple brothers since they always started oldest and introduced the youngest virgins last. My Consort was three of twenty, but he was still too beautiful and exotic to tell just how old that was.

Well. He's older than me, anyway.

My Sister and I watched the crowd and the altar from where we stood. Having already seen the first two chosen, awarded, and fucked — young, Noble caits stumbling on excited, shaky knees off the altar and her cunt filled with seed — the breathing all around was heavy and the air very warm. A few subtle couplings were already going on out on the floor or off to the sides. By the time the rituals ended, most would have found a way to feel release. Then they would start over.

Most would find a way.

Not the Red Sisters, I was guessing. Maybe only later, when the Feldeu came out. I already wished I could grab Callitro for just a little while before returning to the Cloister.

This moment, my Consort lay down obediently upon the altar, his white, flowing hair draping off the side and showing none of the fear and tension I had in that same position.

I tried to watch the room, but soon my gaze returned to the Valsharess as She began at his toes and ankles like the two previous, testing his muscles and leg movement, her aged fingers grazing over the perfect skin. She cupped his pouch and wand between his legs, massaged them, and moved farther up his stomach and ribs until She reached arms to fingers to his lovely face. Finally, She combed her hands through his hair.

Somehow, he kept his expression impassive through all this; I could not read anything, whether he enjoyed it, disliked it, or was sincerely neutral.

Experienced, that one, Gaelan commented. *Perfect control.*

I raised a skeptical brow at that. *Right.*

I remembered him panicking, drawing a weapon on me, defying me with action and words. All the expressions on his face — fear, pain, anger, despair — as he had only reluctantly submitted to me. I enjoyed so many details before and after stuffing that turnip in his mouth. I felt again, in a passing wisp of sensation, how he had struggled *not* to cum inside me, how his magic had mingled with the Priestess' while his cock filled my slit.

My stomach chilled at this point, now with more knowledge.

Gaelan saved me. I would have his child growing inside me now, and I wouldn't be standing here. I'd be somewhere in the Sanctuary.

Maybe Gaelan hadn't seen most of what happened at the farmhouse, but I knew all of that had been genuine. For me, it had been nothing like the soft doll he was here with the Queen. How often did the elite females see a Consorts' genuine responses? Or did they even care?

"Unsoiled perfection," the Valsharess announced, and another Priestess stepped up to take over.

Unsoiled, huh? I bet he's relieved to hear that.

It took that extra moment to recognize Wilsira, and my mouth gaped a bit to hear her call forth Houses Lospure, Qevren, and … Itlaun.

Of course, it must be House Itlaun.

I felt an instant, hot dislike for Curgia, irrationally hoping she wouldn't get "my" Consort, and the surge of emotion shook me.

Fuck. I took a slow breath out. *No. That has to go away. It must.*

What I'd done coming back from the wilderness didn't matter anymore, except when Elders D'Shea or Rausery, or the Red Sister Prime, said it did.

Still, I watched Curgia gesture to another Elf who had to be her younger sister; she whispered something harshly and nudged her forward. The younger sister was prettier than Curgia but inexperienced in the ways of Court; it was clear she did not know exactly what to do and had been hastily filled in — perhaps kept intentionally ignorant by her elders.

I smirked to myself, aware of the irony in my own experience, while more than one Noble House noted the sudden switch. I forgot to keep sweeping the crowds as I focused on Priestess Wilsira, Curgia's little sister, and my Consort. I suppose I justified it in that D'Shea would want to know about this especially; it tied in directly to a recent report of Jaunda's, and my Lead wasn't here to witness.

Wilsira began to chant and invited the three Davrin Nobles to touch the Consort; her smile when she looked at Curgia and at the sister again told me that Curgia's House would be awarded him for certain. At least the suspense was over for me; I could swallow my nonexistent pride and observe the interaction itself.

He's not mine.

The contrasts between the Houses invited was apparent. The other two Nobles were higher than Itlaun but lower than D'Verin who'd had this male last. They touched him now with entitlement and less reverence, their exploration heavy-handed, as if he was not their first choice anyway, being well-used, and higher Nobles than them being given some of his traits.

My Consort subtly shrank from these Nobles, and his member did not grow for them. Whether this was an instruction he was following from Wilsira, I didn't know, but those two Nobles weren't especially impressed.

Perhaps the Priestess simply chose those who couldn't surprise her.

The younger Itlaun sister, on her first trip to Court, was in plain awe of him, her mouth open as she gazed on his face. As she lightly touched his fine jaw and the edge of his ear with the soft tips of her fingers as if she expected him to chip like fired clay. I saw a small shift in his sex. He was half-erect by the time she smoothed her palm over his cheek, and he turned his lips to kiss her fingers. She gasped and nearly yanked her hand away as if surprised he had moved on his own.

Wilsira nodded once and gestured for the other two to step back. "Braqth has spoken!"

Maybe as air through my ass.

"Tulia of House Itlaun, will you accept the care and devotion of this gifted Consort for one decade? Will you protect and keep him in good health, and breed him with your family line in the name of our Valsharess and the beauty of the Davrin race?"

Curgia's sister dragged her gaze from my Consort and blinked at Wilsira before it struck her that she'd somehow been awarded his service. She glanced at Curgia once then nodded vigorously.

"Yes ... yes, Priestess! We p-pledge to care and honor him while he is in our keeping for — for one decade from this eve, my Priestess!" She made a bow to her and to the Valsharess. "Our eternal thanks and gratitude, in the name of Braqth."

"Then let the Court witness the bonding of him with House Itlaun."

I glanced at Curgia. Her jaw was tight, and she was probably gritting her teeth; she was trying not to look at Priestess Wilsira. At the same time, she nodded encouragement when Tulia hesitantly began to remove her dress in front of the crowd.

I reflected that I had been watched a lot in my time — about equally desired or not — and I was tempted to roll my eyes watching Tulia try to be modest. Then again, perhaps even I would have quavered a little at an entire Hall with hundreds of eyes all focused on me, waiting for me to mount a coveted cock and beg his seed out of him. I knew as well that Curgia wished this was her, but she did a good job hiding it. That made two of us when Gaelan looked curiously over at me, testing my own reaction.

I smiled, shrugged, and gestured, ★Aren't they cute?★

Tulia had a lithe, dancer's form, and was probably barely old enough to be at Court. The Royal bua had the vast sexual experience between them. He was already rigid for her, waiting patiently as she climbed up onto the altar to straddle him. He waited until her hands smoothed over his shoulders before he reached to touch her haunches.

She was trying not to look at the audience as she had to gather some of her own spit to make herself wet enough and, with his guidance, she slowly eased his pole inside her body. Then my Consort thrust upward, prompting her when she didn't move first, encouraging her with his smile, and reaching one hand at an awkward angle to massage her clitoris. He nodded up at her as if to say, *"The sooner we cum, the sooner they'll stop looking at us."*

Such a lucky Third Daughter. And she had no idea how this had happened, how this had been arranged. She was a pawn, but one that a lot of females would have gladly swapped places with for the rest of the Ball, including me.

"Ohh," Tulia breathed, eventually releasing her nerves and falling into the pleasure. She closed her eyes, bouncing up and down on her blessed gift, grinding her hips and squeezing her breasts with both hands. Her moans were breathy, and it occurred to me to wonder if she felt any of his magic entering her?

Maybe he's helping her to relax and get closer to the edge.

It wasn't clear to me how close she was until she suddenly stopped and hunched over her partner, clutching his chest and making such an abrupt, orgasmic squawk that it *had* to be genuine. There were more than a few chuckles in the front rows; what had lacked in grace had made up for it in entertainment.

My Consort smiled, however, holding her hips and bracing his heels against the altar to thrust up harder just as Tulia was coming down. The laughter in the crowd disappeared entirely when he orgasmed; they were captivated by the way he tensed and threw his head back, his hair waving, and by the raw, enchanting cry that escaped his lips as he gave Tulia's womb his seed at last.

A quiet beat passed before most of the audience exhaled at once, and I could tell which couples continued their standing fuck after the pause as several calls and encouraging hoots rose up.

"Show Us," the Valsharess commanded as She stood from her throne once again. Her voice was the perfect pitch of anticipation representing the rest of us.

Tulia swallowed and made as if to climb off the altar, but Wilsira held up her hand immediately.

"No. Present on the Altar. Stand above him."

The young Itlaun nodded, mumbling an apology as she recollected the next part of the ritual the crowd had seen twice before. She stood up with her ankles against her bua's ribs, and she bent over at the waist, her hair falling to brush his face. Her hands reached back to part the cheeks of her backside, presenting her soggy sex to the Priestess' and the Valsharess's full view.

I couldn't see detail from where I was, but I watched Wilsira reach to touch the wetness between Tulia's legs. The Nobles almost always flinched when that happened, and this young one was no exception. The elder Priestess ritually glided her finger across her tongue with a grand nod.

"May House Itlaun be fruitful with whole, magical seed, as evidence of Braqth's favor. Know that if you spurn Her Graces or those of our Valsharess, this award may be retracted."

I didn't miss the glance the Priestess shared with Curgia when she said that, but it was her younger sister who responded with the next line of acceptance and renewed promise.

"Take him. He is yours."

Tulia quickly donned her dress as her gift sat up, and she took the Consort's hand, pulling him naked alongside her to make room for the next ritual, and her older sister breathed out a sigh of relief and nodded. They shared only a few words before retreating with their prize somewhere out of my sight but no doubt still within the Grand Hall. It would be poor manners to leave before the end, and probably reasonably stupid as well. There was so much more to see.

Yes. More to see.

Which Houses were being favored by which Priestess, which ones the Valsharess seemed suspicious of, which Consorts betrayed any emotion whatsoever on the Altar.

I should follow them, I suggested to Gaelan. *Spy a bit more.*

Gaelan frowned. *Don't you dare. Do your duty.*

Damn.

I stood guard and became aware that, even though I was aroused, watching the Nobles have sex with the Consorts now that "my" Consort had left wasn't as potent as it had been the first time I'd seen it. They were repetitive and mechanical and, compared to the Red Sisters, the average Noble lacked the imagination and even a fraction of the passion I'd experienced over the last eight spans. The beautiful toys were in control of their expressions, their acting too obvious.

Frustrating, since I knew something real could be forced from at least one of them.

I grew bored as the Seventh House sat her twat upon the seventh Consort. I started thinking about the wizards again. My invisible wizard, yes, but also the willing and eager Callitro, who could possibly help me find the angry one whose emotions were real, unmasked and bold.

What would it be like to bed *him*, get on top of him and hold him down, whether he liked it or not? What magic would he use in his defense, I wondered? How would I respond?

A spark and a surge of heat bloomed in my gut. Challenge, intensity, and intelligence. Not to mention honest, raw emotion. That was how I wanted it if I could have it, from male or female. The Sisters had proven to me that I could take it as well as serve it, and where once I failed, I could always try again.

I had no choice but to simply wait for the Worship Ball to end at this point. Even the five new virgins being presented to Noble society, with their nervousness and wide-eyed gazes at the Valsharess were of no interest to me anymore.

Chapter 20

The Worship Ball neared an end at last. All the Consorts had been given away as proven studs, and all of those honored House members retired to their quarters at Court, granted leave to begin exploring and getting to know their new pet. I had noticed my Mother — or rather, my former Matron — and a few others had left with that first group, even without a Consort.

Not that Matron Thalluen needs one. So, who did she choose this time to puff up her belly for her?

Kaltra hadn't come. Neither had the Head Guard so I could guess which one of them was running the plantation while Mother was here.

Matron! Not Mother. Damn it.

The Priestesses remained while the Valsharess took her leave, some of them inviting their Sathoet into the Grand Hall now that no Consorts were remaining. A Noble orgy had begun as the final indulgence, but, interesting to me, Gaelan seemed no more entranced by it than I was.

Although far less orchestrated by age than when I'd been chosen, and without the compulsory magic which now gave me a tremor, I could still see that the Priestesses somehow gained something from it, and I could see the inherent contradiction among the Nobles.

Paranoid enough to assume no one follows the rules when out of sight but trusting enough to believe the rules will hold in public.

I supposed I came by it naturally. I looked for Wilsira and Kerse when the next directive came.

Time. Qivni's voice. *Next station.*

Gaelan and I split up. We were to watch the outer area of the Grand Hall as the Lead directed, discouraging anyone from trying to slip in while so many were distracted. The halls were mostly empty, with a few, furtive trysts occurring in small side rooms nearer to the festivities, which I knew weren't bedrooms.

I patrolled in silence, my footfalls refined enough that boots were now as quiet as dancing slippers. I practiced earing "past" the sex on either side of me rather than focusing on it, and it wasn't as hard as I might have thought once. I just had to remember I wielded my cunt, it didn't wield me.

At least, not anymore, I wanted to think.

I'd reached the far end of my patrol where the hallway torches hadn't been lit for several marks at least — not even an impression of the usual Radiants against the wall behind the stanchions — and I was about to turn back when a soft, directionless hiss caught my ear.

I turned around in place, my eyes piercing the dark until I spotted the faint outline within. I didn't have to wait; once I focused on the shape, the void filled with heat and strong life energy immediately. It was a Sathoet.

Then his scent hit me.

Kerse.

The demonblood wasn't in the Grand Hall with his Mother, and I wasn't sure Wilsira hadn't left as well before I came out here. I glanced around for another outline but spotted none.

Shit.

Elder D'Shea had instructed me to avoid this one. Following her orders now meant that I walk away without interaction, but that would put my back to him. Would he attack me? That depended on why he was here, and whether Wilsira sent him. My Elder and I had argued about whether he could do anything independent from her.

307

I might be about to find out unless Qivni answered me quickly.

I reached for one of the message pellets in my third pouch, and Kerse crouched lower, his yellow eyes narrowing, the white mane along his spine rising as he opened his mouth wider in another hiss. He looked about to charge.

I held up my other hand straight out, palm forward. "Whoa. Stay."

"No ssspiderss," he demanded, muscles at his shoulders bulging in tension.

I didn't understand but agreed. "No spiders, Kerse. Just this." I pulled out the pellet, holding it between my thumb and middle finger. "See? Harmless."

He sniffed in my direction suspiciously and snorted in alarm when I squeezed the pellet, breaking it to release the tiny spark of magic. At the same time, I whispered, "Qivni, aid me. Fourth side away from the altar."

The magic swallowed up the words and took them away to my chosen set of ears. Kerse wouldn't know what I'd said; he would only see my mouth moving.

"Sssirranna," the Sathoet rumbled.

I took a step back when he stepped forward. He seemed to like that; his mane relaxed.

"Ssissterrr," he hissed with a smile, crouched and ready to spring. "Rrred."

I didn't respond. I wanted to ask his intent, or if he knew I'd been watching him rut Curgia, or if he was here as a command from his Mother. I resisted directing him or exchanging any word at all. D'Shea would eventually find out about this.

Kerse's blank, yellow eyes drifted over me. "Wanntsss."

I shook my head. "No. Return to your Mother."

He grinned. "Busssy."

That didn't tell me as much as I thought at first. Only that Wilsira supposedly wasn't present and Kerse wanted to fuck again. He growled low, and his mane raised up again as I drew a dagger and a longer, fighting blade from my belt.

"Do not attack me," I commanded, brandishing both.

He chuckled and licked around his mouth, flexing his long, clawed fingers. I narrowed my eyes, locked gazes with him.

"Kerssse."

I drew out his name, mimicking him as he had said mine, trying to sound soothing although my heart pounded, and my muscles ached from inaction. He perked up a moment before shaking his head and growling.

"Kerssse," I said. "Your Mother will be displeased. She did not command this."

"Shhee diid." Another chuckle and I could see his teeth clearly in the dark as he opened his mouth, panting.

Had she? Could he lie outright, or was he twisting something he'd heard her say as an excuse? Neither was good, but the only thing truly clear to me was that this Sathoet hadn't forgotten about me as D'Shea had hoped.

Where is Qivni?

"Kerssse. Not now."

He sniffed the air, his lip curling. "Yesss, now. Hott cunnt." He gestured as if jamming two clawed fingers in a female's snatch. "Sssmell it." His eyes lingered on my drawn blades. "Ffight ffor it."

No. I won't fight. If I hurt a Priestess' son, D'Shea will answer to Wilsira.

It was also terrifying to know that he could impregnate me by force. What would happen to me, then? Taking a risk, I sheathed both weapons, abrupt and decisive. I stood up straight, confident.

"Kerse. No."

His hackles lowered down; he hesitated, looked confused. That was progress, but my message must be clear as crystal. With all the willpower I could muster, I turned my back on him and walked away. My heart pounded harder for doing it, and if his ears were as good as his nose, then he knew I expected to be attacked.

Like any of Davrin blood, he interpreted it as an invitation.

I flung myself to the side at the last instant when he was about to collide, and instead of his weight, I felt his claws rake at my torso as I was thrown off balance. He continued forward, and I heard his claws skidding on polished stone.

The Sathoet and I scrambled to be the first upright; I was a fraction faster with less momentum built but didn't have a planned response so at best it gave me the chance to draw my dagger and dodge him again.

Kerse didn't roar as he had in the candle chamber; he was amazingly quiet. He struck me on his third try, and we slammed to the ground, the wind knocked out of me though I still gripped my dagger. I didn't want to get pregnant but hesitated to stab him, cursing in my rigid mind when someone spoke aloud, harsh and grating.

Kerse flinched and threw himself away from me, champing in pain, and Qivni stepped into my field of vision, her intense, red eyes burning into the Sathoet. Her teeth bared.

"*Kerser'in'chowcz. Haganidtezj!*"

The Sathoet glared balefully at my Collector, whining in pain, and then he all but vanished from view. A moment later I heard his feet padding down one of the smaller halls. I'd just about regained my breath when Qivni stepped close to me with a scowl and knocked the toe of her boot against my ribs.

"Get up."

I felt myself smiling as I rolled to push off the ground. "Impressive. I need to learn ... how to do that."

"You can't," she said with finality, and added as I stood up, *Use sign.*

I took another breath and straightened, looked at her stern face. My hand moved. *You received my message but waited to watch?*

She nodded, owning it easily. *I told you the Priestess would resent what you did to her son. Now she will harass you.*

Did she send him?

She must have.

I didn't argue, but I wasn't so sure. At least I knew that Qivni had witnessed my attempt to disengage from the Sathoet, that he had attacked me first, and that I didn't stab him when I had the chance. Qivni might be tightly wound and did not appreciate my "quirks," whatever they may be, but I knew she wouldn't lie to Rausery about what she'd seen.

My Collector motioned with her head for me to follow her, and we moved in the opposite direction Kerse had gone. We entered a tunnel where we'd be less likely to run into wandering attendees in the halls. I could also speak quietly as Qivni walked in front of me.

"What about the Worship Ball?" I asked.

"It is over. Lunent Agalia will manage as I make sure you return to the Cloister without disappearing."

It couldn't be that bad already, could it? I barely knew anything.

"What would you do about this in my situation?" I asked her.

She turned her head and blinked in surprise. "I wouldn't have tried to overbear the will of a Sathoet in the first place."

"Too late for that." I frowned in confusion. "And you just did."

She huffed a short laugh and shook her head. "Not quite. It's an approved spell. It makes them leave under their own power. However they came, and it hurts if they resist." When she glanced at me and easily read my next question, she repeated, "You can't learn it."

"Why?"

"Don't act dumb. You're not a mage."

"It's not only you in the entire Sisterhood who can wave off a Sathoet if needed, is it? What if you die?"

Her eyes narrowed as she looked again out of her periphery. She answered grudgingly. "No, it's not."

"Then what do the other Sisters do?"

"Mostly watch them and avoid them. But seeing how one is watching you and you cannot seem to avoid it ..." She shook her head. "I will leave this to your Elder. You obey her, whatever she says."

"No recommendations at all? Nothing to suggest to Elder Rausery?"

Qivni was outwardly agitated with my questions. "That will be between her and me. Be silent, Sirana."

"But —"

"Keep talking, and I'll convince Elder Rausery your training requires a solitary fight with a Drider," she seethed.

My Collector was so much fun.

Gaelan somehow caught up to us. As she closed the distance in a very quiet sprint, I could see she had been actively searching for me. "What happened?"

"You should be helping Agalia," Qivni reproached.

My Sister straightened and saluted with respect. "Lunent gave me leave. The Nobles are staggering back to their rooms, they have it under control."

Qivni narrowed her eyes, and the same thought which probably passed through her mind struck me as well.

D'Shea's orders regarding me would supersede either Agalia or Qivni.

"What happened, Lead?" Gaelan asked again. "Why are you escorting Sirana back now?"

Rausery's Lead shook her head, her usual frown stuck in place. "She drew attention she shouldn't have. Let her explain it to her Elder."

"I didn't draw attention, Lead," I murmured. "He stalked me."

"Save it for your Sorceress, novice."

Gaelan signed for me to let it go, her own interest in events willing to wait. She stayed with me as Qivni led us both back through the secondary passages to the Cloister as deliberate as if she thought we would both get lost without her. I still could, if I wasn't paying attention, but I would also have Gaelan's experience.

Qivni could walk there blind; I only needed to follow her boot steps, so my focus suffered as I was lost in thought along the way.

The Lead was sure Priestess Wilsira had sent Kerse just now, while I wasn't convinced. Either way, this was a result of my first trial to become a Red Sister. It seemed at first that anything I'd done during the tests shouldn't count against me, given my ignorance and lack of instruction, but the next moment I dropped that flavor to the order of things.

Such thinking was a female Noble pretending this wasn't the real game between two of the greatest powers in Sivaraus. If nothing counted in the tests, it implied a Priestess cooperating to give the Sisterhood full ownership of her Sathoet for a while — something I didn't see possible.

Besides, while Jaunda had confirmed the fighter from my trials was already dead, I could poke around for the invisible wizard to see if I could find him. Furthermore, Elder D'Shea had stated she was doing some investigation herself on why that Consort I'd met had been where he was when I saw him. That hadn't been planned.

Neither had Kain.

I shied away from recalling my dreams of late. Qivni herself said they would get tiresome quickly if I drew too much attention there as well. She and Gaelan had already witnessed me making noise in Reverie, which was troubling but about which I knew not what I could do. If they didn't fade or get worse, such a flaw could get me killed if I had to sleep somewhere predators of the Deepearth could hear me screaming.

I could not afford to think that any part of my trials did not count. There were consequences to everything, even if they were arranged or contained, and the aftershocks might be going on for some time.

We entered the eerie dimness of the Cloister where all the stairs disappeared, and we weaved our way toward Elder D'Shea's quarters. She was present — we knew from the mark she had left by the "testing" part of her protective Ward — and Qivni jangled that mark with her finger to let the Sorceress inside know she was there.

I had received some training on breaking simpler Wards of protection, but this one was far too strong to even consider that. Instead, its temporary suspension sucked and pulled at my inner ear for a moment — which could make a Davrin dizzy if they were caught unprepared — and we heard the Elder's voice.

"Enter."

Lead Qivni brought us inside, closed the door behind us, and the Ward went back up. My Elder was at her desk and wearing her robe again, as the first time I'd seen her after taking the black bag off my head. Since then, I had not gotten the impression she was always like this, or at regular times but seized the opportunity when she could. She enjoyed her finer things more than anyone else here. If Rausery's Lead judged her for it at all, it was completely hidden.

Elder D'Shea scanned us and smiled, her eyes landing on Qivni. "This must be interesting."

My Collector lifted her chin. "I would reconvene with my Lunent soon, Elder, but I escorted our youngest back, else she may have disappeared."

The Sorceress's white brow lifted in an elegant arch. "Mm-hm. You may do so, Lead, but first, say what you will before you go. I'm listening."

Qivni tried to smooth her own agitation. "Only that Priestess Wilsira hasn't forgotten, Elder."

"She never does. I take it Sirana is capable of giving me a full report."

"Yes, Elder."

"Thank you. You may leave to more pressing matters."

Qivni took her up on this and left without hesitation — the Lead wasn't eager to denounce my failings in front of my Elder — and soon enough, it was just the three of us: Gaelan and me with our Elder D'Shea, who nodded to the elder between us.

"Your report, Gaelan."

Gaelan glanced briefly at me but backed up before jumping to where we stood now. "No incidents in the Grand Hall that required interference from the Sisterhood, Elder. It was a peaceful and successful Worship Ball, as planned."

D'Shea nodded. "Did the Valsharess speak to either of you?"

Gaelan shook her head. "No, Elder."

"Any of the Priestesses?"

Gaelan said, "Not to me." And looked at me.

I cleared my throat. "No Priestess spoke to me, Elder."

"Not one?" D'Shea's smirk turned wry as I confirmed it again. "I see. Hold that thought, Sirana. Gaelan, from previously discussed, was there anything unexpected in how and to whom the Consorts were doled out?"

"No, Elder, it was as you estimated. The new buas went to the highest Houses, while all fifteen of the older ones went lower than they had been."

Elder D'Shea nodded and looked at me. "What about your Consort, Sirana? Where did he go?"

I swallowed, almost denied the implication of attachment, then answered the question. "The former D'Verin Consort went to House Itlaun."

"Ah, did he? Hm."

If Gaelan had been watching the relative age of the males and linking with status, it was quite a drop for him — from Fourth to Tenth — although I didn't know why. If the Priestesses had known about my attack on him, he probably wouldn't have been "re-gifted" at all, or maybe went even lower, into the Twenties. He also wasn't *that* old, I didn't think. Older than Gaelan and me, sure, but much younger than Jaunda.

My Elder asked, "Was Curgia there?"

"She was, Elder, but she directed her younger sister to the Altar to accept him."

"As expected, then."

"Yes, Elder."

Gaelan didn't seem to be in on what Jaunda and I had witnessed about that House. Not yet. She waited patiently while the Sorceress studied me, and our Elder tugged out a blank piece of parchment and set it with a soft lead stylus at the far edge of her desk.

"Write down your notes, Gaelan," she commanded. "Concentrate while I ask your Sister why she might have disappeared tonight."

Gaelan obeyed, but I hesitated as the Elder hadn't quite asked yet, even if that was splitting hairs.

"What happened that Qivni had to escort you back, Sirana?"

There we are.

"Kerse accosted me while I was on patrol at the fourth end, farthest from the events," I said.

D'Shea tilted her head and narrowed her eyes. "He was alone?"

I nodded. "He'd been cloaked with magic. Not invisible as when bending light, but Dark Sight camouflage that mimics the energy waves around him."

"I'm glad you can recognize the difference already. Where was his Mother?"

D'Shea wasn't surprised to hear that Kerse could vanish from view. I wished I knew what else she knew of his abilities. I considered her question from all angles.

"I don't know. The last of the Consorts had been awarded already, and the entire Grand Hall was in lust. At that time, the Priestesses were still present but were no longer confined to the platform. Wilsira could have been anywhere, and I wouldn't know."

"But you didn't sense another in the hall with you."

"No. Kerse also said she was busy."

My Elder did not look pleased. "He spoke with you."

"Yes. And he wouldn't return to her when I told him to."

"What else?"

"He wanted sex." I considered. "I told him Wilsira hadn't sent him, and he said she did, but I ... don't know if I believe him. But he wanted me again. Was willing to 'fight' for it."

"And what did you say? What did you do?"

"I refused, and I called Qivni with a message pellet."

D'Shea clearly approved of my choice, and I relaxed a bit. "What happened next?"

"Qivni didn't arrive immediately. I stalled a bit and kept distance. I'd drawn weapons to warn Kerse off, but it didn't work. I sheathed them and tried to walk away. He charged me from behind, and there was a very brief fight. I almost stabbed him, but that was when Qivni interfered and used the ... words that hurt him if he didn't leave. He got off me, re-cloaked, and retreated."

D'Shea sat still as if picturing it; Gaelan was writing down whatever details she recalled about the rituals but struggled a bit with distraction, glancing at me once or twice.

"Anything else?" my Elder asked.

There was. "He never roared. He was trying to be quiet."

"And you find that significant."

I nodded. "Yes, Elder. He didn't want to draw attention."

D'Shea stared hard at me, her gaze unwavering. "Are you saying that you believe he's stalking you free of Wilsira's will, Sirana?"

I stared back. "I'm saying he was quiet, Elder. For whatever purpose. What do you think? Would he make that effort if Wilsira had really sent him?"

D'Shea looked to make a mental note but didn't answer my question.

"And Qivni? What did she do after interfering?"

"Started leading me back here. She wouldn't give me any advice, though I asked. Just told me it was too late and that I should obey your word on this."

The Sorceress' expression didn't change at all; she was placid, if not at ease with my report. She had me recite the encounter to her again from the beginning, getting all the little details and confirming the order of events. Finally, she seemed satisfied and looked to Gaelan.

"Let us back up. Gaelan, did you speak to anyone at the Worship Ball?"

My Sister nodded. "As you instructed, Elder."

"Who?"

"Rowena of House Kelnic."

"Why her?"

"She is the Aunt of Curgia and Tulia through their sire, and neither Matron Itlaun nor the First Daughter attended. I was told that they had other pressing matters and sent the three of them in their stead. Uncommon, but at least they chose the higher House to represent their Matron. I think Curgia and Tulia's Mother may be ailing."

"Hm." D'Shea glanced between the two of us. "And now the Consort who knows both of you has been assigned there. Very fortunate. We have an easy way to watch these strands of the web for the next decade."

Gaelan was curious; her eyes flicked to me and back. "Sirana knows why this is significant, Elder. What would you have me know?"

D'Shea smiled at the direct cooperation. "Wilsira owns that Consort, he reports to her."

Fuck me. Him, too? Just how powerful was this Priestess?

My Elder chuckled at my expression but spoke to Gaelan. "She is also planning to break Curgia this same turn, to control her, who will help her control Tulia. The Priestess must already know their Matron is weakening, and that something is curious about the First Daughter. We shall find out more than she wants us to."

"Break her this very turn, Elder?"

"Yes. Curgia is likely pregnant by Kerse."

My Sister's jaw was slack, her eyes wide, but she caught herself up quickly. "That explains a lot of what I saw this eve, Elder."

"I figured it would. And I believe I see more of Wilsira's plans."

I cleared my throat. "Elder, what if Kerse had been acting on a … misinterpretation of his Mother's desires? Not on his own, but not exactly what his Mother planned this eve?"

D'Shea was quiet for a moment and granted, "Possible, Sirana. Noted."

I nodded, satisfied with that acknowledgment yet I prodded farther. "Say she knows everything. How does a Priestess try to punish a Red Sister for a personal slight?"

D'Shea shrugged. "Mostly just through undesirable missions."

"What about forcing her to catch? To put her in the Sanctuary."

My Elder's fingers tapped her desk, and her eyes fixed on a point at the side wall. "Curious to hear you go straight there, Sirana. Where did this come from?"

"Elder Rausery told me what happens if I get pregnant, Elder," I said. "Do Priestesses ever try to orchestrate that? Do they get away with it?"

"On occasion. But forcing you to catch by Kerse makes no sense in that circumstance. Any Priestess would prefer a Red Sister catch a pure Davrin."

"Yes, and you said the Valsharess doesn't allow births sired by Sathoet. So, is he or is he not acting on his own wanting to fuck me again?"

The Sorceress narrowed her eyes, annoyed at my verbal trap. "Inform me immediately of any more contact with the Sathoet, of any more information you learn about him. Rest assured you'll be watching House Itlaun and all its connections as if your place in the Sisterhood depends on it, Sirana, because you are making the case that it does. Be prepared to learn quickly."

I bowed a wordless apology and acceptance in one. "Are there ways to simply prevent catching, even if I am forced to take fertile seed like Curgia?"

D'Shea's eyes sharpened enough to cut skin. "That's where we get into politics, Sirana. It shall wait. Use what Jaunda and Gaelan have taught you to avoid being forced in the first place."

I wasn't any happier with that answer than she was with me. "Yes, Elder."

D'Shea returned to our report. "Gaelan, did you speak to anyone else?"

A shake of her head. "No, Elder."

"Very well. Sirana, did you speak to anyone else besides Kerse?"

Oh, fuck.

"My former Matron, Elder," I admitted, and she nodded. I realized that she already knew; maybe I was predictable like the Prime.

"Who approached who," she demanded, "and who spoke first?"

"I did both, Elder."

"What did you say to her?"

"I offered a blessing, of her state honoring the festival."

D'Shea smirked. "Her ... 'state'?"

I nodded. "She is a full turn through a pregnancy."

"Ah. I take it occurred to you that she caught well before you entered the Sisterhood, and she did not send a message to you at Court."

I shrugged at the jab. "It doesn't matter now, Elder."

Her dark eyes still bore into me. "Doesn't it? Why did you speak to her at all?"

"To make my new allegiance clear, Elder. To let her know without doubt that I was no longer part of her House. She acknowledged it without contest or regret. That was all. I walked away."

D'Shea watched me a tick longer then nodded. "Anyone else you spoke with?"

I sighed inwardly. "A battlemage named Callitro who stood with his two Tower-brothers. I approached him after he smiled at me from a distance."

"Tell me about that conversation."

"All flirting. Callitro wanted me to know he was at my disposal at the Worship Ball, I had only to ask. I knew I could not use him for anything then, but he told me how to get in touch with him later at the Tower if I so desired."

"Really," D'Shea said, rather deadpan. "And how will you do that?"

"Requisition the making of a magical item, request him as the maker. He said the contact's name is Phaelous, that he's worked with Red Sisters before. I would have an official reason to visit Callitro in his quarters then."

D'Shea's expression didn't tell me whether my information was trustworthy, but given Callitro's behavior and obvious lust, I was willing to bet on it.

My Elder was quiet for long moments and finally said, "Good work. That may prove useful to me." One corner of her mouth rose a little. "Now comes the question of whether it was *only* flirting which drew you to him, and to ask how to get into the Wizard's Tower. Answer it."

I smiled blatantly back at her, though my teeth were a little tight as I wondered if she may try to block me. I still couldn't lie either way. "I wanted to smell him, to see if he or either of his companions was the invisible wizard from my second trial."

D'Shea let me read her expression clearly. It said, *I thought so.*

"Has it occurred to you that we know who he is, Sirana?"

"Yes, Elder." Of course, it had.

"Why haven't you asked for his identity?"

"Lead Jaunda has made it clear you won't answer." I risked the next reason. "And you haven't forbidden me from looking."

Elder D'Shea did not take the bait. She peered at me for several moments, then shrugged and nodded. "As you wish. Consider it a standing directive to continue the search, secondary to any current assignment. Inform me when you find him."

She just approved the hunt? I smiled tentatively. "Then what, Elder?"

She didn't answer at first.

I repeated, "I shall inform you when I find him, my Elder. But then what?"

I wanted to hear it from her lips.

D'Shea sniffed a laugh. "Pay him back on your terms, Sirana, as you told me in your trial. You are only forbidden to maim or kill him."

A grin formed on my face. "Thank you, Elder."

"And I want reports on anything of note inside the Wizard's Tower."

"Of course, Elder."

Maybe the fallout from my trials would even out if I kept playing the Game. It wasn't as if I had a lot of choices.

CHAPTER 21

THE LAST SPAN HAD BEEN LONG AND TIRING, PREPARING THEN EXECUTING THAT Worship Ball. Gaelan and I retreated to her room for a small break while we could. Despite the repeated couplings upon the Altar, neither of us were rut-ready; my Sister and I were more eager for a rest.

Still, I asked if she could put "it" on. After a pause, she agreed.

"Not too light." Gaelan shivered as I caressed her tool. "Ticklish this eve."

"You'd admit to that?"

A chuckle. "Only to you, because no one believes the new cait."

"You should. Only the new ones are still naïve enough to babble about the sexual flaws of her elders."

"As if you would know. I haven't heard a thing about Rausery or Qivni. I'm not even sure if Elder D'Shea has taken you yet."

I smiled and gripped her Feldeu firmer, stroking slow. I was in the mood to observe nuances, manipulating her tool to help my Sister relax instead of thrash around, and she wasn't rage-aching to get me on top of her. A lot of the contact I'd had with the Sisterhood's magic tool had been hectic, feral, and demanding.

I lathered the plump tip with my tongue, sampling more than sucking, but not too light, as she asked. Muscles in her ass bunched and then softened, and no hands came to take my hair and guide my mouth full on her pole.

"So, when do I get to wear this?" I asked.

"Not mine to say," Gaelan replied. "I am not against sharing with you, however."

"And D'Shea knows?"

"Yes."

"What do I have to do?"

"I don't know."

"What about other Sisters? How do they earn it?"

"I haven't figured out the pattern." She turned her head propped on the low, firm headrest. "Seems different for each Red Sister. Some don't have one."

"Yes, I noticed." I jerked her, coaxing a soft moan from her throat. "Punishment for failure?"

"Sometimes, yes."

"But not based on age when or if you receive one. You were the youngest, and, well." I slurped her phallus between my lips again to finish my point.

Gaelan hummed but didn't respond.

"How did you get yours?" I asked directly.

My Sister wet her purplish-red lips with a bright pink tongue. She swallowed carefully as if she expected it to hurt; she looked at the ceiling. "Mine was linked to my Sisterhood trials. I've had it since then."

My eyebrows went up. I waited.

"Like you, I faced a Sathoet first. I wasn't a warrior, and it happened so fast. How I landed there in the chamber, I hadn't even collected my bearings. It was barely a struggle. He helped himself to all three of my holes before creaming in my netherhole, and I didn't know how to stop him." She glanced at me, her eyes accepting. "Nothing like the confident show you made with Kerse."

"Mm-hm, and that'll come back to stalk me, everyone is saying."

Gaelan shrugged. "Something always does, then or after. Mine was right then. I made noise when he took me. I cried."

"You cried?"

My eyes were wide; my hand had stopped moving on her phallus. Even confessing so weak a moment when all the Red Sisters would have been watching her then, Gaelan's stern glance now down at my lazy hand encouraged me to take my stroking back up. Maybe this thought was believable given what I knew of her, but this Red Sister wasn't that same Dark Elf she must have been.

"What happened next?" I asked, curious how this led to her gaining a Feldeu from the start, which had to be rare.

Gaelan smirked. "Simple. They said if I was going to weep and complain like a male having his netherhole plundered, I might as well be endowed like one. You may have been made to submit to anyone with a phallus in your trials, Sirana, but you remained *female* to us throughout.

"They treated me like I was male, with only the two holes, and a sensitive pole to torment me and use for control. My test was pure endurance, which didn't end until I finally forced another Sister to submit to me. I took her in all three holes like the Sathoet did me."

"Who was that?"

"Not allowed to tell you."

I pursed my lips, rubbing gently along her length. "What about the wilderness? Did they drop you there, too?"

Gaelan shook her head. "No. They knew I didn't have those skills. At least you had Palace Guard training. Mine was being stalked through a controlled area outside the Cloister. I didn't know it at the time, but they herded me toward one of the entrances, I fought back when I had to, and I found escape into the Cloister with my magic. I passed the trials that way and began my real training."

A recruit has to show some resourcefulness. Determination. Not give up.

"And the Elders decided you would keep the Feldeu."

She nodded, smiling but saying nothing else except, "Something you should suck on right now. I'm … closer than you think, and … you can ride on top afterward, if you want."

I smiled and licked my lips. "Done."

I had almost lost track of how long Jaunda had been gone, but I noticed that I missed her style of fucking. I did not have time to touch myself and reminisce or to become too frustrated by the lack because of the gauntlet of subjects on which I would be tutored by my other Sisters available.

I learned more about Wards, how they were put together, and that there were methods to engage and break them without suffering the full effects of whatever the mage had planted. I practiced hand-to-hand in my borrowed reds, blade throwing, became familiar with a small crossbow that fit in one hand.

After vast repetition, I could unpack all my pouches and tools, item by item, say what they were and the most effective uses, and pack them all back up the way they were. And I could do it blindfolded. I could set simple traps, disarm them and a few more complicated ones.

And I still had much more to learn.

The Sisterhood refined the best ways I could move, spy, and remain undetected, but I wasn't going anywhere near the Priestesses again without my Lead or another who could cover any mistakes born of inexperience that I might make.

I also studied more House histories sitting at a table, browsed more lineages, and listened to more politics than ever, even having once been surrounded by it. One of the oddest things to me was that Red Sisters didn't seem to be a factor in how those stories were told. Not unless there was an outstanding execution.

I didn't see how that could be. *D'Shea alone has been mucking around in politics for centuries. Even I can tell that.*

Jaunda had said, "Learn the rules first, novice, before even thinking about how to bend them."

I smirked to myself with hands spread over a scroll. *Qivni would probably blow an eye vessel hearing my Lead tell me that.*

There was no talk yet of a custom-made red uniform for me, although they did allow me to keep the borrowed one. I still wore the black belt with the reds, which set me apart from the others, or I changed my appearance to wear all black. It depended if black or red was better for whatever the Elders would have me do next.

Lately, I wore all black, as I had begun a stake-out of House Itlaun, no less than three cycles at a time; it was a walk to get there, and my lizard riding wasn't stealthy enough yet. I was forbidden from going inside or stalking any Davrin, no matter who they were. The mission was to observe the routines of the House first and take notes.

And test my self-control, no doubt.

I never glimpsed my Consort; he remained safe and sequestered behind the defense wall, inside the manor. Occasionally I thought I spotted Curgia, but the distance was such that even if it was her, nothing she did was remarkable. I wanted to get closer and catch something more interesting than tradesvrin going to and fro, than House Guards doing their drills at certain times of the cycle, but D'Shea had a "tell" stitched into my belt.

"Very sensitive to the spores of the sweet liquor mushroom in Davrin gardens," my Elder had said with a smile. "Which are finicky, you know. The only way you could sneak in would be that way, through the garden. And my patch will turn as blue as your eyes in candlelight."

I hadn't taken her word on it that the garden was the only entry point, but thus far I hadn't seen anything better. Obeying my orders was better. What was the rush, anyway? I could be watching this same plantation for decades. Maybe centuries. At least I enjoyed just being outside, exploring the Great Cavern, finding my own food and drink sometimes, keeping my tools and resources clean and useable.

Ready for anything.

Returning to the Cloister after one such stake-out, I performed my routine with my Elder, setting out all my items for her inspection, to see what I'd used and, if anything, to ask why I'd used it. A proper report then followed, and I waited to be dismissed; to go clean up, eat, and fuck, in whatever order I wanted.

As I waited, betraying some eagerness for I wanted those three rewards very much, D'Shea quietly watched me for a few moments longer, a small smile touching her lips.

What? What are you thinking?

Someone outside touched the Ward, and my Elder lifted her chin and her powerful, mage's voice.

"Enter, Lead."

Jaunda came through the door and grinned widely at me, even as she acknowledged Elder D'Shea. Clearly, she had been in a far more exciting place than me, doing more interesting things. Her armor was soiled with dried blood and flaking, Deepearth sludge; it smelled several cycles old and very unpleasant. She had no marked injuries that I could tell, only minimal damage to her uniform, and plenty of energy reserves, it seemed.

I was a little jealous. She'd seen action, maybe a lot of it. I stood at attention, wondering if I would get to listen in on her report from the wilderness.

"Thank you for your report earlier, Lead," Elder D'Shea said with a smirk, "and for waiting. Sirana is now available to help you settle back in."

Argh!

After we were outside in the hallway, Jaunda gave me a gesture that held no uncertainty for me. I would go with her and assist her with anything she needed or wanted. From wherever she had just returned, my Lead needed to work off stress and, like a good cait, my slit and netherhole tingled as I anticipated one particular duty.

Maybe she could tell me something about her mission if I satisfied her well enough.

My Lead had walked away without even looking behind to see if I followed, and I knew better than to lag. If Jaunda had to turn back to get me, she'd throw me over her shoulder like she had the first time she caught me, but this time I had a lot of tools and pouches and weapons which could get damaged. Working off "negligent magic-loss debt" was a common way for a Sister to get the worse jobs for a span or two.

We moved through the curved hallways and minimal lighting of the Cloister. Jaunda's quarters wasn't too far from Gaelan, as most Sisters shared two or three to a room and Jaunda's teams bedded down closer to D'Shea than to Rausery or the Prime. As a Lead, Jaunda had a place to herself, and when we stood outside of it, her patience faltered at last.

She whirled at the last moment to seize me and haul me inside, murmuring the command to cause the stone door to slide closed with a final-sounding thump. She clasped me to her before I'd taken a step into her lightless quarters and slammed me up against the outside wall beside the door. Pressing her body to me, filling my nose with too many scents, Jaunda stared at my face an instant before she closed her mouth on mine, spearing her tongue between my lips.

It occurred to me that I knew just what to do to get her to stop right then; a pressure point, a new vulnerability I had learned the hard way under Rausery and the Prime.

But I didn't. I yielded my mouth to the exploration even as I wondered what had her surged up like this.

When she stopped, we were breathing hard for air, and our eyes had adapted to the dark. She said, "You look great in red. I heard Rausery loaned that for the Ball, but you still got it. Have to tell me how that went. After."

I smiled, about to reply when she took hold of my hair at the nape and pulled my head to the side, leaning to bite my neck and nibble on my jaw and earlobe before champing her teeth in again. I winced but in a good way. Her appetite was dominant as ever, and I gasped at her attention, aroused, glad she was back, even with the Deepearth stink clinging to her.

"We'll get a uniform made just for you," Jaunda murmured, gently kissing flesh that I was sure was bruised and teeth-marked by now. "We'll have to replace this black belt."

As she spoke, she undid that belt and let it drop gently, avoiding breaking anything. She began stripping me from the waist up with an intense clash of efficiency and impatience; though I was jerked around, I stood cooperatively, anticipating being naked. Her heavy breathing and especially the low growl from her throat as she next kneeled, peeling down my pants to be at eye level with my white thatch, had me squeezing my thighs together.

My Lead smiled, glancing up at me with eyes intense as magma, even in colorless Radiants, and she leaned forward to push her nose into my white fur.

Goddess …

She scented me, humming in pleasure, purely focused on her desire as she extended her tongue, lashing it across my folds. I swallowed a moan, but my thighs relaxed, yielding as my sex swelled to aching against her mouth. She pinched the soft parts of my inner thighs, waking up my nerves further with pain, and hissed how much she would enjoy fucking me so hard that I'd waddle to my next duty.

I missed this, I realized.

Then I wondered whether I had missed *her*?

Would she enjoy hearing that, or would that be the same as crying like a sodomized male?

I said nothing as Jaunda stood up and put her rough, dirty hands at my waist, my ribs, and then my tits. She leaned down, restrained herself a little as she took more time there, biting my breasts and sucking on my nipples to make them hard. A mewl slipped out of me.

After I closed my eyes, after I foolishly let down my guard, she swept my feet out from under me. Only recent training helping me to break my fall and land without injury, though I blurted a cry as I went down. Jaunda grinned at me.

"Good. Been paying attention. Silence is better, though."

She bent and seized my ankles, pulling my legs up. I lay still on my back upon the cold stone as Jaunda took off each of my boots before yanking off my leather. That was it. No more clothes. I was a naked novice again, as the first time I'd been beneath her getting fucked.

My Lead was still fully dressed; she hadn't even removed her cloak, and she stared hard down at me. One gloved hand briefly rubbed her sex through her leathers, and she still held my left foot. Then, using both hands, Jaunda massaged my foot for more than a few flicks, bending down to nibble on my toes — which felt good but tickled — then bite the inner arch.

I winced again but managed not to jerk my foot out of her hands like I had the first time. She made an approving sound and went back to sucking on my smaller toes, her fingers digging into my ankle as I gripped the grit of the bare, stone floor. Then she wanted to switch sides, and

I knew better than to be too slow lifting my leg when she was ready to sample that other foot. Gaelan's comment about being ticklish came back to tag me as I whimpered one more time.

"Open wide," she growled, releasing both feet at last. "How I like it."

My gruff, superior Sister enjoyed some posing and performance from her subordinates. I stretched my legs up straight and together toward the ceiling, opening them slowly until my hands were bracing my thighs. I held the position with my toes pointed toward the sides of her room. She gazed hotly down at me, drew the obsidian dagger at her belt and kneeled between my legs.

Fuuuck.

Jaunda also enjoyed testing me. Again and again.

I held perfectly still, tried not to make it obvious I was holding my breath as my Lead lifted her dagger, barely touching the tip of her blade between my netherlips, watching me with that familiar intensity. The whisper-light prod didn't hurt or cut; at worse, it felt like an incomplete itch. I focused on controlling my breathing because I had to breathe; I held still, waiting.

I felt the flat of the cool, black glass press to one side of my cunt, and then the other as if it were a blind thing trying to find its way inside. The very tip tickled as it was dragged so lightly over my naked netherlips to barely touch my clitoris before moving to ruffle and reverse the lay of my white mound hair. I couldn't prevent a shiver or the tiny bumps rising on my ass and thighs. It had been a while since she'd done this.

I whispered, *"No demons but us."*

"What was that?" my Lead asked. Her arm and wrist were always in control of her weapon, no matter what it was.

"No demons but us," I repeated louder.

"Mmm." She was pleased. "Damned right."

Jaunda pressed the flat of the blade to my thigh as she leaned down and suckled my slit. I sucked in a breath, enjoying those moments while I could before she straightened up and tugged on my patch of curls. I felt the air on my damp skin, a hot hole already wishing for her cock.

Instead, I watched her pull pinches of white fur up away from my skin.

Jaunda made small, sharp cuts, carefully trimming my hair with her blade. She liked it on the short side, and I had not been doing it myself while she'd been gone. When she was finished, the hairs would be short, straight, and laid flat, the shape pointing toward my slit like an arrow instructing: *Fuck here.*

"Saw something I never thought I'd see this time out," Jaunda murmured, her eyes gleaming as she groomed me to her standards.

I blinked, brows rising with interest. I felt some strain holding my legs up and opened wide like this, but I could manage for a while. Sometimes she told me about some action from her missions, nothing secret, but it had always been *after* the sex.

I wondered why she was bringing it up now.

"This time out?" I repeated. "Where have you been?"

"The Elders or the Prime didn't say?"

"Not in my hearing, Lead."

Jaunda grunted. The smooth leather of her red gloves tantalized me as much as her words had. She caressed and petted my mound, dragging her fingertips along my netherlips and brushing off some loose hairs from her blade-trimming. Ignoring her own hints, Jaunda stared at me like she hadn't drunk water in whole cycles, and I was the river. The short, white hair atop her head was touched with dried mud.

Removing her gloves to set them aside, Jaunda touched me slower than I would have anticipated, using my own moisture to trace along my slit and circle my nub.

"Mmm," I hummed.

Then she slowly poked her slickened finger inside my hole, holding it there. Curling.

"Oh … !"

That felt good. Her white teeth showed in her dark face when she noticed my naked toes flex.

"Nice to be home," she said.

Any response was stuck in my throat as Jaunda added a second finger and leaned over; she nipped at the skin of my thigh and covered my nub with her mouth again.

"Goddess ... Lead ... !"

Her fingers slipped out of me, and her thumb replaced her tongue on my clit, only so that probe could extend down to my purple pucker, swirling around and jabbing it. I gasped again, my netherhole clenching down by reflex. She chuckled.

"S-so where did you go?"

My hands still had a firm grip on my thighs while I braced myself on my elbows, and my legs remained straight and far apart.

"Up."

She kissed my sex, inhaled the scent, and sucked again, her hand still massaging between her own legs. She had never lavished attention on me quite like this before. That was my duty, to use my mouth so long and usually with her Feldeu lodged in my throat.

"Up," I repeated, expectant. "H-how far?"

I knew there were many caverns, many sprawling passageways above Sivaraus and the Great Cavern; there were probably almost as many leading down, or out in each direction a Davrin could face. I had heard from my long-ago tutor that those pathways were always changing.

Cave-ins created another dead end or revealed a new shortcut to another level. Hot spots melted rock, pushing new rivers of magma, sometimes meeting water and cooling to form odd, sparkling tunnels. I had only been outside the city that one time so far; I could hardly imagine where my Lead had recently set her boots.

Jaunda lifted her mouth, her lips glazed with my juices as she considered me. "First tell me how far up you think we can go."

My toes wiggled again, this time from nerves just thinking about it; still, she noticed, and it amused her.

"Umm. Some say we can go so far as to leave the caves altogether. Where there's no longer any stone above our heads, but vast ... space."

Her eyes probably would have twinkled had there been any light whatsoever. "Got a name for that 'space,' novice?"

"The Surface," I said.

A place so far away, so alien and difficult to imagine that most of the Nobles I knew merely didn't spare the time. Not when there was plenty in Sivaraus to fill the turns.

My Lead winked. "Good enough."

I swallowed, noticing the hard knot in my middle. "Did you go there? Just now?"

Jaunda saw my legs tremble and tapped at them to indicate I could fold one over the other and turn over. I did, crawling to her pallet without being told, and my Lead seized my hips just as my knees moved off the bare floor and onto her sleep space.

"Just like that," she ordered, her voice husky as strong fingers massaged my bottom.

I looked over my shoulder before she pried my buttocks apart with her thumbs and dove in, her tongue again tasting and exploring my asshole. I blurted a cry of pleasure, my sex swelling further, my tight ring spreading to her familiar, probing tongue, clutching at it without my conscious will. My cunt grew hotter when she slipped two fingers back inside.

"G-Goddess, Lead," I stuttered, forgetting the topic in her hungry exploration. I only knew she was going to fuck one or both holes and fuck them hard.

I spread my knees a bit more, arched my back, making it clear I was willing. Jaunda chuckled deep in her throat as her tongue left my pucker damp and sensitive.

"Kinda wonder how it mighta gone if the pale Elf had been as smart as you, Sirana."

*'The pale Elf'? A … **pale** Elf?*

The lust haze cleared from my head as my heart surged, my wet sex squeezing around her fingers with shocked surprise. I was tempted to twist, to face her directly but she held me in place, gripping me by my slit, and I didn't fight.

Could she even talk about this? Should I say something? I didn't want to dissuade anything she might say. I justified it thinking perhaps D'Shea had planned it this way, even instructed Jaunda to talk to me. I'd been explicitly made available to slake my Lead's urges, after all.

"What do you mean, p-pale?" I asked, my curious mind in direct battle with my body as her fingers moved inside me. "*Argh* ..."

She coaxed such arousal, I thought, making me respond that this *must* be a test. Why would Jaunda talk about something this sensitive in foreplay? Practically *as* foreplay.

"I met a pale-skinned Elf," she repeated, self-satisfied as she removed her hand from me and, at last, shed her cloak and belt, taking out her Feldeu and opening her leathers.

My heart pounded as I waited, listening to her motions, keeping my legs open and ass presented to her. I struggled to sort out a clear painting in my mind. There were holes, so many vague spots.

Our artwork around the Palace didn't display anything of the Surface, nor any pale-skinned Elves. I'd never seen a merchant with any pale-skinned slaves to trade. I worked to connect what she'd said a moment before I'd crawled onto her pallet.

"Did you reach the Surface?" I asked again. "Is that where you've been?"

"Yeah, we reached it."

My blood rushed in my ears at the pace of my heart, and I trembled, unable to imagine. "And that's where you saw ... it?"

"Her."

My Lead donned her magic phallus, and I wondered if some of the odd scents and stains on her had been carried all the way back. Jaunda grunted happily as she inserted the bulb end into her twat and whispered the magical command. At the same time, she plunged one finger into my netherhole without warning, successfully distracting me from hearing the word as I yelped. Then she removed it, leaving my bung tingling, wondering what happened, and why there wasn't more.

Jaunda took my hips, shuffling up behind me, her blunt tool nudging at my slit. I rolled my hips to aid her, sucking in air as she mounted me, filling me in one stroke. She held still.

"Mmm, fuck," she sighed, testing a few draws of her cock, making me wait for the story. "Oh yeah, Sirana."

I could feel her leathers and the rough edges of her uniform against my naked skin as, slower than usual, she enjoyed my slit. She was taking her time, not that I had a complaint, as I enjoyed her tool without struggling to catch my breath. My hole welcomed her, stayed wet, enjoyed every thrust, but the teasing about the Surface and the pale Elf had my thoughts batting away any distraction that could lead me to climax.

"Wh-what did she look like?" I risked asking.

Jaunda hummed, grasping my left shoulder for leverage and I took her cock under more force. "Tall, but still … weak. Thin. No combat skill. In torchlight, her skin was like the underside of a mushroom. Her hair was gold. She had green eyes, like Lelinahdara."

She grunted as my hole held tight around her.

"Gold hair?" I asked. "Was she old? Like the Valsharess?"

"Nah," Jaunda gasped, reaching underneath me with both hands to cup my breasts. She pinched my nipples and forced that sound she liked. "Weird coloring, but I saw every bit of her. She wasn't old."

"You saw … every bit?"

"Stripped her naked. Made sure she had no weapons."

I wetted my lips, swallowed to do the same for my throat. I asked, "Did you fuck her?"

"Damned right I did." Jaunda sped up; the memory excited her. "She was comin' into the underground. Our space. Bringing fucking Humans with her. Arrogant as shit. I warned her, that's a bad idea."

Humans?

Jaunda pulled out of my sopping cunt and aimed then for my pucker, as I'd fully expected. She pushed; I relaxed, bore down gently. My netherhole stretched easily now, sucking her Feldeu in, and the familiar friction made my vacated twat tingle. I moaned, unable to ask about the non-Elves as I braced to have my ass reamed.

"Goddess, you're such a slit," she growled hotly, adding to her grip on my shoulder by reaching for the back of my head. Fisting my hair, she pulled my chin up as she buried herself deep in my ass. "You embrace this."

Out. Then in again.

"Oh, yes," I agreed, content that pleasing her was so easy on me.

Nothing like it had been with my older sisters; I truly never thought I would get so wet for another female, much less being dominated by one. But that first time with Jaunda, when I'd begged her after she'd "won" me, had proven otherwise.

It was the manner of domination, I thought. The desire in it; her reason to seek it with me. Somehow, it was opposite of what it had been at my House, the opposite of what the females at Court practiced, and even different from what Corpora Thena and her Red Sisters preferred.

Jilrina, Thena, and the others all wanted *fear*. They wanted humiliation, forced subjugation, and to feel the more significant power, the "better" female to the one underneath her.

Jaunda wanted to control the sex but didn't care about any of that other stuff. I knew she had tested my nerves at my House and was pleased I had held stubbornly to them. Later, she had encouraged me to become stronger, not weaker, by training in the Palace Guard.

When I proved strong enough to join the Sisterhood, her pleasured enthusiasm to "welcome" me was undeniable, even if I had little say in where I'd take her tool. She wanted me *because* I was strong in her eyes. Not weak. When I submitted to her, it was to enjoy the moment. Both of us, if I only wanted it that way.

To my surprise, there was room for my mind to absorb this new concept — to believe I could show the pleasure I felt. To risk a trust that she had no desire to hurt or injure me for her entertainment.

The Sisterhood had shown me it was possible, and Jaunda had taught me well.

I grunted as she lunged, my mind fogging and my asshole stretching, tightening around the repeated penetration. Her thrusts were fierce, yet she took her time. I gave in to my urge to reach between my legs, pressing the flats of my fingers on my mound. Desperately I hoped to rub out that building tension without interruption.

"Sexy cait," she whispered, releasing my hair and my shoulder to let my head droop in concentration. She leaned forward, holding my hips with both hands, and I rubbed harder as she spoke in my ear. "Enjoying my Feldeu that much, eh?"

I managed a moan, a nod as I felt her withdraw and push inside me again.

"Come on, then. Let me feel your shitter ripple, Sirana. Familiar by now, isn't it?"

My breath was ragged, my hips jerking once, trembling as I brought myself right to the edge.

"Do it. Cum on me, Red Sister."

I gasped to hear that, the final shock to my overloaded nerves.

"That's it! Yeah!" Jaunda crowed. "Oh Goddess, cum on my rod. Gonna plug ... your ... tight ... hole!"

She pounded me a few times, and those thrusts pushed me over the edge. I climaxed, crying out in the darkness of her room. A string of growling curses tumbled from my Lead's throat as she wallowed in her own pleasure, her favorite weapon sheathed to the hilt between my cheeks. Her scent was strong as she collapsed on my back, gasping, her sweat heavy and full of musk. She touched my back and flanks, appreciatively mauling the swell of my haunches with her phallus at rest inside my body.

It took us both time to come down, for her to pull out of my sore and satisfied netherhole, more gently than she had to. While she began to clean up, I remained on elbows and knees, aware of my raw, gaping pucker slowly closing, twitching, but my mind cleared much sooner than the afterglow.

"The pale Elf," I panted. "And the Humans. Coming underground."

"Yeah?" she responded, having removed her Feldeu to clean it and her crotch using the wash bowl sitting on a storage block.

I rolled my hips to settle onto my side on her pallet. "You came upon them underground?"

"Uh-uh," she denied. "First saw them on the Surface, my team and me. We watched them, followed them a while. Weren't gonna attack if they didn't notice us and passed by our hideout."

My brows lifted with my interest. "Not attack? Why not?"

Jaunda finally stripped out of her grungy uniform complete to the skin, dumping the Feldeu water down the drain in her floor before refilling it from a pitcher. "Humans don't know we exist. Orders are, we keep it that way. They live too short to remember much from one generation to the next, anyway."

I frowned. "How short?"

"Fifty turns." Jaunda shrugged. "A hundred if they're really lucky."

I stared at her. Fifty turns weren't even full-grown for a Davrin. I was almost one hundred, not quite, and considered old enough to know how to fuck and fight but that was about it. My Lead glanced my way, saw my expression, and grinned as she dipped a cloth to begin scrubbing herself down.

"Yeah. That was my first reaction, too."

"You've seen Humans before this mission?"

Jaunda nodded. "Talked with 'em, even. In disguise."

My stomach tensed with excitement as I thought of doing that. "In disguise. You know their language?"

"One of them. The one they use for trading like we use with some of the caravans down here. Downside to the short lives, their words change fast, and they make new ones constantly. Every time I've gone topside, it takes time to tune my ear again."

I withheld my gasp so as not to sound like a flighty, bubble-headed male. "How many times have you gone up, Lead? Over how long?"

Jaunda chuckled, abandoning a few stubborn, greasy marks on her feet — as if she had been walking around barefoot at some point spans ago — and picked up the water bowl, coming over to lie down next to me. Her feet were pointed at me, and she held out the rough cloth to me. I got the hint, taking it and dipping it to take up the cleaning in exchange for the answers to my curious questions.

"Five," she said. "Over the last two centuries. This was the first time Elder Rausery didn't lead it. She put me in charge."

My eyes and ears felt huge as my perception of Elder Rausery shifted, became more nuanced. *She leads teams to go up, far up, and talk with Humans … Why in the Abyss would the Sisterhood be dividing our strength like that?*

Stupid question. There could only be one reason: the Valsharess wanted it that way.

"Were you … looking for something specific," I asked, "or just observing?"

Another low chuckle. "Whether we were or not, novice, we found something."

A pale-skinned Elf. A blonde female stripped naked after entering the underground. Young, tall, and weak.

I had no doubt it was someone's order that my Lead talk to me, maybe to engage my "too curious" mind. This time, however, it wasn't evident whether it was D'Shea or Rausery. I scrubbed diligently at Jaunda's calloused feet, amazed they didn't twitch or jerk the way mine would have under such treatment.

"We don't want Humans to know we exist," I murmured, "and you watched the group travel without being seen until they went underground."

Jaunda nodded, her smirk receding, so she looked a little more serious. "They entered the same way we came out. The Humans took the lead in most things, but the Elf knew that passage was there. She didn't find it by accident. We had our long-term supplies in there, and she found 'em. I couldn't let that go."

I nodded in agreement. "What were they doing underground?"

"Looking for something. Probably not for us. Even the blonde Elf seemed surprised when she found our stash."

My hand slowed, and I held her foot. My eyes still felt very wide. "You said you warned her. It wasn't a good idea. You fucked her, but let her live?"

My Lead watched the ceiling like she could see through all the way to the Surface. "Yeah. Humans don't know us, but she did. Already knew what we were." Jaunda frowned in what I thought might be confusion. "Almost thought I could understand what she said in her tongue, but … not really. It was only when she switched to the Human Common I got it. She knew that language, too. Better than us."

That worried me for some reason. "What about the Humans? How did you deal with them?"

"Killed them. Wasn't gonna let them go off telling real stories. They'll be forgotten soon enough."

I struggled to follow her logic. "She knew what we were and spoke with Humans better than you. She must be allied with them. They know her but don't know us, and she can tell them about us."

Jaunda shook her head slightly, and I thought a bit more.

"Unless ... she wore a disguise, like you?"

Jaunda hadn't noticed that I'd stopped scrubbing her feet. "Yeah. Her illusion broke during the attack. Might've been the only reason she lived, now I think on it. She was hiding from Humans, like us, even though she was traveling with them."

"Why not choose to bring her here, Lead?" I asked in a carefully respectful tone. "Our Elders could have questioned her."

Jaunda snorted softly. "D'Shea asked the same thing."

I could tell it hadn't been easy for her to explain then, either. I waited, sitting up carefully, rinsing out the cloth and gently wringing out the water. Jaunda listened to the splash and drip like it was quiet music.

"The pale Elf had magic," my Lead said. "She was a mage of some kind. Smelled like flowers, even underground."

"Flowers?"

Jaunda glanced and smirked at me. "Perfumed plants on the Surface, like some of our mushrooms. Draw insects to them with pretty colors and scent."

I frowned. "Draws ... fleas? Flies?"

"Close. Lots more variety on the Surface. True about most anything you could think of that we have down here. If we got it, they got even more of it above."

"How can that be?"

My Lead grinned. "There's an all-important source of light, greater than thousands of candles lit all at once. The whole Surface depends on it moving across the big space above. Why it's only dark enough to leave the cave at certain marks of the cycle. It's too bright, it hurts to see. The scholars call it a 'Sun'."

I stared, my mind working diligently to connect it with any stories I'd heard or read. There were a couple, but no one seemed to pay as much attention as I'd think. No one seemed curious enough to ask for more.

Not as I felt now, looking at Jaunda, knowing she'd *been* there. She'd *seen* it and returned to tell about it.

"How does moving light equal the Surface has 'more' of everything?"

"Light makes things grow on the Surface," Jaunda said. "Food. Shade. Different than down here. Much different. And that pale Elf had odd magic linked to that light." Jaunda paused. "Got the impression she'd die if we dragged her away from the Surface. Like a flower wilts without that 'Sun' giving it light every half-cycle."

My Lead frowned in concentration as I waited, watching her every breath. She absently fondled her netherlips, and I watched that, too.

"D'Shea said something like the plants 'eat' light. Or make food from it, somehow. So blocking the light starves the plants up there. Same thing for that pale Elf."

"You were certain?" I asked, intensely fascinated as a new expanse stretched out far above my head within my mind's eye. "How?"

Jaunda turned her head, stared at the far wall of her room as if trying to put words to her thoughts. "The Sisterhood sometimes kills children. The Priestesses sacrifice the unwanted ones. But under Rausery and D'Shea, we don't use the Feldeus on them. We don't do what your sister did, and a Red Sister who breaks the rule doesn't get off easy. The last two I knew about didn't die fast, but we eventually killed them, because their demon was no longer the Sisterhood but their need for the half-grown."

I looked down briefly, not sure why she spoke about this, though accurate from what little I'd seen so far. The Red Sister punishments and humiliations were only forced on adult Nobles who either needed a lesson or would be an example how to die from shame before dying for real. If there were children who were condemned to die for whatever reason, the Red Sisters weren't called first.

But I didn't see the relevance here.

"What does this have to do with the pale 'flower'?" I asked. "You said she was tall. She wasn't a child, was she?"

Jaunda shook her head. "She had tits. Blonde fur where you'd expect it. She smelled grown, Sirana, in every way. She was built for fucking like the rest of us."

"You desired her?"

Jaunda shrugged. "I was curious."

I watched her ruffle and tug at her pubic fur. So was I, now. "Did she *feel* any different?"

One corner of her mouth lifted. "No. A pink cunt is still a cunt, it seems. So is the rosy pucker of a white ass. Nice and tight, like you." She winked at me. "The pale one also recognized cock when she saw it. She'd taken one before, I could tell."

"Oh?" I was tempted to smile at the comparisons, the similarities. "What sort of things did she say in Human tongue when you showed her your cock?"

My Lead's teeth showed in a dark smile. "Like a Noble. Mostly begging and insults about how the parts don't match."

I let myself laugh at that familiarity — a reaction the entire Sisterhood enjoyed — and for a moment Jaunda joined me. When she stopped, however, I studied her expression.

"But?" I asked, shifting my sore backside. "What else?"

Jaunda sounded rueful. "You're like a mind-reading mage, sometimes, Sirana."

I shifted closer, following the scent. "What else, Lead?"

"Her eyes were different. Green as emeralds, but nothing like our sly Priestess. She wasn't like one of our Nobles, either."

"What? But you just said —"

"I know what I said," Jaunda interrupted. "Except that any Noble we've punished has already done worse things. They might not like it, might want to deny it could happen to them and they might break when it does, but they've always *seen* it before. Ordered it done, or done it themselves. The blonde Elf was …"

Jaunda paused. It was a real exercise to keep my mouth shut.

"She resisted, sure," she continued, "and babbled all sort of things as I fucked her, but she … hm. Seemed ignorant how the world works. Or, at least, how it does underground. Like she'd never seen some of the ways we can kill and fuck each other, let alone acted like she'd already done it to anyone else. I think I was the first cock she'd ever had in her ass, even though she fully expected and dreaded my Feldeu using her throat and her slit."

Again, I tried to smile at the likeness, something I knew about personally, but Jaunda's frown had grown. She stared at the ceiling again.

"My caits had their fun with the Humans, too, before killing them off. Our prisoner could see it, I made sure of that, and ... that really seemed to break her. Didn't seem like she'd even killed before. Everything about that ambush surprised her. Afterward, I didn't take long to decide. I couldn't kill her. And I couldn't drag her back here. I hauled her all the way back to the Sun and threw her out. Told her to never come back."

Now I believed I had enough pieces. Finally. I couldn't help but try to put them together.

"Mercy?" I said, almost squeaked.

It wasn't a word the Davrin used very often.

Jaunda didn't look at me. "Basically, yeah. Elder D'Shea wasn't impressed, but Rausery was. Remains to be seen if they will convince the Prime I don't need a 'lesson in transgression' of my own for making that call. I own it, though."

As I watched her, my chest felt warm. "Elder Rausery was impressed? Why?"

Jaunda smiled a little, looking sideways at me. "She's been to the Surface more than any of us. She's the one who taught us a different set of rules for engagement up there. What works down here doesn't always work up there. And she's never seen a pale Elf, as many times as she's gone. She was glad I didn't kill the Surface Elf or put us in a position where we'd have no choice but to hand her over to the Priestesses. Even if I scared the snot out of her and probably made enemies we don't know about, Rausery said it was the right call."

This was so thrilling of a story to me that I grinned. Jaunda observed me for a few, quiet moments and huffed a laugh.

"Qiv is right," she said, amused. "So fucking curious, Blue Eyes."

"Why did you tell me all this, if I wasn't supposed to listen."

My Lead reached between my legs, nudging between my thighs until

I opened them, and she stroked my sex. It felt good enough that I relaxed and she pushed me onto my back, getting up on her knees and in between mine, already preparing for round two.

"D'Shea's also right," she mused, touching my skin. "You learn enough from us, survive long enough, you might be called on to see the Surface one of these turns."

Chapter 22

A RARE SORT OF MERCY MAY HAVE BEEN AT THE CORE OF JAUNDA'S LAST MISSION, but I knew it wasn't in the next one to which I was assigned. Elder Rausery wasn't present in the torch-lit strategy room when I answered my summons, either, but the Elder Sorceress was.

So was the Prime.

Fuck.

I saluted them both and stood at attention, waiting.

"Strip down, novice," the Prime ordered, jerking her chin toward a table. "Everything laid out there."

I stared straight ahead, first controlling my breath, so my heart didn't race away from me. I removed my cloak, rested it on the table. Then I unloaded the items on my belt, piece by piece, my weapons and pouches neatly lined up on the clean, grey-brown expanse, before placing the belt itself at the end. I removed my boots and socks, worked every piece of cloth and armor, and displayed them for the Prime.

It only took a few hundred heartbeats — mine, not the Prime's, which was no doubt thudding much slower in her chest.

For the first time, I thought, the Prime inspected my gear while Elder D'Shea stood patiently, meeting the Prime's eyes whenever she glanced her way and answering the occasional question. I remained silent, hoping

I hadn't been chosen to alleviate the Prime's boredom.

She checked the sharpness of my blades, sniffed the contents of my pouches and vials, inspected the stitches on my bracers. How grateful I was that I had taken my Sisters' tutoring seriously and all my equipment was in excellent shape.

"Passes muster," the oldest Red Sister stated, faded eyes scanning my naked body as if it was another article on the table — something she'd seen thousands of times before and only used when she had the need. "Glad she can do the basics by now."

By now.

It had been half a turn since Gaelan had swept me up from the Consort's Farm of Solitude. How dumb did she think I was?

Craning her neck to meet my eyes deliberately, the Prime added, "The black belt needs to go."

I hesitated how to answer.

"It shall be, Prime," D'Shea answered, and I realized our superior had been speaking to the Sorceress from the beginning.

Nodding, the old Davrin stepped back to observe as my Elder lifted from the table upon the platform a large, broad, and shallow box made of hammered reed. I didn't see that relatively fragile material often inside the Cloister; I could see it give under her fingers, seeing that it had a lid, as Elder D'Shea stepped off the platform to place the box in front of me. She straightened up, smiling in that unreadable way of hers.

"New items out," she instructed. "Redundant, old items in."

I signed the acknowledgment and went to one knee to turn the lid over to my left, away from the table and my Elder. Inside was a newly crafted uniform made of bright red leather. I stifled excitement and doubt. The others had claimed it would be custom made. I hadn't stood still for any such fitting, so I could only hope that it fit me.

New items out.

I did not have enough room on the long inspection table to lay out a second uniform, the clothing, and the armor, in its entirety. With a third of the items removed, I needed to begin trading items as I could. It became a puzzle of concentration, noting how something new was placed and packed in the box before taking it out, and next returning the old version to fit roughly the same part in the pattern.

The Prime and D'Shea said nothing as they watched. I worked without pause or excess noise, and eventually had all the new pieces switched out for old and the lid back on the hammered reed box. Most of my tools and weapons remained, but I had a new, red belt upon which to thread them.

The Prime jerked her chin. "Show me, novice."

Get dressed.

This was speedier than dressing down had been. Both the new gifts and the fact that my orifices escaped a burning violation had a hand in this. Elder D'Shea was smiling wider now, as she saw the same as I did, each piece fit me very well. Comfortable. Strong. Familiar.

As if it was made for me.

I tested making fists in the new gloves and lifted my chin with a surreal pride I could barely describe. I saluted in lieu of being called upon to speak; I wasn't sure I had the words then, anyway. Not ones I wanted the Prime to hear. The next moment, I heard her grunt.

"She's ready, Elder?"

The Sorceress allowed amusement to show. "We shall soon find out."

I felt a chill enter my middle; again, I breathed to help keep my heart slow. I waited for the orders I did not expect to enjoy.

"We need a confession from House Thalluen," the Prime said bluntly, crossing her arms before her. "And, after you get it, proof of execution."

IF I WANTED TO WALK IN THE SAME WAY ELDER D'SHEA HAD DONE WHEN JIL-rina died, if I tried to order them to take me to any one of their mistress' rooms, they would do it. I could stroll in, request their defenses taken down and take their measure as I saw fit.

But that would give her a warning. A shield to build resistance.

It also wouldn't impress anybody in the Sisterhood.

The Red Sisters dedicated a lot of time and effort gathering intelligence, to find weak points in every House and workarounds to various wards. The Elders possessed a great selection of countering items, created as tools for a specific task, probably crafted under compulsive silence by the Wizards in the Tower. Perhaps that was also how the Feldeu was made.

We hid both our methods and the discovery of any vulnerability; we shared those secrets with no one, not even the Sanctuary. The Nobles and the Priestesses had to feel reasonably secure in their methods defending against themselves and us. We allowed the assumption of "common practice" to work in our favor because then we seemed unstoppable when enforcing the Queen's Will.

If one of us arrived unannounced, our target would spend precious focus and time fretting where their defenses had failed, weakening their will before we had even begun.

Jaunda had even used that tactic on me at Court.

While this eve was not my first time alone and outside the Cloister, it *was* my first entering a free-standing House rather than a wing or room using the spyways of Court. I felt ready yet wary, both aided and pressured by the fact that I was familiar with the grounds of the plantation and the mansion itself. And those within it.

First, I rode a lizard mount to the outskirts, its only tackle being the chew-proof bridle. There I left it behind, crossing the land on foot, knowing it would wander back to the sentry border if it weren't collected in a cycle. Nothing on the plantation was very tall so the House Guards would see a massive, dark lizard and rider slinking along the road, but if it was only me, my cloak masked much of my life sign and, from afar, a crouching Sister could mimic a humble boulder quite nicely.

During my training, I'd grown more sensitive to the presence of wards, runes, and circles from repeated exposure and the discomfort they caused. This was the area of skill where I had spent the most time with D'Shea one-on-one, and while she was not my only tutor in this regard, she was an exacting one.

Now I felt I could be glad about that. If the magic ring on my left hand

and beneath my glove did not warm pleasantly, indicating it protected me from setting off the alarm, then I could choose to break a pellet from my pouch which opened a brief, counter-magic disruption through which I could step. That second option wasn't my first choice; it made the magic waver, even if it did not destroy it, and a sensitive mage would sense it.

There are no sensitive mages at my former House.

Still, I didn't want to risk it. I preferred the climbing and picking of more mundane locks to using too many magical tools anyway, even if I wasn't foolish enough to think I could get by without them. Affinity to magic was inherent in our bodies and our culture; our very society encouraged the development of new tricks and methods to overcome them. Knowing how to use the tools one had access to was essential, even if one was not a mage.

It had been a long time since some attack had happened at this House, I knew. The guards were bored in a way I recognized and, as I expected, loitered a bit while changing their watch. That was my opportunity to scale the three stories directly beneath the room I sought.

She could have changed bed quarters since the last time I was here, or the last time a Sister had made any notes, but this didn't concern me. Part of this assignment was to report every known change and make those notes on the Matron and House Thalluen myself.

The decorative glass of the window was rare and a marked expense from a time when House Thalluen must have been rising in status. Jilrina had always preferred the room on this account, probably because she couldn't have the Matron's suites herself yet, which had a heavily protected balcony with glass doors. Web-frosted panes rested in a gold frame which I knew was in good repair but lubricated the hinges all the same and tested for silence as well as Wards.

My ring warmed strongly beneath my glove as I paused with my hand on the glass. When the sensation became pleasant, I smiled, tugging on the window. It didn't open.

Physical lock. Maybe she's not so stupid after all.

What most Nobles didn't realize — indeed, I hadn't — was that locks of this design were stronger from the inside than from out. A new handhold, a new leverage tool, and a sound muffling pellet later, the lock gave way, and I opened the window, climbing in and sliding into the deep shadows of the bedroom.

Like many Nobles' bedrooms, it was dominated by a large, wide bed, layered with fine sheets, and covered with a canopy with veil-like drapes. I recognized her form even from where I crouched, lying next to a resting, male companion.

My nose told me I'd just missed their activity, and neither had bathed yet. A wine pitcher and two glasses, one empty and one still mostly full, had been placed at the bedside table. By his breathing, the companion was deeply asleep. I supposed more than a few paranoid Nobles sedated their mates if they Reveried together.

As I crept closer, I was relieved to see that he was mature. One of the House Guard. Not as young as I'd been.

Still. Odd to see him here.

I drew an obsidian blade and stepped silently toward her. Any of my Sisters would have been awake and aware by now, but this one still had her eyes closed. It seemed far too easy when I pressed the tip of the dagger into the hollow of her throat.

Coup counted.

Her eyes snapped open, and I looked straight at her. Given a moment for her vision to adjust, she recognized me. Her eyes filled with hatred.

"Hello, Kaltra," I whispered, pressing harder. "Swallow that indignance. You'll impale yourself."

My sister gasped in disbelief and hissed, "W-what are you doing back?"

"It was time for a visit."

"You weren't invited. I know you weren't." She glanced down at the hilt of the blade which kept her pressed to the bed for the moment. She wasn't wearing any clothes, only the thin, white sheet covered her. "You shouldn't be anywhere near Mother, especially now."

"Nor should you be," I murmured. "I hear she hasn't been well."

Kaltra pursed her lips briefly. "Yes, it has been a difficult pregnancy for her. She's older now."

I smirked, knowing Matron Thalluen was easily two centuries younger than Elder D'Shea, probably four from Elder Rausery. "She's not *that* old. And no trouble from the three before? Quite curious, don't you think?"

Kaltra's eyes oddly flicked to the side. My jaw tilted, but I didn't blink, didn't look away from her and kept the obsidian in place.

"Something off?" I asked.

"You haven't been here, what would you know?" she spat. "Even when you were, you only acted for yourself. You killed our sister and got away with it, you cunt. Jilrina would have made our House powerful again, not let it stagnate under a weak Matron!"

"Stagnate," I said. "That's a big word, Kaltra. Did you mean stalagmite?"

That moment of self-doubt in her eyes was what I had lived for as a youth. And when had we ever been that powerful, anyway? I grinned, and her lower lip trembled a little, but not in fear.

"You don't even deny it, do you?" she said, her voice caustic as acid.

"Jilrina died, Kaltra, but not by my hand. We won't say the same for you."

Her eyes widened, and she slapped clumsily at my wrist as she made the motion to sit up. I allowed it to be knocked to the side and stepped back, giving her room to get to her feet. She seemed so slow. Had I truly once been terrified of her?

Kaltra seized a robe, choosing not to parade defiantly before me though I'd seen her naked so many times. I gave her just enough time to slip into it. As soon as her fists clenched, her face contorted, and she drew breath to speak, I whispered the word to light one of the lamps to full glow in a few flicks. My former sister cursed at the brightness, covering her eyes in reflex.

It was the same trick I'd used against her more than once to slip away into the hall.

Still the same after all these turns. I could have killed her twelve times by now.

No faster than she'd ever been, Kaltra wrenched her hands away, blinking to grow accustomed to the new brightness. She froze when she saw the red leather, and as she recognized me once again in a new form, her expression changed from rage to confusion to horrified disbelief.

"Impossible," she said. "No."

If I had killed her in the dark, I wouldn't have seen that face.

My shoulders shaking in silent laughter, I pulled out a small, amethyst crystal rod to hold in my other hand, the dagger remaining in the other. My target watched as though hypnotized as I tapped it against the obsidian, causing a small chime and activating the spell D'Shea had placed on it. I sheathed my blade and held the crystal forward.

"As one of the Red Sisters, I declare you've been feeding your Matron and her unborn child a slow poison to prevent competition to your inheritance. Do you confess?"

Her bottom lip started to tremble again. This time it was pure fear.

"Not this," she whispered. "It cannot be this! Should not be!"

I shook my head, tucking the crystal in a tight, flat pocket on the torso of my new armor. "That's not an answer. Try again."

I took one step toward her, my hands now free, and Kaltra whirled and lunged on the drugged male in her bed.

"Wake up! Wake, damn you!"

He didn't respond, and she gripped his limp wrist and hand, twisting and preparing to break one or more of his fingers. It was a method of shifting both pain and blame, one with which I was familiar.

Swiftly I closed the gap and snatched her wrist, pressing a point where she lost all strength in her grip and pain shot straight up her arm. Kaltra screamed much louder than I had the first time, and she let him go.

"I've never heard you cry like that before," I said, dragging her away from the unconscious male in her bed and toward the dining table closer to the window.

"Help! *Help!*"

She struggled hard and, once, her vicious strikes had been enough to make it not worth being near her.

"Mother! *Guards!*"

It wasn't nearly enough now. I laughed out loud in disbelief and threw her into a chair at the small table. She almost fell over backward. I placed my hands on my hips as she recovered her balance.

"Kaltra. I know thinking is hard for you, but have you ever seen a House Guard attack a Red Sister because a Noble said so?"

She was shaking so much she didn't even try to stand back up out of the chair.

"On the contrary," I continued, "didn't they look the other way while a Red Sister had some fun with you? I bet I can describe the dirty things she did. Magical phallus, right? And you yielded like a good little servant. You were held down while she used whatever hole she wanted for her pleasure, right?"

Kaltra made a face of distaste as she gripped the arms of the seat; even more, it looked like the memory physically tasted terrible.

"Ohhh, did my Sister make you taste your own shit?" I chuckled, rubbing my mound through my leathers. "Plunged deep in your burning pucker, roughening that up some before she pulled out and made you suck it?"

Kaltra's eyes grew rounder as I let her see my own lewd response to what I described. For as long as I had hated her, I wished I could have watched at least one time. Still, she had not suffered anything more than I had.

She shook her head in angry denial, and I came closer, only to see it move faster. My cloak and stance seemed to block her in, I seemed to tower over her, though with her speed, she was not close enough to have a prayer of snatching any weapons from my belt. The amethyst crystal was still listening.

"Too bad you couldn't use the same spell-brewer that Jilrina did," I said. "She kept her silence rather well. The one you picked has already cried your name and what she'd given you multiple times in the dungeon. Brewmistress Whelery."

Kaltra went stiff as a corpse.

"Using Murhalla weed extract, right?"

My former sister refused to make a peep. I shifted my weight casually.

"Very subtle. It just took too long. Do you confess?"

"Wh-what does it matter?" she said. "You have always hated me. You have already judged me."

A shake of my head. "My Elders sent me. They've judged you."

"You are here to punish me. L-like that other Red Sister."

My smirk twisted with disgust. "Thank you, but I'll pass. It would be fun to watch you spread your smelly cheeks for another Sister but, fortunate for you, the others are busy this eve."

Kaltra's dark face was ashen and pinched in confusion; her knuckles were grey from gripping the chair as she waited. I took a lean against the table, seemingly relaxed, watching her with a small smile. The lack of fear I felt, the lack of hatred, was astonishing.

She was so small, so lost in the chair. I could wait all eve for her to crack. I wasn't afraid.

She is nothing.

"You poisoned your Matron while she is pregnant," I repeated. "Do you confess?"

Her nostril curled in loathing as her eyes narrowed at me. "What happens if I confess?"

"You already knew that when you chose to do it. Valsharess' law is clear, isn't it?"

Kaltra swallowed. "What about what *you* did?"

"If you're still convinced it was something, then I suppose you'll never truly know."

SOMEONE HAD HEARD KALTRA'S SCREAMING. SOMEONE HAD TOLD MATRON Thalluen, but no one signaled at the door while I got what I needed from her. It had taken a long time for my Mother to reach the door herself, and she opened it, as she could open any entry in the mansion.

The pregnant Davrin leaned against the frame as if the mere act of getting here had exhausted her. Her face was gaunt, the white hair at her temples was damp. First, one hand cradled the large, hard swell of her belly, then both as she caught her breath, and her eyes teared up as she glanced at Kaltra's bloody body in the chair.

Tears?

Tears for a stupid retch who got caught was the last thing I expected to see from any female, but our Matron always had shown weakness in odd ways. Kaltra hadn't been entirely wrong about that.

"Kaltra Thalluenduv confessed to poisoning you, Matron," I said formally, cleaning off my blade using part of the pale eve's robe before sheathing it. "You and your unborn. My Elders didn't want her taken in. They are satisfied with her death."

"Sir ..." my Mother began, then stopped, licking her lips. "Sister. The Sisterhood comes again to my House unannounced."

She might have wanted to say more, but it looked as though she might vomit instead.

If she has anything in her belly not already claimed by the little cait.

I withdrew a vial from my belt provided by D'Shea and met Rohenvi Thalluen at the door. I held it out to her; she glanced cautiously at it.

"A message from my Elder," I said. "This should neutralize the poison over the next cycle. Healing potions will work again. Remember to eat. You're losing weight, and the child you carry is female. You can't die until you have birthed an Heir, Matron. There's no one left to defend the House but you."

Word-for-word, as the Elder Sorceress had instructed me to say. Privately I marveled at the spark of fight I saw in my former Matron's eyes, how those words seemed to recapture more mind and spirit than I thought she had. She reached out and took the vial, avoiding the blood stains my glove had left near the bottom.

She asked me, "All at once?"

I nodded.

Matron Thalluen drank it as I watched, gagged once and only kept it down with effort. I retrieved the empty container from her and replaced it in a pouch, and she nodded, licking her lips and perhaps searching for something to drink. She didn't seriously consider the open wine container by the bed, I didn't think, but she noticed the House Guard unconscious in Kaltra's bed.

"Oh, Sibron," she breathed out, walking into the room and around me with a respectful nod.

I could have assisted her but was curious what my Mother intended to do. I watched as, like Kaltra, she also tried to wake him with a shake. The Matron merely said his name and checked his pulse instead of threatening to break his fingers.

The Matron knows him by name, hm?

Yet I couldn't place him. It had been too long for me being away from here, and that assumed he wasn't one who had just come of age.

"He hasn't stirred since I arrived, Matron," I said. "Do you need assistance moving him somewhere else?"

Breathing carefully, she nodded. "Yes, Red Sister. I would be ... most grateful."

"Where do you want him?"

"The healer's quarters, if you please."

I smirked at the irony. "Your House healer was condemned with Brewmistress Whelery. He told you he went out for supplies, but he won't be back."

My former Matron held still, again leaning to better bear the weight of her huge gut. "Who can I trust, then, Red Sister?"

I shrugged. "Rao'mino, for sure."

She sounded baffled, even as she kept her eyes on Sibron. "The kitchen's assistant?"

"I was told he provided the lead the Sisterhood needed to follow the connections. He is young but loyal to you."

Slowly, she nodded. "I see. Can you still move Sibron to the healer's quarters, Red Sister?"

"As you like, Matron."

As I once had for an intoxicated young male back at Court, I gathered Sibron close to me after sitting him up. He was naked as Kaltra had been. I bent and pulled him over my shoulder, preparing to carry him out of Jilrina's former quarters. Per my instructions, I would be leaving the body; I already had the proof of execution.

Now they are dead. Both of them.

I felt so strong, standing there with the male Guard braced across my shoulders.

"What will you do when we get there, Matron?" I asked curiously.

"I will tend him until he wakes."

I almost laughed at that but just held it, imagining she didn't realize that might include cleaning up his waste if it wasn't soon enough.

I glanced at her with a confident smile. "Only after you eat something, Matron."

On cue, her belly grumbled, and she nodded with grace even weak as she was. On our way there, however, I noticed we were being followed while taking the staircases leading from the third to the first floor.

"Who's that?" I asked, shifting Sibron's body for balance.

Matron Thalluen carefully looked behind her, scanned the darkness and spotted the small, pointy-eared form now peeking around the corner.

"Natia," she said, sounding dizzy. "Go back to your room."

"No, Matron," she whimpered. "Don't go with her ..."

Again, my Mother's eyes shone with moisture, and she blinked them rapidly. Her voice was much more commanding on a second try. "Return to your room. I will come to you soon."

Very reluctantly, the cait shrank away and returned to the second floor. Sibron's dead weight was becoming a strain, and I urged we move on, even as I kept one ear back for anything else that had changed about this place.

"Who was that?" I asked again. "Do you mean to tend every Davrin in the House this eve by your own hand, Matron?"

The Elf who had given birth to me heard the edge of brittle sarcasm, I knew she did. However, as it had always been before between us, she pretended not to.

"That is Natia, a child of one of the House Guards. She was orphaned recently, and I mean to keep her close to me as a handmaid."

My Mother breathed in, then out, holding her distended stomach as it seemed to clench without her meaning it to. I watched with more fascination than I should have. How close I'd been to this path, too, after attacking that Consort.

I could be watching my belly swell and clench like that, after growing up believing that I never would.

Now I still couldn't catch; not unless I wanted to meet the Priestesses up close, as I had every Red Sister so far.

"Very soon, thanks to the Sisterhood and the Valsharess," my Mother said, "I will need a spare pair of hands and quick feet like hers. A new handmaid can aid me."

Thanks to the Sisterhood.

A new handmaid. A newborn Daughter.

And the tormentors of my own childhood dead.

I was reminded how everything handed to me now was a test of being a Red Sister. I wanted to know more; I thought perhaps I should stay and talk, ask questions, even though my mission was complete. I could only report more to my Elder if I knew more, right?

Yet, I also knew I *shouldn't* be this engaged in what was going on within these walls.

Not anymore.

"Sounds like you shall need all the aid you can get, Matron."

I walked without error to the healer's quarters, placing Sibron upon a cot, and admitted to myself that I wanted to know more about the "handmaid" that my Mother had promised she would meet soon, in her bedroom on the second floor and not the servants' quarters. I also wanted to know who had sired my unborn sister, and why Matron Rohenvi had chosen him.

By the Abyss, I even wanted to know why the Matron knew Sibron's name, why she said it with familiarity as if she was concerned about him.

Why he was in Kaltra's bed?

It only struck after acknowledging that curiosity that perhaps my now-deceased sister had been trying to test her own fertility before her Matron succumbed to the poison. Only one fertile and ruling female now remained, because Elder D'Shea had sent me.

All will be different from how it was when I lived here.

My Elder would be curious to know how much I cared, no doubt. She'd watch how much attention I paid to this. Perhaps the drama here was best left to another Red Sister. One who did not feel what I felt that moment, threatening my new focus.

"Will you be staying at our House for a time, Red Sister? Do we wait for anyone to set the pyre?"

I listened to her voice, eyes resting on the sleeping male. The Matron was good. I couldn't tell if she had a preference. Hiding a reluctance like I'd seen in the little squeak upon the stairs, I shook my head.

"No, Matron Thalluen. I will be leaving now. You may set the pyre for the Second Daughter at your convenience."

CHAPTER 23

GAELAN WAS WAITING WHEN I RETURNED TO THE CLOISTER. HAD SHE BEEN carrying a pole-net in one hand, I'd have thought she watched for me like a flashing bug, ready to stalk and catch if I tried to avoid her.

Come, she signed. *D'Shea wants a report.*

I tapped her shoulder. *The Elder's quarters are the other way.*

Both her expression and tone of hand were sarcastic. *Is it? I'd forgotten, novice.*

That moment I felt like anything *but* a novice, resentful that she did not even ask where I'd been or if she knew of my accomplishment, and my irritation showed.

Annoyed with our Elder again? I signed back as a barb. *Still won't say why?*

Fuck your ear, she replied and sped up to where I'd have to speak aloud at her back to say anything else.

I knew the tension in my closest Sister rose quickly when our Elder provoked her — often on purpose, and about things I knew little about, because they didn't argue in front of me. Gaelan couldn't always let it go, even once D'Shea was no longer present.

Definitely the case here.

Smirking, I hustled out of the Cloister after her. Our hoods up,

Gaelan and I weaved along sunken paths carved out at the bottom of magically masked crevices. Our elevation and the illusions obscured our comings and goings from chance observers. There were roads and fields within sight of the Cloister, off in the distance and below us. So many Wards, traps, and secret passages lay between them and us, however, that we were rarely worried about moving too many of Red Sisters or mounts too fast and drawing their attention.

To caravans, slaves, and commuting Davrin, our hill looked like an unusable swath of igneous rock they'd seen well offroad for centuries. It was not worth building upon or adjacent, though they would have been hard-pressed to explain why without being able to say they were too late. The Sisterhood had already constructed something underneath.

The Wizard's Tower and four of the wealthier Houses and their plantations were situated between our Cloister on one side of Sivaraus and the massive Palace-Sanctuary complex on the other. Quite a distance to move between, but we used hidden transport rings and magical entries into the spyways of the Valsharess's complex. They were worth whatever price was paid in resources and skill it took a sorceress to build.

This moment my Sister and I didn't take a ring which brought us closer to either Wizard's Tower or the Palace but farther away from them. We jumped past the sentry perimeter and landed on the edge of the wilderness where darkness was near complete, and we stood in a bubble of silence but for the throb of the Deepearth. Suddenly, I was nervous.

Why does our Elder want my report way out here?

Gaelan noticed I covered the hilt of a dagger at my belt and eyed her. She grinned as my response lifted her ill humor. It didn't help.

Hand off the weapon, Sirana, she signed. *Don't get paranoid.*

Easier signed than performed, I remarked. *It's not stupid to keep one's guard up.*

True. But don't get paranoid.

I made a face. Clearly, there was a difference I was missing.

As we kept climbing upward, I tried not to let my mind wander to Jaunda's recent journey to the Surface. It was harder than I thought.

She was gone for spans and spans. How much of that was climbing like this?

How would she know she was any closer to the blinding light and open space? Why wouldn't she just hit one dead end after another?

I shook my head, imagined D'Shea's voice in my head.

Report. Focus.

I was climbing to report on House Thalluen, far out from both the city center and the Cloister. Although, regardless of what Gaelan said, that "paranoid" part of my mind left it open that perhaps this wasn't the case.

Still, I breathed in and out slowly, quietly, while bringing recent faces to mind — Kaltra's, just before she died, and my Mother's, just before I left. I kept the Deepearth scents in my nose, scanned the tunnel walls around us, and listened as we eventually reached a source of running water. My eyes had long since adapted to the ever-present Radiants. Challenging as it might be given the quality of a Red Sister cloak, I could still make out Gaelan's form separate from the water-carved stone, even after she stood still, waiting with her arms crossed. I took a moment to fill my empty flask with water, test it, and swig a needed drink.

The running water muffled any footsteps there might have been, so Elder D'Shea's appearance out of one of two tunnels in a fork I'd missed startled me. The Sorceress gave me a look reminding me I was, indeed, still a novice, and gestured for both of us to follow her. We went left at the fork, D'Shea retracing where she'd just been; she brought us to a stone door masked as well as the crevices leading us away from the Cloister.

Inside, she motioned.

I found a small but familiar version of the "cache room" where Gaelan had first taken me after dragging me off the D'Verin property and away from their prized male. Like that other, larger spot, this could be used as an interrogation space, as storage for cached weapons and supplies, or just as a place to rest if one was out on assignment in the area. Among a few sturdy and unpadded furnishings was a bench that could be used as either a low table or a place to sit.

Or a place to lay out tools.

As if she'd heard me, my Elder gestured to me and spoke. "Show me."

I laid out my equipment in the pitch dark, managing to fill the surface of the bench as I added the warm and squishy pouch last. Then I stepped back and waited.

D'Shea called a small, orange light, just enough that the three of us didn't flinch, and stepped closer to the items. She scanned all of them, studied a few a bit closer, used a cantrip or two to cause a few of the things I'd used to illuminate in an odd, fluorescent glow. She lifted the empty vial with the antidote to the poison, from which my Mother had drunk without question. She put it down, then lifted the oiled, liquid-proof pouch containing my evidence.

"Obsidian carving blade, long dagger, barbed knuckle-wrap," she murmured more to herself, weighing the evidence in her palm before she raised it, so she was clear. "Who quaffed the vial I gave you, Red Sister?"

"Matron Thalluen, Elder."

"Before or after you executed the Second Daughter?"

"After, Elder."

"Ah." D'Shea tugged open the pouch and placidly looked inside it. "And you made my statement to her?"

"Yes, Elder."

"Before or after she drank the contents?"

"Before. Otherwise, she may not have drunk the contents."

The Sorceress' intense eyes flicked up to catch my expression, and she smiled. "Your presence and purpose weren't incentive enough, Sirana?"

I remembered to breathe. "No, Elder."

"Hm." My Elder cinched up the evidence and attached it to her own belt, glancing over my tools again, at Gaelan, back to me. "Report. From the beginning."

I described and confirmed the entry point, offered the basic layout of the bedroom and those who were in it. At D'Shea's insistence, I recited most of the conversation with my former sister.

"Did you cut her the first time before or after she confessed?"

"After," I replied truthfully.

"Did she receive any other injuries before then?"

I thought back without flinching. "Bruises. I had to haul her around a bit."

"What caused her will to break?"

I glanced at the amethyst crystal that my Elder still hadn't picked up. It held these answers in the laced sound captured by her magic. "Talking about the First Daughter."

The Elder Sister looked at Gaelan and smiled back at me. "Indeed. And you could without shouting?"

I returned the smile. "For a long time, I couldn't so much as whisper talking about her. Shouting wasn't necessary. Repeating it like a chant was, rubbing in how easy it was for me to speak what I'd always thought."

"Impressive, Sirana. Did you tell her how you killed her?"

Nice try, Elder.

I smirked. "I didn't kill her, Elder."

The Sorceress chuckled, changing the subject. "Who was the male in the bed?"

"Sibron. House Guard."

"Could he have heard any of this?"

"No, Elder."

"You're sure?"

"He barely breathed and didn't move at all the whole time. I think Kaltra overdosed him. I wasn't certain he'd live after I left, though the Matron intended to try her hand at healing."

D'Shea perked up. "Back up, novice. You imply Matron Thalluen came to the room herself?"

"She did, Elder."

"Alone?"

"Yes, Elder."

"No House Guard attending her."

"No, Elder."

"This wasn't odd to you?"

"No, Elder. The Matron often walked where she pleased on her own plantation. She seemed to fear nothing but Jilrina."

D'Shea's gaze sharpened, the dark red seeming lighter in the orange light. "And? Continue."

"I stated my business there, and the Sisterhood's sentence. Offered the Matron the vial, which she drank. She saw Sibron and seemed … concerned. I offered to carry him out of the room since Kaltra's corpse was still there. Waiting to be burned." I couldn't help smiling a little again at this. "She accepted, and I took him to the healer's quarters."

"Which you knew would be empty," she added. "Is that all?"

I nearly said yes, but I hadn't yet learned to lie while staring my Elder in the eyes. Not with any confidence. She could see it.

"A little cait I didn't recognize followed us on the stairs. When I challenged this, the Matron tried to send her away, but she defied her. Begged the Matron not to go with me."

"Oh?" D'Shea stepped around to my other side. "Thoughts why?"

"Either she recognized the uniform or saw our likeness," I answered, "and saw me as a threat like Kaltra. The Matron bribed her with a promise to visit her next if she obeyed. Which she did. Only when I asked did the Matron tell me the cait was an orphan of a House Guard who would serve both her and the new heir after she's born."

"Why was this significant to ask?" the Sorceress asked.

A test. How much did I care about this?

"Not many Matrons I knew would be willing to tend the nerves of children in a nursery," I said. "Particularly orphans of House Guards."

"Does this behavior not suit your former Matron?"

"On the contrary," I said. "She knew Sibron's name. She wanted him out of Kaltra's room. She has often done things like this. She could be … closer to the lowborn than the First Daughter. Not aloof, or distasteful of them. I think that is how the Matron outlived Jilrina's schemes. The House Guard especially are difficult to turn against Rohenvi of House Thalluen, as she did not flinch at their dirt."

D'Shea smiled slightly. "And now? With the healer's betrayal a crucial part of Kaltra's scheme to prevent an heir and quicken her inheritance."

"Kaltra found a weakness in him and exploited it," I said. "I don't know what it was."

"That's true, she did." My Elder hadn't blinked since I began my report unless it coincided with one of mine. "Anything else?"

"The Matron asked if I had another purpose or if she should expect more Red Sisters. I informed her neither was the case, that she could arrange the pyre. I took my leave."

Elder D'Shea nodded, stepping away to study my equipment again. She lifted the amethyst crystal at last and pocketed it without activating the sound-capture spell.

"You asked no questions of your own?"

Her tone was lightweight. Mildly curious, unconcerned. I took the hint; I'd better not do the same.

"I asked who the orphan was," I admitted. "She looked old enough to have been born when I was sent to Court, but I didn't know her."

"And?"

"Matron Thalluen gave me a name. Natia, child of a House Guard." I thought back. "That was all."

"Was the House Guard the mother or the sire?"

"I didn't ask."

"No?"

"No, Elder."

"Did you ask anything else?"

I lifted my chin. "No, Elder."

Her eyebrow quirked. "Did you want to?"

"Yes, Elder."

"Tell me," she commanded. "What other questions?"

I wet my mouth a little. "I wanted to ask who was the sire of the unborn heir."

"You can go to our records for that."

"Yes, Elder. Why it wasn't important enough to ask Matron Thalluen."

A striking spark of humor entered the Sorceress' eyes. "What of questions only Matron Rohenvi could have answered? Had you asked before you left."

Fuck.

"Why she was concerned for Sibron," I said. "Familiar enough to know his name, to check his pulse and be willing to tend him all eve.

Why Kaltra had him in her bed in the first place."

"Those are good questions. Particularly if Sibron is still alive."

"He may not wake up, Elder."

"You didn't stay to confirm this, novice, so I shall have to send another. If we're lucky, we can still get a sample of that tampered wine you left on the bed stand. I'm curious what was used, and it would tell me the likelihood of survival better than mere unconsciousness. Fortunately, one female is still alive to ask. If she doesn't know, perhaps one of the House Guard does."

My heart sped up despite my efforts to control it. Damn it. So, did my Sorceress Elder want me to be curious about my former House or not?

"Anything else?" she prodded, her strength of will like a solid rod poking the middle of my forehead.

I glanced down and clenched one fist in my red gloves. They felt very new. "I fulfilled my mission as stated, but I did not ... feel balanced to remain and conduct a thorough interrogation for you."

Elder D'Shea nodded, seeming satisfied. "You did not fail in your mission, Sirana. I acknowledge that. Any other discoveries would have been nice, but I've learned to tailor expectation within the Sisterhood, even if they have been with us for a century."

Relaxing at this point would have been a mistake. I remained in position, at attention as the Sorceress stepped closer. She tilted her head to meet eyes.

"This excuse of performing the mission only as stated will not always work with me, however," she said. "I expect more from you. Every mission has an opportunity, and you have the ability to spot it. Your trials demonstrated this without any doubt on my side. Your poise dealing with Kerse again at the Worship Ball, and your thoughts afterward, prove this to me. You will *not* ignore your instincts in the future, Sirana, no matter if you 'feel' unbalanced."

I swallowed without blinking. "I apologize, my Elder. I will do better."

The Sorceress smiled fully. When she was genuinely pleased, it was surprisingly beautiful. "A Red Sister held to a higher standard climbs the ladder faster. I foresee you will appreciate this truth more than others."

I saw the quickest flick of her eyes to Gaelan, and I knew my Sister would take it as another barb. If her mood had improved at all from when I'd first returned to the Cloister, it was no doubt souring again. I could not yet look at her myself, however. I only heard her weight shift, felt her tension behind me. For a split instant, I imagined Gaelan drawing a dagger and aiming it at my back.

Don't get paranoid, she said.

That was an impossible task in Sivaraus.

I SAW THE QUEEN'S EYES AGAIN IN REVERIE, NOT LONG AFTER I HAD EXECUTED Kaltra. Darkness within darkness, there hovered an impression of a semi-transparent face floating in the air above an open expanse. Uncountable pricks of light spread above me in a ceiling of impossible height.

The Surface, I realized.

No burning ball hovered overhead. I stood at that point of the cycle when the Sun wasn't overhead, when Davrin could explore more comfortably. Had I dreamt of this before Jaunda had ever left and returned to tell tales?

My feet were wide apart on the shifting sediment, and I wore no clothes. Someone caressed my cunt from behind, and I believed I recognized my Lead.

I was just thinking of you … Oh. Just like that. You know how I like it.

I got down on all fours, willing to give a pleasurable ride, and felt my body penetrated with no hesitation. I groaned, bracing for more force. My chest froze when he spoke.

"Kwernish toug, Davrin?"

I stared at the ground; it gave as my fingers gripped it.

~Why are you doing this? Your Goddess magic is stronger than me. Release me, whore.~

"No." I shuddered, remembering how disgustingly good that thick, short prick had felt. In my mouth, my ass. Now it moved inside my slit again, stretching it open.

"Get off me, Kain. Goddess, make him go away!"

A Goddess answered, perhaps. The male hunched over my back grew larger, although he never released my hips. The shape of him changed, still deep inside me, and I heard a rumble, then a hiss as he drooled on my bare back.

"*Ssirranna.*"

"Kerse!" I grunted. My fingers sank deeper into the red grains beneath me as the Priestess Wilsira's Sathoet rutted me. Somewhere behind him, a mature, Davrin female laughed at my predicament.

"See to my son's needs," she said. "Do you not feel his power? Far better than any pretty Consort. Deny me, and you deny Braqth."

Then someone I couldn't see gripped my hair and jerked my head up, pushing the soft glans of a penis against my lips.

"Suck me," my invisible wizard demanded. "Arrogant Noble."

I'm not a Noble. Not anymore. I am more. I have proven myself.

I couldn't speak, however, as both held me as if on a spit. I had the skills to break loose, I knew that I did, but my limbs were stiff as their cocks, refusing to move or bend. Wilsira Tachnathon chuckled again though I couldn't see her. I raised my eyes, and the Valsharess's Gaze had disappeared from the light-pocked darkness surrounding me.

Surrounding us. My throat full of the wizard; my cunt speared like Curgia's, just a Noble ready to be bred. Another House controlled by Priestesses.

No! I'm not of House Thalluen anymore! I'm a Red Sister. They can't control the Sisters.

Not unless I became pregnant.

"I can tell you are no commoner, Mistress," my Consort said, his voice immediately soothing, cooling the fire in my holes. "Please *think* what you are doing. There will be consequences."

There were always consequences.

Kerse and the invisible wizard vanished. Once freed, I attempted to gain my feet. I failed the first time, stumbling, but the beautiful Consort took my arm and helped me up. I could barely look at him; he was too lovely. He watched me with concern, not unlike my Mother looking at an unconscious Sibron. Both baffled me.

And somehow, I resented it.

"What injured you, Mistress?" he asked, far too gently.

I stared at his beauty. I could not give him an answer.

I AWOKE ALONE, AND THE FIRST THING I DID WAS STAND AND CHECK THE LOCK and ward upon the tiny room in which I'd chosen to rest.

This wasn't Gaelan's room, nor Jaunda's, and Elder D'Shea hadn't called on me to attend her in quite some time. For the first time, I tried to sleep without them.

It was dark and quiet. As I became aware of the dampness cooling between my legs, I sighed in surrender, glad no one had witnessed another fitful Reverie like that even as I ached for a Sister's tool to enforce discipline and focus.

What was I doing here?

I was haze-walking at Court. Nothing to do but drink, breathe incense, and fuck in between plots for revenge.

Elder Rausery's response had been, "Why do you think that would be any different here with us?"

Perhaps she was right, yet there was Elder D'Shea's recent riposte.

"I expect more from you."

There were demons everywhere, within the Cloister and without.

There were those I could touch and their ethereal counterparts inside my head. Demons who were dead but wished to be remembered. Of them all, only one could matter to me if I was to survive, to thrive where I now belonged. Our motto alone made that clear, and I had taken it to mean I must reject all but the red uniform.

All demons had begun as something to fear; a child could not help but be tense and wary when they were around. Through the time my demons compelled me to silence, I loathed their control of my will. It had happened once, D'Shea warned me, and it could happen again with Wilsira, or any Priestess.

For the first time, however, I felt attracted to some of these other demons, whether approved by my Elders or not. Jaunda, Gaelan, the Royal Consort, the unnamed wizard. Even Kerse.

And I wondered.

My childhood solitude is gone. D'Shea has seen to it. Yet demons will always be here. I can't avoid them in Sivaraus. I'll meet them again and discover new ones. I can't reject them or remain apart, or I miss opportunities as I did at my Mother's House.

I scrubbed down my skin and began to equip myself.

Jaunda had said it: Red Sisters with another demon overtaking her will above the Sisterhood were killed by her own kind. This didn't mean other demons didn't linger in our thoughts. The existence of the competition and the struggle was proof of this.

If I cannot avoid them, what might happen if I explore and tame them instead?

Soon, I was dressed, equipped, and ready. I left the sparsely furnished, little closet with a smile on my face. When Lead Qivni saw it and lifted one nostril, I wanted to laugh.

I *did* laugh, still astonished how intense this release could be.

Another cycle, another awakening. Here I was, on the cusp of my second century, just following another exchange of Consorts and the shifting of heirs among the Matrons. Old and frayed threads of Spider Queen's Web had been shed, the gossamer designs throughout Sivaraus refreshed.

With the Sisterhood at my back, I could walk this new design. I could explore all that Jilrina tried and failed to keep from me, and I no longer needed my Mother's name to pursue ambitions.

My demons were still here and perhaps would be for a while. The Sanctuary would try to exploit them but, for now, had been pushed out by a wreath of red cloaks and daggers.

I had lived to count my hundredth turn. The next hundred promised to reach heights of which I'd once not dared to dream.

No demons but us.

The helpless Noble I was once is no more. I am Red Sister Sirana, watching my city from the shadows.

Read Treasure Revealed: Sister Seekers Book 2 now!

Thank you for reading about Sirana and the Davrin Elves of the deep! Help others to find the dark fantasy they want and leave a review for Book 1 on Goodreads, Bookbub, or your favorite retail site!

Sister Seekers is an adult epic fantasy with an ever-broadening scope. Found family is a core theme throughout. Perfect for fans of entwined plots, challenging themes, immersive worldbuilding, and elements of erotic horror. Sexuality and inner conflict play into character growth with nuance, intrigue, action, and magic.

[Follow Etaski and Subscribe to her newsletter at her website]

Do you enjoy fantasy maps, timelines, and glossaries? Do you love to read extra tidbits about the characters and places in the story?

[Be sure to visit Etaski's series lore at World Anvil!]

Read the next book in the Sister Seekers: Treasure Revealed

Once silent and disposable, I've found my place among the Sisterhood of Sivaraus, coarse, crude, and stirring to my blood.

In crimson uniform I walk among sensual consorts, studious wizards, and sadistic Priestesses. I am an initiate with true influence in my underground city, a power both freeing and addicting.

Everyone keeps secrets which bind them up if they jerk the web too much, and none are more vulnerable than novices wielding new power. Should my own secret fall into the wrong hands, I cannot survive alone.

I shall not give up what I've found. Neither will the Sisterhood. Sivaraus will always need new Red Sisters, no matter what strangeness we bring with us.

In *Treasure Revealed*, A.S. Etaski weaves threads of intrigue and action in this second tale of the Sister Seekers.

ACKNOWLEDGMENTS

My heart-felt thanks goes out to my beta readers, fans, peers, and friends who had a direct impact on this first book.

Ile Depak, for being a gentleman and wanting to help, for your sharp eyes and proper grammar, and for your kind-hearted and polite correspondence.

Gerrit, for asking specific questions, for rereading so many times to listen for that internal logic and helping me prevent the small things from becoming big things.

Gazukull, for your indomitable humor, for providing that alternate headspace and visual delight, where the ridiculous is cherished and the serious takes a number.

Axelotl, for wanting to make me smile, for providing my very first fan art ever, and for somehow being able to fill in the detail of a paragraph and make the picture worth well more than a thousand words.

NecrosisBob, for being that dry wit, for putting form to your thoughts and making all biology magical, for reading everything I showed you, and making each compliment rare and earned.

Eris Adderly, for picking up what I'm putting down, for the audience commentary and terrible-wonderful puns, for the mounds of advice and generosity, and, of course, for your beautiful cover design.

ABOUT THE AUTHOR

Etaski entertained herself with fantasy stories since the first day she sat on a school bus looking out the window. When hand-written letters were disappearing, she wrote no less than five pages to be worth the postage. Her early stories were written by hand, and she had a writer's callus and three finished novels before graduating high school.

She chose to study science, archaeology, and theater, and she noticed a disparity. Frank discussion of sexuality was rare growing up, so she wrote theories and observations within a story, inviting the reader to contemplate deeper or just be entertained.

History rarely speaks on sexuality, yet biology demonstrates how it sways even basic choices. Drama reveals sexuality but may still fade to black. In the Sister Seekers, the sex *is* the story, and connections made within will forever change Etaski's fantasy world without cutting away.

Etaski's Website: etaski.com
Etaski's Book Page: etaski.com/sister-seekers
Etaski's Series Lore: miurag.etaski.com
Etaski on Patreon: www.patreon.com/etaski
Etaski on GoodReads: www.goodreads.com/etaski
Etaski on BookBub: www.bookbub.com/authors/a-s-etaski
Etaski on Facebook: www.facebook.com/asetaski
Etaski on Mastodon: mastodon.online/@etaski